THE RAINBOW

A CHILTON CROSSE NOVEL

TRACI BORUM

Unlocking New Worlds

ISBN 13: 978-1-940215-40-2
ISBN 10: 1940215404

Red Adept Publishing, LLC
104 Bugenfield Court
Garner, NC 27529
RedAdeptPublishing.com/

Cover and Formatting: Streetlight Graphics

Dedicated to Pat Sandifer Borum.
My mother, friend, confidant, and most loyal supporter.
I love you.

Chapter One

Life seems nothing more than a quick succession of busy nothings.
~Jane Austen

FOR TWENTY GLORIOUS MINUTES AT dawn, the village was all hers. Doves cooed and mist hovered on sheep-dotted fields as she picked up her pace and quickened her breath. When she finally huffed past the dark, empty shops and cobblestone streets, the sun winked through a cluster of trees to signal it was time to head home. Some people hated jogging—the sting of air in the lungs, the irritating burn inside the thighs. But Holly Newbury found it nothing short of blissful.

The running ritual had started six years ago, when she'd quit university to help raise her three younger sisters. She'd craved something she could call hers and quickly found it in a morning jog around the village. Those twenty minutes gave Holly something precious—twelve hundred seconds to clear her thoughts, center herself, prepare for the day ahead. She always felt a hesitant pull toward Foxglove House during that final spurt up the hill because she knew the moment she entered, chaos would ensue. Always the best kind of chaos—people she loved, getting ready for their day as she helped them make breakfast, prepare lunches, find homework from the night before—but her time became theirs again.

A few minutes after this morning's run, Holly stood over the Aga, nudging scrambled eggs inside a pan. As she switched off the burner, she heard footsteps clomp down the stairs.

"No. It's the effing wild berry! I can't find it *any*where!" Bridget shouted, accusing her twin sister as they entered the kitchen, tossing their phones into the wicker basket on the counter. Holly had created the "basket rule" when their father bought the twins mobile phones last year, for their sixteenth birthdays. Holly didn't want them heads down and tapping during breakfast.

"How come it's always *my* fault when you lose something? I don't even use that gunk," Rosalee answered, rolling her eyes and taking a seat at the kitchen table. "It's nasty. Smells like rotten fruit."

"Then you *did* use it!" Bridget pointed.

"No, I only smelled it. But that was, like, two weeks ago." Rosalee poured a glass of orange juice. "It's not my fault you can't keep track of anything like a normal human being."

"Well, it's not *my* fault you're an effing idiot!"

"Enough, girls!" Holly gave her best stern look. She turned to Bridget, waiting for eye contact. "And no cussing in this house. You know better."

"But 'effing' isn't a cuss word," Bridget argued.

"Maybe not, but it's implied profanity."

"Exactly. Implied. *Not* actual," Bridget said to her eggs.

"Well, in this house, 'implied' is close enough." Holly nodded toward the plate. "Now eat something, both of you. You'll be late for school."

She left the twins to their breakfasts, hoping they wouldn't kill each other in her absence, and walked down the long hall. She wondered how much longer this hateful phase of theirs would linger—the twins had never gotten along well, but over the past few months, they barely had a kind word for each other.

Fraternal twins born three minutes apart, Bridget and Rosalee had broken every cliché of twinship since the beginning. As a newborn, Bridget screeched and wailed, while Rosalee dozed through everything. When they were little girls, Bridget was fearless and temperamental, while Rosalee sat quietly in corners and read books. As teenagers, the differences had only grown more distinct—tastes in music, clothing, friendships. Polar opposites. The girls had even worked hard to look less alike. Three months ago, Bridget had bleached her long hair blond, while Rosalee had trimmed hers to shoulder length, keeping it natural brown.

Reaching the sitting room, Holly spotted Bridget's neon-pink backpack crumpled beneath the couch where the twins had finished their homework last night. Holly shook her head at the sight: wrinkled term papers and battered notebooks sticking out of pockets, an open book with a broken spine splayed out on the floor, and beside it—a-ha!—the missing tube of lip gloss. Holly snatched up the book, the bag, and the gloss, and went to check on Abbey. It wasn't like her to be the last one down.

"Abbey! Time for breakfast!" Holly called from the staircase.

"Coming! I'm *coming*!" Abbey emerged at the top, fidgeting with the collar on her sweater—part of the girls' school uniform—and nearly tripped on the first step down.

Petite for her age, twelve-year-old Abbey still seemed like an awkward little girl. But Holly was grateful for the awkwardness. Too many of Abbey's schoolmates were eager to grow up fast, experimenting with makeup and showing off their midriffs, already begging parents for piercings or tattoos. But not Abbey. She'd rather play outside, watching a ladybug crawl on a frond, than worry about boys or makeup. She also wore glasses that fit her personality, made her look as bookish as she was. An old soul.

When Abbey reached the bottom of the stairs, Holly adjusted her sister's collar and followed her to the kitchen.

"I smell bacon. Mmmm," Abbey said as they went. "Is it the maple kind?"

"Yes. Just for you," Holly whispered then rounded the corner and set the backpack beside Bridget's chair. "I found your lip gloss. Second pocket," she added, then poured another cup of coffee.

Rosalee, newly absolved, tossed a self-satisfied glance in Bridget's direction.

"Five minutes," Holly announced as she saw the time and watched them gulp down their food.

Holly remembered well the first breakfast they'd had when she returned to Foxglove House six years ago. A somber morning, where the only sound had been the quiet clanking of flatware against plates. She knew nobody wanted to be there, sitting at that table. Her sisters would much rather have been up in their bedrooms, grieving privately. Staring out windows and gulping back tears. Wishing their mother had been at the head of the table, where she belonged.

But Holly had insisted on that half hour, knowing back then the importance of it. Coming together as a family, if only in silence. And since that first morning, those breakfasts had become a steady routine, something the girls could count on. Something Holly could count on, too.

Over the years, though, they'd turned into little more than bickering sessions, an inconvenience the girls rushed through. But maybe this particular morning's squabbling could be blamed on the fact that school was back in session after a long break. Perhaps the girls needed time to readjust to the early morning routine.

"Outta here," Bridget announced first, disappearing in a neon-pink streak.

"Don't forget your umbrella. It's going to rain!" Holly called after her.

"I'm gone too," Rosalee said, sipping the last of her juice and pushing back from the table.

"Wait for your sister," Holly said, receiving an impatient sigh in return.

"I'm eating as fast as I can!" Abbey insisted through a mouthful of eggs.

"That's gross," Rosalee said then asked Holly, "Can I go to the bakery after school?"

"As long as you take Abbey. Do you have money?"

Rosalee nodded. "Couple of fivers."

One last bite and Abbey scrambled to catch up to Rosalee, who was already halfway down the hall. They slammed the front door, taking all the energy of youth along with them.

Thankful that she could trust their tiny Cotswold village, Chilton Crosse, to provide the girls a safe walk to school, Holly sat at the corner desk to check her laptop for her next assignment, another staple in her morning routine. As much as she would love to open the French doors wide, linger against the doorframe and sip her coffee for hours while she watched the garden change in the light of a mid-April morning, there wasn't that sort of time today.

She drummed her fingers, waiting for the slow-moving university site to open, and let her eyes wander over to *it*. Something she'd received in yesterday's post. Something she'd intended to throw away. Sondra's wedding invitation, propped against the edge of the counter, asking Holly to look at her own life and compare it with someone else's. This had been the third invitation in six months—two for weddings, and one for a baby shower. While Holly had created an odd sort of life here in her childhood home, raising her sisters, her university friends had moved on, meeting new guys, getting engaged, having children of their own.

Standing, Holly took the few steps to the counter, snatched the thick, expensive card, and chucked it into the receptacle. *Good for Sondra,* she thought, shoving down her jealousy.

Envy is a poison, her mother had once told her. Indeed.

Returning to her laptop, she heard the grandfather clock's chime echoing down the hall and realized she only had an hour before visiting Gertrude's. Barely enough time to start brainstorming that research paper. Or to emotionally prepare for the visit to come.

Clutching the oatmeal raisin bread she'd made the night before, Holly stood at the door of the cottage and wondered *why* she put herself through this torture. She already knew every one of the probing questions she would get, as well as the rote answers she would be forced to offer. These interrogations always turned her inside out.

Gertrude Middleton, her father's cousin, lived in Hickory Cottage down the road. Though only in her early seventies, Gertrude seemed at least a decade older: the grey hair she refused to color, the cane she leaned upon because of arthritis, the general crankiness with which she approached each new day. Holly often questioned why her father displayed such loyalty to "just" a cousin—especially a grouchy, ungrateful one—by stopping in to see her every week, when he didn't have time.

"It's the right thing to do," he'd once told her. "She's family."

So, Holly had taken over her mother's duties six years ago, visiting Gertrude at least once a week to check in, to give her someone to talk to. Gertrude had so few visitors. Really only Mildred, her housekeeper and caretaker, ever came to the cottage.

Realizing she would be chided for her three-minute tardiness, Holly put on a cheery face and gave a jovial knock before walking inside.

"I'm hee-eere," she called as she entered the parlor.

As usual, Gertrude sat rigidly in her straight-backed chair, stroking Leopold, the black miniature poodle who ate gourmet biscuits from his mistress's fingers. Holly was always amazed the dog wasn't two hundred pounds.

"I made some raisin bread for you." Holly held up the wrapped bundle.

"Put it over there," Gertrude demanded, pointing a withered finger in the direction of the table. "I'll have it with my tea when Mildred arrives this afternoon."

Holly took her usual spot on the button-backed couch with the scrolled wooden feet and clasped her hands in her lap. She never seemed well dressed enough in this house of antique furniture, of old lace draperies and doilies. Like something out of an Elizabeth Gaskell novel. No television, no computer, no technology at all—only basic electricity and running water. The cottage had an eighteenth-century atmosphere, and Holly supposed she should be wearing a flowing, high-waisted dress to better fit in. Along with some long, white gloves and a fan.

"How are you feeling today?" Holly said loudly, so she wouldn't have to repeat herself, as she normally did.

"You don't have to shout." Gertrude scowled. "I'm not deaf." She shifted uncomfortably, forcing Leopold to cling to her lap for dear life. "The weather change is making my knees worse, I can tell you that. And my hemorrhoids are back with a vengeance."

Now it was Holly's turn to shift uncomfortably, racking her brain for a valid enough excuse to leave earlier than planned.

"Tell me." Gertrude tapped her cane on the floor as a judge would a gavel. Commanding, arrogant. "Do you have a young man?"

The same question she asked Holly during *every* visit. So, Holly offered the same answer as every visit: "I'm too busy for that. Plus, I haven't found the right person yet."

As always, the answer wasn't good enough.

"Well, you're not getting any younger. How old are you now?"

"Almost twenty-eight."

"Remember, every tick of the clock is a minute closer to staying a spinster."

Holly bit the inside of her cheek to avoid a snide response. And a chuckle. The irony struck her. Gertrude had never married, yet there she was, lecturing Holly, judging her "spinsterhood."

Hypocrite, thy name is Gertrude...

Eager to change the subject, Holly remained undauntedly cheerful and leaned forward. "So, I have a delicious bit of news. I heard it from Mrs. Pickering yesterday."

"Do tell." Gertrude drew in, visibly eager for a generous piece of gossip to munch on later with her afternoon tea.

"Apparently, our little village is about to be famous. A film crew is going to set up at Chatsworth Manor and make a film. Isn't that exciting? The rumor is that it's *Emma*."

"*Emma*?" Gertrude crinkled her brow.

"Yes. Jane Austen. *Emma*. The matchmaker who pairs up people unsuccessfully?"

The look of confusion remained. "Never read it."

Holly sucked in a breath and unclasped her hands. "Oh, you *must* read it! Jane Austen's best work and my favorite book in the world since I was fourteen. My mother gave me my first copy. I've lost count of how many times I've read it."

"Humph," Gertrude said, raising her nose to the idea. She slipped another biscuit to Leopold, who snatched it greedily. "In my opinion, books are only for those who cannot think for themselves."

Holly's cheeks prickled with heat. She could accept the rude judgments of her social life, could even take being labeled "spinster"— but a lack of respect for books, for Jane Austen, and thus, for her own mother's memory? That was unacceptable.

"Well, in *my* opinion," Holly started, trying to contain the tremble in her voice, "those who detest literature have small minds and narrow views of the world. Jane Austen once said that. Or something like it."

Gertrude sat higher in her seat, face horrified, and said with another rap of her gavel, "Then this 'Jane Austen' is clearly a fool."

Holly stood and tried to breathe, remembering who she was talking to. A blood relative, an elder who deserved respect. She monitored her tone and kept it as even as possible. "Honestly, Gertrude, I think you're wrong. And to prove it to you, I think we should start a book club."

"A what?"

"And I think that our first book should be *Emma*."

"For goodness' sake, you have got to be—"

"And that this book club should meet right here. In Hickory Cottage. Once a week." For the first time in her life, Holly saw genuine panic on Gertrude's face. Holly took advantage of the moment, reveling in her own boldness. "This will be the best way for you to decide if Jane Austen's work is trash or treasure. I'll round up some interested readers this week and we can have the first meeting on Monday. I'll take care of everything."

With that, Holly pivoted and headed for the door, half proud and half petrified of what had just happened. She knew the shocked expression would remain on Gertrude's face for the rest of the day. And something about that gave Holly a wicked rush of satisfaction.

Fat drops of rain spattered above Holly's head, tap dancing on her green umbrella as she skipped over puddles. Storey Road, the cobblestoned main street of Chilton Crosse, glistened on rainy days, like a watercolor painting. Holly inhaled the dewy scent and browsed the street, savoring how the rain altered the quaint limestone shop-fronts from a pale sand color to a darker taupe. A stone gazebo stood in the middle of the road, usually occupied by tourists taking pictures or eating lunches. Holly always loved this view of the village: pristine shops lined up in a neat row, multicolored flowers peeking out of window boxes. All brought to life, even on a gloomy day.

She approached the art gallery, which was sandwiched between the post office and clock shop across from Joe's pub, and shook out her umbrella. Though Holly's father insisted she didn't need a job—she was busy enough looking after her sisters—she believed otherwise. It was important to earn her own money, to set a good example for her sisters. So, four years ago, Holly had filled out an application for part-time work and had been hired on the spot by the curator, Frank O'Neill.

Today, Holly arrived early, thanks to her unusually fast escape from Gertrude's, and opened the gallery door, the sharp tinkling bell announcing her arrival.

She spotted the new piece immediately, a Bath landscape painted by the gallery's owner, Noelle Spencer. Noelle was the great-niece of the late Joy Valentine, the famous and ever-mysterious Cotswold artist, and original owner of the gallery. The first time Holly had seen a painting of Noelle's, she'd known the artistic talent had been completely genetic.

"Still raining?" Frank asked as he approached.

Holly twisted the dripping umbrella at her side to show him the answer then placed it inside the umbrella stand with a clink.

"Ahh. Probably why it's been so dead all morning." Frank rolled his brown eyes and scratched the top of his angular nose. His frame was slender, bordering on skinny, and he always wore the same ensemble to work—a dark jacket of either navy, brown, or black, perfectly creased trousers, a starched white shirt, and suspenders. As with Gertrude, Holly often felt underdressed in the presence of Frank—even today, with her flowing broomstick skirt and silver jewelry.

"What's on the agenda?" Holly asked, nudging aside a damp wave of auburn hair from her cheek.

Frank clasped his hands. "It's been slow, so I've done the paperwork already. Nothing left for you at the moment. Maybe you should even go home? With this weather, I doubt you'll have much to do here."

"No," Holly said. "I have a project for us."

She motioned for him to follow her back to the supply closet, where she paused and pulled a dozen sheets of printer paper from the shelf, along with a couple of thick black markers. "I'm starting a book club. So I need to make some posters to place around the village—at the pub, the bakery, even here, if that's okay."

Frank's expression was unreadable, and for a moment, she thought he would refuse. Or, lecture her for doing personal work on "company" time.

But then he asked, "What sort of book club?"

"It's *Emma*. In correlation with the film that's being shot at the Manor soon."

"Oh, I heard about that. Mary Cartwright mentioned it yesterday when she came in to look at Noelle's new painting. Terribly exciting!"

"Isn't it? And with this book club, we can be a small part of it, in our own way. What do you think?"

"Is it females only?"

Holly hadn't thought that far ahead. In her vision, she hadn't actually pictured any males sitting in Gertrude's parlor, discussing the social and romantic conundrums of early nineteenth-century British society. But why not?

"Anyone can join," she decided.

"Then count me in." He threaded his fingers together, his index fingers pointing at his chin, and got a faraway look. "Let's do this right, with the posters. No markers." He waved them away and sat at his laptop. "I can design them here, and we can print them off. I see big, bold letters with some sort of hook to reel them in, something eye-catching. Dramatic."

"Frank, you really don't need to do all that. It sounds like too much work," she protested.

Laptop already opened, he clicked on a blank document. "Nonsense. I'm good at this sort of thing. No trouble at all." He paused and brought his focus back to her. "One condition, though."

Holly stared suspiciously. "What?"

"That you say 'yes' to a night out. Nothing fancy, just supper at the pub."

She was aware of an awkward silence but didn't know how to fill it. Finally, she gathered her courage and asked—"This isn't a… date?"— then wished she hadn't. Awkward silence had been less awkward than that question.

During the last four years, Frank had dropped some incredibly subtle hints that he might be interested in her romantically. So subtle, in fact, that they were unverifiable. An occasional lingering look, or an extra smile—all things that could be interpreted as "friendly." No matter the case, sweet as he was, there wasn't a single molecule in her body that was attracted to Frank that way.

"Heavens, no," he said. "I just know that you rarely take a night off for yourself. And while we're at the pub together, putting up the posters, we could... have a spot of dinner. That's all."

"Oh."

"I bet you can't recall the last time you've been out by yourself. Without your sisters."

"That's true," she said. "I really can't."

"Then it's settled. A casual supper at the pub. It'll have to be tomorrow, after I close the gallery. We'll even go halves."

With that, she couldn't think of a single reason to turn him down. "Okay. Now, what can I do to help with these?" She pulled up a chair beside him.

"Feed me some information about the book club—dates, address, those sorts of things—and I'll include it in the posters. Let's advertise!"

Chapter Two

Reflection must be reserved for solitary hours; whenever
she was alone, she gave way to it as the greatest relief.
~Jane Austen

WITH A YANK, HOLLY TORE the sheet of foil from its roll and covered the still-warm pan of delicious leftover chicken breasts. Baked in a cream sauce with garlic and a few pinches of salt, the dish had become one of the girls' favorites.

Years ago, when Holly had first moved back home again, mid-semester, all she had known how to do was heat up a bowl of soup in the microwave. But quickly, she'd researched a few basic dishes to feed her sisters and father something nutritious. If she couldn't heal their broken hearts, at least she could fill their empty stomachs.

To give herself a break in those days, she'd proclaimed Fridays as "takeaway" days and gotten something from Joe's pub, or the Indian restaurant, or even Mrs. Pickering's market, ready-made. It later became tradition to eat and then follow the meal with a Game Night. Her father would occasionally join in, when he was able, making it a real family tradition. Since last year, when the twins turned sixteen, Game Night had steadily declined into Lie-in-Front-of-the-Telly Night. Holly couldn't remember the last time they'd brought out a board game and spent an evening laughing together.

"Daddy's home!" Abbey shouted from the sitting room as the front door slammed, earlier than expected.

Holly finished crimping the foil around the pan's edge then went to greet her father. Rounding the corner, she watched Abbey snuggle into Duncan Newbury's damp overcoat as he squeezed her shoulders tight.

"How was your day, pumpkin?" he asked in that unmistakable raspy voice.

All that pipe smoke, her mother had once blamed as the culprit.

"I came in second in our spelling bee!" Abbey's face contained a specific glow only reserved for her father. It showed itself in the corners of her smile, the warmth in her eyes.

"Did you? Well, that's no surprise. You got forty-eight words right when I quizzed you on Saturday."

"Forty-*nine,* Daddy."

"Pardon me," he said with a grin.

He waited until Abbey released her grasp before removing his coat, still covered in translucent beads of rain.

Holly reached out to take it and folded it over her arm. "The chicken is still warm, Dad. Do you want a plate?"

"Thanks, honey. I'll take it in the study."

He poked his head into the sitting room, giving a wave to the twins.

"Hey, Dad," they said in perfect unison, glancing up from their phones momentarily.

Thinking no one was looking, her father rubbed his eyes with his fingertips and inhaled deeply, then shifted toward his study. Holly knew it took every effort for him to hide his exhaustion each evening. He often worked fourteen-hour days, even at his age, to keep his prosperous financial-planning business running. Three of those fourteen hours were devoted to the London commute. He had once considered moving the family closer to make it easier, but he couldn't bring himself to uproot them that way. Especially not from Foxglove House, which had been in his wife's family for more than two centuries—a sprawling estate with six bedrooms, a sitting room, a front parlor, a dining room, a study, a spacious French-style kitchen, and a three-acre garden. There was no way Holly's mother would've given up her family home, and when she died, no way her father could have sold it.

Holly hung his coat on the nearby rack and headed for the kitchen to make up his plate.

Minutes later, approaching his study, she paused. Sometimes when she entered this room, especially when she saw her father tired and haggard, she had to swallow an uneasiness at the back of her throat. This room represented something dark. Even now, all these years later. The ghost of her father's mourning still lived in these walls.

Holly would never forget, years ago, creaking the door open to see him behind that sturdy oak desk—his salt-and-pepper stubble growing into a fuller beard day-by-day, the wrinkles and lines in his face deepened by sorrow. She was watching him grow older, literally. And losing him with every tick of the clock.

After the funeral, he spent his days either staring with hollow eyes at the warm spring weather outside, or listening to the album his wife had recorded when she was in college, just after they'd met. Hannah Newbury had been part of a trio of girls who'd gotten a lucky break, recorded an album, and had a hit single at number fifteen on the U.K. charts. One-hit wonders, they disbanded when Hannah had become pregnant with Holly.

Holly suspected her father hadn't heard the album in years, maybe even decades. But when his wife died, he dusted it off and played it in a continual loop in his study, sometimes mumbling along to the words, "Whenever I'm near you / I get a feeling love is nearby..."

Holly would pause at the door before going in, lean her forehead against the wood doorframe as she mouthed the words too, waiting for the song to end, giving her father a chance to rub away the tears.

Then she would enter, set the food tray on the desk, remove the untouched one from the meal before, and brainstorm what she could do to reach him. He wasn't her father anymore—not the one she remembered. The husky laugh, the mischievous eyes, the wicked wit— all of it had disappeared.

Holly tried to make excuses to her sisters, tried to banish the look of worry from her own face as she reassured them he was fine—that he'd simply chosen to work from home for a while. But she knew they knew otherwise, even at their very young ages. The girls couldn't help but sense the oppressive weight of grief in that house. It sat in every crevice, dissolved itself into the air they breathed. What the girls sensed most was their father's absence. Even on the rare occasion that he emerged from his study, he was a shadow of himself, going through the motions. The girls hadn't just lost one parent; they were losing two. And Holly was helpless to stop it.

Concerned, she had asked the family doctor to examine her father, to give her some guidance. Dr. Andrews made a house call and examined his patient for over an hour. Holly could hear him through the door, asking her father questions and hearing only low grumbles in reply.

When he'd finished, the doctor shut the door behind him and told Holly, "Other than some sleep deprivation and loss of nutrition, Duncan is physically fine. It's pure grief. Depression. His mind is still in shock, and he's on autopilot right now. Try to get him some fresh air now and then. And see that he eats."

He offered some sedatives to ensure that Duncan slept, which Holly was sure her father never did.

She followed the doctor's orders, but still, her father was a stubborn patient. Though he was never snappish or quick-tempered with her, he hid his pills in drawers or pushed food around his plate to fool her into thinking he was eating. Just enough to give Holly some hope.

Then one day—one strange and miraculous day—she awoke to find him shaved, bathed, and dressed, standing in the kitchen and ready to eat a full breakfast. A new man. Other than his still-gaunt cheeks, he *looked* like the former version of her father, but the change was so sudden Holly almost didn't trust it. For the first time in nearly two months, he made actual, steady eye contact with her.

"Thank you" was all he said. But that had said everything.

She'd read about people who handled grief in odd ways. Perhaps this was one of those. An odd way. He'd risen up suddenly out of his grief, with a burst of energy—like someone coming to after a hypnosis session. *Snap!* Rather than question it, Holly had fallen into his arms, tears splashing onto his shoulder, and whispered, "I missed you."

To this day, her father had never spoken about what made the change in him, what had brought him back to his family so rapidly. She wondered if she would ever know.

Holly shook off the memories and balanced the plate of chicken with one hand, pushing open the weighty door with the other.

"Smells delicious." He cleared a space on his desk for the plate. "I'm famished."

"Hard day?"

He gave a chuckle. "Aren't they all?" He picked up a fork and took the first bite, talking through it. "This merger is on the verge of falling through. And Wilson is about to get his ass sacked."

"Serves him right, from everything you've told me."

"Well, I'll give him one more shot. He can prove himself in tomorrow's meeting or hit the door. I'm running out of patience."

Duncan had a ruthless reputation when it came to business, which was how he had built a million-dollar company from the ground up by the time he was thirty-eight. But he also had a reputation for being fair-minded, which earned respect from nearly everyone. Especially his daughters.

Holly had always wondered if it bothered her father, not having any sons to share "son things" with. His house had always been filled with females. Lots and lots of them. But if it bothered him, he never gave a hint of it. A domineering lion at the office, he saved all his softness, all his tenderness and kindness for his girls. Growing up, the only time Holly had ever seen him cross was when any of the girls had dared to disrespect their mother—with a word, a tone of voice, a disobedient action. Then, they saw the fire in his eyes, adequate enough to get the message across. The lingering disappointment in their father's expression was often the only discipline they needed.

"Were you able to finish that paper?" he asked Holly between bites. "The one on business strategies?"

"Almost. It's due tomorrow, so I'll probably stay up late and finish it when the girls are in bed."

"Mm." He nodded.

"Oh!" She pulled up a chair. "I almost forgot. I've started a new project."

"For school?"

"Nope. This one is the 'Gertrude Middleton Project.'"

He raised an eyebrow and took a sip of red wine. "Go on."

Holly told him about this morning's visit to Hickory Cottage and the bold way she had announced that *Gertrude* would be hosting the new book club—there, in her own cottage.

"I even ordered a large-print copy of *Emma* online tonight. Now she'll have no excuse!"

Duncan snickered into his glass. "She told me about it when I dropped by this evening. You're a wicked girl…"

She recognized the sarcasm and smiled. "Do you think I overstepped?"

"Not at all. It'll be good for her," he said with a wink.

"Well, I don't expect a big crowd—probably just me, Gertrude, maybe Mildred, and Frank."

"Frank?"

"Ehh, don't ask," she said, rolling her eyes. "I'll tell you another time."

She eased up from the chair, feeling the weight of her research paper calling her back to the laptop. "I'll let you finish."

"Night, Hollybear. Thanks for dinner."

Holly had been waiting all day for this. To open the blue door and walk into this three-hundred-square-foot space knowing the only sound she could expect was the soothing patter of rain. She'd waited past dinner, past seeing the girls off to bed, even past the research paper, to enter her cottage, her getaway.

Hideaway Cottage sat behind Foxglove House, built for Holly by her father the week after she was born. Proud to be the father of a little girl, his first-born, he didn't want a playhouse for her. He wanted *the* playhouse. He never did anything small, and the cottage was no exception. Adult-sized in height with a stone exterior that matched the main house, Hideaway Cottage contained a sitting room, complete with custom-made kiddie furniture and bookshelves. Since Holly had been an only child for the first eleven years of her life, she'd spent endless hours in this cottage, talking to her dolls, telling them secrets, reading them books.

When she moved back home from university to take care of her sisters, she realized the twins were too grown-up to enjoy Hideaway Cottage, and Abbey was uninterested in it altogether, preferring to spend her playtime outdoors. So, Holly transformed the cottage into a more mature hideaway—a haven from those early, daunting everyday duties. She redecorated, replacing the kiddie furniture with her mother's rocking chair, a petite wood table she found in the attic, a beautiful antique lamp on sale at Mrs. Mulberry's antique shop, and all sorts of other odds and ends, such as candles and silk flowers to dress up the space. She boxed up the toys and children's books and replaced them with knickknacks from her dorm room and all of her favorite books. Pleasure reading. No textbooks in this cottage. Or laptops or mobile phones or iPods. Only silence.

Here, most of all, she could strip away the good-natured mask she wore on everyone else's behalf. If she felt anxious, grumpy, knackered, it didn't matter. Here, she could just *be*. The moment she stepped over the threshold, her entire body relaxed.

Tonight, she had a specific mission. She shut the blue door and went straight to the bookcase to find her thirteen-year-old copy of *Emma*. Though she'd read the book a dozen times, it had been years ago, as a child and teenager. She hadn't opened this precious copy since before her mother passed away. A time when her world, and her future, had looked entirely different.

Holding the beloved copy now, touching the raised wrinkles in its cover and the soft dog-eared pages in between, Holly recognized a strong pull to revisit that Jane Austen world. To take a peek inside a familiar place, to be in someone else's skin for a while.

Chapter Three

Nothing ever fatigues me, but doing what I do not like.
~Jane Austen

HOLLY FROWNED INTO THE FULL-LENGTH mirror, wanting to blame the piece of glass for her dilemma.

"What do you wear on a *faux*-date?!" she asked her reflection. Especially a faux-date that involved Frank. Yes, he had assured her this wasn't a real date. But in the twenty-four hours since he'd asked, Holly had grown more suspicious that he was lying—at least to himself. That deep down, he hoped this dinner would turn into something more.

In preparation, Holly had considered wearing no makeup, leaving her hair disheveled, and maybe donning something frumpy. Anything to put him off the idea. She'd even considered more than that. Staring at the phone, she contemplated again: Fake cough? A couple of sniffles thrown in for good measure? Surely, over the phone, she could pull it off.

But she knew better—Frank would only hold her to their original bargain some other time. Best to get it over with. Deciding on jeans and a sweater, she figured it didn't matter what she wore. Her attire wouldn't change the fact that this was an outing with potentially disastrous consequences.

The entire day had seemed utterly disjointed, from the moment Holly awoke in Hideaway Cottage and realized the time. She'd stayed up until the wee hours reading *Emma*, falling asleep with the lamp on. The crick in her neck had lasted all day, a reminder of her foolishness.

Thank goodness an annoying bird whose call she couldn't identify had the good sense to alert her in time to wake the girls and prepare them a hasty breakfast. And thank goodness she'd submitted her research paper last night *before* entering the cottage, instead of deciding to finish it this morning, as she'd been tempted to do. Still, her jog had been sacrificed, which seemed to set the tone for everything else.

She lost count of all the little things that had gone wrong—from the mug she dropped and shattered, to the dentist appointment she completely forgot, to the house keys she misplaced, making her late to work. And finally, to this "thing" with Frank.

Walking downstairs, she heard mock whistles as she passed the girls watching telly in the sitting room.

"Holly and Frank sittin' in a tree..." Bridget sang, out of tune.

"Hilarious," Holly called behind her, turning the corner to the kitchen in search of some chalky Tums to calm her anxious stomach.

Relieved to find them in an upper cabinet, she uncapped the nearly empty bottle—but before she could tip them into her palm, a rap at the back door startled her. She spilled the last two tablets onto the floor.

"Bollocks," she whispered, picking them up, chucking them into the garbage. The five-second floor rule might have applied when she was a child but not so much anymore.

She looked toward the French doors and recognized the silver hair immediately. Her face softened. It was Mac.

"Hey," she said, opening the door. The cool evening air sifted through her sweater, and she rubbed at her arms. "It's chilly—come in and have a coffee." Even as the words left her lips, she realized she hadn't actually *made* any coffee, and that she didn't have time to make a pot before she met Frank.

It didn't matter. She would make time for Mac.

He remained where he was, removing his cap as he always did. "No, thank ye. I only came by to check on the hot water."

"It's perfect. Thanks again for repairing the system. I don't think I could've taken another rant from Bridget. That girl needs her hot showers or else!"

Mac chuckled, squinting his grey-blue eyes. "Glad to be of service. If you have any trouble, give me a shout." He started to leave but then added, "Everyone well? Your sisters? And your pa?"

"Everyone is great. Busy, though. School's back in session."

"Aye, that'll keep those lasses out o' trouble, then."

"I'm hoping so. You sure about the coffee?"

"Aye. Must be going. I'll take a rain check. Have a good evenin'."

She shut the door and noticed the acidy sensation in her stomach had lessened. Perhaps Mac had been just the Tums she'd needed.

The family's gardener-slash-handyman, Mac MacDonald had looked after Foxglove House for the past thirty years. Though he knew the family well, he always kept to formalities, never divulging anything much about his own personal life. Come to think of it, Holly knew next to nothing about him, except that he was an excellent gardener and a loyal friend to her father. And that she often had trouble understanding his words through his thick Scottish accent.

Even with the formalities, though, there was something warm about him. She'd seen it when her father had gone through his "rough" months and Holly had felt so incapable. Mac had caught her crying one day, muffling sobs into the sleeve of her shirt so nobody would know she was falling apart. Mac closed the gap between them and offered his shoulder.

Then, he offered solutions. He sat at the breakfast table and listed all the things he could do to help out around the house—practical things, such as repairing a leaky patch in the roof, changing impossible-to-reach light bulbs, even helping Holly budget the household accounts. Things her father would normally have done. Mac was a godsend, an angel her mother had sent in the nick of time.

Putting an arm through her jacket sleeve, Holly heard the doorbell and paused. Knowing one of her sisters would answer, she stayed frozen, listening for who she hoped *wasn't* on the other side.

But after a few seconds, there it was—Frank's distinctive voice, in her home, echoing down her hallway.

"Seriously?" she muttered. They were supposed to meet at the pub. This was *not* the plan.

Thrusting her other arm through the jacket sleeve, she hurried to the door. The longer Frank stood in the hall, the more likely it became that Bridget would either insult his obnoxious laugh or sing that blasted "kissing" song again.

"Frank!" Holly forced her best I'm-not-irritated expression. "What are you doing here? I thought we agreed to meet at the pub."

He wore a pea-green blazer she'd never seen before, and his hair was slicked back with some sort of mousse or gel. It resembled motor oil.

"Well," he explained, "it's a lovely evening. I thought the walk up your hill would do me good."

Holly heard giggles, so she waved Frank back through the doorway, following him outside before he had a chance to process her sisters' childishness.

The intermittent rain had stopped again, but the fresh scent lingered. They walked in silence down the hill toward the village. From here, inside a luminescent sunset, everything looked picturesque. The glossy-wet cobblestone street, the vivid green hues of towering trees beyond the village, the one ray of hopeful sunshine backlighting the row of quaint shops—no wonder tourists flocked here each summer, cameras at the ready.

Joe's Pub sat in a prominent spot near the end of Storey Road, offering respite for tourists and locals—a cozy, casual environment for a non-date. Or so Holly had assumed. When she entered with Frank and recognized most of the patrons, she knew it was the worst of all possible choices. Not only would she have to sit through a meal with a man she didn't care for, scrambling to think of things to say—but she would have to do it in front of people she knew.

"Holly!"

Lizzie, Joe's wife, appeared with a bright smile—which changed abruptly to confusion as she saw who stood with Holly in the doorway. Once upon a time, Lizzie would've been the first person Holly called about the Frank "situation." As teenagers, Holly and Lizzie had worked together at the antique shop and had become fast friends. But time and distance, as well as life's growing responsibilities, had pulled the friends apart.

"Umm." Lizzie gave an awkward smile toward Frank. "Will you two be needing a table? Or a space at the bar?"

Holly preferred the bar—more active and lively, less chance for intimate conversation—but Frank would no doubt prefer a table.

"Table's fine. So, how've you been?" she asked, following Lizzie along the bar toward the back corner.

"Amazing!" Lizzie said, beaming, then leaned in with a whisper. "We're trying to get *pregnant*."

"That's… great!" Holly said, trying to hide a cringe. Too much information, even for a former best friend.

"Here you are," Lizzie said, placing menus on the table, then took their drink orders as they sat. "Oh! There's already some buzz around your posters." Lizzie pointed with her pencil to the nearby wall, and Holly saw it—one of the colorful posters Frank had finished and printed this afternoon.

"I've never read *Emma* before," Lizzie confessed. "But I can't wait for the book club to start."

Since Holly and Frank already knew what they wanted, Lizzie jotted down their orders—a club sandwich and crisps for Holly, spareribs for Frank.

"I'll be back in a jiff with this." Lizzie's long, brunette ponytail swished as she left.

"So." Holly threaded her fingers together on top of the table as though she were about to conduct a job interview. "Did Mrs. Aimes ever ring you back? About her collection?" Talking about work was the safest route. Even if it was an overly obvious one.

Frank shook his head. "Not yet. I'll ring her again this weekend, after my trip."

"Trip?"

He inched closer in a bashful whisper, "I'm going on a butterfly hike with a couple of friends. I haven't told you, but my passion—well, besides art, of course—is entomology."

"Ento-*what*-ogy?" she asked.

"Collecting insects."

"Eww." Holly scrunched up her nose then realized he was serious. "Oh. Sorry."

"I know how it sounds, believe me. But it's a real science, a true art form. The iridescent wings of a White Admiral butterfly, the perfect polka dots on the back of a ladybird. I prefer the rare species, of course. They're more challenging to find." He cleared his throat, apparently preparing to offer a full lesson on the joys of entomology. "There's nothing more exhilarating than finding that insect you've been searching for for months, even years. It's a lifetime pursuit."

"I can imagine." She reached for the lager Lizzie had just set on the table, hoping it would stifle the giggle rising in her throat.

"I've been interested in insects since I was a small boy. My father gave me my first kit. He and I would go to the countryside each Saturday, stalking praying mantises or Rosemary beetles. Quite an adventure. I would pore over biology textbooks before our trips, bookmarking pages and memorizing the genus names ahead of time."

Holly tried—really tried—to discipline her mind to listen to Frank's story. She owed him that courtesy, at least. But as he droned further on about his passion for bugs, all she could think about was how lame the last episode of *EastEnders* was. Or how she should add cornflakes to her ongoing grocery list. Or how perfectly a pair of yellow sandals would go with Abbey's new church dress—

"Holly?"

She paused, utterly caught. "Sorry, what did you say?"

"Your courses. I was asking what you were taking."

"Oh." Guilt forced her to sit up straight, make eye contact, and commit to being fully present for the rest of the meal. Even if it killed her. "I'm taking one course this semester, business administration, and I've already signed up for a summer course. Small business."

Frank approved. "Very practical."

"Yes."

Practical was good. Holly was on track, excited to finish her final courses in autumn and finally graduate. She'd always been good at math and had originally focused on business to follow in her father's footsteps, inspired by his success. But she still didn't know how exactly she might end up using her degree. Or how it could alter her home life with the girls. She only hoped inspiration would hit before her last semester.

Lizzie walked toward them, balancing two hefty plates. The meal kept Frank and Holly from saying much more, and Holly was glad of it, seeing as Frank had a difficult time keeping the rib sauce inside his mouth. By the time he'd finished the meal, the crimson mess was all over his fingers, his chin, his napkin, even on his glass of ale in sticky fingerprints. Holly couldn't have stomached watching him attempt to talk through all of that.

Frank tried to buy dessert, but Holly turned him down, saying she should return to her sisters. Abbey needed help with her algebra.

They split the bill, and as they stood to leave, Frank reached out to hold her coat up. "You really are a good mother figure to those girls."

Taken aback, Holly thanked him. No one had said that to her in a long time.

When Frank opened the pub door for her, she saw the almost-full moon, shining low in the sky.

"Beautiful," Holly whispered.

"May I walk you home?" he offered hopefully.

"Oh. No, Frank. I'll go on alone. It's not far."

"I insist."

Knowing he wouldn't give up, she said, "All right," and moved toward the road.

Halfway up the hill to Foxglove, amidst the quiet shush of leaves rustling around them, Holly noticed a hand at her elbow. She paused and saw Frank staring at her. She wished he would say something. Anything was better than silence. The moonlight was strong enough to light up his expression—a hopeful smile, bright eyes. His shadowy face leaned in, and she shifted away. Just in time for his lips to graze her cheek.

She stepped back, realizing this had been a terrible mistake. All of it. The dinner, the conversation, the walk back home. She should have never accepted his invitation in the first place.

"Frank, I—"

"No," he said quietly, eyes downcast. "It's fine."

But she knew it wasn't fine. If she let this moment go, if it were allowed to fester, she would never be able to face him at work. In fact, this very moment might eventually force her to quit a job she so enjoyed.

"Frank, I'm sorry."

"No. I'm the one who's sorry," he said, finally able to raise his eyes again. "I promised you this wasn't a date, and yet, I've turned it into one. I'm embarrassed."

"Please, Frank. Don't be." She reached up to clasp his hand. His gaze had darted back down again, and she wanted to make sure he heard this, loud and clear. "Our friendship matters to me. I want it to continue without awkwardness. Please tell me this won't change anything."

"It won't. I'm fine," he said once more, but the hasty removal of his hand from her grasp told her otherwise. "Have a nice evening. See you next week." He pivoted to walk away.

She watched him go then wrapped her arms around herself, suddenly chilly, and headed home alone. What she hated most about what had just happened, besides hurting Frank, was the irony. For six long years, she had been utterly dateless. Man-less. And now, the first "date" she'd had in years was with a man she didn't care for. Didn't harbor a single romantic or sexual feeling for.

Not that it mattered, anyway. Even if Frank *had* been a true romantic possibility, her priorities still remained with the girls, her sisters. This life. Someday, she would have room for a guy. He would be her priority. But not yet.

Still, here she was, breathing in the crisp air of a romantic moonlit night kissed by a thousand stars… all alone. Feeling small. Feeling lonely and vulnerable. And so, walking home, she let herself want someone. She daydreamed about what a perfect date *could* be—sparkling conversation over untouched meals, giddy smiles as he grabbed her hand on the walk home, breathless anticipation as he leaned closer for a lingering kiss.

Long ago, that man had a face. Liam, her first love, the one she thought she would marry. Liam, the boy she'd met in her Humanities seminar, the one she'd dated for almost a year. He was her future, *the one*. During a weekend home, Holly had even told her mother, "We're meant to be," with visions of wedding cake and bridesmaids dancing in her head.

But only two weeks later, the bubble of that idealistic, romantic university world had been permanently pricked by a late-night phone call—her father's quivering voice telling Holly to rush home immediately. Her mother was gone.

Holly never did return to Kingston University. And, after the funeral, never saw Liam again. Three years ago, she'd heard from an old university friend that he'd gotten married in London. Surely by now he even had a kid or two. While Holly sat here, treading water. Stagnant in a life that looked exactly the same as it did six years ago.

Arriving at Foxglove, approaching the wooden gate that led down the cobblestone path to the front door, Holly knew she couldn't go in. By now, tears had surely stained her cheeks, and she didn't need all the questions tonight. So, she changed her course, walked around the house, past the luscious gardens to her cottage, and opened the blue door, unsure why all these unresolved emotions had suddenly bubbled up.

Like a river breaking cracks in a dam, the lingering doubts and questions from all these years threatened to break wide open. And Holly wasn't sure what kind of damage it might do.

Chapter Four

The person, be it gentleman or lady, who has not
pleasure in a good novel, must be intolerably stupid.
~Jane Austen

"WHEREABOUTS DO YOU WANT THESE, lass?" Mac held a heavy, wrought iron chair at each side.

Holly skimmed the room and pointed. "There. And... maybe over there. Thanks!"

She watched him thread through the group of twelve ladies, chatting and munching on pastries Holly had brought to the first book club meeting. *Twelve!* Amongst them, Mrs. Pickering, Mildred, Lizzie, and Mary Cartwright, the postman's wife. Minutes earlier, after running out of the folded chairs that Holly had asked Mac to bring, he'd located the wrought iron chairs from the garden, to compensate. Holly hadn't even asked Gertrude's permission—she was probably already in hot water over the book club anyway, so a couple of borrowed chairs wouldn't make much difference.

Holly watched Gertrude now, sitting in the far corner like a black rain cloud, holding Leopold and eyeing these people who had the gall to take over her house. The new copy of *Emma* sat beside her, and Holly doubted Gertrude would ever crack it open and glance at the first page. Even out of curiosity, even after they'd all gone home.

Noticeably absent was Frank. Holly hadn't seen him since their date-mishap last week. She had never been more grateful for her part-time schedule of Tuesday through Thursday than now. It had given her more than a weekend to avoid him, though she'd have to face him tomorrow, promptly at 11:00 a.m.

Scanning the overcrowded parlor, Holly suddenly realized how "in charge" she was. These women would have no guidance, no direction, except from her. Usually at these kinds of gatherings, Holly's shy side kicked in and she would sneak to a place in the back, content as a mere observer. But since she had been the one to instigate this meeting in the first place, she would now have to put her money where her mouth was and facilitate every moment.

"Ladies?" she called, too softly at first.

This got Dorothea's attention, who tugged at Mrs. Pickering's sleeve.

"La-dies," Holly said again, louder, and watched a few more faces turn in response. In a matter of seconds, everyone but Mrs. Pickering— still chatting away—stared at her.

Holly cleared her throat. "Thank you all for coming. Please, take a seat and get comfortable."

Sensing another pause as the ladies sat and stared once more, Holly scanned her notes for comfort—then decided to improvise.

She asked who had read *Emma*. Surprisingly only four ladies raised their hands. Next, she asked about their experiences with Jane Austen in general. Two ladies shared—both had been assigned her works back in school, back when they didn't fully appreciate them. And over half the group had seen at least one film based on the books.

As Holly told them her story—the day she fell in love with Jane Austen—she relaxed.

"It was my fourteenth birthday. I'd torn open all my presents and was ready for cake. But Mum slowed me down and handed me one more present. A rectangle wrapped in smooth, gold paper. She looked at me and said, with big, dramatic eyes, 'This is a book that just might change your life.' Curious, I ripped open the package and saw this book."

Holly held up her old, ragged copy. "I've lost count of how many times I've read it. Not an 'easy' read for a fourteen-year-old, but that's what I like about Jane Austen. I think she rewards readers, the ones who invest time in her books. And I think that's what Mum meant, about changing my life. I don't know if 'change' is the right word. Maybe... shaped. I didn't know it back then, as a girl, but I really believe this book has affected the way I look at relationships, at men, even at life in general. I can see little bits of myself in these characters. They're quite dear to me." She peered down and flipped at the corners with her fingernail, hearing the tick of the pages. The shyness had returned, especially as Holly thought about her mother. And as she realized she'd started to bare her soul to the group, unintentionally.

"I understand what you mean," someone said.

Holly looked up to see Mildred.

"Characters can seem like real people sometimes, can't they?" Mildred's nod extended to the entire room, encouraging reciprocal nods.

Holly wanted to cross the room and hug Mildred for saying the perfect thing at the perfect time. For giving her validation.

Her confidence fully restored, Holly opened her beloved text. "Why don't we begin with Chapter One?"

Early this morning before the book club meeting, Holly had taken a detour during her sunrise jog. She'd heard that the *Emma* film crew had arrived last night. So, she tackled the steep hill that led up to Chatsworth Manor on the outskirts of Chilton Crosse and puffed her way to the entrance, stopping to peer down the wide, elongated pathway lined with statuesque elm trees. The Manor stood at the end, waiting for her. From the distance, she could see people scrambling about, even at that early hour, hoisting equipment from lorries into the Manor. As much as Holly wanted to go further, investigate, there wasn't time, so she turned back around to start the girls' breakfast.

But now, after the book club, and after Holly had finished some textbook reading and a load of laundry, she found there *was* time. Rather than walk, or even jog, she chose to take her bike.

By the time she reached the Manor again, her thighs burned from the uphill climb. She kept close to the road's edge as another lorry passed by. People still scrambled about, carrying equipment and furniture, while a couple of men—one using a megaphone—directed the traffic. She noticed a handful of other curious villagers under the shade of a tree, sitting quietly on blankets, eating apples or sipping beverages, enjoying the show.

Unsure of how to proceed but sensing the urge to explore, Holly dismounted her bike and walked it to the opposite side of the road, propping it against a tree trunk. She didn't know the procedure—whether "civilians" were even allowed this close—but until she was told to leave, she would tiptoe around the edges and people-watch.

These days, the renovated Chatsworth Manor served as an elaborate hotel, where tourists could have a getaway retreat or business executives could hold important conferences. But it also happened to be the perfect place to film a film—with two ballrooms, three sitting rooms, a richly decorated parlor, and a restaurant, all surrounded by gorgeous, original fourteenth-century architecture and formal gardens in the back.

Taking a peek inside the main entrance, Holly noticed blockades and barriers around certain areas, guiding film personnel to one area and hotel guests to another.

Deciding to keep to the outside for now, she wandered around to the back gardens and wondered when the actors would arrive. Perhaps Gerard Butler as Knightley? Ioan Gruffudd as Frank Churchill? Not *completely* beyond the realm of possibility, as big-name actors often threw in a classic period piece to bulk up their resumes. But somehow, she doubted they would end up gracing her little village with their glamorous presence.

Reaching the outskirts of the gardens, Holly wished she'd visited more often. She adored their formality. Luxurious and immense, the gardens served as a stunning backdrop for daydreaming. She paused to stare at the cypress trees standing in perfect alignment, tall pointed tips waving in the wind. The trees surrounded a stocky fountain at the bottom of a wide stone staircase that rose up through the Italian gardens, adding a second level. Holly moved along the fringes, drifting, just as the passing clouds drifted above, casting shadows on the manicured lawn.

Selecting her favorite oak tree at the far edge of the garden—and noticing that big, sweaty men with cables and camera equipment had entered the area—she squatted down, invisible, settling at the base of the trunk, shifting to get comfortable on a patch of grass, still slightly damp from this morning's mist. She wished she'd brought along a blanket, maybe with a picnic lunch.

Her mother used to bring her here as a little girl. The gardens were always open to the public, so the two of them would pack picnics and spend hours beneath shady trees, munching on peaches and strawberries, and rubbing the velvety-warm summer grass between their toes. She remembered her mother removing a notepad from her bag. Inside the blank pages, she would compose poetry about what she saw—a bird, or a flower, or even the picnic basket—and read it to Holly. Sometimes they would write a poem together, her mother writing one line, then handing the notebook to Holly for the next, back and forth.

Holly had found the notebook in a drawer a few weeks after her mother died. Even now, the memory of it made her eyes burn hot with unexpected tears. Memories of her mother always seemed to come in odd surges. Periods of drought made Holly feel guilty, as sometimes a whole day went by without thinking of her mother in a specific way. But when the memories did come, they came incessantly, vividly, like waves reacting to a strong tide.

Holly pushed herself up to stand again, to wipe the tears before they had the chance to fall.

Still wishing to remain invisible, she lurked along the garden's border, listening to the men bark orders at each other. As she approached the backside, past the garden's staircase, the men's voices grew softer. But other, newer voices replaced them. Ahead of her, beyond some nearby trees, she could hear a conversation. Of sorts.

She stopped to listen—one voice low then another in response, an octave higher. It might've been a woman, but it didn't quite sound like a woman. The tone was too artificial, too forced.

Curious, Holly stepped closer and saw someone pacing in the distance, waving one arm as he spoke. Her eyes searched for a second person but didn't find anyone. Just the one man, in his early thirties or thereabouts. He had thick dark hair and wore jeans and a navy shirt, and held something in his left hand.

"I don't under*stand*!" he said to the air, in his too-high, mock-female falsetto.

Holly stifled a snicker as she drew a few steps closer. Even knowing it was wrong, eavesdropping, she couldn't help it. He held what seemed to be a rolled-up script. Practicing lines? Role-playing, maybe?

He cleared his throat then lowered his tone to what she assumed was his natural one. But his accent was hard to make out.

A poor attempt at being British, she thought. All his vowels flat and twangy.

"I realized something while I was gone," he read, making "gone" sound more like *gah-hawn*. "Being apart from you, I'd left a piece of myself behind. My dearest Emma, you have my friendship, but I must know—will you take my heart, as well?"

With the last word, he raised his hand and froze. His eyes had found Holly.

She was caught, royally.

In that split second, Holly had a choice—run away, or stay and face the consequences of her eavesdropping. She chose the latter.

She stepped out boldly from the shadow of the tree and into the brilliant sunlight. "Well," she said, deciding to cover her embarrassment by being cheeky. "I wouldn't mind being friends, but I'm afraid I don't know you well enough to take your heart."

He bowed his head, shaking off his own embarrassment.

"And my name isn't 'Emma.' It's Holly." She grinned.

By now, his expression matched her own, and she noticed two dimples tucked away at the ends of his smile, as though someone had dotted them there with a pencil. His warm brown eyes locked onto hers. "How long have you—"

"Been standing here, being horribly rude and spying on you?" Holly finished. "Only a few seconds." She moved closer. "Sorry if I startled you. I promise I'm not a stalker."

"I probably looked like an idiot." He batted the rolled-up script softly against his thigh.

"Not at all," she half-lied. "You're American, aren't you?" She'd suspected as much the moment he flashed those brilliant white teeth, but his accent was the dead giveaway.

"From Texas," he admitted.

His profile and mannerisms earlier had been deceptive. From further away, his jaw had looked more angular, and the shadow of stubble had made him look older. But seeing him close up as he squinted into the sun, Holly changed her mind. He had a boyish quality that made him instantly approachable, almost shy.

She was glad she hadn't run away.

"I'm Fletcher. Hays," he said, offering his hand.

"Nice meeting you, Fletcher." She returned his gentle handshake. "So, you're an actor?"

He seemed confused until he looked down at the script again. "Oh. Definitely, no. I'm a writer. This is actually mine." He raised the script for clarification.

"Yours?" A light dawned. "You wrote the *Emma* screenplay?"

"Yeah. Well, sort of. I co-wrote it with Finn, my writing partner. He's in London, trying to get us a new gig, some ghostwriting thing. Anyway, the director asked me to stick around the set as story consultant. So, I'm trying to get the lines right, see how they sound."

"I think that's *amazing*, writing a screenplay. What does 'story consultant' mean?"

Probably tired of squinting, he reached for his sunglasses. "Nothing too glamorous. I'll mostly hang around set, stay available to the director, actors, producers. Answer questions about dialogue or make changes to the script."

"How long is the shoot?"

"Four months or so. Shooting all around the Cotswolds, but mostly here at the Manor."

"So, you get to live here? At the Manor?" Holly hoped her questions weren't too obnoxious. She normally wasn't this inquisitive, especially with perfect strangers. But she'd suddenly become fascinated with the behind-the-scenes process of filmmaking.

Fletcher chuckled and shook his head. "I wish! No, writers are on the low end of the totem pole. Just the actors and producers—the 'important' people stay here. I'll be at some place in the village called Joe's?"

"Yeah, Joe's got a couple of rooms above the pub. Smallish, I think. But nice. Cozy." For the first time, a silence lingered. She didn't want to keep grilling him with questions, though she still had a few. "Oh, blast," she said. "What time is it?"

He looked down at his chunky watch and announced, "3:05. Why?"

"I need to get going," she said with a reluctant wince. "I forgot about this teacher's conference. For my little sister, Abbey."

"I should probably get back to this, anyway. Can't seem to get the final scene right."

"Where Knightley and Emma reconcile." She nodded. "The most important scene in the book."

"That's the one. It's gotta be perfect."

"You'll get there," she said, having no idea if he really would. She started to leave then said, "It was nice meeting you, Fletcher Hays. Maybe I'll see you around the village sometime."

With a friendly goodbye wave, she scurried back through the trees, retracing her steps around the edges of the enormous garden until she finally reached the Manor again. Drained from an overly active morning, she somehow still bubbled with new energy. Whether because he was a newcomer from the States or because he was an accomplished writer, Holly was instantly fascinated by this Fletcher person. She hoped they indeed would cross paths again soon.

Chapter Five

My idea of good company... is the company of clever, well-informed people, who have a great deal of conversation.
~Jane Austen

NOT ONCE IN FOUR YEARS had Holly hesitated at the gallery door. Of course, not once before today had she feared what was on the other side.

It had been five days since her faux-date with Frank, and now the gavel would fall. In those five days, she'd gone from thinking the best—that Frank would be unaffected by her avoiding his kiss—to the worst—that he would be *so* affected he would sack her on the spot. Realistically, she knew, it would probably be somewhere in between.

Grasping the brass handle, she braced herself and walked inside.

"Holly, nice to see you!"

Noelle Spencer, the gallery's American owner, stood at the front table. Petite and blonde, dressed in a sweater and jeans, she greeted Holly with a warm smile. When Noelle had first arrived in the village, Holly had recognized a kindred spirit in her right away. It wasn't until months later, though, that Holly discovered they had a more profound connection. Noelle had also lost her mother, at nearly the same age Holly lost hers. And although they hadn't discussed their mothers past that one conversation a year ago, it changed things for Holly. They now spoke a language no one else could speak. A knowing tone, a secret handshake. Holly could go to Noelle, if she ever needed to.

Usually, Noelle stopped by the gallery once a week to check in and sometimes to paint. Two years ago, she'd turned the space back into a working gallery, where artists, including her, worked on their paintings while patrons observed. Unfortunately, Noelle's gallery days always seemed to coincide with Holly's days off.

"Noelle! How are you?"

"Really good. How are your sisters?"

"Oh, they're great. Busy with school, just the usual stuff."

Before meeting Noelle, Holly had always pictured Americans as stuck-up or cold. Or arrogant. She wasn't sure what had perpetuated the image. Maybe just a collection of observations she'd made, or propaganda she'd swallowed over the years from the media. But Noelle shattered Holly's American stereotypes. Perhaps it was her easygoing California upbringing that made Noelle so naturally gregarious. Or maybe it was her infectious happiness, a direct result of her move to England. Nearly three years ago, Noelle had uprooted her life from the States and moved to the Cotswolds after inheriting Primrose Cottage—and this art gallery—from her famous-artist aunt, Joy Valentine. Since then, Noelle had settled comfortably into village life, becoming involved in committees, helping renovate the local school, and saving the gallery from bankruptcy. She'd also married the love of her life, Adam Spencer, last summer. Nearly the entire village, Holly included, had turned out for the ceremony.

"Oh!" Holly remembered. "Did you hear about the book club?"

"Frank just told me. I've been in London with Adam until this morning. But sign me up for the next meeting. I'll be there!"

"We had a nice turnout yesterday."

"I love the idea of a book club. And *Emma*'s my second-favorite Austen book."

"*Pride and Prejudice*, the first?" Holly guessed.

"Yep," Noelle admitted. "I can't help it. I fell head over heels for Mr. Darcy at fifteen."

"Sounds exactly like how I fell for Knightley."

They shared a smile just before Frank walked around the corner, and Holly remembered her anxiety again. He avoided eye contact and spoke directly to Noelle, asking her a budget question.

So, there it was. Holly was invisible to him. That told her all she needed to know. This would be a long afternoon.

By Thursday's shift, things still hadn't warmed enough between Holly and Frank for him to treat her as a human being again. But it didn't matter, because today, she had the whole gallery to herself. When she'd arrived this morning, he'd met her at the door and said, "I'm going to Bath—hold down the fort," then brushed past her to leave, as though escaping a small fire inside.

She didn't need further explanation. "Going to Bath" meant he was in search of new artists, scouring galleries for additions to the collection. Holly was perfectly capable of "holding down the fort" for those few hours. Still, he could've at least been cordial, asked if she had any questions, or given her the usual quick rundown of his own shift, before abandoning her so curtly.

Relieved he was gone and looking forward to a quiet morning, she stepped into the back room, prepared to finish whatever leftover paperwork Frank had begun this morning.

But before she could even sit down to assess it, she heard the tinkle of the bell. Rolling her eyes, she put on her best customer-service face and rounded the corner again, hoping this was a self-sufficient tourist. One who would browse quietly then leave.

"Oh. It's you!" she said, her courtesy smile warming to something genuine as she saw Fletcher Hays close the door behind him. His stance was awkward, hesitant, as though he'd mistakenly walked through the wrong door and had been caught. He wore a khaki blazer and jeans, and this time, she noticed cowboy boots.

"Holly, right?" He pointed at her. "What a coincidence."

"I normally would agree, but since I work here, maybe this is only half a coincidence?" she offered.

"And it *is* a small town."

"Very small."

"So, I guess coincidence isn't really the word." He shrugged. "A pleasant surprise, then?"

"I'll take that."

He shifted his weight, and she noticed he held the script again. She wondered if it was attached to his hand permanently, like a tattoo.

"Some beautiful stuff here." He walked deeper into the room, browsing the first painting—the one Noelle had finished last week. He paused and tilted his head.

"Do you like art?" she asked.

He made a "sort of" gesture with his free hand then turned back around to face her. "I took a course in art appreciation once. But that's about as far as my appreciation goes."

"Where'd you go? To university, I mean?"

"Oxford."

"Seriously?"

"Why so surprised?" He smiled, his dimples appearing. His country twang deepened. "Y'all probably think us dumb Americans could never make it at a posh place like Oxford."

Holly felt her cheeks go warm. "No, that's not what I meant. I'm only surprised you've been in England that long. I assumed you'd only been here a few months or something."

"Nope. Been here nearly ten years. Went to Oxford as an exchange student for one semester and didn't wanna leave. So I finished out my degree and worked some odd jobs then landed a writing gig at the BBC."

"Seriously?!"

"Again, with the surprise! You're giving me a complex."

"You have to admit. The BBC? That's pretty amazing."

"Yeah, but it's not as glamorous as it sounds. High-pressured, getting stuck with teams of writers. Lots of egos, backbiting. I lasted about four years, until Finn and I decided to write this *Emma* script. It eventually got accepted, so here I am. You officially know more about me than most people."

"Well, I'm honored." Feeling a pause she didn't know what to do with, she suddenly went back into gallery mode and added, "So... you're welcome to look around at the pieces. Joy Valentine's are displayed upstairs. She's the gallery's original owner."

Something in his expression had changed—an ease in his eyes replaced by... she couldn't tell what. Discomfort? She watched him lean in slightly and half-whisper a confession, "To tell you the truth, I was only looking for a quiet place to work. The pub is a bit... raucous for the creative process. Loud music, people talking. I thought a gallery might do the trick."

She played along, whispering, too, "You mean, like one of those bookshops with cushy seats, where they let customers sit there all day and read?"

"Well, yeah. Sort of." His eyes searched hers, maybe to see whether he'd insulted her.

"Hmm," she said. "Well, that's not *quite* how it works here. I mean, people come from all over England to view our fine gallery. To get some culture."

"Fair enough." Fletcher took a step backward. "Well, I can go, then."

Holly reached to grab his sleeve with a chuckle. "I'm only having a laugh—I thought you knew. You can stay. Of course you can stay. In fact, you're in luck. We happen to have an enormous cushy chair in the back that's not in use at the moment."

Watching his comfort level return as he contemplated it, she actually favored the idea. Especially with Frank out of the way. He would never have allowed this—a script-toting American squatter in *his* gallery. But Frank wasn't here right now, was he?

To convince Fletcher further, she said, "Seriously. Stay. I'll just be doing some paperwork in the back, anyway. You'd be keeping me company."

"Only if I won't get you into trouble."

"You won't," she reassured, leading him toward the back room. She pointed to the aubergine plush chair. "All yours," she said then sat at the table, determined to make a dent in the pile Frank had left behind.

From the corner of her eye, she saw Fletcher sink into the chair and spread out the script on his lap. After a minute, he looked up and stared at the wall. "What's that?"

Holly heard the chimes. "Oh. There's a clock shop next door. Dozens and dozens of clocks, all set to chime at the same hour."

"Every day? Doesn't that drive you nuts?"

"I hardly hear them anymore."

"Can you imagine having to set them for daylight savings?" Fletcher snickered.

"Old Mr. Rothschild actually hires someone to help him. They spend half the day setting all the clocks in the shop. Lots of grandfather clocks, but then, all sorts of other ones, too—watches, alarm clocks, table clocks. Probably a couple hundred, in all. He's a stickler for it. Every single clock must hold the accurate time. I think he was in the Navy or something. Or has OCD. Maybe both."

As the last chime rang out, Holly lifted the first receipt, and Fletcher settled in, flipping a page of the script.

Holly only made it to the second receipt when she heard the front door's bell tinkle again. This time, it came with a familiar voice.

"Holly! Where are you? Look!"

Abbey bounded around the corner, waving a piece of paper. She plopped down in the seat across from her sister, out of breath.

"Well, I can't see it if you don't hold it still." Holly grabbed the paper. "Oh—your exam?" she asked, even before she looked. She remembered the crash algebra study session that had kept them up until 2:00 a.m. a few days ago. Holly had tried to explain quadratic equations to her frustrated, tearful sister—in vain, she'd thought, until she looked down now and saw the red-circled A.

"Outstanding!" She gave back the paper and leaned in for a warm hug. "I *knew* you could do it," she whispered, smelling the strawberry shampoo Abbey was so fond of.

Abbey squeezed her back, still slightly out of breath. She must've run all the way from the school.

"Why are you out so soon?" Holly asked, backing away, remembering the time.

"Teacher training. They released us early. Rosalee and Bridget went home, but I had to come here and show you this first."

"I'm glad you did. I'll be home right after work, and we can start an early supper. Maybe with a special dessert to celebrate?"

"Okay!" Abbey folded the exam and noticed Fletcher. "Oh. Hello."

The wall had come up. Abbey had never been very good with strangers.

Fletcher put down his script and flashed a smile. "Hello."

"Who is *that*?" Abbey whispered to Holly but loudly enough for Fletcher to hear.

"That's my new friend, Fletcher Hays. He's from America."

Abbey's eyes widened behind her glasses, as though Fletcher had transformed into some kind of alien in front of her eyes. "America?"

"That's right," he confirmed. "From Texas."

"Do you have a ranch?" Abbey asked him. "With horses and cows? And servants?"

Fletcher looked confused and said, "No, none of those."

"Oh." Abbey seemed almost disappointed.

"I think she's thinking about *Dallas*," Holly explained. "She likes to watch the re-runs."

Fletcher chuckled into his fist and shook his head. "I see. Unfortunately, not all Texans have ranches or horses. Or even wear cowboy hats."

"But, you're wearing boots," Abbey countered, pointing down, her timidity all but gone.

"True. But that's only because they're comfortable. I've never been on a horse in my life."

"Well," she said, scooting back her chair. "It's very nice to meet you. I'm Abbey Newbury. Holly's my sister."

"It's a pleasure to meet you, Abbey Newbury." He rose and took two steps while reaching out his hand.

When he sat back down, Abbey whispered to Holly, "I like his accent. He says my name sort of funny."

"I'll bet he thinks the same thing about us," Holly whispered back.

"You're probably right," Abbey agreed. "Well, I have to go," she announced in full voice. "I told Rosalee I'd be home by now." She stuffed the exam into her backpack and, with a final wave, disappeared around the corner. "Bye, Fletcher Hays!"

"She's adorable," he told Holly.

"Thanks."

"Is Rosalee another sister?"

"Yes. And her twin's name is Bridget. They're sixteen."

"Wow, big family," said Fletcher. "And teenagers. Your mom's got her hands full."

Holly paused, caught off guard. "Yeah, well…" She had a big decision to make in a split second. She hadn't planned on having this particular conversation today. Still, rather than lie or avoid the issue entirely, she decided to say it. Nothing to hide from or be ashamed of. Just a fact of her life. "Actually, Mum passed away. Six years ago."

His eyebrows rose as he processed the information. "I'm sorry. I had no idea."

"It's okay. I live with my sisters. And my father. We take care of each other now."

"You're lucky," Fletcher said.

"Lucky?"

"To have each other, I mean."

"Yeah. I guess we are."

Somehow, Holly's admission about her mother broke through the social wall that normally exists between near-strangers, and she and Fletcher spent the next two hours talking. The usual polite standoffishness was waived, the shallow chitchat bypassed, in favor of deeper conversations that actually meant something.

Fletcher still held his script, and Holly still held her receipts, both intending to return to them at some point. But they never did. She found out Fletcher had a sister and older brother, that he had a scar on his shin from a car accident years ago in which his best friend had died, and he had an inexplicable fear of clowns. Holly confessed her love of cheesy classic eighties films and her embarrassment about singing horribly off-key. She also revealed her feelings of incompetence with her sisters—always measuring her own care of them against what she thought her mother's would've been—and that the burden of it nearly suffocated her sometimes.

Inside those two hours, not a single tourist came through the door. This happened periodically, no visitors at all, for a whole afternoon. But when the bell's tinkle finally came, Holly sucked in a quick breath, thinking it might be Frank. She knew he wouldn't fire her for this, but the thought of him coming in right now, seeing her with Fletcher and not having made a dent in her work...

Fortunately, it was only an elderly couple from Australia, wishing to browse. When Holly returned after greeting them, Fletcher was on his feet.

"I'd better go. Thanks for this," he said. "Letting me sit awhile."

"But you didn't get a single ounce of work done," she protested.

"Neither did you."

"It's okay, though. I enjoyed our chat."

"Yeah, we should do this again sometime. On purpose. Maybe at the pub."

"Definitely."

When they walked toward the front door, an idea struck Holly. "Would you be interested... well, there's this book club thing," she explained. "We're discussing *Emma*. We meet at a cottage. My dad's cousin Gertrude—"

"That grumpy woman you mentioned? With the high-strung dog?"

"That's the one. I was wondering if you might be the guest speaker at our next meeting, Monday morning. I think the ladies would love to hear about *Emma* from an expert."

"Not sure about the expert part." He shrugged. "I think we have a director's meeting then, but I'm not sure. I'll check and let you know."

"Brilliant. So, it's at 10:00 a.m., if you can make it. Hickory Cottage, at the bend in the woods, south of Storey Road, our main street."

"What's your cell number? I'll phone if I can't come."

She recited the number as he tapped it into his mobile. "Oh," she added. "If you *are* able to come, wear your boots."

"Why?"

"Just trust me."

Poor Fletcher. He really didn't know what he was in for, meeting Gertrude.

When he left the gallery, Holly revisited her receipts, utterly bored by them. Her thoughts still lingered on the lovely talk with Fletcher. Her mind hadn't been that stimulated with adult conversation in ages, and it left her satisfied, filling up little gaps inside that she didn't realize were empty.

Chapter Six

*At my time of life opinions are tolerably fixed. It is not likely that
I should now see or hear anything to change them.* ~Jane Austen

I T WASN'T UNTIL SHE PRESSED the doorbell that Holly remembered:
she'd worn the earrings Gertrude always mocked. A pair of lovely
gold hoops that, inside Gertrude's cottage, were referred to as
"circles."

"Why do you insist on wearing 'circles' in your ears?" Gertrude would
chide. "If you're going to wear earrings, wear proper earrings—hanging
pearl drops. Or diamonds. Something classic." Then she'd cluck her
tongue and mutter, "Your generation…"

Not in the mood for a confrontation, Holly removed her 'circles'
and tucked them inside her skirt pocket then found the scribbled notes
she'd made this morning for the book club in case Fletcher weren't able
to attend and take over as guest speaker.

Her phone buzzed impatiently from the other pocket, so she reached
to check it and saw a mysterious text. A number she didn't recognize.

Turn around.

How bizarre.

Curious, she obeyed. And there stood Fletcher, grinning, phone
in hand. Relieved, she watched him shut the gate and amble up the
stone path.

"You made it," she said.

He joined her on the step. "Yeah, the director didn't need me after
all. So, I thought, why not come and meet the infamous Gertrude? How
bad can she be?"

Holly faced the door. "You're about to find out."

Before she could reach for the bell again, Mildred cracked open the door and invited them in.

As Holly tried to make the introductions in the foyer, a bellowing, "Who is that?!" came from the other room. "Come! Show yourselves."

"We've been summoned," Holly whispered with wide eyes.

Fletcher followed her into the parlor to find Gertrude at her finest. Wearing a long, brown dress with a lace collar, she clutched at Leopold, a yipping little maniac wriggling out of her grasp at the sight of Fletcher.

"Leopold doesn't like men," Gertrude announced, reining him in. She looked Fletcher up and down then locked eyes with him. "You are the young man Holly told me about. The American." She crinkled her nose, as though something putrid had just wafted through.

"Guilty as charged," he said, closing the three steps between them. He offered his hand, well out of Leopold's reach, and added, "Fletcher Hays. Pleasure to meet you."

Gertrude likely decided propriety wouldn't allow her to refuse it, so she placed the noncommittal tips of her fingers lightly into his palm then returned them to Leopold, who had assessed by now that this stranger wasn't a threat.

That was when Gertrude saw the boots.

"A true *cow*boy," she exclaimed. "I was informed of your Texas roots."

Fletcher glanced back at Holly, clearly understanding her odd request of footwear, then told Gertrude, "A cowboy? Well, ma'am, that's a matter of opinion. In some people's uninformed minds, cowboys are twangy, uneducated hicks who've never read a book in their lives. As that description is the exact opposite of me, I must say that the answer is decidedly, 'No.'"

Gertrude's lips parted slightly. Holly caught a snicker under her breath.

Gertrude cleared her throat and narrowed her scowl. "Young man. I would like you to state your exact intentions with Holly."

"Intentions?"

Holly needed to step in before this all went incredibly wrong. "Gertrude, I told you. We're just fr—"

"What Holly's trying to say"—Fletcher reached down to thread his fingers through hers—"is that friendship has blossomed into something else. We are, as you've suspected, dating. And my intentions are purely honorable."

Now Holly's lips were the ones parted in surprise. Gertrude glanced from Fletcher to Holly, then back again. "Well. Be sure that they are. Or you'll answer to me."

Attempting an obvious rescue operation, Mildred chirped from the kitchen, "Come in here, you two, and I'll make you some tea!"

Holly untangled her fingers from Fletcher's and nudged him toward the kitchen.

"Hey, that was fun," he said a minute later, as Mildred handed him a cup.

"Why did you *do* that?!" Holly attempted the same scowl as Gertrude's but knew it wasn't effective. She didn't have a dark enough soul to match it.

"Umm, probably for the same reason you told me to wear boots?"

"Fair enough."

"Besides, isn't that better than her thinking you're an old maid? You said she calls you 'spinster' all the time." He took a sip. "I thought I was helping, getting her off your back. But, you know, I can go in and tell her the truth, if you want." He'd set down his tea and was already halfway to the door when Holly yanked back his sleeve.

"No!" She pictured weeks and weeks of pity-free discussions ahead. In fact, was it possible she might even receive a smidgen of respect in place of the pity, for once? "Okay, fine. You're my pretend-boyfriend. But only around Gertrude."

Mildred raised her cup, hiding her smile.

"Done. But," Fletcher added, "there could be trouble up ahead. She might blow a gasket when she realizes your 'boyfriend' is abandoning you in four months to go back to the States."

"But what about Finn?" Holly asked. "I thought you said he was in London. Getting you more work in the U.K. after *Emma*?"

"Yeah, but I can't count on that. He's sort of flaky, God love him. Unless he gets us something solid, I'm probably going back home. I've been working on a couple of good leads in Texas."

A knock at the door broke into Holly's next question and sent Mildred scurrying back through the house to let the book clubbers in. At the same time, Fletcher's phone buzzed. Holly watched him peer at the screen in his pocket and clench his jaw.

"Be right back," he told Holly and slipped into the adjoining dining room. She wasn't straining to hear but could still catch fragments of the conversation: "Not now… I told you yesterday… It's too late."

When he returned, Holly busied herself with lining up the napkins into a perfectly square stack, hoping to seem absorbed in her task. Before she had a chance even to peek at Fletcher's face and read his expression, Mildred had ushered three women into the kitchen and started the introductions. Holly now had social permission to stare at Fletcher, but all she saw was warmth as he shook the ladies' hands. No trace of the tension in his conversation with whoever that was.

Minutes later, thirteen members buzzed and circulated around Gertrude's parlor—Noelle had joined them, and Frank was still a no-show. Holly called the meeting to order and presented their surprise guest.

At first, Fletcher seemed adorably nervous, stumbling a bit, searching for words—just as Holly had, on her first day of the book club. But once the ladies generated questions about the script-writing process, or asked his take on Mr. Elton or the reason Knightley was his favorite character, Fletcher relaxed. He stood and used gestures to explain his viewpoint, making eye contact, asking them questions, too. Instead of a presentation, it became a lively exchange.

At one point, Holly snuck a glance at Gertrude and saw her paying attention. Not fawning over Leopold or grunting and scoffing but actually watching Fletcher, even nodding a couple of times at something he'd said. Could he possibly have won her over so easily?

"You were quite the success," Holly proclaimed an hour later, accompanying Fletcher outside. "I measured it by the Gertrude Scale. I saw her pretending not to listen at first, but then she couldn't help herself. From a one to a ten in only an hour's time. You had her mesmerized."

"I don't know about *that*." Fletcher opened the gate and let her pass through.

The noonday sun had dimmed behind thin clouds, creating patchwork shadows on the ground. Fletcher was due back at the set, so Holly would walk with him until the fork separated their journey, leading her back to Foxglove House.

"So. You want to talk about it?" Holly said, playing a gentle version of hopscotch with the shadows as they walked.

"What?"

"That call you got in the kitchen, before we started? It seemed a little... intense," Holly said, then added a quick, "Not that I was listening in." When he didn't answer right away, she wished she hadn't brought it up at all. "Sorry. I have this awful eavesdropping habit. Forget I said anything. Terribly rude."

"Naw, it's fine. You're right. It was intense. The call was a girl I used to know." He paused and dug his hands into his jeans pockets. "More than that. A girl I used to be engaged to, for about half a second. Eight months ago." His tone was matter-of-fact, but a darker undertone punctuated his words.

"Fletcher, you really don't have to talk about this. I shouldn't have brought it up."

"Maybe it'll be good for me." He resumed a leisurely pace. "Stacy. She was English, worked at the BBC with me. That should've been my first clue," he muttered through the side of his mouth. "Never date a co-worker. Anyway, after a few months, I finally convinced her to go out with me. We were together nearly two years. I thought it was time to make things official, so I proposed."

"So far so good," Holly prompted.

"She accepted, but something was 'off.' She started acting weird. Distant. Turns out she'd been sleeping with one of the other writers. I found out the same day we got the green light for the *Emma* gig."

"Oh, wow. Bugger. I'm so sorry."

"That was probably the most surreal day of my life. The best news and the worst news all at once. Hard to process either one."

"So," Holly prompted, "that was her on the phone earlier? Stacy?"

"Yep. She called last night. First time in months. She and the jerk writer broke up and now she suddenly 'misses me.' Wants to get back together."

"Blimey. What did you say?"

"That it's too late. That the damage she did was permanent. That I can't trust her anymore."

"Good for you. But, I don't understand. Why did she call again, today?"

"Just being persistent, seeing if I'd changed my mind. And I hadn't. I hope she believed me this time," he grumbled, more to himself than to Holly. "You know the worst thing is—" He paused again, this time looking far beyond her to the fields, as he explained. "I've always been this really trusting guy. Like, to a fault. And the worst thing is that her cheating… changed me. It turned me into someone I didn't expect to be."

"How do you mean?"

He moved his gaze back to Holly. "Well, I hate this stupid cliché, but I'm having trouble trusting people now. Women, especially. I never used to be that guy—suspicious, cautious. Putting up walls. Jaded."

"I'd say you're doing pretty well with me," she offered.

"You're different, though. In a good way," he clarified. "Easy to talk to. And you don't want anything from me. It's just… I'm protective now. I don't wanna feel the way I felt with Stacy. Ever again. Sucker-punched." The frustration pricked his voice.

"You just need time," Holly said, aware she was offering yet another cliché.

Fletcher kept walking, stepping on his own shadow along the path. "I guess. Taking a break has helped."

"Break?"

"From dating. I need to get my head together, focus on other things." Fletcher removed his hands from his pockets and shook them out then folded them across his chest. "See? You're easy to talk to. Almost too easy. I never talk this much about myself. Okay, your turn." He peered at her sideways. "What's your story? Who was the love of your life?"

"Well, that's a loaded question." She smiled. "But I guess I owe you a story. Love of my life. That person would have to be Liam. From university, at Kingston."

"College sweethearts?"

"Yes." She could see them nearing the fork in the road up ahead but wasn't ready to part yet. "The short version is that we were madly in love, dated for a year, and I thought he was it. The one. And then… I got the call about my mother. So I came home straightaway. Never returned to university."

"And Liam?"

"We tried to make it work at first." She remembered the funeral, how Liam had dutifully comforted her but then went back to school that afternoon for an exam. And stayed there. Then, the hasty and infrequent emails he would send, written between busy university activities—studies, parties, girls? Leaving her to speculate whether the distance was an excuse, whether he was ever really "hers" at all.

"But I knew my place was here in Chilton Crosse," she continued, "with the girls. The distance was too much, and besides, Liam and I were young. So, I sort of made the decision for us. To let him off the hook. I didn't want him to sacrifice his university days for me."

"He didn't fight you on it? Try to make it work, long-distance?"

"No…" she said, thinking back to that final three-minute phone call four months after the funeral—how devastated she was that he *hadn't* tried, hadn't fought for their relationship. "He said he was hurt but that he understood. We haven't spoken since."

"Guess it's my turn to be sorry," Fletcher said.

"It's okay. We weren't meant to be. Another cliché!" she groaned. They'd reached the fork in the road. "Well, thanks again for helping out. At the book club, I mean."

"Do you think there's room for one more member? Is it female-exclusive, this club?"

"Well, there's supposed to be one male attending, but he hasn't shown yet. Frank. We'd love to have you there. I'm sure Gertrude would enjoy it."

"That's reason enough to join. Plus, we can keep up our ruse that way. Being a pretend couple."

"Clever thinking." Holly shaded her eyes from the sun to look up at him. "Would you like to come to dinner sometime? To the house, I mean? You've met Abbey already, but the twins would be there, and possibly my father."

Fletcher pondered it then said, "Yeah. I'd love it, actually. Joe's pub food is amazing, but I've ordered the same thing three times in a row."

"Tomorrow night? Say, seven-ish?"

"Perfect." He glanced at his watch and pointed down the road. "I'd better take off. See you tomorrow night?"

"See you then."

She continued up the hill to Foxglove, loving the idea of having someone over to the house. A guest for dinner. They hadn't had a guest in... well, years. Her mother used to love to entertain, to invite friends over for supper a couple of times a month, at least. Foxglove House needed this. Needed someone to prepare for, to make a special dinner for. The house needed life again, someone new. It would be good for the girls, meeting Fletcher, forced to be on their best behavior. Good for everyone.

Chapter Seven

Ah! There is nothing like staying at home, for real comfort.
-Jane Austen

THE STRAPS FROM THE CLOTH bags bore into Holly's shoulders, and no amount of shifting would ease the burden. She should've taken her bike, or even the family car—rarely used because everything was in walking distance at the village—but she'd thought she could handle the load of groceries on her own. Knowing that a special guest would be at the table this evening, she'd made a stop at Mrs. Pickering's market after work, paying close attention to the menu. Pork tenderloin, assorted vegetables, and an all-American apple pie. Holly had hoped to have a larger attendance this evening by inviting a few more guests. But in the end, Mac had a job in another village, and Joe and Lizzie had to work, so the party would be small and intimate.

Even so, she wanted to make it special, so before work, she rang Mac to ask about setting up a table in the garden, just as her mother used to do. Mac had access to things like tiki torches and sturdy tables for such an occasion and offered to deliver and set them up before he left for his other job. Holly had also checked the forecast and noticed a rare mild evening with no rain. Dinner in the garden, it was!

When Holly entered the kitchen at Foxglove House, Mildred was there to help relieve her heavy load.

"Oh, dear. Let me get this." Mildred reached out.

"Thank you. I couldn't have made it another step."

Mildred Smith had been Gertrude's caretaker and housekeeper for over a decade. Last year, Holly's father had asked Mildred to help out at Foxglove once a week, even knowing Holly and the girls were capable of handling the household chores together. When Holly questioned her father, he told her the real reason for the decision—the medical bills for Mildred's brother were piling up. She was a proud woman and would never take a handout, so this was a small way they could help. Holly had agreed.

Secretly, she enjoyed having another adult in the house, even if it was only once a week. Besides, Mildred wasn't a housekeeper. She was more of a family friend. She and Holly would often chat about village goings-on, share tea during breaks, exchange recipes. In her late fifties, Mildred looked older than her years. From what Holly knew, she'd lived a hard life—battled cancer and won in her early thirties; never married or had children, but wanted both; and now spent her days caring for her ailing brother who lived with her. And, of course, she worked for Gertrude. Holly pitied anyone who had to put up with that woman's balking and griping on a daily basis.

"Is Dad here?" Holly asked Mildred now. About six months ago, her father had begun working from home on Tuesdays. It kept him from having to commute so often.

"He was here earlier," Mildred motioned, unloading the groceries. "But then he left. Some dinner meeting in London this evening. He'll be home late."

"Shame…" Holly mumbled then clarified. "I was hoping he would be here for our party. You're coming, aren't you?"

"Oh, I *wish* I could," Mildred said in her slight Irish brogue. "Perfect evening for a party, isn't it? Lovely, cool spring weather." She paused. "But my brother needs me. In fact, the doctors are talking about hospice care."

"Oh, Mildred." Holly set down the frozen broccoli and placed a cold hand on top of Mildred's. "I'm so sorry. What can I do?"

"Nothing, love. Thank you." She sniffed back tears and reached for the next item. "It is what it is. We'll get through it, won't we?"

"Yes." Holly squeezed her hand. "Yes, we will."

"So. Is the American coming to this party of yours? Fletcher?"

"Yes. In fact, he's the whole reason for it. I figured he needed a home-cooked meal. Plus, he still feels like a stranger in the village, I think. This was just a friendly gesture."

"Mmm-hmm." Mildred raised an eyebrow.

"Mildred, you *do* know we were joking, about that whole dating thing, with Gertrude? It's all a big act. Strictly for her benefit."

"Whatever you say, dear." Mildred reached over to place the margarine into the fridge.

"Abbey! Get the door, please!" Holly called, removing the buttered wheat rolls from the Aga.

An hour before, Holly had looked a right mess, her hair twisted into a messy knot, dark blue T-shirt dusted with patches of flour. Under other circumstances, she would've been fine with Fletcher seeing her that way. He wouldn't have cared, and neither would she. But this was a proper garden party, and she wanted to dress the part. So, minutes ago, Holly had scurried upstairs, slipped into a favorite skirt and top, brushed out her hair, spritzed her arms with a little body spray, and dabbed on some lip gloss.

"Hey," she heard now, from behind.

Fletcher stood with Abbey, who held his hand and positively beamed. Holly remembered that it had been ages since a man had been in the house—one besides Mac, or their father. Their dinner guest would become quite the spectacle this evening.

Tonight he wore jeans and a dark blazer, along with his cowboy boots, and gripped a bottle of wine in his left hand.

Holly shook her head and pointed a pot-holdered finger at him accusingly. "You weren't supposed to bring anything."

"It's nothing special," he countered. He released Abbey's hand with a squeeze and set the bottle down. "Smells amazing in here." He joined Holly at the counter as she spooned the veggie mixture into a bowl. "How can I help?"

"Maybe the salad? Lettuce and dressing are both in the fridge," Holly said, back to business. "Abbey," she called behind her. "Would you go find your sisters? They're supposed to be setting the table."

Fletcher carried the lettuce head to the cutting board beside Holly then found a knife and carved out the core, removing it with ease.

"You've done this before," she said.

"Once or twice."

The twins filed in, looking annoyed about their new table-setting task—until they saw Fletcher. Just as Holly suspected, the girls were rendered dumbstruck at the first sight of those dimples.

"Hey there. You must be Bridget?" he said, pointing to Rosalee. She shook her head. "Rosalee," he corrected himself. "Then, you're Bridget? I'm Fletcher."

Seeing that the girls had no intention of responding, Holly took the initiative. "Okay, girls, please set the table. Dinner's nearly ready."

The kitchen bustled with activity during last-minute preparations. Holly directed everyone out the back door to the garden, each carrying heaping bowls of food or baskets of bread. As Holly stepped over the threshold, she had to stop, take it all in. She hadn't seen it all come together, at least not in this twilight setting—the flittering lights of the tall, slim torches strategically placed around one long table, donned with crisp, white linen. The sun had set minutes ago, casting an orange glow beyond the trees. Even the breeze cooperated, offering a hint of cool air on Holly's cheeks. The recollection of her mother's parties struck her in a way she wasn't prepared for. She stepped back in time several years, saw her mother dressed in white—always, in white—making the rounds about the table, making sure everyone was comfortable. Then, throughout the evening, steering conversations and laughing that pure, uninhibited cackle when something struck her as hilarious.

Blinking, bringing herself back to the garden, without her mother in it, Holly wondered if this had been such a good idea.

She felt a nudge at her elbow and saw Fletcher, his eyes browner and warmer than usual in the dusky light.

Her expression must have betrayed everything, because he whispered, "You okay?"

Holly remembered why she'd set up the party in the first place and found a half-smile. She could do this. "I'm great. Thanks."

Fletcher reached down to take the heavy glass pan she'd forgotten she was carrying and walked it to the table for her.

When they all got settled, Fletcher said a brief prayer of blessing over the food, then the dinner guest quickly became the center of attention. The girls tossed questions at Fletcher, mostly about the film set—*Which actors are playing the roles? Can we watch the scenes being filmed? Can we be extras??*

Fletcher fielded them well, obviously comfortable with becoming the entertainment for the evening. Holly remembered that he had a sister of his own. He was used to this.

She also noticed how well-behaved the twins had become. They hadn't been this cordial to each other in... well, a lifetime. They displayed pristine table manners and hung on Fletcher's every word.

By the end of the meal, Holly's sisters had hogged every Fletcher conversation. Holly hadn't spoken a single word to him since they sat down. And she probably wouldn't be able to afterward, either. She had another term paper due in the morning.

Taking advantage of a rare lull, she pushed back from the table and lifted her plate. "Anyone up for dessert?"

A chorus of "*Me!*"s went up.

"I'll help," Fletcher offered, taking her plate and reaching for Abbey's, too.

"Thanks," Holly said. "I'll go get the pie."

A minute later, he met her in the kitchen with a stack of dirty dishes.

"Sorry the girls peppered you with so many questions about the film set." Holly scooped vanilla ice cream into petite dessert bowls. "You only *thought* tonight would be an escape from work."

"I didn't mind. They're adorable. I had no idea so many people would be this interested in the movie. The whole village is buzzing."

"I guess it gives us small country folk something exciting to do with our mundane days," she teased, licking her finger.

"Dinner was amazing, by the way."

"Thanks. I—"

The slam of the front door distracted her, and she saw her father enter the kitchen, toss his keys onto the table.

"What's for dinner?" he bellowed then looked at Fletcher. "And the better question is—who is this stranger standing in my kitchen?" His tone was entirely playful. One side of his mouth even crooked upward into something resembling a grin.

"Dad, stop that. Don't scare the dinner guest. This is Fletcher Hays, a new friend of mine. He wrote the script for *Emma*, the film at the Manor."

"Well, *co*-wrote," Fletcher said, stepping forward to extend his hand. "Nice to meet you, sir."

Her father caught Fletcher's hand in a hearty shake. "He's American," he told Holly.

"Yes, Dad. He is. Be nice," she muttered, enforcing the request with narrowing eyes.

Fletcher played along. "American by birth, British by choice, sir."

"Whereabouts are you from, son?"

"Texas. San Angelo. Small town, far west of Austin."

Holly's father nodded and tried to ask another question when the girls came in to see what all the commotion was about. Within seconds, their dad became the most important male in the room again.

"This ice cream is melting," Holly announced, shoving dessert bowls into their hands and ushering them all back outside.

"Dad, I'll make you a dinner plate," she offered.

"Absolutely not. I'll do it myself," he insisted. "I have some work to do. You go back outside and join your friend."

Though surprised by his offer, she decided not to question it. "Thanks. I will."

"Your family is great." Fletcher stood in the doorway, running a hand through his thick hair. "They remind me of my family."

She knew, with that statement alone, that her dinner party had succeeded in the only way that mattered. To make him feel at home.

"I'm not sure if you got the most accurate picture, though." She winced, remembering the twins' incessant squabbling at breakfast this morning. "They were on their best behavior tonight. Trust me, they're not usually this... tame."

"A little spunk is a good thing. You've done a wonderful job with them. It's obvious how much they love you."

"It is?" Holly felt an unexpected sting of tears.

"It is. They feel comfortable with you. I'm sure it's hard, not knowing whether to be their sister or authority figure. You seem to have balanced those really well."

"Thank you," she said in a whisper, not able to trust that her voice wouldn't crack.

"Well, duty calls." He stretched his arms behind him. "I've got some revisions waiting for me. Hey, y'all should come up to the Manor soon. Watch one of the scenes."

"The girls would love that. And so would I."

"Well, you've got an 'in' whenever you want. I'll give you a behind-the-scenes pass. Just ask for me at the entrance, and they'll bring you back." He started to walk off into the night air. "I'd better get to the pub. Thanks again for tonight," he called back with a wave.

Holly waved too then shut the door and wondered if this was how her mother felt after a dinner party—blissfully exhausted.

In the kitchen, Duncan stood at the counter, reaching to place the dry glasses into the cupboard.

"What are you doing?!" Holly asked.

"Can't a man put away glasses in his own kitchen without it being national news?" He closed the cabinet and turned around.

"I like the effect Fletcher has on this household."

"Maybe you should invite him over more often, then."

"Dad."

"What? I think it's about time. Your having a 'friend' over for dinner."

"That's right, a friend. A mate. *Only* a mate." She joined him at the counter and turned on the tap.

"Whatever you say, love..." He kissed the top of her head and disappeared around the corner toward his study.

By the time Holly entered the garden, she could see that the girls had already cleared the entire table. She hadn't heard a peep from any of them since she'd said goodbye to Fletcher and assumed they were in their rooms, tapping away on their phones or computers—or, she hoped, finishing up any leftover homework. Using a folding chair, Holly stood to extinguish each of the torches. Mac would come by in the morning for the tables and tikis, and with the mild weather, she could leave them where they stood. She gathered the tablecloth, folded it, and went back inside, closing the door on her first official garden party.

Creeping upstairs a few minutes later, she heard a small voice call out her name. She tipped open Abbey's door across the hall and peeked in.

"C'mere," Abbey said, waving Holly inside.

Holly obeyed and perched on the edge of her sister's bed. The lamp cast a soft glow, illuminating the lime-green quilt. With her right hand, Abbey clutched a stuffed lamb, her bedtime companion given to her by their mother a few weeks before she died. *A Wrinkle in Time* sat, splayed open, beside her.

"Did you finish your homework?" Holly asked.

"All of it. Even the algebra. And I didn't need any help."

"Good for you." Holly combed a stray hair away from Abbey's cheek. "So, how did you like our little garden party tonight?"

"Such fun. I like Fletcher. I'm glad you invited him."

"Me, too."

"Holly, is he your boyfriend?" she asked, her round, blue eyes unblinking behind her glasses.

"No, he's just my friend."

"But, why just a friend?" She almost seemed frustrated, disappointed in Holly somehow. "Don't you think he's dishy?"

Holly smiled. "He's very dishy. But that doesn't mean we *have* to be boyfriend and girlfriend. Sometimes it's nice to be friends. Sometimes, it's best to be friends."

"Adults are confusing."

Until now, Holly hadn't needed to give inquiring minds any reasons that she and Fletcher were "only" friends. And until now, she hadn't genuinely stopped to answer that question for herself. "Well, I think it's partly because I'm so comfortable with him. I don't have to pretend with him or put on a show for him. I can be myself."

"And you can't do that with a boyfriend?"

Holly tilted her head. "Well, not all the time. A boyfriend is someone you try to impress, show more of your best side to."

"That sounds exhausting."

Holly chuckled and tucked the quilt around Abbey's legs in a cocoon. "It is. But I don't have to impress Fletcher. It's very natural with him."

"I guess that makes sense."

"And besides, he's not staying in our village. He'll have to leave someday."

"When the film wraps?"

"Exactly. So, even if I fancied him 'that way,' it would be rather futile."

"I wish Fletcher would stay." Abbey removed her glasses and rubbed at her eyes. "Maybe we can change his mind."

After tossing around for a while, Holly decided to let insomnia win. Strange, that her body experienced the euphoria of exhaustion while her mind refused to turn off. Rather than fight sleep, she threw off the covers and wrapped up in a thick robe, heading downstairs to Hideaway Cottage. Perhaps reading a chapter of *Emma* would help.

The garden was bathed in luminous moonlight, and Holly wanted to linger in it. Even at the beginning of May, the evening held a chilly snap, so she was glad she'd worn this particular robe, fleecy and warm. Holly sat on the step leading up to her cottage, facing the house. She always loved this view. Foxglove was so charming, even for its grand size. It never felt anything but cozy. She remembered the night she'd left Foxglove for university, recalled the ache in the pit of her stomach at the thought of not sleeping in her own bed. Of leaving behind something so comfortable and familiar.

But she had gotten used to it, so that whenever she came back to visit during those university years, returning home was... odd. Foxglove House wasn't hers anymore, not the way it had been. She was a guest. A lodger. There was a formality in the air she couldn't shake. Sometimes, even now, she didn't quite know where she fit in. Or what her role was, or how long she could stay in it.

Lately, in the back of her mind, far into the hard-to-reach corners, was the thought, "How long?" How long would she live in this space, be this person who ran a house that didn't really belong to her?

"As long as I need to," was always the dutiful answer she gave. But that answer was becoming inadequate, thin. And she didn't know why.

Holly picked up a pebble and chucked it, watching it bounce off the stone steps like a rock skipping on a lake.

The low hoot of an owl came from somewhere deep in the forest beyond the edge of the property. Hearing it brought Holly out of herself, back into the moment. Back to this spot where the warm, gold shaft of a hall light inside the house reflected elongated rectangles on the grass.

So what, that her life didn't look the way she thought it would by now. Did anyone's? Surely she wasn't the only one in the world with something missing. Something just out of her grasp that she couldn't see or name.

So what, that she didn't have what she'd expected to have by now: a husband and baby, a home of her own, a university degree with solid plans for a career. It shouldn't mean she couldn't appreciate what she *did* have. She named them now in her mind, ticked them off, one by one: active, healthy sisters; a supportive and loving father; a satisfying job; a book club; and now, someone to throw garden parties for. A fake boyfriend. A true friend.

And for now, in this moment, it was more than enough.

Chapter Eight

Nobody, who has not been in the interior of a family, can say what the difficulties of any individual of that family may be.
~Jane Austen

"WHY HAVEN'T WE DONE THIS for ages and ages?" Abbey licked a dollop of cookie dough from her finger.

"That, little sister, is an excellent question." Holly pulled the third batch from the Aga, and the sugary blast of warm air made her blissfully lightheaded. Almost enough to distract her from the incident with Abbey that had happened thirty minutes ago.

"Mmm. Those are the best yet," Abbey decided, watching Holly coax hot cookies onto the cooling rack with a spatula after they'd cooled.

This Baking Day Saturday was all Abbey's idea. The twins had scampered out the door for Chatsworth Manor first thing this morning, to see if they could spot any famous actors. And their father was spending his afternoon helping Mr. Peterson with some financial questions about his fledgling business. So, today was Holly and Abbey's day. They would bake cookies for Abbey's Sunday school class then join the twins at the Manor.

A few years ago, when it had been obvious that Abbey felt left behind watching the twins do older-sister things, Holly made a point of spending one-on-one time with her at least once a week.

Abbey seemed at her most relaxed during these times, and as she got older, their talks evolved into deeper topics. Things Holly imagined

Abbey would've talked over with their mother—crushes on boys, or what God looked like, or what she wanted to be when she grew up.

"Do you think I'm pretty?" Abbey whispered now. She nudged her glasses back with a floured index finger then used a cookie cutter to carve the dough into star shapes.

Holly studied her, unsure of where the question had come from. "You're beautiful. You look more like Mum every day. Your hair is turning her shade of auburn, and you have those striking blue eyes. Why would you ask that?" She tried to be nonchalant, lifting a limp angel from the dough and placing it onto the empty pan.

Abbey shrugged, moving on to the next shape. "Carly Weatherall told me my nose was too big."

Instantly livid with this other child, one she'd never met before, Holly focused on Abbey. "Look at me."

Abbey blinked and raised her eyes.

"You *are* beautiful," Holly said in a quiet, even tone. "Your nose is perfect. And this Carly Weatherall person has an inferiority complex if she says any differently."

"What's that?" Abbey frowned, pushing another cutter into the dough.

"It means she's jealous of you."

"Of me?" Abbey said, skeptical. "How do you know?"

"I studied it in school. In a psychology course. When people are mean to other people, nine times out of ten, it's because they feel bad about themselves. Picking on other people makes them feel better."

"Well, that's stupid."

"It certainly is."

Satisfied that the embers of a poor-self-esteem fire lit by Carly Weatherall had been squelched, at least for the moment, Holly let her mind drift back to the incident an hour ago. To the confusion on Abbey's face as she'd held the peach tight, and the strength it took for Holly not to explain everything to her right there and then. They'd all kept quiet for so long, but she knew the day would come. Perhaps sooner than they were ready.

After the last of the cookies were cooled and placed into bags, Holly and Abbey took them to the crew members at the film site.

"Look, there's Fletcher!" Abbey called out at the end of the long walk that had brought them to the Manor.

He stood with his back against a tree, strumming a guitar.

"Fletcher!" Abbey waved, then ran ahead to meet him.

When he saw them approach, he looped the guitar strap back over his head, balancing the neck against the tree.

"You made it," he said, reciprocating Abbey's hug.

"Yeah, we thought we'd come check out your 'office,'" Holly said. Gesturing toward his guitar, she added, "I didn't know you were a Renaissance Man. You write screenplays, you play guitar... what else can you do?"

"I can do some killer donuts on a three-wheeler."

Holly pictured sugared treats sitting on three tires. "I have absolutely no idea what that means, but it sounds impressive."

"Just another redneck 'thang' we do in Texas." He grinned. "The twins are here. I put them to work as extras in a scene. Hope you don't mind."

"Mind? It'll win me major brownie points for the next ten years. They'll love that."

"I see them!" Abbey exclaimed. "Can I go?"

"Sure," said Holly. "Just don't get in the way. And do what they tell you, if they ask you to move."

"Okay," she agreed, sprinting toward the Manor.

"Aww, you brought me cookies," Fletcher said, hand on his chest.

"Well, they're not all for you, but you can sneak one." She opened the bag. "Or two."

He reached inside and drew one out. "I don't know the last time I've had homemade cookies." He took a bite. "Delicious."

Holly's gaze drifted away, followed Abbey as she met up with the twins, far in the distance.

"Hey," Fletcher said, waving a hand. "Where'd you go?"

"Sorry." She sealed the cookie bag and let it swing down at her side. "It's nothing."

"It's clearly something."

"Well, it's sort of something. It happened this morning. It was..." She searched for the right word. "Unexpected. And it's a little weird to say out loud, actually."

"Now you *have* to tell me. I'm intrigued." He leaned against the trunk and took another bite.

"It's Abbey. It's actually something good, if you see it from a certain angle. I should probably be grateful and not question it. But I wasn't ready for it."

"Totally not following you so far."

Holly shook her head. "Right. Sorry. Here it is. So, this morning, before we made the cookies, I looked out the window and saw Abbey under the peach tree. It's that giant tree far over to the left of the garden? Anyway, she picked up a peach that had fallen and turned it over in her hand, and smelled it."

"Still not following. A peach?"

"I'm getting there. Okay, maybe I need to back up." This was harder than Holly thought. She hadn't told this story to anyone. Not even Lizzie or Mildred. "Abbey was the only person who witnessed my mother's collapse. It happened outside while she was playing—she was only six—and Mum was thinning out the peaches from that tree. Abbey's never told us the details, but it was clear that Mum collapsed while picking the peaches. She had an aneurysm, we found out later. She died instantly. There, in the garden."

"Oh, man." Fletcher's expression shifted to warm and empathetic.

"Anyway, Abbey was able to scream out to Mac, who was inside repairing something in the kitchen. He came out, saw Mum lying there, and tried to do CPR. But she was already gone."

"And Abbey saw the whole thing."

"Yes. But she doesn't remember any of it. She knew Mum had died, but she sort of blocked out how it happened. But even with the memory loss, Abbey has avoided that peach tree all these years. Won't go near it. Dad's first thought was to 'cut the son-of-a-bitch down,' but he figured cutting it down might confuse Abbey's subconscious, or agitate her. Plus, Dad was hoping that one day, when she got older, maybe Abbey would work through everything and be able to face it."

"Sounds about right."

"It's so strange, how her mind protects her—even the mention or sight of a peach seems to be a trigger. She sort of shuts down. So, all these years, we've treated peaches almost like an allergy—never bring them into the house, never have them as ingredients in food."

She looked down, tracing a mangled tree root with the tip of her shoe. "I told you it was weird. It sounds extreme, the allergy thing, but we wanted to do what was best for Abbey. Sometimes I wonder if we've been enabling her, protecting her from what's inevitable. But we wanted her to have a normal childhood. Well, as normal as one can be without a mother."

"So then, this morning, Abbey had a peach?" Fletcher prompted, finishing off the cookie and wiping the crumbs on his jeans.

"Yeah. I watched her from the kitchen window. She brought it up to her nose and looked confused, searching for a memory. I froze, wondering what to do. But then she dropped it on the ground and came back inside as though nothing happened."

"It sounds like her mind is trying to unlock itself. You did the right thing, not pushing her."

"You think?"

"Absolutely," Fletcher nodded firmly. "And I'm glad you told me."

"Yeah. It felt good, telling someone." Holly realized how much she'd needed to talk about it. How saying something aloud, explaining something hard to explain, had removed a pressure, a weight.

"So. Why don't you let me give you a tour of this joint?" He grasped her hand then picked up his guitar and pulled her in the direction of the Manor. "Let's go see what they're filming."

Watching a scene being filmed didn't match Holly's high expectations. Sure, at first she enjoyed seeing the twins in their costumes—Bridget looked right at home, playing dress-up, while Rosalee seemed uneasy and insecure. And Holly did enjoy the excited thrum of energy as actors found their marks, gaffers adjusted reflective screens, and makeup ladies powdered noses and cheeks. Then later, as everyone on set held a collective breath while the clapboard was tapped—"Take one!"—and the director shouted, "Action!"

But seconds into each scene, something—an off-camera noise, an actor flubbing a line or missing a mark—would occur, causing the director to issue a frustrated "Cut!" Actors would then grumble and whip out mobile phones or cigarettes from the folds of their dresses or deep pockets, and the Regency-era atmosphere would quickly dissolve.

Another disappointment arose as Holly studied the actors and couldn't name a single one she recognized. She'd known it was a long shot, hoping to see Rupert Friend or Joseph Fiennes, but this was a low-budget film, so only underpaid unknowns were present.

Still, this was *Emma.* Beloved characters in a beloved novel, coming to life right in front of her eyes. It was surreal, being transported inside this time machine, back to a gentler era where women were feminine and dainty, and men were chivalrous and cut fine figures in their frock coats.

Surprisingly, the best source of entertainment ended up coming from the twins. Bridget pranced around the set in costume, making her onlooker friends jealous, while Rosalee stood in place, soaking everything up. Holly noticed how mature Rosalee seemed—years older. It suited her, being in Jane Austen's world.

The twins' only job was to pretend to chat while standing in the background of a two-minute scene. Holly could see the impatience building on Bridget's face between each take. Eleven, at last count. She'd gotten creative, turning her down time into something more useful than texting—flirtation. She'd been making eyes at one of the actors, a striking blond, at least twenty years old. A young Brad Pitt. Holly could see, even from this distance, that the handsome actor had noticed Bridget as well. She did that hair-twirl thing she always did when she saw a boy she liked, and it was working.

When the director yelled the final "Cut! Print!" the actor gravitated toward Bridget and lingered beside her, even as the other actors darted to their trailers to remove their itchy wigs. Bridget drew out her mobile from the folds of her dress and tapped something out while the actor whispered something into her ear—probably his number.

Holly didn't like the look of it, the quickness of it all. But Bridget would turn seventeen this year, would soon fill out university applications. She was old enough for some harmless fun.

Seeing Abbey raise her groaning, sleepy self from the grass, Holly knew it was time to go home. The afternoon had become quite warm, and a cold drink in the shade of Foxglove's garden—with another cookie—sounded lovely.

"So, this was… fun," Holly told Fletcher as she stood, stifling a yawn.

"You're a terrible liar." He smirked. "You were bored stiff."

"Not stiff. I'm still bendy. See?" She posed in a runner's stretch.

"Hollyyy!" Abbey called, already rounding the side of the Manor.

"She's a demanding little thing, isn't she?" Holly told Fletcher.

"Wonder where she learned that?" Fletcher cleared his throat.

"Hey." Holly play-punched his arm then jogged away to follow her pint-sized dictator home.

Chapter Nine

Death… a melancholy and shocking extremity.
~Jane Austen

THIS WAS HOLLY'S LEAST FAVORITE kind of rain. The misty, drizzly sort that didn't require an umbrella but still managed to dampen the hair along with the spirits. She rather preferred a good downpour to this. At least you knew where you stood with a downpour.

She crossed the street, relieved that at least one thing had gone right today. Frank, after nearly a month of doing his best to ignore her, had finally ended the standoff with an actual, "How is your family?" conversation. She hoped the freeze-out was nearing an end.

She approached her destination and waved at the elderly man sitting in his blue chair. Come drizzly rain or beautiful shine, old Mr. Bentley sat at the entrance of the bakery, protected from the weather by a green-striped awning, handing out free bite-sized samples of scones or teacakes. He'd been at his post, spreading sunshine, as long as Holly could remember. He had to be ninety now, at least.

"Good afternoon," she said, shaking his extended, withered hand. Surprisingly, the older he got, the tighter his vise-grip of a handshake became.

"Miss Holly Newbury," he replied with a bright smile. "How are you on this fine day?"

"Very well. Yourself?"

"Nary a complaint." He raised a plate of miniature blueberry scones. She chose one then entered the building.

Mr. Bentley's daughter, Julia, ran the bakery, though she was rarely seen. And for good reason. Unlike her gregarious father, Julia was cold and anti-social. Though she had pretty features—fair skin, dark eyes, sandy hair—she never smiled and rarely spoke to the customers. The only time Holly ever saw Julia was when she appeared through the swinging door with a tray of biscuits or tarts then returned to her cave like a grumpy bear. She wisely hired perky young university students to man the counter, a natural extension of Mr. Bentley's cheery greeting when customers first arrived.

Fortunately, Julia wasn't around, so Holly approached the counter with ease to select an after-dinner sweet for the girls.

"Hi, Holly." Theresa appeared from behind the counter. "Sorry I wasn't able to make it to the book club yesterday. Had to work. What did I miss?"

"We spent a while talking about Emma's governess and how her friendship with Emma is changing. We're reading the next three chapters for Monday."

"I'll be sure and make it. I don't want to miss another one."

Behind her, Holly heard new voices. She turned to see characters from *Emma* walk inside, clutching toothpicks from Mr. Bentley's tray. Ever since the film actors had arrived, it had become quite common to see them traipsing about the village, in full Regency costume, whilst on breaks or stand-bys. Holly got a kick out of watching tourists react to men in frock coats and women in gowns and bonnets, sitting on pub stools drinking lagers, or smoking on a bench outside. They probably thought it a normal, everyday occurrence in a small English village.

As Holly pointed to the chocolate pie under glass, someone tapped her shoulder—Mrs. Cartwright, the postman's wife.

"Holly, did you hear?" she asked, her voice solemn and low.

"Hear what?"

"Mildred Smith's brother. He passed away, just this morning. About an hour ago."

"Oh my. No, I hadn't heard. I knew the end was near but not quite *so* near."

"I was going to take something over to her now," Mrs. Cartwright said. "Would you join me? We could walk together?"

"That sounds perfect. I'd love the company."

Holly decided to forgo the pie and instead ordered chicken salad sandwiches for Mildred. Taking the paper bag from Theresa, she stepped aside for Mrs. Cartwright to place her order, too.

"Fletcher!" Holly whispered. She'd forgotten to check her texts to see whether he could meet her for a late lunch. They hadn't seen each other since Saturday at the Manor—Fletcher had skipped yesterday's book club because of a director's meeting—so she had texted him this morning, asking about lunch at the pub.

She saw his reply. *Sure. In an hour?*

That was over an hour ago.

Holly told Mrs. Cartwright the situation and asked if they could meet outside the pub in about five minutes.

At Joe's, Holly found Fletcher sitting at the bar, frustrated, tapping his phone. When he saw Holly, he said, "Don't tell me. You're canceling."

She set down the bag and crawled up onto the stool.

"I have to. It's Mildred. Her brother passed away this morning."

"Oh. Gosh." He shook his head. "Sorry to hear that."

"It's not really a surprise—she's been caring for him about two years, now. And the hospice workers had been going to her cottage the past few days to see him. It shouldn't be a shock, but somehow it is."

"I think death is always a shock."

"I guess so. Nobody's ever ready to let go of somebody they love, are they?"

"True."

"So, I need to go to her. See if there's anything I can do. I suspect she'll need help with Gertrude." Holly rolled her eyes. "That's a job, if ever there was one."

"Heh, no kidding. Want me to come with you? To Mildred's, I mean."

"Mrs. Cartwright's waiting for me. We're going together. I'll just send Mildred your condolences." She grabbed the handles of her bakery bag and slid off the stool then paused. "You looked a little... irked when I came in. Were you mad I hadn't answered your text?"

"Naw, of course not. I was doing a sort of… purge. Ridding myself of some memories."

"Stacy?" Holly guessed. "Have you heard from her again?"

"Nope. But this morning I was sorting through some old photos and realized I'd kept a few of us, from a long time ago. All smiles, at holidays and at work. Here's one where I'm putting the ring on her finger." He tilted the phone to show Holly the photo. But before she could process the details—a blonde with her hand covering her mouth in surprise and the back of Fletcher's head—he tapped the picture into cyber oblivion.

Holly wasn't sure what to say, how to encourage him. He seemed so confident that he didn't want to keep even a single piece of evidence that he and Stacy ever existed as a couple. Holly still had a couple of pictures of Liam, buried way back in her wardrobe somewhere. She hadn't looked at the photos in years but couldn't bear to tear them up, throw them out. As painful as the break-up had been, a purging would be an attempt to erase a whole section of her life. And she wasn't willing to do that. Weren't the bad parts of a relationship every bit as real and meaningful as the good parts? Getting rid of a few pictures wouldn't change that.

Just as Holly remembered Mrs. Cartwright and started to leave, Fletcher said, "Oh, did you hear about Rosalee? The good news?"

"No, what news?"

"The part. It's only a few lines, but she beat out several other girls."

"I have no idea what you're talking about," Holly said, cocking her head, trying to make sense of it. "What part? You mean *Emma*?"

"Oh, crap. I assumed she would've told you by now. Yeah, after you left the set on Saturday, the director put out a spur-of-the-moment casting call. The actress playing Elizabeth Martin was rushed to the hospital that morning for gallbladder surgery, so the director was desperate to fill the role."

"And Rosalee got the part? Are you serious?"

"Yep. The director handed it to her right after her audition. Didn't even want to see the rest of the girls. I'm surprised she didn't tell you."

"Me, too." Holly saw the clock on Joe's wall ticking down the time. "I really have to go. Sorry about lunch. Rain check?"

"Absolutely."

When Holly arrived with Mrs. Cartwright, she hadn't expected anyone else at Mildred's cottage.

But on the way there, Mrs. Cartwright reminded her that Julia had rushed to Mildred's side when she heard the news an hour ago. Holly had forgotten that Mildred had practically raised Julia, whose mother passed away when Julia was only an infant. With no children of her own, Mildred had offered a widowed, heartbroken Mr. Bentley her support and time.

At Mildred's front door, Holly and Mrs. Cartwright took turns hugging Mildred tightly then followed her into the reception room to see someone else Holly hadn't expected—her own father. While Julia and Mildred took the food into the kitchen, Holly made her way toward him.

"Dad," she whispered. "I didn't realize you'd be here."

His hands were clasped respectfully behind his back, his expression grim. "Mildred got the news when she was at our house this morning. I was working at home and gave her a lift over here."

He must've parked at the back of the cottage. "That was kind of you," Holly said, threading her hand through his arm. She loved this side of her father. Compassionate, helpful.

When Mildred and Julia returned, Holly tried to fill up the silence. All the things you were supposed to say—even knowing it sounded hollow, "I'm so sorry about your brother. Is there anything at all we can do?"

Mildred did take Holly up on her Gertrude offer. Holly would go there immediately and help out today and the next day, at least.

"It's no trouble at all," Holly said, trying to convince herself. "Really."

After a few moments of Mrs. Cartwright offering some spiritual comfort to Mildred, Julia decided to leave, and it became clear that Mildred probably wanted solitude. So Holly stood and offered another warm hug, and Mrs. Cartwright followed suit.

"Please, call if you need anything at all," Holly told Mildred, still clutching at her sleeves. Seeing tears well up in Mildred's eyes, she added, "Anything."

Fully expecting her father to fall in behind them, Holly noticed he was still seated.

"Oh. Are you staying?"

"For a bit. You go on. I'll be there in time for supper."

"Okay." Holly headed for the door with Mrs. Cartwright and suddenly dreaded the rest of her afternoon. With Gertrude. How would she survive it?

With every additional chore she was ordered to do—sort Gertrude's medicine, change Gertrude's sheets, dust Gertrude's curio cabinet—Holly's respect for Mildred skyrocketed. It wasn't that she was afraid of hard work. Holly did these sorts of things on a routine basis in her own household. But it was the *way* they occurred, here at Hickory Cottage.

Gertrude would hobble about on her cane, follow Holly room to room, and tell her all the things she was doing wrong.

"You missed that spot of dust there." Gertrude would scowl, pointing with her cane.

"That's not where the hand towels go."

"Haven't you ever folded sheets before?"

Holly's tongue was metaphorically sore from biting it the past three hours.

Now, they were in the kitchen, the last room that needed care. Holly rushed through the dishwashing so she could finally leave, desperate to breathe oxygen that wasn't poisoned by insults and jabs.

Gertrude had eased into a chair in the corner, propping her cane against the cabinet and adjusting Leopold in her lap. "Tell me more about this young man of yours."

Holly swiveled the plate in her hand, drying the edge with a towel. "You mean Fletcher?"

"Who else could I possibly mean? Of course Fletcher."

"What do you want to know?"

Gertrude ignored the question and made a face like she'd tasted a lemon. "*Hideous* name. Fletcher."

"I adore his name. It's so... American."

"Precisely! Even worse. Let me warn you, child—he's likely to have a negative influence over you. Those Americans have wild ideas about things."

Fed up, Holly set down the heavy plate with a thud and folded her arms to face Gertrude. "Fletcher has a degree from Oxford. He's not some country hick. He's smart and he's kind. And he's funny."

Gertrude grumbled and fed Leopold another biscuit.

Knowing that trying to prove Fletcher's worth would accomplish absolutely nothing but raising her own blood pressure, Holly resumed her drying then folded the damp towel and looked around. "Well, I think I'm all finished here. There's leftover chicken in the refrigerator for you. If there's nothing else, I need to get home to the girls. It's suppertime."

Gertrude waved her on without a single thank you—not that Holly had expected one.

Walking out the front door, Holly doubted she could make it through one more day of being Mildred's substitute. But, remembering the sad circumstances, she knew she would muster the strength. For Mildred.

Chapter Ten

*Friendship is certainly the finest balm for the pangs of
disappointed love.*
~Jane Austen

"MORE TEA, MRS. MULBERRY?"

"Oh, yes, dear. Thank you." She held her cup steady while Holly poured.

Nearly the entire village had turned out for William Smith's funeral two hours before. Seeing the generous crowd spill over at the church, Holly was glad her father had offered Foxglove House as a place to hold the reception afterward. Mildred's cottage would never have sustained even half the guests.

The service itself had been brief but emotional, with Mildred bravely sitting through the testimonies and stories of longtime friends: the vicar, who had made frequent visits to the cottage throughout William's illness; Mr. Elton, who had given William his first job nearly fifty years before; even an elderly Sunday school teacher who had taught William when he was a boy. Mildred and her brother had grown up in Chilton Crosse, had even lived together as adults in the same cottage where they were both born. And though Mildred was now officially alone, she undoubtedly knew the support of everyone sitting in that packed, overheated church.

The turnout reminded Holly of her mother's funeral, of all the lives her mother had touched during her too-short years. Today, during Mrs. Bates's solo, Holly's eyes wandered to the place where she'd sat with her father and sisters, at the front of the church on that horrible day. The only thing she remembered was how hard she tried *not* to look at the casket. Because looking at it would mean it was real.

"This was lovely," a voice said now, and Holly pivoted to see Noelle in the hallway, standing with her husband, Adam. "I'm sure Mildred appreciates you for doing this."

"I'm glad you both were able to come," Holly said. "It meant the world to her, seeing the village turn out today."

"That's what I love about this place." Noelle agreed. "Everyone is so supportive."

Adam squeezed his wife's shoulders. "Yeah, I'm always itching to get back here whenever I have to venture into the bowels of London. This place is a haven in comparison."

After Noelle and Adam left, others filtered out of Foxglove, offering final condolences to Mildred on their way out. The twins had become bored an hour ago, so Holly had nudged them upstairs, knowing they could keep themselves busy Facebooking or Tweeting, or whatever it was they did these days.

But Abbey had chosen to stay downstairs, and Holly enjoyed watching her sister stick closely to Mildred most of the time, protective. Abbey later helped Julia in the kitchen, replenishing the food trays and fanning out white paper napkins. Later, when Holly asked if Abbey was a little nervous about being around stoic Julia, Abbey only shrugged and said, "She was nice to me. I think she's just misunderstood."

Near the end, when only a few guests remained, Holly's phone buzzed—a text from Fletcher: *Meet @ pub? Late lunch?*

On paper, it sounded crazy. Already mentally drained, Holly still had clean-up to do, and the last thing she wanted was more socializing. But she knew she didn't have to put on "the face" around Fletcher—that frozen, robotic half-smile that told everyone she was in a consistently pleasant mood. Maybe a trip to the pub wasn't so crazy.

What Holly loved most about Joe's pub wasn't its traditional heavy wood beams attached to the low ceiling, or the light jazz playing, or even the heavenly smell of Joe's potato soup simmering. It was the crackle and pop of the flames in the rustic fireplace at the back of the room. Winter or summer, that fire was always ablaze, some eternal flame one could always count on. She'd never seen it unlit. Consequently, the table in front of the fire was also the most coveted one in the place, and Fletcher held it for her now.

Still in funeral clothes, she walked over to him. After Fletcher's text, she'd spent an hour cleaning and saying goodbyes and getting the girls settled so she could leave with a clear conscience.

"How did you score this spot?" she asked as he stood. "It's always occupied by the old men, smoking cigars and playing Spades."

"Here, let me have this." He helped her out of her light raincoat and placed it on the rack behind him. "I ordered you a pint."

Holly chided herself for failing to add "perfect gentleman" to her list of Fletcher-traits when defending him to Gertrude the other day.

She sat opposite him in the squeaky leather chair. "I'm not very hungry. I've been snacking all afternoon."

"Maybe just some soup?" Fletcher suggested.

On cue, Lizzie arrived with the pints and took their order—potato soup for both.

"How was the funeral?" Lizzie asked in a whisper. "I was heartbroken I couldn't be there."

"It went well," Holly answered. "I think Mildred's pretty numb right now."

"Poor thing," Lizzie said with a "tsk."

When she left with their order, Holly stared deep into the fire, letting the warmth envelop her face. There was something terribly hypnotic about watching flames lick the air.

"You okay?" Fletcher asked.

Holly blinked. "Oh, yeah. Knackered, is all."

"I can't imagine why." He teased. "Sorry I couldn't make it, either. The director called at the last minute for some script changes. There was no getting out of it."

"That's okay. You didn't know Mildred's brother, anyway." Holly took a drink of her pint then said, "As funerals go, it was nice. I tried not to let it remind me of my mum's, but it wasn't easy."

"Understandable."

She crossed her legs under the table and leaned back, resting her head against the edge of the chair. "Change of subject, please. Distract me. I want to know how your job is going."

"Some meetings, occasional questions about the script. Nothing exciting. I'm required to be on set most of the time, but there's not much to do. You should drop by tomorrow. Entertain me."

"I might do that."

"Oh, and I'm working on a possible job lead." He tapped a finger on the table's rich, dark wood.

"In England?"

"The States. My brother has this connection. Something in real estate."

"That doesn't sound like you. I mean, I'm sure you'd be great at it, but it doesn't sound very... creative."

"No, but it's immediate work. It would pay the bills. And it's flexible. I could have time to figure out what else I wanted to do."

The soup arrived, and before she lifted her spoon, Holly asked Fletcher, "But Finn could still come through? Find you a job here?"

"Unlikely. He's not answering my messages. I can't wait around on him much longer. And my lease at the Bristol apartment is up in two months, so there's a real time factor involved. Gotta make some firm decisions."

Not knowing what else to say, Holly focused on her soup and sipped enough spoonfuls to empty her entire bowl.

"That was outstanding," she said, wishing she could order another but knowing how sick it would make her. "Joe makes a mean potato soup." Seeing Fletcher grin, she tilted her head. "What? Something on my face?"

"No. I just thought you weren't hungry."

"Well, I guess I was. Can't a girl change her mind?"

"Yes, ma'am, she can," he said, tipping an imaginary hat.

In the hush of silence that followed, Holly grew suddenly pensive again, recalling the funeral, the vicar's words about the grieving process. About the importance of keeping those we love alive in memory.

Seeing her expression change, Fletcher swallowed his last drop and set down the lager with an exaggerated slam. "Let's get out of here."

"Where?"

"You need a surprise."

She hesitated. "Oh, no, no. I don't like surprises. Really, I don't."

"You'll love this one. I promise."

The reassurance in his eyes melted her resolve. How could she resist? "Okay. I'm in."

By the time they'd walked to their destination a quarter-mile outside the village, Holly had forgotten to care about the surprise. She was enjoying the slow pace of their stroll and the clean spring air. Every flower in the village had blossomed in the past week without her even realizing. Now, she had time to notice them in the late-afternoon sun.

She and Fletcher hadn't said a word since the pub. With anyone else in her life, even her own family, Holly struggled to fill awkward gaps in conversation with more conversation. It made her uncomfortable, holding silence with a person nearby. But with Fletcher, even the empty spaces felt full.

"Mr. Elton's farm?" she asked when Fletcher stopped at the edge of the property. "This is my big surprise?"

"I never said it was big. In fact—they're actually quite small," Fletcher said cryptically, opening the rusted metal gate.

"They?"

Fletcher led her along the dirt path to the edge of the farmhouse. "Around here, I think."

Holly could hear the squealing of some sort of animal—several of them, in fact.

"Someone on set told me about them today." He pointed to the wooden kennel, where a little boy stood on tiptoes, peering over the top.

Holly stepped closer to look inside. Seven puppies, black and white, squeaking and biting each other's ears and tumbling about in the dirt.

"Border Collies," she said, feeling a smile rise.

"Six weeks old."

Fletcher reached in to scoop one up. It wriggled in his hand, whining as Holly reached out. The puppy quivered as it sniffed her fingers then stuck out a tiny pink tongue and gave her a hesitant kiss.

"Ooooh," she said, unable to resist, reaching out. "You adorable little rascal," she cooed as Fletcher passed the puppy to her.

She brought it close to her chest, stroking it. Almost instantly, it fell asleep, snuggling into the crook of her arm with a puppy-sized sigh. She looked up at Fletcher and saw him cross his arms with satisfaction.

"Admit it. Good surprise."

"Okay. I admit it," she whispered. It had been an eternity since she'd held a puppy. "They're gorgeous. How could I not love this?"

Mr. Elton, the wrinkled old farmer, approached them from behind. "Chosen that one, eh?"

"You have no idea how tempted I am," Holly said. "But, no. We only came to look. Way too much responsibility, raising a puppy. They're beautiful, though."

"They'll have all their shots in two weeks' time, if you change your mind," he said, placing a dirt-caked hand on top of the kennel. "They're going fast. I've already got two of 'em promised."

"I'll keep that in mind," Holly said, wishing she could take this one home with her right now. But the rational side of her brain knew it wasn't a wise move. She simply didn't have time for yet another living creature to take care of.

She had already become too attached, so she handed the puppy back over to Fletcher, who rubbed its velvet ears and returned it gently to the kennel.

"Thank you," she told Fletcher as they walked away. "You have no idea how much I needed that today."

"I think I do," he said, opening the gate for her again.

Chapter Eleven

*His person and air were equal to what her fancy had
ever drawn for the hero of a favourite story.*
-Jane Austen

*Grocers
Read Chapters 16 & 17
Call Mac about garden
Make new dentist appt*

"WHAT ELSE...?" HOLLY CLICKED THE end of the pen
twice then thought of something:
Abbey—new shoes

Satisfied, she pushed away from the table and tore the list from the
pad. That would certainly be enough to fill the afternoon. Anything else
could wait for another day.

Seeing the clock, she realized if she left the house in the next two
minutes, she would be right on time for work. She usually said goodbye
to Mildred before leaving on Tuesdays, but she hadn't seen her for a
while now. Probably upstairs, Holly thought, changing the girls' sheets
or replenishing towels. Holly had called Mildred that morning, told her
to please take a couple of weeks off from the chores at Foxglove, but
Mildred said it was good for her, keeping a routine. And that being in
that empty cottage without her brother was nearly unbearable.

Finding her bag, Holly walked toward the door, planning to pass by
her father's study quietly. She didn't want to disturb his work.

But today, his door was cracked open, and from inside came voices—soft whispers. Knowing she shouldn't but unable to resist, Holly tiptoed to see through the crack. Her father stood beside his desk, with Mildred's hands clasped in his. He spoke something to her tenderly, and she responded with nods. Then, they embraced.

Holly took two steps back, out of sight. She knew her father and Mildred had been acquaintances all these years but real friends? Her mind darted back to her father's attentiveness at Mildred's house last week. How her father had driven her there, then lingered…

She noticed the time again and headed quietly out the front door, still mulling things over on her walk to the gallery. The embrace was simply an act of comfort between friends in a time of grief. Mildred was still mourning, after all. Her father could certainly relate.

In fact, the two of them now had something undeniable in common. That kind of grief, the loss of someone important, could bind people like nothing else. And, Holly's father could be very tender when he wanted to be. Besides, what was he supposed to do when someone was vulnerable and weak? Walk away? No. Her father was a compassionate man and would give his shoulder to anyone in need.

Yes. That was it. That explained everything.

Satisfied, Holly carried on her way, reaching for her pen to scribble down one more item on her list.

"What if, instead of, 'How highly do you regard him?' she says: 'How greatly do you *esteem* him?'"

Fletcher considered Holly's suggestion and made the change with his pencil, which had worn down to a nub. "I like it. Sounds more feminine."

A clap of thunder startled Holly, making her spill tea onto the rug. "Blast!"

"Here, use this." Fletcher passed his napkin over and she blotted it, grateful it hadn't spilled onto her precious copy of *Emma*—or Fletcher's precious script, spread wide on the table.

Earlier, he'd rung her at the gallery, desperate for help. The director was finally making Fletcher earn his keep, ordering a major scene revision by tomorrow afternoon. After laboring on it all morning, Fletcher had given up. The panic in his voice wasn't something Holly was accustomed to.

"I'm stuck!" he'd told her. "I need your opinion on a couple of spots. I've *got* to get these right."

Since she'd finished yesterday's list and had nothing pressing this afternoon, she agreed, and they met at Foxglove when she got off work an hour later. She'd picked up two roasted chickens from Mrs. Pickering's, ready-to-eat, so she wouldn't waste time making lunch. Now, nearly three hours later, sprawled out on the sitting room rug, they took turns reading the script aloud, trying to act it out, hear the lines. It took a while to stop feeling ridiculous, to quit stumbling over words, or giggling at Fletcher's horrid attempt at a British accent. But finally, they'd developed an easy rhythm.

"I didn't even think of this till now, but we should've asked Rosalee to act out the lines for us," Fletcher said. "You wouldn't have had to double up for Miss Bates. And, it would give her some practice."

"She'd never do it." Holly had given her sister several chances over the past week to share the good news about getting the part, but she never did. Finally last night, catching Rosalee in the kitchen without her twin, Holly had snatched her opportunity.

"Congratulations," she'd said, expecting at least a third of a smile. Instead, she got a blank stare as Rosalee looked up from her glass of milk. Holly specified, "On winning the part."

"How did you find out?" Rosalee asked.

"Fletcher told me. Why didn't *you* tell me? That's so exciting!"

"Yeah. I guess."

Frustrated but refusing to show it, Holly continued, "When do you shoot your scenes?"

"Dunno yet. The director's supposed to call and let me know." She took a sip.

"Well, I think it's amazing. You're going to be on the big screen!"

"Thanks," Rosalee whispered, then stepped past Holly to leave the room. And to leave Holly puzzled about how Rosalee had done on her audition, to get the part in the first place. Surely, she'd shown more enthusiasm, more sparkle and gumption than this...

"Why wouldn't she do it?" Fletcher asked now.

"What? Oh, read the lines? Well, she's shy. I think it's the Bridget factor."

"Bridget factor?"

"Yeah, she doesn't want to outshine her sister. Rosalee's so used to being in the shadows I'm not sure she knows what to do with the spotlight."

"Ahh." Fletcher flipped several pages into the script. "So, you've spent all this time helping me, but are you up for one more scene?"

He pointed to it and as Holly skimmed the dialogue, she recognized it as the one Fletcher had been working on when she'd met him that first day at the Manor's garden.

"I still can't seem to get these lines right," he said. "This scene has to be perfect—where Emma and Knightley realize they're in love."

A crack of thunder drew Holly's eyes to the window.

"It's getting bad out there." She watched raindrops pummel against the crisscross panes. "We should take a break before we tackle the scene. More tea, maybe?"

"Sure, hit me up." He handed her the mug.

The girls had arrived from school twenty minutes ago, mere seconds before the worst of the storm rolled in. Bridget had begged to go to the Manor, but Holly insisted that homework came first. Aggravated, Bridget had stomped upstairs, mumbling "Damn it" loud enough for Holly to hear.

Fletcher had confirmed that he'd noticed Bridget at the set every day last week, flirting with "that actor" during breaks. At this point, as long as Bridget paid attention to her schoolwork, Holly was still okay with it. She remembered being that age, having the thrill of a new romantic attachment.

Let her enjoy it, Holly reasoned.

"Here. It's hot," she cautioned, setting Fletcher's refill on the table they'd pushed aside earlier, giving them room to sprawl out, or even stand and act out scenes.

This was Holly's favorite room of Foxglove. The sitting room had her mother's stamp all over it—her warmth, her quirkiness. The eclectic mix of items seemed entirely disjointed but oddly worked together—the crimson antique couches, the collection of windmill figurines on the bookshelf, the tapestry on the wall of a mother rocking her child, even the Oriental teapot she'd bought on a trip to Japan before Holly was born. And the rug, plush and soft and perfect for playing board games, or watching telly, or spreading out while reading a script.

Fletcher rested his head back on the couch cushion and closed his eyes. "The thunder reminds me of home," he said dreamily.

"It does? I don't picture Texas as particularly stormy."

"Are you kiddin'? We get storms all the time. Terrifying ones. Especially now, in the spring. That season is always the worst. Usually we get tornadoes too."

Holly's eyes widened as the word brought forth images of Kansas and Dorothy and houses spinning in the air. "Do you have basements to hide in?"

Fletcher opened his eyes. "Not in West Texas. But we probably should. It's something when the sky turns this eerie mustard color right before the tornado is spotted."

"Sounds horrifying. You miss it, don't you? Not the tornadoes. Texas, I mean?"

Fletcher rubbed at his neck. "Yeah. I do, sometimes."

She thought of him returning to Texas. It was hard to imagine sustaining a friendship an entire ocean away, even by text or email. It didn't seem enough. She'd gotten used to Fletcher in her life just when it was probably time to start letting him go.

Holly watched him highlight a line of text and thought how brave he was, how interesting his life choices had been, living in a foreign country. And how glad she was, that those choices had brought him here, to the rug of her sitting room floor.

A *thud* in the hallway snapped their heads in the same direction.

Holly stared at Fletcher. "That wasn't thunder."

"Ohhh!" someone groaned.

"Abbey?" Holly scrambled to get up.

Fletcher followed, and they entered the hallway to find Abbey, wincing in pain and pointing to her leg.

"It *hurts*," she said, on the verge of tears.

Holly kneeled to get a better look. "What happened?"

"Something slippery… on the stairs. I fell."

"Probably rain water," Holly said. "I told the twins to take off their wet shoes, but I guess they didn't listen."

"Where does it hurt?" Fletcher asked, kneeling beside Holly.

"Here." Abbey pointed more specifically at her left foot, the top of it already red and starting to swell.

"Can you move it?"

Abbey's cringe showed she was trying, but then she shook her head "no" and bit her lip. "It hurts."

"It's okay, sweetie. We'll take care of you," Holly reassured.

The twins appeared at the top of the stairs, peeking down.

"Looks like we're going to the doctor's," Holly called up to them. "It's Abbey's foot. Stay here and we'll be back soon."

Holly moved to stand, the thought hitting a second later. "Oh! We don't have a car. Mac picked it up yesterday for brake repair."

"Here," Fletcher said, repositioning himself closer to Abbey. "Can you put your arms around my neck?"

She nodded, and Holly moved out of the way to watch him scoop up her sister from the floor with ease.

"Transportation solved. Where do we go?" he asked Holly.

"This way." She scrambled to grab an umbrella and step into some shoes before clicking open the front door.

"I lost my glasses," said Abbey.

Although glasses were the last thing they should be worrying over, Holly knew they were important to Abbey, a security blanket of sorts. So, she took a few seconds to skim the floor.

"Got them!" She snatched them up and ushered Fletcher out the door.

Dr. Andrews's cottage/office stood at the outskirts of the village about a quarter of a mile away. In pleasant weather, it made for a lovely walk. But for Fletcher, holding eighty-something pounds and fighting against the battering rain, Holly could imagine it was anything but. She wished she could do something to ease his load, but aside from blinking away raindrops and occasionally shifting Abbey in his arms, he seemed fine, carrying on as though rescuing injured damsels was an everyday occurrence.

The first dozen steps, Holly had tried to shelter them from the rain with the umbrella, but they were getting wet in spite of her efforts. Plus, Fletcher seemed encumbered with someone close at his side, maneuvering an umbrella awkwardly above his head.

"*You* use it," he shouted through the thunder.

"That would be silly," she replied. "Me, dry, and you two soaked through. We're in this together." She closed the umbrella, her bare feet squishing inside her sneakers.

"Beautiful day for a walk." He smiled into the rain.

When they reached the office, drenched and soaking the carpet, Mrs. Cox left her post behind the desk to help guide them to the exam room, where the doctor was fortunately available.

Half an hour later, Holly and Fletcher walked—while Abbey hobbled on crutches—back into the waiting room. Two X-rays had showed a possible hairline fracture, one that wouldn't require a cast. Dr. Andrews had bandaged her foot then recommended, "Ice and elevation," before letting them go. He wanted to see her back next week.

"Daddy!" Abbey said, spotting her father in the doorway. "You came!"

She wobbled toward him, and he caught her before she fell, again. "Of course I came. Rosalee called me. I was on my way home, as luck would have it. Nearly had to swim to get here. How are you feeling, pumpkin?"

"Better. It doesn't hurt so much anymore."

"What say I drive you all back? You need some dry clothes."

Abbey told him, "Fletcher carried me. All the way here."

"In the pouring rain," Holly added.

Her father raised his eyebrows at Fletcher. "Is that so?" He extended his hand. "Thank you, son."

"My pleasure, sir."

Back at the house, Duncan helped Abbey upstairs while Holly sifted through his wardrobe to find suitable dry clothing for Fletcher. She couldn't send him back out sopping wet. In fact, she would offer him dinner and a drive back to the pub in her father's car. She owed him that much.

After a quick change of her own, she returned to where she'd left Fletcher waiting by the fire in the sitting room. Shifted sideways, he rubbed at his scalp with the plush towel she'd tossed at him before she'd gone upstairs.

Shirtless.

She couldn't help gawking. He had *the* perfect chest—slightly chiseled, not too skinny, not too bulked up, and not at all what she expected of a self-effacing, good-natured country boy. This was not the body of a Fletcher. This was the body of a film star. A Greek god.

Still gawking, she noticed something else... chest hair! And not a meager "soul-patch" tuft of hair, no. It looked thick and soft, in perfect proportion. Unusual, seeing full chest hair on a man her age these days. Somewhere over the years, it became a trend to shave it all off. Holly never understood how a purposely bald chest could ever be attractive and even remembered having a debate about it at university. Her flatmate had proclaimed chest hair "completely disgusting." But Holly argued that men shaving their chests was vain and unnatural, even prepubescent.

"Hey," Fletcher said, breaking her thoughts. Thank goodness he couldn't read them.

She cleared her throat and walked to him, holding out a cotton shirt and khaki trousers, her eyes drifting to the floor. "I think they're close enough in size."

He tossed the shirt upward, catching it and shaking it loose of its folds, before placing it over his head. Then he reached to unbuckle his belt, but paused.

"Oh. Right. Sorry," Holly said, bumping into a chair on her way out. "I'll be in the kitchen if you need me," she called, imagining his dimples appearing behind her back.

"Are you sure you won't let me drive you? A cold front came in with the rain."

They were standing in the open doorway, Holly folding her arms across her chest to ward off the chill, Fletcher carrying his rolled-up script in one hand and a ball of his damp clothes in the other.

"No, it's fine. I'm hot-natured, anyway. And, it stopped raining."

"You won't stay for dinner? We could finish that scene..."

"Naw, I'll grab something at the pub. I've still got some notes to type up. And we can save that scene for another day—it's not due tomorrow. Besides, staying here would only tempt me to avoid work. Your cooking is too good."

Holly suppressed a blush and leaned her head against the doorframe, smelling the air. "Mmm. I love that fresh scent after a storm."

"Exactly. See? A walk in the fresh air will do me good."

He leaned down to give her cheek a soft peck, catching Holly pleasantly off guard, then stepped backward over the threshold. "I'll see you sometime."

"Okay," she agreed. "Sometime."

Holly lingered, intoxicated by the heady scent. She looked upward and saw a sliver of a distant moon, enjoyed the shreds of cotton-candy clouds drifting past it. The calm *after* the storm was always the best part.

Chapter Twelve

Seven years would be insufficient to make some people acquainted with each other, and seven days are more than enough for others.
~Jane Austen

"I FOUND IT, I FOUND IT!" Abbey's voice crescendoed all the way across Mrs. Mulberry's antique shop, echoing off the pristine wooden floors. Fortunately, no other customers were there to hear it.

"I'm coming," Holly called, before Abbey could yell again.

Two nights ago, Abbey had been her adorable, klutzy self, knocking over their mother's glass Tiffany lamp. Granted, she'd been trying to maneuver the sitting room with her crutches and had simply lost her balance. But she'd cried herself to sleep over the incident. The next day, Holly assured her they would replace the lamp, find a similar one at the antique shop.

As Holly rounded the corner, she saw that Abbey's discovery was remarkably similar to the broken lamp. The colors held the same dark purples and golds, and although their mother's lamp had contained red butterflies embedded in the stained glass, this one had red dragonflies. Close enough.

Holly saw Mrs. Mulberry approaching and told her, "We'll take this one, please."

"A lovely choice." She lifted it gingerly from its place on the shelf and walked it up front. "I'll wrap it up for you."

Satisfied, Abbey asked Holly, "Can I go to the Emporium? I need to buy a new brush."

"And some licorice, no doubt," Holly teased. "Do you have money?"

"Yes," Abbey said, already on her way out the door. She'd abandoned her crutches only an hour ago, after Dr. Andrews and one more set of X-rays had given her the green light. She was already back to her bouncy self.

"I'll come find you in a minute," Holly called before the door slammed shut.

Mrs. Mulberry stood behind the counter at the back, wrapping the lamp in layer after layer of tissue. Knowing this would take some time, Holly decided to do some browsing. She knew the shop well, better than any in the village, except for the gallery. Years before, Mrs. Mulberry had groomed Lizzie for the "family business," requiring her daughter to work at the shop nearly every day, weekends included. But Lizzie quickly tired of being around antiques all day, and when her mother began looking for someone else to add to her staff, Lizzie insisted that Holly would be the perfect choice. For two-and-a-half years, the girls had worked within these walls, taking inventory, waiting on customers, pricing new items, ringing the cash register.

Since those teenage days, the layout hadn't changed a bit. It wasn't just any box-of-a-building. It had character, charm. As she browsed now, Holly admired its structure—the towering, crisscross windowpanes at the back that spilled a kaleidoscope of sunlight into the room, the rustic wood trim and paneling, and especially the numerous quirky nooks and crannies. Those had always been her favorite places as a little girl. Her mother used to bring her at least once a week for a treat, and Holly would wander about, getting lost amongst the shelves and antique furniture.

On the north wall was a sunken area, a cozy niche where the children congregated to play jacks or marbles while their parents browsed. Many lasting friendships had been formed in that niche. On the opposite wall stood furniture—entire bed sets and dining sets, even quaint sitting areas set up to look inviting and cozy. As a child, Holly had often wondered if anyone would miss her, should she decide to stay behind one night after the doors were locked. She could hide out, much like the children in *From the Mixed-up Files of Mrs. Basil E. Frankweiler* did at the enormous museum. She'd have everything she needed right here. A place to sleep, books to keep her company, even snacks, always available on the counter for customers.

"Holly, I have your package ready!" Mrs. Mulberry called now.

Wishing she could linger, Holly pulled away from the niche and entered adulthood again.

"The shop looks wonderful," she told Mrs. Mulberry. "It's been too long since I've visited."

Mrs. Mulberry paused, still holding the plastic straps of the bag containing the lamp. "Between us," she said, her voice hushed, "I think it might be time to retire."

"Already?" Holly asked. Mrs. Mulberry was only in her early sixties, at best.

"Yes," she confirmed, her face a little downcast. "Mr. Mulberry has some new health problems. I feel my time would be better spent by his side. And as much as I love the shop, the upkeep and the running of a business… well, it's exhausting sometimes. I'm not getting any younger."

Holly never knew what to say when older people said this. Agree with them? Politely disagree? Both seemed equally inappropriate.

But Mrs. Mulberry continued before Holly could find the right response. "No decisions have been made yet. It's only something to think about."

"I'm sure you'll make the right decision when the time comes," Holly said, taking the handles from her. "Thank you for the lamp. It's a perfect fit."

Leaving the shop, she could almost hear her little-girl self, clapping "Mary Mack" with Lizzie inside the niche. Rather than linger, Holly closed the door on the memory before it could take root and change the tone of her day.

After two unanswered texts and a voicemail regarding this morning's missed book club, Holly knew a face-to-face visit was in order. Fletcher was probably busy writing, but it was unlike him to be so inaccessible.

She didn't have anything urgent to tell him—no drama she needed his advice about, no disaster or emergency he needed to rescue her from. But after shopping with Abbey then spending the rest of the day with some household chores, she had nothing left to do. The time she would usually spend on school was empty for now. She'd submitted her final paper yesterday, finishing the course, with a week off before a new summer course would begin, a small-business course online. So tonight, she felt the specific itch to celebrate the time off, away from the house. Perhaps Fletcher did, too.

So, at ten o'clock, after seeing the girls off to bed, she opened the pub door to a whiff of ale and shepherd's pie. Even late, on a weeknight, the pub was boisterous. Her ears rang with the volume of laughter and music and voices marinating together. She recognized most of the faces but didn't see Fletcher among them. Reaching the mahogany bar, she squeezed in between two stools and waved to Joe, a picture of calm in a raucous sea of customers.

"What'll you have, love?" he shouted.

"Two pints, please," she answered. She caught his sleeve before he reached for the mugs. "Have you seen Fletcher around? Do you know if he's here?"

"Saw him going up to his room. 'Bout an hour ago."

Holly paid for the drinks and walked around the bar, maneuvering her way behind a game of darts, trying not to spill. Making it to the edge of the game, she thought she was safe, but a man at another table pushed back his seat. Dodging the chair abruptly, she splashed both drinks over the rim.

"Oh, I'm sorry," the man said, trying to steady her.

"No problem." She forced a smile in spite of the warm ale dripping down her fingers, onto her jeans.

Gripping the mugs tighter and carrying on, she finally reached the narrow staircase and managed to climb up—slowly—without spilling another drop.

She reached Fletcher's room and stopped. She could hear a voice, harsh and angry. Then, a long pause. He must have been on the phone? For a second, Holly thought she had the wrong room—anger seemed very un-Fletcher-like—but then she heard the "y'all" and knew it was him.

Debating whether to stay or go, she waited until he ended the call then tapped at the door lightly with the tip of her foot. There was no way she was coordinated enough to shift the heavy mugs to one hand to knock.

The door flew open, and Fletcher stood, looking cross, his usually warm eyes scrunched into a glare. When he saw Holly, his face softened a bit but not enough to convince her he was all right.

"Oh. Hey," he said softly, stepping back to let her inside.

When he saw her struggling with the mugs, he reached out to take one, holding the door with his elbow as she walked inside.

He took a lengthy sip and closed the door. "How did you know I needed this?"

"I'm clairvoyant," she said.

He motioned for her to sit at his desk while he took the edge of the bed. In all these years, she'd never been inside one of the pub's rooms. Smartly decorated, with cotton striped curtains and a matching bedspread, it was cramped but homey. A wrinkled shirt lay across the bed, with two pair of shoes on the floor. Empty crisps wrappers lay next to Fletcher's open laptop.

"I had a bit of an accident," Holly said, pointing to the wet stains on her thighs. "A dart game gone awry."

"Hang on," he said, tapping her knee before disappearing into the loo. He reappeared with a towel.

"Thanks." She set down the mug and blotted her jeans, wishing she could change out of them. They reeked of ale.

"What's the occasion?" he asked, balancing the mug on his knee as he sat again.

"Nothing, really. I felt antsy, wanted to get out of the house. I didn't mean to bother you."

Fletcher blew out a puff of air and scratched his jaw. He hadn't shaved in a day or two. "Naw, it's fine. Just been a rough night."

"I can tell. I heard your voice through the door. You sounded upset."

"Pissed off is more accurate."

In the several weeks she'd known him, she could always count on Fletcher to be the cool, levelheaded one. It was almost unnerving, watching him be this out of sorts. Something in the universe had shifted off balance.

"You want to talk about it?" she offered, prepared for the likelihood that he wouldn't.

He set the now-half-empty mug on the floor then leaned forward and clasped his hands. "That phone call was Finn. Finally. He's been in London all this time, but he hasn't been working on our next project. He's been working on *his* next project. He got hired as a ghostwriter for Lily Allen's tell-all. Without me."

"Oh, wow."

"Yeah. We were supposed to be a team. But I guess he didn't see it that way. Now it's obvious why he's been avoiding my calls. Sneaky son-of-a-bitch. He had no intention of including me in this. It's a million-dollar deal, too, apparently."

"Wow."

"You keep saying that."

"Sorry. Is there anything you can do? I mean, legally? Was there a contract?"

"It wasn't that kind of partnership. Although, looking back it would've been smart—make it legal, have a binding agreement. But I didn't think it was necessary. I mean, he was my friend." Fletcher stood and folded his arms across his chest, let out a frustrated grunt. "I knew it was possible he wouldn't come through for us, that he wouldn't find us work after *Emma*. But I wasn't prepared for this. Leaving me behind, going out on his own and not having the nerve to tell me until after the deal was signed. Now my future career is one big question mark. This changes everything."

Holly knew exactly what that meant, without having to ask. He was going back to America for sure now. The door to England had been firmly shut, nothing left to keep him here after *Emma*. Thanks to Finn.

Fletcher sat back down, locking eyes with her for the first time since she'd arrived. For a second, he looked like a little boy, helpless and vulnerable. She wanted to save him, to say the perfect thing that would remove the black clouds, brighten his outlook. The way he'd brightened hers so many times since the day they'd met.

"Fletcher, you are so talented. And even though you can't see this now, you *will* land on your feet. This is only a stupid bump in the road. Trust me."

"It's not talent. It's luck."

"What do you mean?"

"I feel like every writing job I've had, I've been riding the coattails of somebody else. At the BBC, I was part of a writing team. I didn't even write the *Emma* script on my own. I had someone else helping out."

"But that doesn't mean they did all the work. You contributed."

"Yeah, but it's not the same. It wasn't all mine." He pointed at his chest. Staring down at the bed, he twirled a loose string from the quilt around his finger, then snapped it off. "I even tried writing a novel, right out of college. Never finished it. Didn't have the guts."

Nothing else she could say seemed right enough or wise enough to pull him out of this funk.

"I didn't even tell you the other bad news," he said, looking up again.

"What?"

He smirked and shook his head. "The movie is in trouble. That's the rumor going around set. Lack of funding could shut us down."

"Is that even possible? They've already shot, what, a third of the film?"

"Movies can tank at any step of the process. Happens all the time. You'd be surprised."

"Well, maybe it's only a rumor. It could be one person who misheard something and spread it around. Maybe it's nothing at all. Try not to worry."

"Easier said than done. But I get your point. I have enough on my plate right now."

"Exactly. I'm sorry about everything. What can I do to help?"

"You already did it. You showed up at my door at the perfect time. With alcohol. I needed somebody to vent to. You really are clairvoyant."

As Fletcher reached for his mug to finish it off, Holly got an idea to change the mood. "Hey, are you up for some darts? A game was ending when I came up here. Maybe they're finished."

"Oh, I'm really bad at darts," he said between swigs. "I don't know if I wanna be around people right now."

"Hey! I'm not just 'people.'"

"I know. You're more than that. You're… you've become…"

Holly felt an unaccountable urge to fill in the pause, but before she could, he finished his thought.

"Invaluable," he said.

She tilted her head and smiled. "What a lovely thing to say."

"It's true. And in this really concentrated period of time, too. How did that happen?"

"I have no idea. But I'm glad it did."

Chapter Thirteen

*And you have forgotten one matter of joy to me... and a
very considerable one—that I made the match myself.*
~Jane Austen

FRANK WOULD CERTAINLY BE PLEASED. The supply closet had
never been so organized. Holly stepped back to examine her
progress, realizing she'd forgotten to account for the oversized
box of pencils she'd bought at a discount last month.

"Bollocks," she muttered.

Luckily, one empty hole remained, and after shifting a couple of
items to make room, she squeezed the box snugly into it.

Frank had taken his lunch break thirty minutes ago, leaving her at
the gallery to do—well, nothing. Periods of inactivity were common,
but Holly always tried to utilize them somehow. She felt guilty for being
paid to sit around and twiddle her thumbs.

With the supply closet finished and nothing else to do, she resolved
to become useful in another area. She could log onto Frank's laptop
and access her new course. Her online professor had created a Facebook
study group for the course yesterday. Once upon a time, years ago,
Holly had a Facebook account she never used, so she'd deleted it. To
participate in the new course, she'd re-registered early this morning.

She logged on now and saw her first notification. A schoolmate,
Lily, asking Holly about an in-person study session next week. Lily and
two other students lived nearby, also in the Cotswolds, and wanted to
get together. Holly usually shied away from study groups, but this one

sounded halfway promising. Lily had posted an invitation and the other two Cotswold students had already declined. Feeling bad for Lily, Holly clicked "Accept" without thinking, and the date was set.

She looked closer to see Lily's profile picture and noticed she looked older than Holly—mid-thirties, with light ginger hair and squinty eyes as she smiled. Pretty.

An idea presented itself as Holly clicked through Lily's profile, through photos of family—sisters, parents, two cats. No husband. No children. Perhaps Holly had immersed herself in too much *Emma* lately, but the thought was too delicious to ignore. A sweet-looking, studious woman who lived in a nearby village, matched with an eccentric, cultured man who worked in an art gallery.

What would it hurt? Holly could simply crack open a door and let fate do the rest. Invite Lily here to the gallery for their study session during a time she knew Frank would be here. All perfectly innocent. All perfectly legitimate.

She poised her fingers to type a message to Lily, suggesting a change in venue. The moment she clicked "Send," Frank came back from lunch. Holly clicked off her Facebook window, closed the laptop, and popped up from the chair, feeling suddenly guilty. She wasn't good at keeping things from people. And, as much as she hated surprises, she apparently had no problem inflicting them on others.

Hoping to look productive, she snatched an invoice from the table and stared at it intently. "Good lunch?" she asked, not looking up, hoping Frank wouldn't notice it was upside-down.

"Fine." Frank removed his jacket.

"Oh, come here, look." She walked past him and showed off the closet, extending her hand in a sweeping gesture. "Now we can find everything!"

Frank put his fingers to his chin and studied the shelves. "You've been busy."

She wasn't sure whether he meant that as a good thing or a bad thing.

"I like it," he then proclaimed.

She'd been so glad to see the old Frank return entirely about a fortnight ago. The wall had crumbled, and he spoke to her in warm tones, as he had before their disaster-date. Perhaps, just perhaps, he was ready to look toward someone new.

"I might have a few pieces for you to check out next week," he said, back to business. "In Bath. I'll let you know ahead of time. Still a few calls to make."

"Sure. Whatever you need," she said.

A new customer pulled Frank's attention away, and Holly became bored once again. But Noelle was due in five minutes, an instant cure for boredom. It fascinated Holly, watching Noelle paint, single brushstrokes coming together, transforming a canvas into something beautiful.

It reminded her of a quote she'd read a couple of months back. Noelle had published it in a coffee table book about her Aunt Joy. Unable to remember the quote well enough, Holly went to find her copy now, one she'd left inside a drawer to peruse.

She flipped through it and found the page she'd bookmarked: a photo of Joy Valentine's Cornwall seaside painting, with a caption. Holly read it softly aloud, "In life, just as in painting, you can only experience it one stroke at a time, moments building on top of each other. Until one day, you step back, and it's become something full and whole and beautiful."

Maybe one day, Holly could step back and finally see the canvas she'd been painting all this time.

"That's one of my favorites," a voice said.

Holly saw Noelle walking around the corner with a wide smile. "Hi! Are you painting today?"

"Sadly, no. I wish I had time, but I'm just here to pick up some papers Frank left for me." Noelle paused, holding her stomach.

"What's wrong? You look a bit... green." Holly guided Noelle to a chair.

Noelle sat down and chuckled. "I wasn't going to tell anyone—it's too early. But can you keep a big secret? Well, it's only a little secret right now."

Holly already suspected what Noelle was about to divulge.

"Adam and I are having a baby."

Holly's immediate squeal said everything as she hugged Noelle, issued her joyful congratulations. "I couldn't be happier for you."

As the words came out, Holly realized she meant it. Not a hint of envy inside her. Adam and Noelle were her favorite couple—first loves who had reunited, a storybook romance—and now, a baby on the way. Holly couldn't be anything but happy for them. "And I won't tell a soul. It's our secret."

"Thanks. We're so excited. I'm only about two months along, but we'll probably tell people shortly. At least before Mrs. Pickering finds out and announces it for us."

"Everyone will be thrilled, trust me. I wonder if the little she—or he—will get your Aunt Joy's 'art' gene."

"You know, that's a possibility," Noelle said. "It seems to skip a generation, though. Only time will tell."

Holly waited and tapped again.

"Rosalee?" she called then twisted the brass knob and cracked open the bedroom door. This was Holly's favorite bedroom because of the view—two generous windows facing the back garden, with a sitting area for reading. Rosalee had recently plastered the other three walls with posters of Robbie Williams, Leona Lewis, and One Republic.

Rosalee sat on the bed, head down, eyes closed, bobbing to whatever was playing on her iPod at the moment. Once upon a time, this room—the largest, except for the Master—had belonged to Holly. But when the twins became toddlers and needed more space, this room was the obvious choice for them. Holly never minded. She rather enjoyed smaller spaces, the safety inside them. When the twins turned ten, Bridget insisted on having her own room. She had her eye on the one farthest from the others, at the end of the hall, the most private and with its own toilet. Rosalee wanted to stay where she was anyway, so their father approved. Given this garden view, Holly always thought Rosalee got the better end of that deal.

Holly drew closer, waving her hand as she approached the bed. Rosalee opened her eyes and tugged at her earbuds to fall to her shoulders.

"Who are you listening to?" Holly asked.

"Some Travis. I'm in a mellow mood, I guess." She sat cross-legged, papers splayed out around her.

"What's all this?" Holly pushed some pamphlets away so she could sit.

"Applications and stuff. For university." Rosalee rolled her eyes. "I never thought it would be this complicated."

"I can't *believe* it's already time to start thinking about university." Holly picked up the brochure for Cardiff and began flipping through it. "Where did the time go…?"

"Yeah. It's still a year away, but Mrs. Palmer says it's smart to think ahead. Says it'll be here before we know it."

"She's right. I heard about one girl who missed out on an entire first semester because she messed about and got her applications in too late." Holly picked up another brochure and noticed some courses had already been circled.

"Can I ask you something?" Rosalee asked.

"Of course."

"Well." She leaned against the headboard and stared at the ceiling. "What if a person wanted to do something… nonconformist? Radical, even. And what if that person was risking the wrath of a certain *other* person for doing that something?"

"This is so hypothetical, I'm not following. Can we get more specific?"

Rosalee shifted her focus back to Holly. "I want to study theatre. At university. But Daddy would be completely against it."

"Ah." Holly smiled at the thought of her conservative sister even thinking of doing something "radical." Rosalee was surprising her more every day. First, the film role, and now this. "So, I guess you've caught the acting bug, then. When do you film your scene?"

"In a couple of weeks." Her eyes came alive. "I love it. Being on set with all these quirky, creative people. There's this… spark. And energy. And it's *not* about the fame." She was adamant, unnecessarily. Anyone who knew Rosalee knew the last thing she sought was fame. "I never in a million years thought of doing this before, acting. But now it's all I can think of. Being someone else. Acting like someone else. It's a rush I can't explain."

"I'll tell you what," Holly proposed. "I'll speak to Dad on your behalf. If you want me to."

"You would?"

"I'd be happy to try."

"Thank you!" Rosalee flung her arms around Holly's shoulders in an uncharacteristic display then backed away.

"No guarantees, of course. You know how Dad can be. But I'll do my best," Holly reassured. "So, is Bridget looking too? At universities, I mean. Are you trying to attend the same school?"

"You know better than that." Rosalee smirked. "Bridge would never be caught dead going to the same university as me. Plus, I don't even know if she wants to go at all."

"Why would you say that?" Holly said, hoping it wasn't true.

"I haven't heard her talk about it. Like, at all. She's more interested in boys these days."

"Speaking of," Holly said, shifting her knee up to the bed to get more comfortable, "I wanted to ask something. About this boy Bridget's seeing. This actor."

"Colin. She's there now, you know. With him. At the Manor."

"Yeah, she texted me right after school. Said she didn't have any homework."

"Do you believe her?"

Holly shrugged, not knowing what to believe.

"She totally changes when she's around him," Rosalee said. "It's really annoying."

"How do you mean?"

"You know, tossing her hair around, giggling in this high, irritating voice. She's a different person with him. Like an alien suddenly took over her body. I don't like it."

"Me either," Holly admitted. "Tell me more about Colin. What do you know?"

"Well, he's fit and gorgeous, anyone can see that. But he's older. Like twenty-one or twenty-two. And I see him flirting with other girls when Bridge isn't around. I don't think he cares about her. Not the way she cares about him."

"Have you told her that?"

Rosalee shook her head, wistful, looking down at the quilt. "I didn't want to hurt her. And she wouldn't believe me, anyway."

Holly pretended to sort casually through the brochures as she decided how to phrase the next question. "So, would you consider doing me a favor?"

"Does it involve hard labor?"

Holly grinned, looking up. "No. In fact, it's quite painless. Physically, at least."

Rosalee looked suspicious.

"Well, I'm concerned about Bridget. And it sounds like you are, too. So, I was wondering if… whenever you're there with her on set…"

"You want me to spy on her?"

"No, not spy! Well, not really. Just—watch out for her. That's all. Nothing sinister or underhanded."

"Do you want me to report back to you?" she said with a raised eyebrow, unconvinced. "Should we have secret codenames?"

"Funny. No, but… if you see something wrong, or out of hand, then yes, I want to know about it." Holly dropped the brochures and made eye contact. "Look. I'm worried. That's it. And it wouldn't hurt for someone—someone who loves her—to keep an eye out. Watch her back. Wouldn't you want the same done for you?"

"Not if it included someone spying on me."

"Would you stop using that word? We're not spying. Not exactly. And I'm not putting a gun to your head. Think it over. Okay? That's all I'm asking."

"Okay." Rosalee uncrossed her legs. "My foot's asleep," she said, wiggling it in circles.

"You've been sitting here awhile. How about some chocolate?"

"Before supper?"

"Sure. Why not. Let's be nonconformist."

Three hours later, Bridget came home with a boy. But it wasn't Colin. It was Riley, a mate from school. Holly had seen him once before at the house, a couple of weeks ago. Bridget's study partner for A-levels, Riley had ash-blond hair that hung down in his face, imperfect teenage skin, and a gawky demeanor. But he seemed sweet and, from what Holly could tell, had an enormous crush on Bridget. And she was either totally oblivious to it, or knew, but didn't care.

Tonight, they sat at the kitchen table after supper had been cleared away, studying elements of literature while Holly checked her email at the writing desk nearby. Lily had emailed her back—next Tuesday at the gallery was a "yes."

"Pathetic fallacy?" Riley said.

A pause, then Bridget answered, "A fallacy that's pathetic?"

Holly chuckled with Riley then cleared her throat and pretended to go back to her email.

Seeing their reactions, Bridget slumped her shoulders in defeat. "I don't know, dammit."

"Bridge..." Holly warned.

"I know, I know. Watch the language. Sor-ry," she said.

"It's all right, you'll get it," reassured Riley. "Pathetic fallacy. It's sort of like... well, when nature reflects what's going on in people's lives. Like nature brought to life, with human characteristics."

"I don't get it." Bridget pouted.

"Remember in *Othello*? When he's just murdered Desdemona?"

"Yeah. That was horrible."

"Well, remember the part when he talks about the moon? How there should be some huge eclipse, the moon hiding its face from him, because of this horrific thing he's just done?"

"I guess..."

Holly could hear the shrug in her tone.

"Well, that's pathetic fallacy."

Bridget paused then tried to sort it out, "The moon can't actually hide its face. So it's kind of a personification? Of nature?"

"Yes. That's a good way of looking at it."

"Okay. Next one," Bridget said.

Holly smiled into her computer, loving the impact Riley had on her sister. And wishing desperately the moon would quit shining so favorably on Colin and transfer its affections onto Riley.

Chapter Fourteen

What wild imaginations one forms where dear self is concerned!
How sure to be mistaken!
~Jane Austen

TREASURED DAYS, FRIDAYS. HOLLY WOULD usually take a jog, set the girls off to school, savor a third cup of coffee in the garden, do some leisure reading, finish a little housework and a little homework, then maybe take another jog before the girls returned from school. No rushing to get to work and no serious studying or cooking, thanks to Takeaway Night.

This Friday was supposed to be even more treasured. Mildred had taken over her Gertrude duties again, and Holly was hoping Fletcher would meet her for lunch somewhere. Plus, the pristine, sunny June weather had lately put everyone in a good mood. But from the moment she awoke, Holly could tell this day would be nothing but a challenge.

First, the girls were required at school an hour earlier than usual for special testing. Holly had forgotten this fact and failed to set her alarm accordingly the night before. Abbey had burst into Holly's room this morning to shake her awake in a panic. Holly grunted and scurried downstairs, without even changing or brushing her teeth or glancing in the mirror.

Then, halfway through preparing the girls' breakfast, still blurry-eyed, Holly got the call from Frank. He had taken ill, and Noelle was in London and unable to open the gallery, so "Could you work a full day?" he'd asked.

Her heart dropped at the thought, but her voice said, "Of course. No problem."

An hour later, hearing the rumble of thunder, Holly sat at the desk at the back of the gallery, making doodles instead of working, or reading, or even playing a bit of solitaire. She was utterly unmotivated. And she knew exactly why. She drew a birthday cake with candles and icing and wondered if positively *everyone* had forgotten. Not that birthdays should matter, at her age. At twenty-eight, she was a full-fledged adult, no longer in need of birthday parties or special gifts, or even general "Happy Birthday" greetings left as voicemails or issued from random people she might see throughout the day. No, she should be mature about this. Understand that everyone had busy days and it had simply slipped their minds.

Apparently *all* of their minds.

Minutes stretched into hours, and finally, Mr. Rothschild's hundred clocks chimed the five o'clock hour through the wall—the gallery normally stayed open until six, but Frank had told her to close at five if traffic was slow. So, Holly flicked off the gallery lights, locked the door, and mulled over how to spend her evening. She'd gotten a call from the twins at lunch, asking to attend a slumber party. Holly said yes. Abbey had already made plans to sleep over at her best mate's house. Even her father would be gone—he'd told her yesterday that an intense and lengthy meeting tonight would keep him in London late. So late, in fact, that he wouldn't be coming home at all. He would stay the night at a London hotel.

For the first time in perhaps years, Holly would spend the night entirely alone in that great big house. On her birthday.

She had texted Fletcher earlier to see what his plans were. But that was hours ago, and he hadn't texted her back. In fact, she hadn't seen him in days. She didn't know whether he was pulling away on purpose or was just too busy with work.

Pushing away the urge to sit at the end of Joe's bar, lost in a pint of lager, drawing circles with her finger on the mahogany surface as she snacked on stale peanuts, she decided to take control. She would celebrate her own birthday. It was up to her whether she had a crap day or a good one. She entered Mrs. Pickering's market with a new attitude, in search of cake mix and a cheap bottle of red wine. She could pick up some curry on the way home. It was Takeaway Friday, after all.

Even trudging home under the load of her groceries, she noticed this beautiful day around her—scented flowers lining the shady path, a couple of sheep along the stone wall baaing at her, a mockingbird standing atop the highest branch of a tree, singing her a song.

As the sun set an hour later, casting golden rays on the clipped green grass in the back garden, Holly took another sip of wine as she leaned against the open French door. She loved this time of day. Things winding down, pulling to a close, twilight on the horizon. People hunkering down in their homes, having dinner with loved ones or reading the paper by the fireside. Or, spending birthdays alone in a big empty house.

The timer dinged, signaling the cake was ready. She almost didn't have any room left after gorging on the curry, but she couldn't resist a slice. She opened the Aga door to remove the pan with a mitted hand, the smell of buttery cake intoxicating.

She listed the distinct advantages to being alone in the house. She could listen to any sort of music she wished, for instance. Including Coldplay, which Bridget despised. Holly could also watch anything on the telly now, and she intended to watch *Miranda* reruns, which Rosalee always mocked. Most of all, she could enjoy the quiet. Normally, every hallway in this house was filled with some sort of noise at any given moment—music or arguing or the clatter of footsteps. But not tonight. And she was determined to enjoy it.

After the cake cooled, Holly spread the icing on top and cut a slice. She shut off the Coldplay and carried her plate, with the wine, into the empty sitting room, singing quietly, "Happy birthday to me," and wishing she'd bought a couple of candles, too.

Even coming from a box, the cake tasted outstanding. Finishing her piece in a few bites, she knew another slice was in order. She went in for seconds and came back to the sitting room, squatting on the rug beside the fire. The only thing she could hear, besides the crackle of flames, was the tapping of fork tines against the plate as she scraped off the last bit of icing.

"Mm," she hummed, full and content, leaning back on both hands, crossing her ankles and listening to the nothingness.

But it only took a couple of minutes for the nothingness to become oppressive. Too quiet. Too peaceful.

Holly pushed herself up, collected the crockery and walked it to the kitchen sink, then carried her half-empty glass of wine through the French doors in search of fresh air. The house seemed far too big for one person right now. The sky had just emptied itself of every last trace of sun, and a half moon shone in its place.

She knew the only thing more pathetic than spending one's birthday alone was going to sleep on one's birthday before nine o'clock. But the boredom was too strong, and she'd started to consider it. Then, she remembered *Emma*. Things had been so busy this past week that she'd neglected those characters. How could she be the leader of a book club if she'd failed to do her own reading? They were heading into Week Seven. She still had three chapters to read before the next meeting, only two days away.

Clicking open the blue door of Hideaway Cottage, she turned on the lamp and made her way to the rocking chair. Her copy of *Emma* sat perched, waiting for her, and she found the scene where Mr. Elton and his new wife treated Harriet with particular rudeness and arrogance.

"Contemptible," Holly muttered, settling in to read.

Normally, the simple act of opening the cover thrust her firmly into Jane Austen's world with other people's dilemmas. But tonight, Holly reread the same sentence four times and knew it was time to quit. Perhaps it was the wine, making her head fuzzy. Or perhaps it wasn't.

She shut the book and gave up, gulping the last drop of wine. Closing her eyes, she conjured a memory of another birthday on which she was ignored. She had turned twelve that day, her first birthday no longer an only child. The twins were a few months old, and Holly knew her mother's focus was on them this year. It had to be. They made their demands in shrieks and wails, in need of constant attention. It had been that way since the moment they'd come home from the hospital.

Holly had retreated to Hideaway Cottage when the twins cried for their breakfast that morning. She had a birthday tea party alone. An hour later, her mother tapped on the door and entered the cottage with something in her hands.

"A cake!" Holly had said, her face unable to contain the joy. Her favorite kind—pineapple upside-down. It even had a candle perched on top.

"I made it late last night," her mother said, setting it down on the kid-sized table in the center of the room. She sat on the floor with Holly, both cross-legged, and pulled a matchbook from her pocket. "Now," she said, in a hushed voice. "Make a wish."

She lit the candle and Holly stared at the flame, knowing her wish had already come true.

It wasn't long before her mother was called away again, to help Duncan change two dirty diapers. But for Holly, the cake had been enough. It was an acknowledgment that, amidst the flurry of twin activity, she hadn't been forgotten. That she was still important.

"Oh, Mum," she whispered to the air now, tears brimming. "Why can't you be here, right now, with me? I miss you so much."

She let the grief have its way, let the tears finish their course. The wine was partially to blame for this maudlin mood, but the ache in her chest, the desire to have her mother there, just for a moment, was very real.

Her head throbbed, and crying only made it worse. It was time to get up, get out of this cottage, away from these memories. She decided to go to bed—turn the page on this depressing day and begin another one tomorrow.

With great effort she stood, tired and woozy, clutching her glass and headed for the door. But before she could reach the handle, a loud knock made her shriek and drop the glass. It shattered near her feet. Thank goodness she wasn't barefooted.

Adrenaline pumping, Holly braced herself, irrationally afraid to open the door. Another disadvantage of being alone at night was having fewer people around to help fend off a prowler.

"Holly?"

This was no prowler. Recognizing the voice, she tiptoed to the side of the broken glass and opened the door.

"Fletcher! What the bloody hell are you doing here? You scared the life out of me." She could still hear her pulse thumping in her ears.

"Sorry," he said, his arms crossed in front of him. He looked... odd. "Are you gonna let me in?"

"Sure," she agreed, suddenly realizing he was entering her sacred abode. She wasn't certain she was comfortable with someone—anyone—crossing the threshold of Hideaway Cottage. "Watch the glass," she added, pointing down as he stepped around it. As she shut the door, she stooped down to pick up the four largest pieces, gingerly placing them into a small trash bin nearby. She could clear the few remaining shards in a bit. She noticed Fletcher standing in the middle of the room, his arms still crossed.

"You've been crying," he said.

She joined him and waved a hand. "I'm fine. Just some old ghosts lurking that decided to come out tonight. So, why are you skulking about? And how did you find me?"

"I wasn't skulking. Only British people skulk. Texans... loiter." He smiled at his own joke. "Anyway, I knocked on the front and back door of the house and nobody was there. So, I went through the garden and saw your light on."

His jacket twitched in the shadow of the lamp, drawing her attention. "What's the matter with you? You're acting a bit barmy, if you don't mind my saying."

"Well, there's a good reason." He uncrossed his arms and opened his jacket fast, like a flasher, revealing a whimpering, fluffy, black-and-white fur ball.

"Happy Birthday!" he said.

The puppy squirming inside his jacket looked terrified, his whole little body trembling as he sniffed the air. Fletcher dug his hands inside to lift him out. Holly let out a squeak of delight that scared the puppy even more, then reached out, taking him carefully from Fletcher's arms.

"What have you done, Fletcher Hays?" she said, letting the puppy sniff at her fingers.

"Do you like your present? His name is 'Rascal,' if I remember right."

She cuddled the puppy and looked up. "Is this the same one? That we saw three weeks ago?"

"The very same. I phoned Mr. Elton that night and asked him to reserve him for me. I knew you had a birthday coming up."

"How?"

"Lizzie mentioned it."

"I can't believe this," she whispered, nuzzling her nose into the puppy's soft fur. She felt him gnawing on her index finger with little razor teeth.

"Are you angry with me?" Fletcher asked.

"Angry? Why?"

"Well, what you said then, about the responsibility of a pet. I knew you'd turned him down once, so I took a chance that you really didn't mean it."

"Well, tonight you've caught me with some wine in my system, you lucky bastard. I *might* regret this in the morning, though." She smiled, making cooing sounds at her new present.

"Look how relaxed he is with you," Fletcher noted. "He belongs here."

"Well, I can't very well let go of you now, can I, little one?" she asked the puppy, scratching his ear.

Fletcher reached out to scratch the other one. "I'll build you a doghouse if you want. Just to give him a little outdoor space of his own. I've already asked Mac to help out."

"I think that would be lovely. Even though I can already tell this dog will be an indoor dog. The girls will make sure of that. They'll fall in love with him, especially Abbey." She made purposeful eye contact with Fletcher, her rescuer-from-bad-birthdays. "Thank you."

"You're very welcome."

"Not for the puppy—well, yes, for the puppy. But that's not what I meant." She paused, tried to sound less foggy and more coherent. "Thank you... for remembering."

"What?"

"My birthday." Ridiculous tears flooded her eyes again. She wiped them before Rascal could lick them away.

"More tears?" Fletcher reached out to touch her cheek.

"Nobody remembered," she said. "Not Frank or Gertrude or Mildred—not even my own father or any of my sisters! Nobody." She realized how petty it all sounded. But she was past caring now.

"Come here." He pulled her into him, the puppy squirming between them. Resting her head under the curve of his neck, Holly felt Fletcher stroke her hair. His shirt smelled sweet and clean. It calmed her instantly, human contact. The warmth of another body.

"*I* didn't forget." His voice resonated inside his chest.

"I know," she whispered.

He backed away enough to look at her, still touching her hair. "Look, people get busy. They become preoccupied. It doesn't mean they don't love you."

"You're right." She rolled her eyes. "I mean, I've done it lots of times myself, forgotten people's birthdays. It happens. I guess I'm vulnerable today. And it just hit me."

"What did?"

"My life. This." She backed away, still holding Rascal, and extended her hand to point all around her. "I'm pushing closer to thirty. And I'm celebrating a birthday all alone. Well, not anymore, of course. But really, look at me. I've got no family of my own, no house, no husband or kids, no career. I'm standing in the middle of a child's cottage, for heaven's sake." She chuckled. "Honestly, I'm twenty-eight, and what do I have to show for it?"

"Three sisters, which is more than most people have. And a father who adores you."

"And who all forgot my birthday."

"Okay. How about a job you actually like?"

"One that's generally boring and stagnant. No room for upward mobility."

"Well, you've got—a brand-new puppy."

"This is true," she said, peering down at her wriggling bundle. "But I think he has to wee." She looked up at Fletcher. "Seriously. You're right. I'm being ridiculous."

"Not ridiculous. Tipsy, maybe. But never ridiculous."

"I've managed to turn my birthday party into a pity party, haven't I? Do you want some cake to celebrate?"

"I thought you'd never ask."

Chapter Fifteen

Know your own happiness. You want nothing but patience;
or give it a more fascinating name: call it hope.
~Jane Austen

CRAWLING UP OUT OF THE fog of a heavy sleep—especially a sleep of the hangover kind—was always a challenge. Somewhere in the faraway corners of her brain, Holly could sense the wet licks on her feet, could even hear the front door open and voices grow louder, but her eyes refused to budge. They felt hollow and heavy, as though small bags of change had weighed them down all night.

She rubbed her throbbing forehead and then her dry eyes. How many glasses of wine *had* she had? No more than three, surely.

She groaned as she tried again to open her eyes.

"Holly!" Abbey's voice shrieked in a pitch and timbre that only worsened Holly's headache. "What is *this*!?"

Abbey's presence forced Holly's eyes open, but the image of her sister was blurry. She watched the figure bend over the settee and reach for another equally hazy blob—the puppy.

"A present," Holly whispered. "From Fletcher."

Fletcher. Holly reached back in her memory to figure out what had happened to him last night. They'd shared a piece of cake and a glass of wine in the sitting room, settling in to chat for hours, it seemed. First about Finn, then about America, then about lots of other things. She remembered becoming groggy at one point and lying back on the couch, nodding at something he was saying. Then, nothing.

Now, she saw the twisted-up blanket that lay over one leg. He had probably covered her up, then snuck out to leave, always the Southern gentleman.

"I can't believe he got you a puppy!" Abbey yelled, sitting on the floor and patting the rug, the puppy pouncing at her hands. "What's its name?"

"Rascal," Holly replied, moving to a sitting position. But even slow movements made her headache worse. Her whole body seemed to throb. "He probably needs a pee."

"I'll take him!" Abbey offered, scooping Rascal up to carry him out to the back garden. If Holly had any reservations that she alone would end up caring for the dog, Abbey had just put them all to rest.

Next, she heard her father's voice and realized she must look like absolute rubbish. She combed through her hair with her fingers then rubbed beneath her eyes to remove the possible smudges of eye liner.

"Hey, Dad," she said as he entered. He carried a bouquet of assorted flowers.

"Am I forgiven?" he asked as she struggled to stand.

"What for?"

"Your birthday. I remembered it as I was driving back to the hotel last night. It was too late to call. Damn sorry about that. My days got mixed up. Helluva week."

"Oh, no worries," she said, flicking her wrist in a no-big-deal sort of way. "I didn't even notice."

"Well, here. I hope this makes up for it." He handed her the flowers. She sneezed.

"I'll put them in water," he offered, backing out of the room awkwardly.

"Thanks, Dad. Very sweet of you," she called after him.

She could hear him meeting Abbey down the hall, could hear her continued peals of joy over the puppy. It suddenly dawned on Holly how her father might feel, having a dog in the house.

Craving a shower, Holly headed for the staircase and nearly ran into the twins, who'd walked in the front door. They had cards and unwrapped books in their hands. She imagined that her father had called them early this morning, strongly suggesting they buy something at the Emporium rather than arrive home empty-handed.

"Happy Birthday," they said in unison, offering their gifts.

"Thank you, girls. Did you have a nice time at the sleepover?"

Rosalee nodded, but Bridget sighed. Must've been some unexpected drama amongst the girls. Either that, or the sigh reflected her desire to be with Colin rather than a roomful of schoolmates.

"Look!" Abbey told them, shoving Rascal into their arms. "Fletcher got him for Holly!"

Too sluggish to attempt another smile, Holly took the first step up the staircase. "I'm off to take a shower. Back in a bit. Look after the little guy, will you?"

Thirty minutes later, refreshed from the shower, Holly padded in her bare feet and towel to her bedroom mirror and tapped concealer under her eyes to banish the dark circles.

Then, wriggling into her jeans, she heard a sharp tapping outside. Curious, she threw a T-shirt over her head and went to the window, from which she could view one large corner of the back garden. Abbey bounded around with Rascal. And at the other end… Mac's silver-grey head? And Fletcher stooping beside him? They looked hard at work, hammering wood beams together. She remembered the doghouse and scurried downstairs, hair still damp, make-up half done, to join them.

Her father sat outside, leaning in a chair against the side of the house, observing their work. A pipe hung out the corner of his mouth, smoke escaping out the other corner.

"Look at you, the lazy spectator," Holly teased as she approached.

He looked the part—sunglasses on, legs crossed at the ankles. The only thing missing was some white sand and a piña colada.

"I find that manual labor doesn't suit me. Besides, I signed a new client last night. Worth ten million. Doesn't that earn me a bit of R and R?"

"It certainly does." She leaned down to kiss his unshaven cheek. "Oops—wet hair."

"No problem," he said, taking another puff.

She motioned toward Abbey and Rascal. "You don't mind, do you? About the dog."

"Whatever makes you happy," he said, his eyes showing through the top of his glasses. "And if a dog makes you happy, I'm happy."

124

"Thanks, Dad." She squeezed his hand and squinted, watching the workers and wishing their job was a less noisy one. The aspirin she'd swallowed before her shower had begun to take effect but only barely.

"Hey!" Fletcher shouted.

She noticed he was sweaty and out of breath. And, once again, shirtless. Holly ventured out into the warm sun to join him. "You sure didn't waste any time. With the doghouse, I mean."

"I have the day off. What better way to spend it?"

"Mac, thanks for your help," Holly said, seeing him pause, too. "How'd Fletcher talk you into it?"

"I overheard him yesterday, asking Joe about a doghouse. I knew a bloke who had extra lumber and needed to get rid of it." His Scottish "r" trilled. "Consider it a belated birthday present from all of us."

Mac wiped his forehead, sending Holly into hostess mode. "Well, I'm getting you two something to drink. And some sandwiches. We can have a picnic!"

The idea took root, and before long, Holly was in the kitchen concocting a grand spread—turkey sandwiches, fresh fruit, potato crisps, even a batch of lemonade. Before she knew it, her headache had vanished, and she was a new person, vibrant and energetic.

She commissioned the twins to help carry out all the food, and soon, they were all sitting on blankets in the garden underneath the shade of an oak tree, munching on grapes and sandwiches and enjoying the peerless day. Unfortunately, Fletcher had put his shirt back on for the meal, but Holly had every hope he would remove it again later on to finish the doghouse.

During the picnic, Rascal became the entertainment, as he went from person to person, trying to steal food. He even let out his first piercing "Yip!" and made everyone chuckle. Even Bridget was distracted from her texting long enough to reveal a smile. Holly suspected the textee was Colin, and her suspicions were confirmed when Bridget asked their father if she could leave and go to the Manor set for a while. Their father gave permission, and off she went.

Holly wished she'd been close enough to Bridget to give her some words of advice, about moving a relationship forward too quickly. About striking a balance between boys and everything else that was important at her age. But she and Bridget had never had that sort of relationship, though not from Holly's lack of effort. Anytime Holly gave Bridget something resembling personal advice, she got an eye roll in return. After a certain number of eye rolls, Holly stopped trying so hard.

Bridget's contact with Colin seemed to be intensifying rapidly these days—Rosalee had recently confirmed that she saw a "major kiss" take place between them in a corner of the Manor gardens. Bridget was also starting to disengage from her life. When she wasn't with Colin, she was uninvolved in the household, staying up in her room most days, claiming homework but probably texting, and she rarely talked—or even fought—with her sisters anymore. She even quit returning her friends' phone calls. These days, Bridget's life centered only around Colin.

The picnic lunch devoured, Mac and Fletcher finished the doghouse while Rosalee helped Holly clean up. Inside, after chucking paper plates into the garbage, Rosalee said, "So, did you ask him?"

Holly popped one last crisp into her mouth. "Ask who, what?"

"Da-ad," Rosalee said, shoulder slumped. "About school. About theatre courses?"

Holly dusted crumbs from her fingers. She'd spoken to her father two nights ago, and there was a very good reason she hadn't told Rosalee yet. He'd said "no." As many different angles as Holly had tried to argue on her sister's behalf, her father could only associate acting with something fruitless, vapid. He went so far as to say that if Rosalee chose to focus on theatre courses, she might even lose his financial backing for university. His way of forcing the issue. But Holly couldn't tell Rosalee this. Couldn't bear to.

"Holly?"

"Yeah. Well, you know Dad. He's a little stubborn."

"He said 'no.'"

"Not exactly."

"But he didn't say 'yes,' did he?"

"Look, don't worry about it. Let me handle things. He'll come around. I know he will."

"Thanks for trying." Clearly gutted, Rosalee switched on the tap to rinse the flatware.

Abbey rounded the corner with Rascal bundled in her arms, panting. "I think he needs some water."

"I'll get it," Rosalee offered, already at the sink.

Holly clamped down the lid on the tub of fruit, musing over the subtle changes taking place in Rosalee. Bridget's preoccupation with a certain actor seemed to have a positive impact on her twin. In Bridget's absence, Rosalee seemed more in tune with the family than ever. She seemed softer, more willing to help or to join in. She even spent more time with Abbey instead of treating her like an annoying gnat to be swatted away.

An hour later, the doghouse was finished. Mac departed, taking the tools and extra scraps of lumber with him, while Fletcher painted the doghouse a pale white and Holly sat with her father and held a sleeping Rascal.

Yesterday's pity-and-moan party had been replaced by today's unexpected family time. It was what Holly needed all along. She looked around at the sun-washed garden, at her life, and felt nothing but gratitude.

Chapter Sixteen

*If I had not promoted Mr. Spencer's visits here, and given
many little encouragements, and smoothed many little
matters, it might not have come to any thing after all.*
~Jane Austen

HOLLY MUNCHED ON A BISCUIT, thrilled that the seventh week
of the book club had come to *this*. She had only posed one
question at the beginning of the meeting—about Emma's true
feelings for Mr. Churchill—and the ladies, as well as the men, Frank
and Fletcher, took off with the question, diving in, overlapping each
other in eager discussion. Holly no longer had to bear the burden of
facilitator, thinking up discussion-worthy questions and fearing there
might only be crickets as the answer. Today, in fact, she had to pause
and wait on someone else before voicing her own opinion. The book
club officially had a life of its own. And the gathering had grown larger,
a packed house today at fifteen. Even Julia, from the bakery, had started
to attend.

Weeks ago, Frank and Noelle had decided to trade off Mondays, so
that one of them could join the discussion while the other opened the
gallery. Frank's turn this week, he now edged the discussion toward Mr.
Elton, who had brought his new wife to town in Chapter Thirty-Two.

"Elton's snubbing of Miss Smith is unconscionable!" Frank insisted
as he flipped through his text. "And the way he parades his new wealthy
wife around... no wonder he's such a despised character."

Fletcher caught Holly's gaze and discreetly raised his eyebrows at Frank's passionate diatribe. She had to look away, for fear of giggling.

"I disagree," a new voice came bellowing from the corner. A voice that hadn't once, in seven weeks' time, spoken at this book club before. Gertrude tapped her cane defiantly, startling Leopold, who had been sound asleep in her lap. "Mr. Elton was entirely practical, marrying that woman."

"How do you mean?" Frank asked, after finding his voice again, seeming rattled by Gertrude's signature scowl.

"What I mean, young man, is that Mr. Elton was incredibly wise, marrying for money rather than love. He and Miss Smith would have been positively miserable together, mark my words."

Holly returned an eyebrow raise toward Fletcher. Somewhere along the way, without anyone knowing it, Gertrude had not only started reading *Emma* but had actually begun caring enough to get riled up.

"With all respect, ma'am," Frank continued on thin ice, "marrying for love is the only happiness, I believe."

"You are a fool to think so." Gertrude tapped her cane again. "Marrying for love is impractical and unwise. Even in these current times. Have you seen Britain's divorce rate? It's astonishing."

"Well, yes," he said meekly.

"There you have it. I would dare say that in countries where marriages are arranged—where marriage is *not* based upon love, but upon financial considerations—the divorce rate is practically nothing."

Frank shifted uncomfortably in his seat, clearly unable to argue further on the matter.

"Therefore..." Gertrude raised *Emma* to emphasize her point. "Mr. Elton is one of the wisest characters in this entire book."

"Well, I wouldn't go *that* far," another voice whispered from the opposite corner. Holly shifted her eyes to see the voice's owner. Mildred!

"What was that?" Gertrude asked, squinting in her direction.

"I do see your point," Mildred answered with growing confidence. "However, the attitude of Mr. Elton as he 'paraded' his wife about, under Miss Smith's nose, knowing exactly how she had fallen for him... well, in my mind, that makes him rather an inconsiderate character."

Gertrude stared down Mildred from afar. The entire room grew silent, and Holly wondered if anyone was even breathing.

Finally, Gertrude gave a firm nod. "Quite right," she said. "Sensible, Mr. Elton was..." She wagged her finger. "But not considerate. He is a *man*, after all."

The remark was met with giggles from the women, and fortunately, Fletcher had the good sense to smile, brushing off the sexist insult as he would lint on his jacket. But Frank... Holly wasn't sure he would ever return to the book club after that.

An hour later, the members had cleared out of the cottage, and Holly left Mildred in the kitchen to dry the rest of the dishes.

Holly hugged her copy of *Emma* close to her chest and approached Gertrude. "That was quite a discussion."

"Who invited that Frank fellow to these meetings? He has no sense." Gertrude scoffed.

"I did. He's the gallery curator, remember? My boss. And he's the one who helped organize this club for me. He even made posters to put up all over the village so people would know about it."

"Well."

"So, you're enjoying the book?" Holly asked, knowing she was pushing it.

"It's all right." Gertrude sniffed then leaned in, motioning Holly closer.

She stepped forward and bent down, curious.

"Have you noticed anything odd going on with Mildred?" Gertrude pointed toward the kitchen.

Holly thought about it and said, "Well, she was a little outspoken this morning. But I think that's good. It means she feels comfortable, opening up."

"Yes, of course. No, I meant something else," Gertrude continued to whisper, her breath hinting of strong tea. "Mildred has been... whistling."

"Has she?"

"Yes. I constantly hear her whistling some dreadful tune as she's stripping the sheets or cleaning up after Leopold."

"Well, that's hardly a crime, is it? Whistling? Perhaps that's a good sign. Maybe she's starting to heal a little. You know how awful things have been, after her brother's passing."

"Yes. Excellent point." Gertrude agreed. "Still, I find the whistling highly suspect. You should keep an eye on her. See if she whistles at your house, as well."

Holly suppressed the urge to roll her eyes and tried to say goodbye. But clearly, Gertrude was in a rare chatty mood.

"Tell me," she said, clutching her bony fingers around Holly's wrist to keep her there. "How are things going with your young man?"

"You can call him 'Fletcher.' He won't mind." By now, Holly felt silly, upholding their ruse, and had come close to setting Gertrude straight. But she knew she'd be better off playing along. She continued, "He's perfect. Things couldn't be more wonderful."

"When is he going to marry you?"

"Marry me? Well, that's hardly a question to ask at this point. I'm not thinking about marriage right now."

"Well. Perhaps you should." She emphasized each word, weighted them, punched them with deeper meaning: *If you don't catch this man and hold onto him, there will never be another, and you will end up nothing but an old maid.*

"Look at the time." Holly glanced at her other wrist then remembered she'd forgotten to wear a watch. "I'm sorry to cut this short, Gertrude, but I need to run. Have a nice day." She wriggled out of Gertrude's grasp and walked away.

Opening the front door, Holly breathed free, fresh air for the first time all morning. That cottage positively suffocated its inhabitants. She didn't know how Mildred stood it every day. No wonder she whistled.

"Here are the ones I'm having trouble with." Lily Griffin pointed to the list she'd printed off before she came. "Can you quiz me on them?"

"Sure." Holly took the paper, frustrated that Frank had chosen the fifteen minutes before now to take his break and run an errand. Lily, the student from Holly's online course, had arrived at the gallery precisely on time for their study session at the gallery. She'd been sweet and cordial and was just as pretty in person as on her Facebook page. Holly had no doubt that—should Frank ever return—he would be smitten.

"Let's see. The first one is…"

Rather than bringing relief, the tinkle of the front bell brought alarm. Holly hadn't thought this through, what to say to Frank when he *did* arrive. She hadn't prepared him for Lily at all. This could actually backfire.

Frank rounded the corner in mid-conversation. "I tell you, I've never once, in my five years at this village, seen Julia crack a smile." Holding a coffee and a petite paper bag, he stopped short when he saw Lily sitting at his work table. Holly watched his face change but couldn't tell what it changed to.

"Oh, hello," he said softly. He looked to Holly for an explanation.

"Frank O'Neill, this is Lily Griffin. From Malmesbury. She's a student in my course. I hope you don't mind our—"

"So lovely to meet you," Frank said, cutting Holly off, setting down his bag, and offering his hand.

Holly noticed that Lily's expression—the warm, shy smile—mirrored Frank's expression almost exactly. They shook hands and held each other's stare, seconds longer than was normally polite. *Could it really be this easy?*

"I wish I'd known about your friend coming," Frank said, breaking his gaze to speak to Holly. "I would've bought you both a coffee."

"It's okay. In fact…" Holly stood and gathered her bag from the other chair. "Why don't I make a quick run, myself?"

"Fine," Frank said without protest, taking Holly's seat.

"Lily was telling me how much she loves the Cornwall painting in the window," Holly prompted.

"Yes," Lily confirmed. "The colors are so vibrant. My family often went to Cornwall for our summer holidays when I was growing up…"

Sneaking away, Holly opened the gallery door as quietly as possible, deciding she would take her time, linger at the bakery, perhaps stop by the pub and see Fletcher. Maybe even take a browse at the Emporium. She was in desperate need of light bulbs and a few other essentials, anyway.

Chapter Seventeen

Surprises are foolish things. The pleasure is not enhanced,
and the inconvenience is often considerable.
~Jane Austen

"STUPID MOUSE," HOLLY ACCUSED, SEEING the red dot winking. She had thought a wireless mouse a wise idea—until it started running out of batteries about once every five weeks. Perfect timing, too. She had a term paper to finish and couldn't lose a minute. Even to go hunting for batteries.

Still basking in the glow of a seemingly successful match—Frank and Lily had *still* been chattering away when Holly's shift ended—Holly had returned to Foxglove House an hour ago only to remember her paper was due this evening by midnight. She'd forgotten to double check the due date and thought she had at least two more days.

Fortunately, today, when the house should be full—her father's day to work at home, Mildred's cleaning day, the girls home after school—Foxglove had been gloriously empty, allowing her to write in peace. Her father had a half day's work in London, while the girls went off to the Manor and Mildred ran some all-important errands for Gertrude.

Scooting back her chair with a grunt, Holly went in search of batteries. While she rummaged around, Rascal whimpered at her ankles, begging for attention.

"Not now, baby," she cooed, closing one drawer and opening the next. "Damn it."

Cursing apparently made Rascal squeal louder, so she stooped to pick him up, carrying him with her to different rooms of the house. She could feel his velvet-soft tummy rise and fall as he breathed his quick puppy breaths.

Desperate, she searched the space under the staircase, recalling that sometimes odds and ends hid out there.

"Ah-ha!" she exclaimed, seeing an old box of batteries, but hesitated when she saw the fuzz that had gathered on them. Too old. Plus, they were the wrong size. She shut the door and moved on, hoping she wouldn't be forced to use the laptop's horrid and cumbersome touchpad.

Rascal seemed amused by their scavenger hunt and chewed happily on her finger.

"Ouch! Stop that, silly bugger."

As a last resort, she entered her father's study, knowing that sometimes he kept batteries in his desk for his own wireless mouse. He wouldn't mind if she did a quick look-round, stole one wee battery from him.

Setting Rascal down on the plush rug, she rounded the desk and started opening drawers. She'd made it through three with no success before finding his secret battery stash in the bottom drawer. She heard the front door slam and glanced up to see her father in the doorway.

"You're home early," she said.

He nodded but stayed put, looking a little lost.

Perhaps a deal had gone sour, or he'd finally had to sack Wilson after all. Rascal tugged at Holly's trouser leg, growling, and she set her battery on the desk to reach down and snatch him up.

Her father finally entered, rubbed at his stubbled chin, and eased into the leather seat on the opposite side of the desk. "We need to talk."

"Okay," Holly said. "What's wrong?"

Rascal yawned and settled on Holly's lap for a nap.

"Nothing. In fact, it's the opposite of wrong, but I'm afraid you won't agree."

"Dad, you're being cryptic. Tell me. I can take it."

When her father couldn't look her in the eye, she knew it was serious. He tapped the top of the desk with his index finger in Morse-type code, as though practicing the right words in his head before he said them. "I've been sort of... seeing someone."

Holly tilted her head, a bit like Rascal did whenever he heard a new sound, trying to isolate it, figure out exactly what he was hearing, make sense of it. *Seeing someone?*

"You mean, dating?"

"Yes. Dating."

Holly was hit with a bizarre mix of shock and foreknowledge—as though somewhere in her brain, she already knew this was coming but still wasn't prepared for it. At all.

"For how long?" she asked, trying to think of how he'd possibly had *time* to date anyone. Or how he'd kept it such a secret.

"Not long. But it's turned serious."

"Who is she?" Holly pictured a business associate, or maybe a secretary back in London. Those were the only females her father would be around on a daily basis. But seconds after the question came out of her mouth, she knew. The pieces fit. The whistling... the tender embrace... the whispers exchanged. "Mildred." *Of course, Mildred.*

"How did you know?" His expression held surprise.

"Call it a lucky guess."

Rascal nuzzled his nose inside Holly's elbow and sighed deeply.

"I need to explain," her father said.

Holly felt caught, somewhere between strong curiosity and a none-of-her-business dismissal. But curiosity won out, and she said, "Okay."

He stood and began to pace. Her mother had always called it his "Thinker's Walk." He talked to the floor instead of the person, punctuating his words with hand gestures, watching his own feet shuffle.

"About seven months ago, as you know, I decided to work from home on Tuesdays, which happened to be Mildred's day here, at the house. Pure coincidence. I'd also run into her at Gertrude's occasionally, when I stopped by for a chat."

He paused to glance at Holly, probably trying to read her face, then continued.

"So. Mildred would sometimes come in to my study on those Tuesdays, offer me some tea, and we'd chat a bit. About the weather, about Gertrude, casual things. After a while, I found I looked forward to them—those chats. I enjoyed having another adult to talk to. No offense." He waved in her direction, still looking at the floor.

"None taken," Holly said, trying to be patient, trying to let him finish before drawing her conclusions.

"Well, one day, here in the study, Mildred broke down and cried. I offered her a tissue, and she told me about her brother—how he wasn't doing well, how he was writhing in pain from the cancer, how she knew it was only a matter of time. She was watching him die. She hadn't told anybody these things before, and... well, I felt bad for her. I realized what a strong woman this was, what a gentle, kind woman this was. My eyes were opened that day. I can't explain it. And I guess she felt the same way."

He planted his feet and held onto the back of the chair for support, still unable to look Holly in the eye as he finished his tale. "After that conversation, I wanted to see her more often than Tuesdays. I would make up an excuse and call her from the car on the way home from London, and we would talk for the entire commute. It turned into every day, a ritual. We were becoming friends. And after her brother died, well, we got even closer. She leaned on me, and I could understand that kind of pain. You know, with your mother..." he trailed off.

"Dad, why did you hide it? And why did you wait until now to tell me?"

"I tried. Well, I meant to try. Mildred's been urging me for ages, and I guess I've waited too long." He took his seat again and leaned back, threading his fingers together. "At first, it was nice, having it be between only us, this... friendship, whatever it was. No judgment from anyone. This village loves its gossip."

Holly knew it was true.

"And then, when it unexpectedly became something more, I didn't know *how* to tell you. I didn't know it would get this far this fast. That I would purchase a ring..." He clamped his mouth shut.

Up until this moment, Holly had actually started feeling little bubbles of happiness rise up for her father and for Mildred. He'd found love. He was happy.

But a *ring*? This soon?

"You've proposed to her," she said flatly.

"No, of course not." Her father stood again, scratching his head. "I wouldn't ask her without getting my girls' approval."

"But you purchased a ring," Holly countered, sensing the bubbles pop, one by one.

"Yes, but—"

"I don't understand. Why the rush?" Her words had a bite to them, sounded angrier than she'd meant them to—but wasn't she? Angry? Didn't she feel betrayed that he was springing all this on her now, an enormous life change for *all* of them, without a single hint beforehand? Not to mention what this might do to the girls when they found out. "Tell me why this has to happen now."

He shrugged, his tired eyes squinting with a half-smile. "I'm in love. I don't see the need to wait. I want Mildred as my wife. It's that simple."

Holly knew this side of her father well. The unbending side, the logical side. The one that, once it made a decision, would never back down or change its mind. In spite of the ripple effects it might have for anyone else.

"Simple for you," she whispered, thinking again of her sisters. If Holly was experiencing such a confusing mess of emotions, there was no telling how the girls would handle the news.

Holly fidgeted, frustrated. The taut leather squeaked beneath her, waking Rascal. It was all too much to process. But instead of going backward to make sense of it all, her mind raced ahead. Dating was one thing. But with a ring involved—a marriage involved—everything would change. Suddenly, permanently.

Would Mildred live here, at Foxglove? Would the girls call her "Stepmother"? Would they even need Holly anymore? The pace of all this became dizzying.

"Honey, I'm sorry I blurted it out. And that I waited so long to tell you." His voice cracked under the weight of what sounded like guilt. "But I didn't know how. I never expected to find someone. I wasn't looking for it. And, I'm not good at these sorts of things… talking about feelings and such."

"No kidding."

"Okay, I'm complete crap at these things. Better?"

"Yes, much."

She noticed the weariness in his eyes. He seemed to hit his limit, and his voice softened. "I won't propose to Mildred unless you girls are okay with it. We've been a family on our own all these years, and there's a rhythm to it. Bringing someone else in, a wife, will change that rhythm. Help me out here."

Hitting her own personal limit, Holly needed to escape, to move out of this chair, out of this room. She stood up, balancing Rascal on her arm. "I need to process this. I need some time."

"Fair enough. But will you…" He hesitated, waiting for her to look at him. "Could you tell your sisters for me?"

"Dad!"

"Well, I told you—I'm crap at this. They would take it easier coming from you."

Holly knew it was true but hated the position it put her in. That pseudo-wife role she'd played, off and on, for the past six years. Asking her to do this was asking too much. She could barely comprehend this major shift in the universe—how could she possibly explain it to her sisters?

Rascal squeaked and squirmed in her arms.

"He needs to go out." She picked up the battery and maneuvered her way around the desk.

"Of course."

"And I have a term paper to write. Actually, that's why I came in here in the first place. Looking for batteries for my mouse." She showed him. "I wasn't snooping."

"I never thought you were."

He met her at the edge of the desk.

"Are we okay?" he asked, his expression hopeful.

She couldn't lie to him, so she tried to inject a hint of warmth into her tone as she carefully stated the truth. "We will be. I'm just blindsided. I need a bit of space. I'll tell the girls for you, but I'm not promising they'll be okay with this. You might have to brace yourself for the fallout. But I *will* try."

"Thanks, love," he said, reaching out for a hug, Rascal wriggling between them. "I can always count on you."

Yes, but who can I count on? she wondered. Stepping out of the hug, she went on her way, shutting the door behind her.

Cocooning herself inside a blanket, Holly plopped into the rocking chair and bundled up. She needed to be swallowed up whole by something comforting. Insulated and secure. Now all she needed was a cup of tea and a fire to go with it. But she craved privacy even more than a fireplace. Hideaway Cottage, with its lack of amenities, would have to do.

She stared ahead, finally having time to absorb things. A few hours ago, she'd left her father's study and somehow switched off her emotions to finish her term paper. She had no idea if the words made any sense by the time she sent it off, but at least it was completed.

Then, she'd made it through dinner when the girls arrived home—Indian takeaway, as she wasn't in the mood to cook. There was positively no way she could've spoken to her sisters tonight about this. Not without figuring out how *she* felt about it first.

Remarried. Married again. To someone else, someone other than her mother.

It sounded so odd, put exactly that way. She buried her face deep inside the blanket's gap at her chin and closed her eyes, her hot breath ricocheting back onto her cheeks. Thinking back, she'd handled the confrontation with her father quite maturely. Outwardly, at least.

Never—except maybe when her mother passed away so suddenly—had she been this caught off guard by her own emotions. Or experienced such a sharp paradox—two sides of the same coin: anger and empathy, frustration and compassion—as she heard her father's explanation. Yes, of course, she wanted to see him happy, knew he deserved to smile again, even to marry again. He absolutely did. But on the other hand, she felt overprotective of her mother's memory, of the image of her parents as a unit, forever. That was the only way she had ever seen them. Together.

She'd always known of this possibility, at least in the shadows of her mind. Ironically, Gertrude had been the one to warn Holly right after her mother's death, "Men can't be alone. They must have companionship. Expect your father to find someone else. Prepare yourself for this."

Holly had dismissed the notion at once, and her father had proved Gertrude wrong, as the years rolled by and he remained contentedly single. In that time, Holly rarely thought about the possibility of him remarrying. It seemed less and less likely with every passing year.

But now with Mildred…

Activating the fully rational side of her mind, Holly could see precisely what her father saw in Mildred—levelheaded, practical, compassionate. And strong. Her father admired strength in others, and Mildred had it in spades. Though hers was a quiet strength, a dignified one, not immediately obvious.

Holly thought of her sisters, wondered if they would ever let their own rational side kick in, once they'd heard the news. Abbey was still so young, still fragile over the memory of her mother. The peach tree was a reminder of that. And the twins, they hid it well, but Holly knew they still mourned. And Bridget, especially, would never allow another woman into this household in the role of stepmother. Not without a battle.

Something buzzed under the blanket. Holly always left her phone inside the main house when she came to Hideaway Cottage. But she must've forgotten this time.

Wriggling her arms free, she found her phone. Rather than shutting it off, she saw the caller ID and answered.

"Fletcher, hey." Her voice sounded creaky and unenthusiastic.

"You okay?" he asked.

"Not really."

"What's wrong?"

"I can't really talk about it now," she said. The girls had priority with this information. She would tell Fletcher eventually. "I'm sorry."

"No problem. Anything I can do?"

"I wish. Do you have access to a genie? Or a time machine? Or maybe a crystal ball?"

"Unfortunately, none of those things. But I do have a shoulder to lean on."

"It's appreciated. How are you? Did the scene go well today?"

Fletcher had been asked to make more revisions to dialogue taking place at a party. His admitted writer's weakness was scenes with multiple characters. He always had trouble juggling the overlapping dialogue without it seeming choppy or unnatural.

"I think so. That director can be a real jerk sometimes, though. He's super blunt. No sugar-coating. And he never gives compliments."

"Well, don't let him intimidate you. You're brilliant. And if he has any doubts about that, give him my number. He can talk to me."

"I'll keep that in mind. How's Rascal?"

"Perfectly named." She remembered the kitchen towels he'd managed to yank down from the kitchen table tonight, shredding them into a zillion pieces. "Chewing up everything in sight. Including my favorite pair of sandals."

"Uh-oh." There was a wince in his tone.

"But I do love him, you know. All he has to do is pout with those huge brown eyes, and I melt. He knows exactly what he's doing."

"Good boy. I taught him all about pouting on my long walk over to your house that night. He knows how to get away with murder."

Holly laughed into the phone. "I needed this."

"What?"

"No pressure, just talking. And laughing. I didn't expect to laugh tonight."

"Well, I'm glad I called, then."

"So am I."

"I should probably let you go," he said through a yawn.

"Get some sleep," she ordered.

They said goodbye, and Holly ended the call wishing she *had* told him. Why should she carry this burden alone?

Chapter Eighteen

If there is anything disagreeable going on,
men are always sure to get out of it.
~Jane Austen

"THIS STEADY ENGLISH RAIN COULD drive some people to madness," Holly remembered her mother saying once, then adding, "But I rather enjoy it."

Holly enjoyed it, too, even if it did make this jog a particular challenge. Slugging through mud on an unpaved road wasn't pleasant, but it was necessary—her second jog of the day, in fact. She had felt the pull of it earlier at the gallery, then later, doing housework, waiting for the girls to arrive home from school. Waiting to tell them yesterday's news.

Before they arrived, as Holly folded a second load of laundry, she'd heard the rain begin to patter outside the garden window. She went to find her running shoes in spite of it. Craving solitude, she took the back country roads, with fewer opportunities to run into townspeople to feel obliged to stop and talk.

Slogging along the narrow road that ran alongside Mr. Elton's farm, Holly realized what she loved most about these kinds of days. Certainly not the mud or the raindrops in her eyes. But through them, she could see a beautiful, glossy sheen. The rain made everything look darker, more defined. Tree trunks, flowers, the limestone of the farmhouse. Everything crisp and vivid... and yet, still gloomy. Appropriate for today. Some heavy clouds, a hint of thunder, melancholy rain falling from a melancholy sky. Pathetic fallacy.

Last night, Holly had dreamed about her mother—seen her so clearly that when she awoke, she fully expected her mother to walk into the room. The pain upon realizing it was only a dream knocked the wind out of her. The dream had haunted Holly most of the morning, drifting in corners as she ate breakfast with the girls, haunting her thoughts as she answered an email from Lily asking more details about Frank. Even watching Rascal clumsily shake out his wet fur after a romp in the garden, nearly toppling himself over, couldn't produce a smile.

She knew where this was coming from. It was her father, moving on. She thought she'd resolved many of her strongest feelings last night, after Fletcher had cheered her up. But it was short-lived. This wasn't something she could tuck away somewhere, lock up with a key. This was something messy and emotional.

Her commission today, to tell the girls about their father and Mildred, seemed simple enough. As she jogged, she rehearsed her speech in her mind. Pondered over the words that would soften the blow. But this blow couldn't be softened. It would hit the girls as forcefully as it had hit her, surely even harder.

Now the rain slowed to a drizzle, and when she reversed her direction, to head back down the hill to Foxglove, something drew Holly's attention. Stopped her in her tracks, breathless. The makings of a beautiful rainbow. Subtle, at first, but then she watched it grow and brighten in color. It reached from beyond the hill and arched right above the entire village. A stretch of brilliant Technicolor against a muted sky.

Tears streaked both of Holly's cheeks. It seemed like a sign. First the dream and now the rainbow. Her mother adored rainbows and used to make a game of it, hunting for them at the tail end of a storm, pointing to the sky for little Holly to see.

"There!" she would say, an excited catch in her breath, pointing upward. "Can you find the rainbow, Hollybear? It's God's way of talking to us, reminding us that beauty comes after a storm. There's always beauty. Sometimes it's not easy to find, so we have to search for it."

Not knowing whether the sobs or the jogging had made her so winded, Holly walked down the hill to cool off, settle down before entering the house. The jog had been a good soul-cleanser, a courage-builder, and she was more prepared to face the girls now than she had been this morning.

She couldn't take her eyes off the rainbow, and it didn't start to fade until she reached the edge of the property.

The moment she twisted the doorknob, still drenched, Holly nearly ran head-first into Bridget—hair curled in ringlets, eye makeup dark and heavy.

"I'm going to the Manor," she announced.

"Not yet," Holly said. "There's something I need to talk to you girls about. It can't wait."

Bridget rolled her eyes. "But I'm meeting someone. I'll be late."

"Colin."

"Yes, Colin. Is there a problem with that?"

"Well, there's a problem with your tone right now. I didn't say you couldn't go, only that you couldn't go *yet*. I have to dry off, change clothes. Please round up your sisters and tell them to meet me in the sitting room in ten minutes. This can't wait."

Bridget swiveled back toward the stairs, her ringlets bouncing as she left.

Holly stretched her neck to see through the front window, to find the rainbow again, but it was already gone.

Minutes later, the girls had lined up on the sitting room couch, looking as though they'd rather be anywhere else. Holly took the chair opposite them, her hair still damp and cold and clinging to her neck. She knew she had a limited window of time, so she took a breath, folded her fingers together, and began.

"So, I have some... news," she started. "It's about Dad."

"Is he okay?" Abbey blurted out.

"Yes, yes. He's fine," Holly reassured. "He's healthy and happy. Very happy," she mumbled.

"Can we get to the *point* of this family meeting?" Bridget glared. "I have someplace to be."

"Give me a minute, and I'll explain. This isn't easy."

Holly tucked a strand of hair behind her ear tried again. "So, Dad has apparently been... seeing someone."

After a long beat of silence, Bridget piped up, "Dating? Dad is *dating*? That's disgusting."

"It's not disgusting," Holly corrected. "And let me finish explaining before you jump to conclusions."

"Fine." Bridget crossed her arms and waited.

"So. Dad has been spending time with a… friend. A lady friend. It's happened over the past few months. And it's turned into something… more significant."

"He *is* dating!" Rosalee said.

"Okay, fine." Holly gave up. "He's dating."

The twins nodded together, reading each other's thoughts, while Abbey stared at Holly, confused.

"Who is she?" Bridget asked.

"It's… well. Mildred, actually," Holly said, the atmosphere shifting at the sound of her name.

"The *maid*?!" the twins said together then began talking over each other, questions overlapping. Abbey stared into her lap, unreadable.

"Girls, please," Holly attempted, having to raise her voice to match theirs. "Listen. I'm as gobsmacked as you are. I only found out last night, and he asked me to tell you."

"He's a coward," Bridget spat out.

"Well, yes," Holly agreed. "But it's only because he cares so much about what we think. He doesn't want to hurt us."

"Then he wouldn't be dating at all. Or at least wouldn't have kept it hidden." Bridget stared down at her minidress, her anger deflating into something that resembled disappointment.

Holly couldn't argue with that. "This is confusing, I know. But Dad told me about their relationship, and bottom line, he seems happy. Really happy. And as jarring as all this is, we need to try and find a way to be happy for them."

Bridget looked up, unblinking. "He's going to marry her. Isn't he? That's why you've gathered us here on the couch. It's why Dad didn't have the guts to tell us, himself. They're getting married. Aren't they?"

Holly was unprepared. "Err… well, I…"

"I *knew* it." Bridget stood and waved a hand at Holly. "What a load of bollocks. I can't take this right now. I'm outta here."

Before Holly could stop her, Bridget was out the front door, presumably to seek solace in the arms of Colin.

Holly looked at her other two sisters and wished they would say something. Anything. They wore the same stunned look that she'd had last evening. She attempted to speak, but her throat tightened. Nothing would make things better. And she couldn't lie to them. She couldn't say it would be easy, or that she was willing to welcome Mildred as a new stepmother immediately. But she also couldn't tell them the truth—that it petrified her, not knowing what her *own* future looked like with this new development. A development she had absolutely no control over.

"Is he really," Abbey said softly, making eye contact for the first time, "going to marry Mildred?"

"I think so," Holly acknowledged.

Rosalee stood and left the room. Abbey waited a moment then got up slowly, venturing over to the doggy bed where Rascal slept in the corner. She sat on the floor and scooped him up in her arms, stroking his fur as he let out a squeaky yawn. Holly saw her sister's lip pooch out. What should she do now? Leave Abbey alone? Offer a reassuring hug?

What would her mother have done?

Going on instinct, Holly tiptoed over to join Abbey on the floor. She touched Rascal's ear, and he tried to play-bite her finger. Abbey giggled through tears.

"Hey," Holly whispered, moving to touch Abbey's hair. "It's going to be okay. It really is. This doesn't change how much Daddy loves you. He wants you to be happy. And we want him to be happy too, don't we?"

Abbey nodded then buried her nose in Rascal's fur, dampening it with more tears. Holly remained, stroking her sister's hair, frustrated that words and gestures weren't enough. And equally frustrated that her father wasn't here to see this, the consequences of his secret.

At midnight, hearing her father shut the front door, Holly clicked her laptop shut. She'd expected him to be late, probably hoping the girls would all be in bed when he arrived so he wouldn't have to face them. But not *this* late.

She could hear him in the study, creaking steps on the wood floor.

The longer she'd waited for him, the more she'd stewed. The burden he'd placed on her, telling the girls alone, had been unreasonable. And she wanted him to know it.

She headed down the shadowy hallway, the grandfather clock gonging the hour behind her, sonorous and mellow.

As she entered the study, he looked up, startled.

"Hi, love. I didn't realize you were still up."

"Couldn't sleep." She sat across from him.

"How was your day?"

"Not good. I told the girls."

"Did you?" He shut down his mobile. "How did it go?"

"Not well."

He sat back and exhaled. "I'm sorry, honey. I shouldn't have put you in that position."

"No, you really shouldn't have. It was a struggle."

"How did they take it? What did they say?"

"Well, let's see. Bridget walked out the front door in a huff, Rosalee ran upstairs in a huff, and Abbey sat in the corner and cried."

"Oh." He gazed down at the desk, his eyes hollow, contemplative.

Holly's anger dissolved a little. "Look, Dad, you have to remember we knew nothing of your... relationship with Mildred, until now. It's all so new. Most of the anger we feel is due to the shock. We've had no time to adjust. And we can't help but feel a little betrayed."

"I'm sorry."

"I mean, how would you like it if I came home one day and announced to you I was getting married, and you never even knew I was seeing anyone?" She paused and shook her head. "No, that scenario won't work. This situation is different, because there's a mother figure involved. Mildred will become a stepmother to all of us. Honestly, I don't know what that means for me. Where I'll fit in now..." She drifted off, hating the direction this was going, not wanting to speak her fears aloud. Not yet.

"You'll always be welcome here. You know that. As long as you like."

"Yes, but in what capacity? I've practically run this household for years, and now what? This changes everything. For everyone. Don't you understand that?"

"I do now." He raised himself up and turned, talking to the wall. "Okay. Then it's off."

"What's off?"

He swiveled to look at Holly. "The engagement. Nothing's been promised yet. I haven't asked Mildred to marry me. It won't even have to be undone. She'll never know."

"Dad, that's not what I meant. You don't have to go to extremes." She leaned forward as he took his seat again. "I just want you to understand how *we* feel in all this. You have to be sensitive. Look at things from our perspective."

"How do I fix it?"

The helplessness in his eyes surprised Holly. He genuinely didn't know what to do. His dumping of all this into her lap, making her tell the girls—it wasn't a macho, insensitive gesture. It was pure ignorance. He truly had no idea how to talk to his girls, to relate to them or comfort them. Sure, he knew exactly how to provide for them—put a roof over their heads, food on the table. But when it came to complicated emotions and difficult discussions, he was ill-equipped.

"Honestly, Dad, we're not a problem to be fixed. It's not as simple as that. You can't act like we're your employees, or some business colleagues. We're your daughters."

"I know that. Of course I do. So, what do you propose? What should I do?"

"Talk to them. Tell the girls what you told me last night. Let them hear it from you. You owe them that."

He puffed out a sigh. "I do, don't I?"

"Yes. Because if you leave this all to me, as you did today, you're going to shut your daughters out. And they'll come to resent you for it."

"I never considered that." He paused, got a faraway look, then slapped his open hand against the desk. "I'll talk to them tomorrow."

"That's the spirit."

"Will you be there, too?"

"Of course I will."

"I don't know if I can change their minds. About Mildred, the engagement."

"It's not about changing their minds. It's about letting them in. Showing them you care what they think."

He nodded, satisfied with his decision.

Holly uncrossed her legs and got up from the chair.

"Thanks, love." His eyes shifted to his phone. "You always know what to do."

Wrestling with the sheets, kicking them off, Holly stared at the red glow of the digital clock. She'd been attempting to force sleep for the past hour. And it wasn't working.

Giving up, she stood and flicked on the lamp then found some jeans lying over the back of a nearby chair and slipped them on. Next, she threw on a bulky green sweater, one her father had bought for her on a business trip to Ireland last year.

She found her phone and typed in a text, the buttons clicking loudly in the dead silence of the room: *Awake? Need company?*

She walked to the window. Tipping back the curtain, she saw a cloudless night, with a ripe moon shining right over the Manor, far across the fields. Beautiful. Maybe there really could be beauty after a storm.

The phone vibrated in her hand. Fletcher had texted back: *At pub. Waiting 4 U.*

She snuck out of her room like a naughty teenager running away from home.

Five minutes later, she entered the pub and waved at Joe, who stood behind the bar cleaning a glass. He waved back and pointed toward the fireplace.

Fletcher stood when he saw her, rubbing his hands on his jeans. "Hey." His voice was raspy, sleep-coated, the circles under his eyes defined.

"I woke you up," she said with a pout then sat. "Sorry."

"No problem." He sat, too. "I fell asleep at the desk doing rewrites. I needed a wake-up call." He yawned and stretched his legs out from under the table. A crease in his cheek told her he'd fallen asleep on *top* of his rewrites.

"Holly, what can I get you?" Joe appeared at her side, rubbing his fingertips on the towel slung over his shoulder.

"I think I'll have a coffee. Decaf, please."

"Same for me," Fletcher said.

"Coming right up."

"So, what's with the text?" Fletcher asked Holly through another yawn.

"Will you stop doing that?" Holly said, covering her mouth as she suppressed her own.

"Sorry." He gave a half-grin, revealing one dimple.

Joe returned with the piping mugs and disappeared again.

"It's that 'thing,' isn't it?" Fletcher took a sip and waited, watching her face. "That you couldn't talk about last night?"

"Yes, the thing," she whispered. "Nightmare, more like."

"Tell me."

The late hour and the fire's warmth relaxed her, weakened her defenses. She hadn't come here for this, but she decided to cave. "Okay, here it is. Basically, my dad is getting hitched."

"What? To who?"

"See?" She pointed at him. "That's the face I made when he told me."

"And you had no idea?"

"None."

"I need details."

"It's Mildred."

"*Mildred*-Mildred?"

"That's the one." She was almost having fun with this.

"Wow."

"Yeah. Apparently, my dad has fancied her for the last few months. They got closer when her brother died. He's bought a ring and everything. He hasn't asked her yet, but I'm sure it'll be soon. And that the answer will be 'yes.'"

"I see."

"What do you see?" she asked.

"Well, it makes an odd sort of sense. I mean, similar experiences— her brother, your mom—seem to bring two people together. And, he's probably been lonely for a while."

Holly drank her coffee and thought about it from Fletcher's point of view. "If I step outside the situation, look at everything without me in it, sure, it makes sense. But it affects *me*," she said, the quiver returning to her voice. "And my sisters."

"I know it does." He reached across the table and covered her hand with his.

"I feel six years old, Fletcher. Why is this so hard, so weird?" She let the tears brim over. "Why can't I be mature, levelheaded about this?"

"Because it's not about Mildred. Or even your dad."

She looked into his brown eyes, knowing the words before he even said them.

"It's about your mom."

He said it in a way that cut through everything, the layers and confusion. And he was spot on.

He kept his hand there, rubbing his thumb along hers while she strained to fight more tears. But it wasn't working—his kindness only made the tears splash into her lap. She wiped her hot cheeks with the napkin Joe had left behind.

Fletcher continued, "When she passed away, she left a hole. One that you became used to, probably. You were forced to become used to it. And now, with Mildred, it seems like that hole is about to be filled up. And you're not ready."

"But that's the thing. I should be ready. It's been six years, for heaven's sake. Dad needs companionship. I can't fault him for that."

"Don't be so hard on yourself. You're human, remember?"

"It's not easy to forget. I feel very, very human these days..."

"How are the girls handling it?" He let go of her hand and leaned back.

"Not well. Poor Abbey's hit the hardest. She's so young. She doesn't understand."

"You're one of the warmest, closest-knit families I've ever seen. Nothing is going to fracture that. And I'd even bet that Mildred will end up becoming a special addition to it."

"You think?"

"I do. Your dad couldn't have picked a kinder woman. I barely know her, but her reputation around here is stellar. I think he has good taste in women."

"He does, doesn't he?" Holly said, thinking about her mum. She took another sip of hot coffee and let it warm her whole body. "Thank you. For saying exactly what I needed to hear."

Instead of getting up to leave, she wanted to stay a bit longer. And since Fletcher seemed in no hurry to go back to his room, she changed the subject, wanting to make this conversation less about her. Fletcher was probably tired of hearing all her family drama.

Half an hour later, he walked her outside after insisting on paying the tab, and reached out for a hug. Not a fast, noncommittal goodbye hug but one that swallowed her up, made her disappear into him. The proper sort of hug she craved. Solid, reassuring. She leaned her cheek against his chest and wished she could stay right here for another hour or so.

"Mmm. I'm sleepy."

"Good," he said, resting his chin on the top of her head. "That's what you need. Rest."

After a couple of minutes, he backed away.

"Are you going to sleep? Or work on the script?" she asked, looking up at him in the stunning moonlight. It had gotten so bright that it spilled all around them, creating patches of shadow.

"I'm actually kinda wired. I'll probably work. Want me to walk you back?" he offered.

"Naw, I'll be fine. Thanks again for listening to me ramble," she said. "I'm glad you answered my text."

"I'm glad you sent it."

She hoped he could see her smile widen in the moonlight before she began her reluctant walk up the hill toward Foxglove.

Chapter Nineteen

What is right to be done cannot be done too soon.
-Jane Austen

"THE CHURCH. OR MAYBE THE roses?" Frank looked sideways at Holly for her opinion.

They stood in the art gallery's storage room, deciding which painting should replace the landscape sold to a tourist earlier this morning.

"The roses, I think. They're cheerful. Summer-y."

"Agreed." He picked up the frame at its edge and carried it off to the main room.

Holly was glad to be at work today—it gave her a break from everything at home. Her father had called a family meeting for tonight, finally, and Holly assumed the tension in the house would only worsen. Since she'd broken the news to the girls about Mildred nearly a week ago, things had been eerily quiet. Everyone moved about the house with solemn reserve, not even making an effort to argue or complain. Her father must've told Mildred the girls knew, because she'd left a voicemail on Holly's phone canceling this week's Tuesday workday at the house. Apparently Gertrude needed her.

Frank had reappeared in the doorway, and Holly found the nerve to ask him what she'd been dying to ask for the past couple of weeks. "Okay, I'm about to be terribly rude and pry. But I have to know. How are things going with you and Lily?"

Actually, Holly already knew. Lily had been emailing her, saying she and Frank were talking online more and more often, and had even taken up texting. Still, Holly wanted to hear it from his end of things.

"Well," Frank said, a winsome smile appearing. "We're… chatting. Quite a lot." He inched a bit closer, as though there were a great crowd of people behind him who were trying to press in and listen. "We get on very well. She's amazing. Did you know she plays the cello? Is part of the Cotswold symphony? She has a concert in two weeks."

"No, I didn't know. Impressive!"

"Yes. And, she's agreed to go on a butterfly hunt—that's what *she* calls them—next week with me. Says she's fascinated when I talk about insects."

Officially confirmed. A perfect match.

Feeling bolder, Holly said, "You really fancy her, don't you?"

"I admit it. I do." He looked suddenly years younger.

Holly found it fascinating, how love did that to people—transformed them into giddy teenagers again. Even her father, talking about his courtship with Mildred. It lit up his entire face, softened the edges— even seemed to take away some wrinkles, she could swear.

Pushing her father's situation from her mind, she focused again on Frank, who was busy chattering on about a conversation he and Lily had this morning, via email.

On the way home an hour later, Holly stopped at the market for two packages of bacon and two dozen eggs for a fry-up. Abbey had requested a "breakfast night" for dinner this evening, a Bubble and Squeak—something their mother had started years ago when she'd been too tired to go to the market. Only having breakfast foods and leftover meat, she'd decided to make it into a dinner. Holly thought it the perfect comfort food for the evening that lay ahead.

As Holly placed her items on the counter, Mrs. Pickering gathered them up and tapped the keys on the register. One could never check out at her market without either being peppered with personal questions or receiving the latest bit of village gossip. Whether one liked it or not.

Today, Mrs. Pickering offered the latter.

"Did you hear," she started, "about the fancy dress ball on Friday?"

"No, I didn't. A ball?"

"You know, the filming. *Emma.*"

"Oh, I see. Is there a special scene coming up?" Holly wondered why Fletcher, her inside scoop, hadn't mentioned anything.

"Yes." Mrs. Pickering paused, holding the bacon. "The entire village is getting involved. The word is that they need fifty extras to fill in the gaps at the ball—standing around in the background and such."

"Sounds fun."

"With costumes and hairdos, as well! It should be a cracking good time," she said, beaming. "Bring the community together."

Holly wanted to tell Mrs. Pickering how very dull filmmaking actually was, but changed her mind. Mrs. Pickering could discover it for herself.

"Grab that big plate, will you?"

Unable to abandon the Bubble and Squeak, hot on the cooker, Holly pointed to the plate.

Abbey obeyed, and they worked as a team—Abbey holding the plate steady while Holly slipped the egg/bacon/potato/onion pancake onto the plate in one fell swoop. Next, they added some color by placing grilled tomato halves all around the edges.

"Dinner is served," Holly announced, ready to carry the feast into the rarely used dining room, where the twins had earlier set the table.

"Can I get him?" Abbey pleaded, hearing Rascal's cries and scratches grow louder. During meals, they placed the puppy into the nearby laundry room where he moaned and whimpered and scratched frantically at the door. The outside doghouse was lovely but much too big. Rascal didn't think of it as home. So, the laundry room was the only place in the house he could be safely contained whenever they were busy or gone. That room had no carpets to chew or soil, no furniture to scar with his sharp nails.

"Why don't you go settle him down and give him a chew toy? He'll be fine in there for suppertime. You can play with him afterward."

Holly continued toward the dining room, calling the twins as she went. After setting the table earlier, they'd disappeared again.

Though her father had promised to have "the talk" this evening, he had been unwilling to sit through an awkward dinner first. No, he would time it just right, so that his talk would be given after the meal. In fact, he was on his way home from the office now.

The girls ate in silence, devouring the meal until nothing was left. No matter their moods, a fry-up would always be completely consumed.

Without any communication, the meal was over in a record ten minutes, and the girls marched their plates to the sink to rinse them. Holly ached for this "talk" to be over and done. As with the Frank situation, she wanted things at home back to normal. But what did "normal" even mean anymore?

Holly kept busy with schoolwork until her father arrived, Rascal's gruff puppy bark indicating he was home.

It took him twenty minutes to gather the girls into the sitting room. After he'd sorted through the post, skimmed the front page of the paper, poured himself some coffee, and, finally, run out of time-wasters, he sat on a chair in the center of the sitting room, facing the girls, lined up on the couch. Holly thought they all resembled patients at a doctor's waiting room: uncomfortable, fidgeting, wishing they were anywhere else. Abbey stroked the sleeping puppy in her lap while the twins stared at the ceiling or the floor. Holly, sitting at the end, wished she could channel words to her father as a producer would feed lines to a nervous first-time newsreader. But he was on his own. And that was the whole point. This was his show.

Finally, he cleared his throat and leaned forward. His posture said it all—hunched over, he looked uncertain and ill-at-ease. Hardly the vicious multi-millionaire known for crushing businessmen with a few carefully chosen words.

"So…" he started, staring at his shoes. "I guess your sister informed you about the… situation." He cleared his throat again. "So. Anyway, I wanted to meet with you together, face-to-face, and… sort this thing out." He shot Holly a glance, presumably checking to make sure he was on the right track, then moved his attention back to the floor.

Holly watched him squirm and wished she could help. She could see the wheels turning, knew he was struggling.

"Right." He clapped his hands together decidedly, and Holly saw an inkling of the businessman kick in. "The thing is, girls, I've found someone."

"Mildred," Abbey whispered, her mouth forming into a pout.

"Yes. Mildred. I'm... well, here's the deal. I'm in love with her. It happened pretty quickly. I'm sure your sister explained everything."

"You're going to *marry* her," Bridget stated, looking him dead in the eye now.

"Yes. If she'll have me. And, if my girls can give me their blessing."

He looked from daughter to daughter with measured glances. Receiving only silence, he pushed his chair back so he could pace and talk with his hands.

"Here's the thing. Nobody can replace your mother. Not ever. She was my first love. It wasn't my choice to let her go—but she did go, and we've dealt with it the best we can. As a family. I haven't been the perfect father you needed. I'm a bad-tempered workaholic who would rather run away from emotions than face them. Well"—he stopped mid-step—"here I am. Not running away."

He saw that he had the girls' full attention, and his face relaxed. He sat back down, his eyes warmer, hopeful. The sincerity coated his voice even as it cracked, "I still miss your mother. It's hard not to, when I see bits of her every day in the four of you. Holly, you have these little parentheses around your smile, like she did. Rosalee, you have a particular lilt in your laugh that sounds exactly like hers, the older you get. Bridge, you get your spunk from your mother—she could go toe-to-toe with me any day. And usually won. And Abbey, your sweetness comes from her. The way you respond to other people, your love for animals. Don't you see? Your mother is right here. She's left pieces of herself in all of you. How could that ever be replaced?"

Holly sniffed back tears. Since her mother's death, he rarely talked about her, and certainly never so openly, with such ease. Holly glanced over to see her sisters tearing up, as well.

"Girls..." Duncan stood to walk around the coffee table that separated himself from his daughters and took a seat on it, his knees touching the twins'. "I've given you no time to absorb this... my relationship with Mildred. And I'm sorry. You had every right to know.

It was daft of me to throw it all on you, with no time to adjust. I wish I could do things differently."

"You can't," Bridget said tersely, thin-lipped.

"No, love, I can't. But I can ask you to give her a chance. Mildred is a fine woman. She's been good to this family. She wants to help us, not destroy us."

The pause hung in the air, decisions being made, battles fought.

"*I'll* try, Daddy," Abbey offered quietly.

"Thank you, sweetheart." He put his hand on top of hers and Rascal licked it.

"Me, too, I guess." Rosalee shrugged indifferently.

"Do whatever you want." Bridget bolted up, knocking against his knee as she stood. "You will, anyway."

Before he could form the words to call her back, she'd bounded out the front door. Her father looked at Holly helplessly.

"She'll come 'round," Holly reassured. "Give her time."

He nodded, the tension showing in his weary face.

Rascal play-growled and attacked Abbey's sleeve, gnawing it with his back teeth.

"And what do you think, little man?" Duncan asked, rubbing at the puppy's ears.

"He thinks you deserve to be happy," Abbey said.

For the first time since their mother's funeral, Holly saw the glisten of tears in her father's eyes. He grunted to hide his emotion and got up from the table, tousling Abbey's hair as he moved past her.

"I smell a proper fry-up," he announced brashly. "Anything left over for me?"

Chapter Twenty

But people themselves alter so much, that there is something new to be observed in them forever.
~Jane Austen

TWIDDLING THE PINK HIGHLIGHTER, HOLLY tried to figure out what was important enough to mark, but nothing in the chapter seemed relevant. Or mildly interesting. Shutting her textbook, knowing she'd have to face it again this evening, she capped the highlighter with a sigh.

She heard the front door and was grateful for the interruption. Frank rounded the corner, and she could tell instantly that his first official date—butterfly hunting—with Lily had gone well. Nauseatingly well. The goofiness of new infatuation was stamped all over him.

"So?" Holly pulled out a chair for him. "Tell me everything."

She hadn't exactly meant *everything*, such as the precise shade of Lily's scarf—lime green—or the details of her smile—"It goes adorably lopsided sometimes!"—or the timbre of her laugh—"sing-song-y." Still, it was sweet, seeing him so smitten.

"I never believed in love at first sight," he said, speaking faster than usual. "But, Holly, that's what this is. A feeling, deep in my abdomen"— he said, pointing *to* his abdomen—"that we fit together. That we belong together. I think this is it, Holly. I genuinely do."

"I'm happy for you, Frank."

"And to top it off, we found a magnificent swallowtail butterfly. We weren't even looking for it! I spotted it at the park where we walked after lunch. The most spectacular wingspan and vivid mustard color…"

If Lily could listen to him drone on about bugs this way and not lose her mind, she was either a saint or it truly was love.

Later, on the way home, Holly experienced the same pinch that she had felt on the night of her faux-date with Frank all those weeks ago. That same ache, as though something was missing. She wasn't exactly jealous of Frank. It wasn't so much a "Why him?" but rather a "Why not me?"

Thinking of her father and Mildred, of Frank and Lily, it made her wonder: was there some matchmaking game the universe played, where only certain people were destined to find a soul mate, while the rest of humankind floated about, searching but never finding?

Or, worse, did everyone actually have a soul mate, but some missed their one opportunity—fell through that one crucial crack of time where their soul mate stood, waiting? Perhaps it was all about timing. And once that timing was gone, it was forever gone.

Holly had always hoped that one day, someday, it would happen for her. That the timing of her life would unfold neatly, like chapters in a book. That once her commitment to her sisters came to some sort of clear end—once she was fully free, fully ready for it—then her "love" chapter would start and that "he" would be standing there, waiting. But as the years piled on top of themselves, it was harder and harder to see that "love" chapter ever happening. And even if it did, it seemed too far away to be a reality.

By the time she arrived home, all Holly wanted to do was have a glass of wine, sulk into it, then go to bed. But then she opened the wooden gate, walked down the stone path of Foxglove, opened the front door, and saw Rascal skid around the corner, scurrying on the slick floor with his sharp nails, desperate to greet her. He stumbled and flopped most of the way until he reached her shoes, yipping and panting. She leaned down to pick him up, unable to stop a smile. This was her little man, one who would never make her cry, who was always so happy to see her. Right now, he was all she needed.

"Is Rosalee going to be famous?" Abbey asked as they approached Chatsworth Manor's grand entrance. Twilight had settled by the time they'd arrived, and patches of warm, gold light beamed from the windows, beckoning them closer.

"I doubt it. Not for three lines of dialogue."

"When is it? I don't want to miss her scene!"

"Fletcher said seven. We can check with him first, to make sure…"

Holly could hear guitar music floating from inside the main entrance. *Greensleeves.*

"Do you want to go find the twins?" Holly asked. "I think I hear Fletcher. I'll check with him about the scene."

Abbey had already changed direction, heading back around the Manor. "Okay, bye!"

Inside, beyond the gothic arched door lay a spacious reception area with deep crimson carpeting and oak trim throughout. An elaborate wooden staircase was its centerpiece, with other rooms branching out, leading to a library, dining room, and parlor—where the music was coming from. Holly walked across the thick carpet, beneath the extravagant chandelier, to follow the sound. To find Fletcher, her own Pied Piper.

He sat on a bench in the corner, his guitar propped on his knee as he played. He'd switched to Mozart. Holly paused and watched him, hesitant to interrupt. When he finished, she clapped softly.

"Hey." He leaned his guitar against the bench.

She crossed the room to sit beside him. "That was beautiful."

"Thanks. Just messin' around, killing time." He crossed his ankle over his knee and leaned back.

"I think we're early. I brought Abbey—she's finding the twins now."

"Right. Rosalee's scene. Change of venue, by the way," Fletcher said. "I forgot to tell you. It's been moved to the village. They're getting the dress shop ready now."

"Mrs. Bennett's shop?"

"Yeah. The director thought it would look more authentic—and less expensive—than having to create a set for it. They had the set designers go in and jazz it up, make it fit the era."

"Mrs. Bennett must be thrilled! Can we still watch it being filmed?"

"I don't see why not. There probably won't be much room in there with all the equipment, but I'll see what I can do. We should head down in half an hour, probably."

"Time to kill, then…" She reached across for his guitar. "May I?"

"Of course."

She balanced it on her knees, placing awkward fingers on the strings. "Tell me more about this fancy-dress ball." She strummed lightly. "Eww. I'm terrible."

"Here." He leaned over to place his fingers on top of hers, guiding them to the right frets.

His breath tickled her neck as her fingers created an awkward claw.

"Okay, hold still." He released his fingers.

"Now?" she said.

"Now."

She pressed down the strings until they hurt her finger pads then strummed with her other hand. A beautiful chord rang out.

"Magic!" she said with a smile.

"See? Not so hard."

"Yeah. Not so hard when it's one chord, and you tell my fingers where to go." She handed the guitar back to Fletcher.

He strummed soft chords as he spoke. "The ball. Well, it's Friday night, and we're shooting three separate scenes. It might even take all night."

"I heard that the whole village will be extras."

"Just about. You should be one, too. Dress up in one of those gowns, do up your hair."

"No thanks." She smirked.

"Why not?"

"Too much sitting around, take after take."

"Yeah, but these are special scenes. The most expensive in the script. There's dancing. And a live quintet."

"Really? Well, that does sound interesting."

By now, the random chords had merged into a beautiful series of chords that transformed into a song.

"How are the girls doing?" he asked. "And your dad?"

Holly leaned against the paneled wall. "The same. Rosalee won't talk about the engagement, but I think she's coming 'round. Abbey seems pretty well. She's too transparent to hide much from me. I think I'd know if she was gutted by it. But Bridget, well, that's another story."

"She's here all the time," he said. "Always hanging around with Colin. I'm not sure how mutual it is."

"I'm worried about her. I don't want her heart getting broken."

"I don't think it's as deep as all that, but you might wanna keep an eye on her. She's really cranked it up the last few days."

"Cranked it up?"

"The flirting. She's making it kind of obvious, how she feels about him. And that probably feeds his ego even more. There are rumors he has a girlfriend back in Essex."

"Bugger. I was afraid of that. This could end badly."

"Maybe not. She's a smart girl."

"Sometimes. But, she can be a loose cannon."

"Takes after her sister," he said with a straight face, still strumming.

"Which one?" She raised an eyebrow.

"I'll let you decide that."

She slapped his arm, changing the chord to a dissonant mess.

Surreal enough, watching her sister in Regency attire, standing in the middle of Mrs. Bennett's dress shop, uttering lines Fletcher wrote. But even more surreal for Holly was watching her sister transform into something she'd never seen before. Rosalee had abandoned her usual shy, indifferent expression and replaced it with a focused determination. She knew exactly what she was doing. Certainly, the makeup and costume helped alter her appearance, create the character. But even aside from that, Rosalee's lines rolled off her tongue with a grace and ease Holly hadn't expected.

And she didn't overdo them with wide eyes or a forced lilt in her voice, the way so many brand-new actresses might have done. With every take, she was having a casual conversation. Natural, graceful, as though the camera didn't exist. As though she'd done it a million times before.

In fact, it was the other, seasoned actress who had trouble with her lines. The twenty-five-second scene had been filmed eight times over the past hour, and never once because of Rosalee.

After the ninth take, Holly saw the director mutter something to his assistant, who then pulled Fletcher aside.

"Give another line to the new girl," Holly heard him say. "And take away two from Bernadette."

Fletcher took his pencil and script to the back corner of the shop to make the changes, and Holly seized the chance to give a giddy "thumbs-up" to Rosalee. What she wanted to do was rush up and give her sister a quick squeeze, tell her how proud she was, then sit back down. But she didn't want to interrupt the creative process, or jinx anything for Rosalee.

She wished Bridget could've come, would've come, to the filming. She'd offered some limp excuse about a study group, but Holly, and, most likely, Rosalee, knew it had been a lie. Knew that, instead, Bridget could hardly see straight with jealousy over Rosalee's wee role in the film. Bridget would rather be absent than support her twin.

Holly watched Rosalee fiddle with her white glove and wondered if it bothered her, Bridget's absence. Or even their father's. Holly had texted him this afternoon, but he hadn't responded. Given his view of "actors," she was surprised he'd even allowed Rosalee this small role in the first place.

Fletcher finished his work and carried his revised script to the director, who skimmed it then handed it to Rosalee and Bernadette. They were given a moment to memorize the lines and run through them before filming.

After three more takes, the director yelled, "Cut! Print!" and Holly watched Rosalee remove her bonnet with a satisfied smile.

Late that evening, as Holly flipped channels while on the couch, unable to sleep, she heard a creak behind her. Twisting her neck, she saw Rosalee tiptoeing downstairs.

"Can't sleep?" Holly asked. "I'm sure you're still high on adrenaline. You really were amazing tonight."

"Thanks." Rosalee sat, folding her legs underneath her, smoothing out her cotton night shirt. "So... I have a favor to ask."

"Anything." Holly clicked off the telly and gave Rosalee her full attention.

"Well, I... made a decision. I want to speak to Dad, myself. About university. About theatre courses and acting. And I need you to be there. For support."

"Absolutely. Dad's still up. Wanna do it now?"

Rosalee swallowed hard and blinked. "Now?"

"Why not? Get it over with. I'll be right by your side."

"Well... I guess..."

Holly put a reassuring hand on Rosalee's arm. "You'll do fine. And if you need a backup, or if you get stuck, I'm right there. Okay?"

"Okay."

"You know he's just a big ole teddy bear at heart," Holly whispered as they stood together and approached the study door. She grasped the knob. "Ready?"

"Not really."

Holly knew it was best for Rosalee to do this now, without thinking too much, like ripping off a bandage. Perhaps her sister's acting skills would come into play, giving her the fake courage she needed to talk to their father.

The door creaked open, and the girls walked through to see their father puffing on his pipe, turning the page of a report. He peered at them over the top of his glasses as they entered the room.

"Girls. Come in." He shut his notebook. "I thought you were well asleep by now. After your big night. I'm sorry I couldn't be there, honey," he told Rosalee.

"That's all right."

The girls edged closer to the desk, and Holly nudged Rosalee forward with the tips of her fingers. "You can do this. Courage," she whispered.

Rosalee stood behind the chair and cleared her throat. "I wanted to speak with you... about something important."

"Certainly, love." He removed his glasses, set down his pipe, and leaned back with folded hands.

"Well, it's about tonight. Sort of. About acting, and how I feel about it. Acting."

Holly wished she could help. But this was Rosalee's idea. And she had to see it through.

"Anyway," she continued, "people said I did really well tonight. With my lines."

Holly nodded behind her, hoping the reinforcement might help.

"And, anyway, the director even offered me another audition. For another one of his films."

"He did? You didn't tell me that!" Holly stopped and remembered her own role here. Supporting actress.

She and Rosalee observed their father's reaction. Unreadable.

Rosalee stepped forward, her voice stronger—no stumbling, no hesitation. "I want it, Dad. I want to try. Mr. Abrams sees some promise in me, he said. And I want your permission to try. To go to the audition. I know you don't approve, that you want me to go to university and focus on something sensible. But to me, acting makes the most sense of all. I've found something I love to do, and I want to see where it takes me."

More silence as he rubbed his thumb on top of his other hand. Finally, he spoke. "I respect your candor. And that you didn't try to sneak around and do this behind my back. Therefore, I'll make you a deal." His tone was even, unemotional. "You can go to this audition as long as you make future plans for university. I don't want your education sacrificed for your dream."

"Will you let me study theatre? If that's what I choose?" Rosalee asked, pushing it.

He studied her face with narrowed eyes, chewing at the inside of his cheek as he mulled it over. "After careful reflection, if that's what you choose. Then, yes."

"Oh, Daddy!" Rosalee sprinted around the enormous oak desk to wrap her arms around his neck. "Thank you! You won't regret it!"

Holly watched, stunned. Never in a million years did she think her father would cave this quickly. Or maybe, at all. At the least, she'd hoped Rosalee's plea tonight would etch a few cracks in the wall. But she never imagined this. Perhaps his guilt over Mildred had softened him. Or maybe he couldn't resist the excitement in his daughter's eyes, knowing he held the power to make her happy.

Whatever the case, Holly looked on their embrace as a truce of sorts. And as a real start toward healing this family.

Chapter Twenty-One

To be fond of dancing was a certain step towards falling in love.
~Jane Austen

IN EVERY SINGLE JANE AUSTEN novel she'd read, in every film adaptation she'd watched, Holly could point to specific scenes as her absolute favorites. And they usually involved dancing. And drama. Whether with Marianne in *Sense and Sensibility*, heartbroken at catching Willoughby on the arm of another woman, or with Elizabeth Bennet in *Pride and Prejudice*, rudely refused a dance by the cold and misunderstood Mr. Darcy. But Holly hoped her own evening would be entirely free of heart-wrenching drama, filled only with music and elegance and candlelight.

Tonight, it wasn't the satiny pale-peach dress she wore, or the elbow-length gloves she slipped on, or the pampering by makeup artists to change her into a Regency goddess. It wasn't even the rush of knowing she might get a half second's time onscreen that made Holly glad she took Fletcher's advice to become an extra at the fancy ball.

No, it was entering the Manor's ballroom and seeing how real it was. Or, rather, how *sur*real—walking into a space that had been utterly transformed from the modern hotel conference room to what it originally had been, once upon a time. A glamorous ballroom with candlelit chandeliers and stiff-backed furniture. Of course, the presence of cameras and lighting equipment and crew people dressed in modern clothes tapping on their phones created a bizarre then-and-now sensation. But tonight, nothing could separate Holly from her fantasy. She was a luminous Jane Austen character in a luscious dance scene.

Walking through the grand doorway, she noticed other costumed villagers standing about, proper and sophisticated, enjoying the fantasy, too. In one huddle, chattering away, she saw Mrs. Pickering, Mrs. Cartwright, and Lizzie, all nearly unrecognizable in their fancy dresses and their fancy hair. It all felt like a third dimension, a Twilight Zone containing a pseudo-version of everyone Holly knew.

Far off to her left, Holly saw the twins and Abbey. She wished her mother could see them now, so grown-up. The hair and makeup aged Abbey by three years, at least. And the twins looked stunning in their beaded gowns.

Holly noticed a familiar lanky frame fidgeting beside Bridget—Riley, her study partner, readjusting his stiff collar. He stared at Bridget, opened his mouth to speak, then changed his mind. Bridget was otherwise occupied, craning her neck over the top of the crowd, most likely to try and find Colin. Poor Riley. He had no idea what a lost cause his was.

Inching forward, careful not to step on her own dress or anyone else's, Holly recognized another familiar frame in a faraway corner, seated and leaning on her cane. Gertrude—sans Leopold—garbed in a lovely beige gown with something sparkly in her hair. Still, somehow, she looked as ill-mannered as ever, with that blasted scowl on her face, ruining everything.

If she would only smile, Holly thought. *It would make all the difference.*

"I cannot *believe* you talked me into this," someone said behind her.

Holly turned around to see Fletcher, cutting a dashing figure in his overcoat and tails. His hair slicked back, starched collar grazing the curve of his clean-shaven jaw, he was the perfect Jane Austen leading man.

"Wow," she said, squelching the desire to whistle. She was a lady, after all. "You clean up nice, cowboy."

He bowed and took her gloved hand, lifting it to his lips in a courteous kiss. Then he looked straight into her eyes. "And you're stunning, I'd say."

Her pulse beat faster as their hands lingered for a moment before drawing apart. Even if they were only playing roles, pretending, the magic of the night was infectious.

"Thank you, kind sir." She attempted a curtsey, trying not to jiggle too much. The costume was lower cut than she'd anticipated.

"Quite the shindig." He looked at the growing crowd. "Is that... Gertrude?"

"It is. I did a double take when I saw her. Except for the scowl, she's actually quite beautiful tonight. But from the looks of it, I think she'd rather be having a root canal."

"Let's go say hello." He grabbed Holly's hand.

"Oh, no, let's not," she protested, hanging back.

"It'll be fun," he insisted and pulled her along until she gave in.

Seeing them coming, Gertrude's scowl eased into a frown.

"Ma'am." Fletcher gave a courteous bow. "You look lovely this evening."

"This maddening dress is too tight around the waist," she replied. "It's cutting off the circulation. I told that blasted woman it was too tight. Did she listen? No. She was too busy chewing her gum and yapping to her friend about someone called Daniel Beckham."

"I think it's David Beckham," Holly offered. "But Fletcher's right. You look lovely. Did Mildred bring you along?"

"Yes. She insisted on it. Wouldn't take 'no' for an answer."

Holly saw Mildred across the room, getting some drinks. She hadn't seen Mildred since her father had broken the news about their relationship, hadn't considered what to say to her, what she *should* say to her.

Gertrude broke into her thoughts. "Don't you two make quite the pair." She eyed Fletcher's hand still grasping Holly's.

Before Holly could think of a response, some man in the far corner shouted, "Places, please!" through his squawky megaphone.

Gertrude winced and covered her left ear. "Oh. Dreadful racket. I should be in bed."

Spot on, Holly thought, knowing Gertrude wouldn't last much longer. No more than two takes, she'd wager.

As they called out a quick goodbye to Gertrude, Fletcher put his hand gently on Holly's back, leading her to their spot. Earlier, the extras had each been given specific instructions to stand in certain places around the edges of the ballroom, to watch the actors dance in the center. The extras were urged to turn occasionally and speak with the person beside them, as they might do in natural conversation at a party.

Holly felt her nerves rise as she and Fletcher hit their marks. Though they didn't have any lines or close-ups, this whole process was so unpredictable and new. What if she was caught on-screen during the split-second of a shot, yawning, or fidgeting, or making an unflattering face?

After more shouting and squawking, the director settled everyone down and explained through his megaphone the logistics of the scene. There would be some general chatter from the extras as Emma and Churchill—Colin—delivered their dialogue, then the dance music would begin.

This scene was one of Holly's favorite parts in the book—when the dashing Mr. Knightley asks the plain Miss Smith to dance after she's been cruelly and publicly snubbed by Mr. Elton. Knightley proudly takes her to the floor and shows her off, rescues her. So gentlemanly. So noble. Were there any Knightleys still left in the world?

In the silence before the cameras rolled, Holly saw Colin cross to where Bridget stood—nudging Riley out of the way—whisper something into her ear then disappear to meet his mark. Bridget bit her lip, suppressing a smile.

"Quiet, everyone!"

Holly froze then realized a real partygoer wouldn't resemble a mannequin in a shop. She resolved to be as natural as she could under the circumstances. To enter her fantasy again. Having Fletcher by her side certainly helped. His hand squeezed her elbow, instantly comforting.

The first take was exhilarating. Holly couldn't clearly hear the dialogue from where she stood, but when the music started, she became swept away. The quintet played, and the dancers hopped their choreographed line dance while Holly imagined herself in that era—being asked to a ball, spending half the day dressing for it, then arriving on the arm of a handsome escort.

After the director yelled "Cut!" Holly expected some tedious down time between scenes—fidgeting with dresses and accessories, making small talk, waiting anxiously for the next take—but the director explained through his megaphone that he wanted to maintain the level of "joy" in the scene. And so, he piped in music between takes and asked the extras to enjoy themselves, do some dancing, if they wanted.

The ballroom quickly became a sea of jubilant couples, bobbing up and down to the light piano staccatos while the director pulled the main actors aside to give them notes. Holly wasn't sure if the music was authentically Regency, but it was close enough—airy and buoyant and exuberant.

Fletcher swept Holly up in his arms, pressed her close, and danced. There wasn't room for big, sweeping movements, so they remained in a tight radius close to their marks, swirling and twirling and laughing along with everyone else. When the director cut off the music to start another take, Holly was out of breath and smiling ear-to-ear. Precisely what the director wanted—to place everyone in the proper mood, so that when the cameras rolled, their smiles would be authentic. The fantasy would remain.

An hour into the shoot, take after take, dance after dance, the director finally called for a lengthy break so the extras could get rehydrated.

"May I fetch you some refreshment, m'lady?" Fletcher offered.

"Thank you, good sir." She could get used to all this pampering and attentiveness.

When he left to retrieve the bottled water, Holly glanced at Gertrude's chair to find that she had abandoned it, probably long ago.

"Don't you look beautiful?" a voice said behind her.

Holly spun to see Noelle with Adam, clasping his arms around his wife's waist. Holly noticed a very specific glow around Noelle that had nothing to do with the dancing.

"Thank you! So do you!"

Fletcher arrived at Holly's side and offered a bottled water, opening the top before handing it to her.

"Fletcher, do you know Noelle and Adam?"

He extended his hand to Adam. "We've met. At the pub. But I haven't met Noelle yet." He shifted his attention to her. "I don't know much about art, but your aunt's paintings are incredible. Holly's shown me."

"You're American!" Noelle beamed. "Whereabouts?"

Holly and Adam shared a shrug as their partners chattered on about their shared American experiences. Holly sipped her water and listened to Fletcher talk about Texas, watched him gesture and nod and ask Noelle questions about San Diego. Holly admired how naturally conversations came to Fletcher—with strangers, with everyone. And as Adam involved Holly in conversation too, asking about the gallery, she felt the unique inclusion of standing in a circle of four, part of a "couple" again. Even if it was only a fantasy couple on a fantasy night.

The director nudged everyone back to their marks to film a new dance scene, which meant another two hours of dancing in between takes. Holly had very little dance experience in her life, but Fletcher was an excellent lead. He'd obviously done this before.

"Two-stepping," he confessed during their sixth dance. "And a little country waltzing. It's all the rage in Texas."

By the time the director offered another extended break, Holly was light-headed. She hadn't eaten much for lunch, and the costume was restrictive in certain places.

"What's the matter?" Fletcher crinkled his eyebrows and offered her another water bottle. "You look uncomfortable."

"I think I'm just tired."

"I have an idea." He offered his arm, and she laced her free hand through it. "Let's go get some air."

She followed him discreetly out the ballroom doors.

Fletcher led her outside to a columned marble porch that overlooked the entire garden. Holly felt immediately better, breathing in the cool night air, leaning against the stone railing to view the garden.

In all the dozens of times she'd seen this view, she'd never experienced it at night—the faraway fountain accented with soft light, the manicured hedges creating angular shadows on the manicured lawn. She could stay here for hours. She watched a firefly light up in the distance then disappear into nothingness.

Slipping off her shoes to relieve her throbbing feet, she felt the cold, refreshing stone beneath.

"You really do look beautiful, you know," Fletcher said, leaning his back against the railing beside her. "Or should I say, 'fetching'?"

"You're making me blush." She peeled off her elbow-length silk gloves and placed them into a crumpled pile on the ledge.

The faint chords of the quintet warming up inside drifted through.

"Should we...?" Holly pointed at the door.

"I'd rather stay here, outside. With you."

Nothing sounded better.

"We could still dance, if you want." He offered a hand. "We have a whole dance floor to ourselves now."

She started to accept but paused. "I'm barefoot."

"I'll be careful," he promised. "Better yet, step up on my shoes."

"Really?"

"Yeah. You weigh about as much as a feather. It'll be fine."

She took his right hand while he slid his other hand around her waist, guiding her on top of his fancy leather shoes. His grip was firmer, stronger, than their earlier dances. This particular technique forced their bodies together.

Jane Austen's characters never danced like this, she thought. She held on for dear life as they took their first steps, then let out a small, throaty shriek.

"I've got you," he whispered.

After a moment, she believed him and relaxed into his arms.

She had only ever seen people dance this way in films, usually when one partner was giving the other a dance lesson. The actors always made it look so easy. But it took a great deal of balance. And trust.

She leaned into him, set her cheek against his shoulder, and they danced. Enchanting music floating up from inside the Manor, crickets outside chirping along, the scent of honeysuckle nearby—it was everything a Jane Austen fantasy should be.

Holly lifted out a still-warm towel, freshly tumbled from the dryer, the heat emanating on her face as she folded laundry at the kitchen table.

Pandora played a classic U2 song, and she hummed along. "With or without you..."

She thought about Mildred, about how much she knew, regarding the family drama over the past several days. Surely, Holly's father had told Mildred something. Or, maybe he'd kept her in the dark, too. He seemed to be pretty good at that.

Rascal's piercing yap startled her. She saw a dark figure at the window and recognized the shape. Mac.

Before he could tap at the French doors, Holly reached to open them. "Morning, lass."

"Come in for a coffee," she insisted. "It's time for that rain check."

Rascal growled ferociously but stopped when Mac reached down. After sniffing Mac's hand, the puppy gave a hesitant lick, decided this stranger was harmless, then wagged his black-tipped tail at its usual frantic pace, circling Mac's feet for more attention.

Holly clicked off the music and poured Mac a cup. "Here, sit." She handed him the mug.

"Thank ye. Can't stay long," he warned, sitting and removing his cap. "Came to see if we'll be planting anything new for mid-summer. There's still time. I can get that order in today."

"Honestly, I haven't given it much thought. Can I decide tomorrow?" She joined him at the table.

"Aye."

"I can't believe it's nearly July. The girls are already talking about their summer break coming up. Things are about to get crazy."

Mac smirked and took a sip.

She thickened her accent with fake snobbery. "And then last night, we had that fancy dress ball."

"Did ya, now?"

"It was fun, I admit. I wasn't keen on the idea at first, but seeing all the costumes and that grand ballroom." She lowered her voice to a whisper. "I got a little swept away."

She visualized her ethereal dance with Fletcher and then Abbey interrupting them before Holly was ready to go home. Holly didn't know Abbey had been standing at the window, watching them for half a dance, but the applause at the end gave her away. Distracted, Holly slipped off Fletcher's feet, and he caught her right before she would've tumbled to the hard floor.

"I didn't see *you* there," Holly teased Mac now. "At the fancy ball."

"Nay."

Holly pictured Mac in a jacket and tails, clean-shaven and attempting to look happy about it. He could've been Gertrude's companion.

"I hear you've got a star in the family," Mac said.

"Yes! Rosalee. I watched her film a scene a few days ago. Amazing, how natural she was. She's even trying out for another role in August—the director wants her to read for his next film."

"Aye, Mrs. Pickering told me this morning."

"How on earth did *she* know? We just found out two days ago."

"She has her ways."

"True. Sometimes I think she's got spies around the village."

"Aye." Mac bent down to pat Rascal on the head, appease the whimpering. "Is your father about?"

"He was, but he had to go to London for the afternoon. Business. Can I give him a message?"

"I needed to ask him about the trellis, if he prefers metal or wooden."

"Trellis?"

"'Twas what he'd asked about yesterday," Mac shrugged.

Something for the garden, Holly thought. "Okay, I'll tell him."

Taking his last sip, he grabbed his cap and scooted the chair back to stand. "I best be going. Thank ye for the coffee, lass."

"You're welcome. I enjoyed the chat."

Holly held Rascal back as he tried to chase Mac through the door. When he'd gone, she clicked on the music again, returning to her busy Saturday.

Chapter Twenty-Two

*A man would always wish to give a woman a better home than
the one he takes her from; and he who can do it, where there is
no doubt of her regard, must, I think, be the happiest of mortals.*
-Jane Austen

SHE COULDN'T MAKE A HABIT of this. Of being angry with her
father, constantly surprised at his insensitivity. But, after nearly
three decades of knowing him, Holly still expected more. *People
don't change*, her mother had often told her. So, why couldn't she believe
it was true?

Sitting across the table, fashioning a swan out of her paper napkin,
Holly waited for him to explain. The girls had gone to bed an hour ago,
and Holly had been about to do the same, when her father had
arrived home from a late poker night at the bakery, started by Mr.
Bentley years ago. Her father's attendance was spotty, but he always had
an open invitation.

The look on his face when he entered the kitchen told Holly he was
about to confess to something she might not want to hear.

"I've asked Mildred," he said. No obligatory small talk beforehand.
No segues or transitions. He took a seat. "I gave her the ring on Friday,
and she accepted."

Friday. Day before yesterday. And he was only just now bothering to
let her know. Holly wondered if, once again, he would try to nominate
her as his proxy, to tell the girls the news. If he did, this time she would
say no.

Sure, she'd known an engagement was coming. Eventually. But since her father had only sat the girls down to tell them about Mildred a few days ago, Holly thought he would have waited. Should have waited. Or at least warned them ahead of time. But, in her father's mind, once he'd discussed the courtship in his brief family meeting—during which one of his daughters had stormed out—apparently that was it. He'd met his obligation to come clean, and now he could move on with his life.

Holly fanned out the tail of her swan. "Is there a date set for this wedding?"

"The fifteenth of August."

Holly's hands fell with a thud on the table, crumpling the swan. She stared hard at him. "That's less than two months away."

"Yes."

"Six weeks."

"Yes."

"Were you going to tell us?" She pressed the former swan firmly between both palms, creating a crumpled ball.

"Of course. Things got busy with work. I hadn't had the opportunity—"

"The trellis." Holly's lightbulb came on.

"What?"

"Yesterday, Mac told me to ask you about a trellis. It's for the garden, isn't it? The wedding?"

"Mildred wants a garden wedding, yes."

Holly nodded as though she understood, but really, she didn't. Not any of this.

"The fifteenth was the only break in my calendar," he explained. "It's a busy year."

"Have you thought what the girls might think? That it might be a little too soon for them?"

He rubbed at the back of his neck. "Honey, I'm not getting any younger. I love Mildred. I want her to be my wife, and she agreed. I had the talk with the girls, just as you asked. I don't see any reason to wait."

The anger that had started to bubble now seethed. Holly dug her fingernails into her knees to channel it somewhere other than her words. "Dad. You should have warned us. Or at least told us on the day you proposed. Your tone is so… matter-of-fact. You might as well be telling me about a business meeting that we're no part of at all!"

"As I told you, work was busy. There wasn't time until now."

"You had time for poker," she retorted. "And I really can't help you this time. You can be the one to tell the girls. You're going to have some angry daughters on your hands. Bridget, especially. She's still not come to terms with the idea of Mildred, much less a wedding in six weeks' time."

"She'll be fine," he said.

"Will she? What if she's not?" Holly said, getting louder. "What if she's not ready for you to marry that quickly?"

"Are we still talking about Bridget?"

Holly abandoned the napkin, her voice softening under the weight of his question. "Does it matter?" Raising her eyes to him, she asked, "Do *we* matter?"

His head tilted in surprise. "How could you say that? Or even think it? You girls matter to me more than anyone in the world."

When he sighed, she knew his own frustration was rising. They were speaking two different languages tonight, without an interpreter. He crossed his arms over his chest. "I don't think I've ever told you," he said, his voice low and gravelly, "what snapped me out of my grief six years ago."

She studied his expression, abandoning her resentment for the moment, eager to hear the explanation of a mystery she'd waited for years to be solved.

"Maybe this will clear some things up for you, about Mildred. About you girls." He scratched at his chin and began. "As you remember back then, better than anyone, I was a hollow man when your mother died. I didn't eat, didn't leave the house or that damned study. I was sleep-deprived, a shell of myself. Well, one particular night, I'd been staring at the same wall for hours, unable to stop. My mind was stuck in quicksand, stagnant. And suddenly, there she was, in the room with me. Your mother."

Holly crinkled her eyebrows, trying to understand. "What do you mean? In the room with you?"

"I thought it was a ghost. She was so... luminous." His right hand outlined the figure in the air as he spoke. "She was dressed in this white, flowing gown. I'd never seen her look more beautiful. I stood and stayed like a stone, unable to move. She walked—no, glided—toward me. And then she spoke."

He gazed at the far wall, recreating the scene in his mind. "She said, 'Duncan, I'm at peace. But I can't be with you anymore. This is goodbye. You must take care of our girls. And take care of yourself. Do that for me.' And then, she vanished."

He blinked, closing the memory, and brought his attention back to Holly. "I know what you're thinking. I was delusional. Or insane, out of my head. Or that it was a dream. But it was real. It *was* your mother, right there in front of me."

"I believe you," Holly said. "I've read about these kinds of things. A sort of out-of-body experience."

"Yes, exactly. That's how it felt. There she was, telling me to get on with life. To wrench myself out of that grief, pull myself together. And so, I did."

Holly recalled that next morning, when she saw him, dressed and shaved and looking whole again.

He folded his hands on the table. "The reason I'm telling you this is—well, I *did* what your mother said. I turned my energies back to my daughters, back to my business. I did the best I could to take care of you. I wasn't the best father. But I did what I was able to do, under the circumstances. And now, you girls are older. And I feel that it's... well, my turn. That I have a chance at happiness again, with a woman, and I want to take it. We're not guaranteed tomorrow. Or the day after. If your mother's death has taught me anything, it's that."

Holly wanted to say something, but the lump in her throat wouldn't let her. What was the alternative to August? Was her father supposed to wait until he and Mildred received full, individual approval from all four daughters? That could take months, if not years. If it ever came at all. Her father had a right to a life with Mildred. The girls could cope. They would have to.

"A wasted day feels unconscionable to me now," he added. "Do you understand? Why the wedding needs to be August?" His eyes pleaded with her. He'd never craved her approval for anything before.

"I think so. I'm trying."

He unlaced his fingers and reached across the table to cup Holly's hands. "Then it's okay?"

"We'll do our best to make it okay." She gave him a soft smile then squeezed his hands to let him know she meant it.

Holly wiped the bar down, humming a catchy Pink song. Lizzie had called this morning to see if Holly would be able to fill in for a few hours in the afternoon. She probably should've turned Lizzie down, with all the schoolwork still left to do, but whenever Lizzie or Joe called, it was a last resort. It always meant they couldn't get anyone else. So, she'd said yes. She'd only worked at the pub a couple of times before, so it took her several minutes to get reacquainted with things behind the bar.

Fortunately, the afternoon had been slow, so aside from clearing a couple of tables or refilling drinks, she'd even had time for a few glances at her textbook.

When she swiveled around, she saw Fletcher, doing his best cowboy sidle-up-to-the-bar, which entailed tipping back an imaginary cowboy hat and walking bowlegged for a couple of steps.

"Hey there, bartender—lemme have a cold brewskie."

"You're barmy," Holly said with a grin.

He took a seat on the barstool and reached for the bowl of nuts. "But in a good way, right?"

"I'll get back to you on that." Holly tipped a mug to angle it at the tap. "There ya go. Partner."

"I have some news," Fletcher told her.

"Good news, I hope."

"The best. I finally worked up the courage to speak with the producer this morning. I called him up and told him the rumors, about the lack of funds. He reassured me that *Emma* is solvent."

"That's fantastic!"

"Yeah. He did admit that, at one point, there was talk of financial distress, but he found a couple more backers, so it all worked out."

"No more 'distress,' then?"

Fletcher popped a peanut in his mouth. "Well, not on that end, anyway."

"Things are still bad with Finn."

"He's avoiding all my calls. So, I guess we're over. Like a bad break-up. Except I walked away with nothing and he gets a million-dollar deal."

"Yeah, but he also sold his soul to the devil. Ghosting a tell-all? That's hardly literature."

Fletcher smirked into his lager. "True."

"I predict you'll end up writing the Great American Novel. Or… the Great British Novel?" She wiped the bar in circles.

"Naw, that's only a pipe dream. I've decided to be realistic. I'm thinking seriously about a new career."

"What?" She stopped, mid-circle.

"Teaching. I minored in history and thought maybe… I don't know. I'd have to take a few more history classes and pass some teacher certification test. Probably a dumb idea."

"I think it's a brilliant idea. You'd make an incredible teacher."

"How do you know that?"

"You're charismatic, sincere. You're passionate about the things you love. Students would adore you. They'd love hearing the Southern accent, too." Then, something dawned on her. "Oh. You meant teaching in the States, didn't you?"

"Fletcher Hays! *There* you are."

Holly noticed a Jane Austen beauty sauntering up to the bar—a voluptuous actress in a pale lime-colored dress, complete with a parasol and film star make-up. Holly recognized her from the ball as the actress playing Jane Fairfax.

"Hey, Cindy." He patted the stool beside him. "On break?"

"Mmm-hmm." She climbed up and laid her parasol across the bar, then batted her ridiculously thick—and surely fake—eyelashes at Fletcher from beneath her bonnet. Holly bet those dark-green eyes would look spectacular on the big screen.

"Can I get you something?" Holly asked, prying Cindy's gaze from Fletcher.

"Water, thanks," she said. "With lemon." She leaned in close to Fletcher. "Did I tell you what Mark said today? In the dressing room?" She whispered something into his ear.

Fletcher gave her a flash of his dimples in return. "Ha! Then I guess I was right. You owe me five pounds."

Cindy play-slapped his hand. "Five pence, more like."

Holly slid the glass of water toward Cindy and spotted a customer's hand waving in the corner, beckoning her. She acknowledged the wave then walked around the bar to where he was. She almost offered a "Be right back" to Fletcher, but he wouldn't have heard her anyway, his neck craning to hear more film-set gossip from the beautiful Cindy.

Lizzie returned much later than expected—nearly dusk—with profuse apologies. Holly had reassured her it was fine, but as she began her long walk home, she noticed the toll it had taken. She'd worked four hours *before* the pub this morning, at the gallery, with no breaks. The only meal she'd had all day was a hasty sandwich at the bar.

Her back and feet ached from all that standing, and she knew very well that she wouldn't be cooking tonight. A takeaway was in order.

Minutes later, bags in hand, she stepped out of the Indian restaurant three shops down from Joe's, and bumped smack into Mildred.

"Oh! I'm sorry." Holly took a step back when she realized who it was.

"My fault," said Mildred quietly. "I wasn't watching where I was going."

Holly shifted the bags. "So. How have you been?"

"Oh, fine. Very well, thanks." Mildred smiled, but her eyes held awkwardness.

Holly struggled to find words that wouldn't sound forced. She knew she could easily fill the next couple of minutes with meaningless chitchat about the weather, the book club, or Gertrude. She could be cordial and fake, which would all be quite socially acceptable. But Mildred deserved better.

It had been nearly three weeks since they'd spoken—Mildred, understandably, had been scarce, leaving the girls to sort out things with their father. She'd only left apologetic voicemails for Holly about not being able to work her usual one day a week, offering legitimate excuses each time. She'd even been a no-show at the last couple of book clubs.

Standing here in front of Mildred, hearing her father's recent words echo in her head, Holly made a decision. To test her own maturity. To put away her issues and do the right thing.

"I wanted to congratulate you," she said, relaxing her face into a genuine smile, touching Mildred's elbow. "On your engagement to my father."

Mildred's eyes came alive, filled with surprise. "Oh. Well. Thank you."

"My father told me that you'd set a date?"

"Err, yes. The fifteenth of August." She reached up to touch her hair, something Mildred always did when she didn't know what else to do. "Your father's idea, you know. I urged him to wait. To let the dust settle. Give the girls a chance to get used to things. But, you know your father."

"Yes, I do. Infuriatingly stubborn."

"Indeed." Mildred chuckled. "Do your sisters know yet? About the date?"

Holly shook her head.

"I'm sorry," Mildred said.

"For what?"

"Keeping everything a secret. I felt like such a deceiver, being in that house all that time, talking to you, and not letting you know. I hated keeping it from you, especially. But, I was afraid that... well, that I wouldn't be accepted. Plus, it was your father's place to tell you and the girls. And then these last couple of weeks, I just couldn't face you all. I've made excuses to stay away. Such a cowardly thing to do."

"Oh, Mildred." Holly felt her last defense crumble. "My father loves you. And the girls have known you for years. You will be accepted. It'll take a little time. That's all."

Mildred sniffed back tears.

"I have an idea," Holly said. "Come to dinner at the house. We'll do it properly. Is Monday all right?"

"Oh, I don't know..."

"I think this would be good. For the entire family."

"Only if you're sure. I don't want you to feel obligated."

"I'm a hundred percent positive."

Holly could read the "thank you" in her tearful expression.

Chapter Twenty-Three

*A young woman, if she fall into bad hands, may be teased,
and kept at a distance from those she wants to be with.*
~Jane Austen

"MRS. CLEMENTINE, I DON'T UNDERSTAND." Holly sat, legs crossed, in a stiff high-backed chair at the headmistress's desk. She felt as though she were the one in trouble, instead of Bridget.

Mrs. Clementine coaxed her glasses up the bridge of her nose. "Did you receive the note we sent home last week? About your sister's grades?"

"I don't believe so." Holly wondered if Bridget had hidden it on purpose.

"I was afraid of that," Mrs. Clementine muttered. "Simply put, your sister is in crisis. Her grades have plummeted in the course of a fortnight. As you know, her A-level exams are approaching in the next couple of weeks. It's vital that she scores well, to prepare her for university. But I'm afraid with her current performance, she'll be in danger of failing. Just this morning, she skipped three periods. This is unacceptable behavior. We take such matters very seriously."

Holly blinked and tried to take it in. She knew Bridget had a stubborn streak, that she could be noncompliant and belligerent at home. But her sister had never once shirked her school responsibilities. In fact, Bridget took great pride in being a bright, mostly B student.

"Miss Newbury?" the headmistress continued, her accent clipped and dry. "Did you hear what I said?"

"Yes," Holly responded. "Yes, I did."

"I realize this is a personal question, but is there trouble at home? Can you think of a reason she might be acting out this way?"

Immediately, Holly knew. Of course, she knew. Trouble. At home. Two days ago, her father had finally found the courage to tell the girls about the wedding date but without any preparation or warning. He walked in while the girls were all watching telly, stood in front of it and muted it, folded his hands together and said casually, "I have an announcement to make." Not exactly what Holly had in mind, when she'd asked him to be the one to tell the girls. When he'd told them the date, Bridget had thrown a couch cushion down and stomped away swearing.

"I'm sorry, Mrs. Clementine. I assure you, I'll take care of this. I think I know what's going on."

The embarrassment coursed through Holly's veins. During these times, her mother-figure role became unavoidable. And weighty. She gathered her bag and stood, wishing she could explain further but not wanting their family business to become the village's business. "Bridget's studies will improve. I'll see to it."

She left Mrs. Clementine's office knowing *exactly* where to find her sister.

She recognized Bridget's laugh from afar. That certain laugh her sister used to impress someone—airy, high-pitched, silly. Holly followed the sound to a trailer she suspected was Colin's and pounded her fist against the metal door. A flush rose to Holly's cheeks—partly because of the brisk walk up to the Manor but mostly because of the frustration that increased with each knock.

"Hey, what's up?" Fletcher appeared at Holly's side, probably having seen her stomp up to the trailer, oblivious to all else. He placed a hand on her back.

She tried to stifle the angry quiver in her voice. "I need Bridget. She's in here." Holly pointed at the door.

Since her knocks, the laughter had stopped abruptly. But the door remained belligerently closed. And locked.

"Here." Fletcher guided Holly back a couple of steps. He knocked three times, firmly, and said, "Bridget. This is Fletcher Hays. Please open the door."

Holly both loved and hated how a man's voice seemed to get people's attention so much better than a woman's. The lower octave, the deeper resonance, seemed to command attention. Of course, it made a difference that someone other than Bridget's sister was issuing the request.

Validating Holly's theory almost immediately, the door unlocked and flew open. There Bridget stood, combing down her tousled hair with her fingers.

"What do you want?" she asked, her eyes set on Holly.

"I need you to come home." Holly glared up at the sister she barely recognized anymore. She clenched her fist, trying to remain calm, sensing that this little scene of theirs was being observed by a gathering crowd. "We need to talk."

"I'm busy."

Holly spotted Colin in the shadows, lurking behind Bridget. Coward.

"I don't care. You're coming home. Right now."

"You can't make me!" Bridget suddenly shrieked, an actress in a melodramatic scene. "You're not my mother!"

That last line rendered Holly breathless. Realizing what she'd said, Bridget clamped her mouth shut and waited.

Holly stared at her sister with equal measures of pain and anger but somehow managed a quiet tone as she asked, "Do you really want to do this here? With all these people around? I know about your skipping school. And your grades. I've called Dad. He's on his way home to see you."

Bridget, trying hard to cover the fear in her eyes, rolled them dramatically and said, "Fine. Whatever. I'll be there in a few minutes," and closed the door again.

Holly unclenched her fist, realizing she'd made painful, crescent-shaped dents inside her palm.

"You okay?" Fletcher whispered.

"Not really." The flush dissipated but left her with a splitting headache. She wished she could sit somewhere and get her bearings.

"What can I do?" he asked, guiding her away from the trailer, away from prying eyes.

"Getting her to open that door was like magic. Thanks." She relaxed her expression, reassured him. "I'll be okay."

They stopped behind the trailer, and Fletcher pulled her close. "C'mere."

Her body was rigid. She didn't want to be touched or hugged right now, but feeling the strength of his arms, an embrace from a friend she could trust, she let herself be comforted.

"Call me later, if you want," he said then kissed the top of her head.

Holly closed her eyes and suppressed the urge to sob into Fletcher's shoulder.

When Holly arrived at Foxglove, hoping Bridget would follow after, she'd sent Abbey and Rosalee into the garden to give Rascal some exercise. This wouldn't be pretty.

A few minutes later, as Holly prepared tonight's roast as a distraction, her father arrived home.

"Is she here yet?"

When the answer was "no," he went into his study to wait for Bridget. Finally, nearly an hour after Holly had banged on Colin's trailer door, she heard Bridget come in, slam the front door, then walk to her father's study.

Earlier, during Holly's emotional walk from the headmistress's office up to the Manor, she had rung her dad from her mobile. She'd interrupted a business meeting to tell him everything—about the failing grades, the skipping school, and yes, the boy. And with every word, she recognized a hint of her own hypocrisy. She'd been livid with her father for keeping secrets that affected this family, when all along, she'd been doing something similar, keeping Colin a secret from her father, assuming she could handle it all on her own.

Obviously, she couldn't.

Holly had been so busy believing that Colin was nothing more than a harmless crush that she hadn't seen the reality. But today, at that trailer, observing his influence over Bridget in all its nasty glory, she knew it was good for their father to get involved. Vital, in fact. Perhaps if he'd known earlier, used a firm hand, some of this could've been avoided.

Through the walls, Holly could hear the low reverberations of her father's voice. Good. He wasn't yelling yet.

She turned her attention to the meal, chopping up carrots and potatoes, focusing on the tapping rhythm of the knife. Still, she couldn't help but strain to hear the rise and fall of voices, mostly her father's. She could imagine what he was saying—the words he chose, the strict tone, the demands he would make. She could also imagine Bridget, staring defiantly at the wall behind him, tapping her foot against the desk, crossing her arms in rebellion.

As Holly sprinkled handfuls of vegetables all around the roast inside the enormous pot, she heard a change in volume. Suddenly, Bridget screeched, and the study door flung open.

"I hate you! You can't make me stop seeing him! We *love* each other!" she yelled, her voice shrill and out of control.

She stamped up the stairs, causing the pans hanging from the kitchen rack to vibrate.

Holly wiped her hands on a dishtowel and peered around the hallway. Her father stood at the other end, head down, rubbing his shallow beard. He looked up and put out his hands in a helpless shrug.

Her sympathetic half-smile wouldn't change things, but at least they were in this together now. That counted for something.

Week Ten of the book club, and instead of gaining momentum, Holly was running out of steam. Surely it was because of recent events with her father and Bridget, and had nothing to do with *Emma* itself. But whatever the case, at today's meeting, Holly struggled to concentrate, even with Fletcher sitting beside her, even with Gertrude piping up and answering nearly every question with unexpected enthusiasm.

"Holly?"

She blinked, looking across as Frank said her name. "I'm sorry, what?"

"I asked if you agreed. About the foreshadowing of Mr. Churchill and his... secret." Frank had nearly broken the most essential book club rule, of not revealing spoilers for those who hadn't finished the novel. He'd fortunately caught himself in time.

"Yes, certainly," Holly said, before even knowing whether she did agree. She looked down and flipped through her book, trying to formulate a substantive answer. But she came up empty and looked up at Frank. "Yes. You're absolutely correct. Well-noted, Frank."

The clock on the table chimed noon, so Holly closed her book and dismissed the group with a cheery smile.

"How ya doing?" Fletcher whispered beside her. They hadn't had a chance to speak before the meeting.

"Peachy," she murmured like a ventriloquist, still holding the smile.

They rose together from Gertrude's couch and made their way into the kitchen to help Mildred collect rubbish and cups and plates and do the wash-up before they left.

At the sink, Fletcher handed Holly the sponge while he found a towel. "Catch me up. How's the Bridget situation?"

Holly had phoned him Saturday, a day after beating on Colin's trailer door, more to apologize for causing a scene than to burden him yet again. It was becoming a habit she grew uncomfortable with, unloading her problems onto Fletcher. She never wanted their relationship to be lopsided that way, but it so often was. Of course, Fletcher being Fletcher, he had drawn it out of her anyway, let her vent about everything on the phone. He didn't seem to mind.

"The same," she whispered, seeing Mildred enter from the corner of her eye. Today was particularly awkward, as Mildred didn't seem aware of Bridget's little meltdown or grade troubles. Mildred had a right to know, as a future member of the family, but it wasn't Holly's place to say anything. It was her father's.

"Another good meeting," Mildred proclaimed, joining them at the sink with a stack of cups. "There's talk of continuing the book club. After *Emma* is through."

"Really?" Holly reached for the first cup. "That's an interesting thought."

"I'd better run," said Fletcher, reading a text that had just beeped through on his phone. He squeezed Holly's hand. "Gotta go appease a cranky director. Bye, ladies. Text me later, Holly," he called before walking out.

"Such a nice young man." Mildred took over Fletcher's drying duties.

"Mmm," Holly agreed.

"I think he's good for you. I've seen you two together—here, around the village. He makes you light up."

"Does he?" Holly asked, half-listening.

"Yes. He does. You'll hate me for saying this, and I'm sure you've heard it before, but the two of you are a beautiful-looking couple."

This caught Holly's attention, and she dipped her head. "Not you too, Mildred. I thought we'd put those rumors to rest ages ago. Well, except for Gertrude, but that was on purpose."

"So, you're really only friends, then?" Mildred pushed. "I could've sworn I'd seen a spark or two."

Holly understood Mildred's purpose—knew that people who were giddy in new relationships, themselves, often wanted the same for everyone else. She didn't know if trying to explain things would convince Mildred. Luckily, she didn't have to.

"Someone crushed a biscuit into my carpet!" Gertrude barked as she entered the room, still holding Leopold.

"I'll take care of it," Mildred assured, leaving Holly to finish the dishes. And to realize that talking to Mildred, post-engagement, hadn't been nearly as awkward as Holly had feared. They were already back to their old selves again.

Chapter Twenty-Four

Angry people are not always wise.
~Jane Austen

FIVE MINUTES BEFORE MILDRED'S ARRIVAL, Holly stood at Bridget's bedroom door and tapped softly. Again. "The food's ready. Our guest will be here any minute."

No response.

This had been the pattern for the past three days, since Friday's blow-up with her father. He had confiscated all of Bridget's electronics as punishment for skipping school and as a way to ensure she could have no contact with "that actor." Over the weekend, she'd holed up in her room, refusing to eat or wear makeup or communicate with anyone—including Riley, who Holly had called up for a study session on Saturday night, hoping someone could reach her. But when Riley arrived and Bridget refused to see him, Holly had to apologize on her sister's behalf and watch the disappointment shadow across Riley's face.

Today, Bridget attended school then came straight home, back to her room to fulfill the most painful part of her punishment—to stop being an extra on set, to stop going to the set at all.

With everything going on, Holly had toyed with canceling Mildred's dinner this evening. But she and her father agreed that it would send the message that Bridget had won—that her passive-aggressive behavior had succeeded in affecting the rest of the household.

The dinner would go on as planned.

Not hearing a peep from the other side of the bedroom door, Holly knew that her father would make a scene if Bridget didn't come downstairs. Hoping to avoid the bellowing that was sure to follow, Holly knocked harder. For all their sakes.

"Bridge," she said louder. "It's time for dinner! Dad will come looking for you any minute."

That seemed to work. Within thirty seconds, Bridget had unlocked the door, flung it wide, and swept past Holly. From the quick glimpse, Holly could tell Bridget was unusually pale and unkempt. She hadn't even made an effort. Not a stitch of makeup or a comb through her hair.

Following Bridget downstairs, Holly saw the front door open below and watched her father usher Mildred inside and out of the rain. He had driven to her cottage to pick her up. Bridget pretended not to see Mildred and rounded the banister to walk in the opposite direction.

Holly took the last step down and greeted Mildred with a warm hug.

"May I take your coat?" Holly asked, sounding more formal than she'd intended.

"Yes, thank you."

"It's a bloody mess out there." Duncan removed his cap, beaded with raindrops. "Bit of flooding, down by the creek." He stooped and pecked at Holly's cheek. "Smells wonderful in here, Hollybear."

"Everything's ready. Why don't you two go into the dining room and I'll get the girls."

Minutes later, they sat at the table, their father at the head, Mildred at his side. Holly sat beside her, and all three sisters sat opposite, with Bridget at the other end, as far away as possible.

Holly suggested grace, and her father said a brief prayer over the food.

At first, serving themselves the steaming food was reason enough for silence. It gave them all something to do with their hands, a distraction. But once the portions were set onto plates, the silence grew. It took shape, hovering noticeably in the empty spaces. Holly was afraid this would happen and, earlier, had made a mental list of safe topics to attempt.

"So." She turned to Mildred, who had just lifted a forkful of peas to her lips. "How is Gertrude? Other than the book club, I wasn't able to see her last week."

Mildred lowered her fork. "She's doing well. Her knees are acting up again, and the doctor put her on new medication, which she despises. But she's well."

Another pause, while silverware clanked and ice clinked.

Holly tried again. "She certainly is becoming vocal about *Emma*. I never would've thought she'd enjoy it. I love the way she and Frank bicker about the characters."

Mildred nodded. "Oh, yes. Do you know, I caught her reading *Emma* when I arrived yesterday? She was so absorbed in it she didn't even see me come in! Instead of hiding it immediately, like she's done in the past, she got cranky with me about interrupting her and said she 'positively must finish this chapter' before I spoke to her again."

Holly chuckled. "I can't believe it."

"It's so good for her. Gives her something to occupy her days. Maybe she'll pick up *Pride and Prejudice* next."

"Wouldn't that be incredible?" Holly loved the idea.

If this had been a dinner for two, it would've been considered a success—sparkling, easy conversation, flowing transitions. But there were four other people at the table now who were mere spectators. Perhaps it was time to involve them, as well.

Holly took a bite of mashed potatoes and shifted to Rosalee. "Oh! Did you tell Dad about your audition? That it's in London?" She explained to Mildred, "This director loves Rosalee's work and wants her to try out for his next film in a few weeks."

"I've heard!" Mildred said. "We have a budding young star, here." She focused on Rosalee. "I so wish I could've watched your scene. I'm sure it was superb..."

"Thanks," Rosalee muttered with an attempt at a half smile then took a bite of bread. Holly couldn't tell whether she was embarrassed about her actress role, or whether she was being deliberately cold to Mildred in a show of twin solidarity.

Struggling, Holly moved to Abbey next. "Why don't you tell Mildred about the new addition to our house?"

Abbey stared blankly. "Huh?"

"Rascal," she mouthed.

"We have a puppy!" Abbey's face lit up. "Rascal. He's *so* smart. He can shake and sit, and I can almost make him roll over. Maybe we can play with him after dinner!"

"Maybe so," Holly said then switched to Mildred to explain. "Fletcher bought me a puppy. For my birthday. He's a Border Collie."

"Oh, I had a Border Collie when I was a young girl," Mildred recalled. "Cooper was his name. He lived to be fifteen years old. Such a sweet breed. And so intelligent!"

"They really are," Holly agreed. "Fletcher jokes that we need some sheep so Rascal can herd them."

Holly looked over at her father to see him listening attentively but unwilling to participate. Perhaps it was shell shock, seeing his new love and his daughters occupying the same space, outnumbering him. He admittedly wasn't very good at "these things."

Tearing off a bit of bread, Holly dared to peek over in Bridget's direction, to see her balancing peas on her fork tines.

By the time dessert was served—bread pudding—Holly had successfully managed to fill enough gaps in conversation to keep things flowing for the entire meal. She was mentally exhausted, but it was worth it. Mildred seemed infinitely more comfortable than when she'd first arrived. Her body language relaxed, and at one point, she even reached over to hold their father's hand on top of the table. After a few bites, she asked questions of the girls. She talked to Rosalee more about her audition and asked Abbey more about Rascal. Then, it was Bridget's turn.

"And how have you enjoyed your time on the film set? Mrs. Pickering said you looked lovely at the ballroom dance."

For the first time all evening, Bridget took her focus off her flatware and stared at Mildred. "I don't work there anymore. Or go there anymore," she said icily. "I'm grounded." She shifted toward Duncan. "Or didn't my father tell you? He's really good at that... keeping things from people then springing surprises out of nowhere."

"Bridget Newbury," her father grumbled from the head of the table, his eyes sharp and angry.

"Well, it's true. Or are we not allowed to speak truth at this table? Are we limited to mind-numbingly boring subjects like a stupid dog?"

"That's enough!" he bellowed.

Bridget had already backed her chair away from the table and threw her napkin down on the floor. Her eyes met her father's as she walked toward the door, unafraid. "You don't have to order me to my room. I'm already there."

Her father's grasp was a split-second too late as Bridget slipped away.

He inhaled audibly, controlled, then whispered to Mildred, "I'm sorry, love." He squeezed her hand before he let it go and pushed back his chair. "I'm going to take care of this."

"No," Mildred said, grasping at his elbow. "No, please. Not on my account. Let her be. She needs some space, I think."

He paused, and Holly could tell Mildred was trying to be upbeat.

"I want to finish my delicious dessert. Holly, you've outdone yourself."

Half an hour later, Mildred and Holly stood at the sink, washing dishes. Duncan had gone to Bridget's room while the other two girls played with Rascal in the garden.

The more Holly thought about Bridget and her acidic tongue, the more livid she became. If their mother had taught them anything, even as little girls, it had been grace under pressure. *Always* be a lady. It didn't mean they couldn't express anger or frustration—but that they should channel it as gracefully as possible, pick the proper times and places for it. The kind of disrespect Bridget had shown in this house, at that table—for her father, for Mildred—was shameful. Unacceptable.

Although Bridget had a right to be upset over their father's latest wedding announcement, it didn't give her the right to rebel. To skip classes, to treat her family members poorly, to make guests feel unwelcome. Holly suspected that Colin had been a greater negative influence than anyone had foreseen. Holly had watched him, observed his behavior—on the set, he carried himself arrogantly, spoke sharply to the crew, sneered at his director. His selfish reputation was notorious. And apparently, infectious.

"I've been thinking," Mildred said, rubbing a fork dry, "maybe we should postpone."

"What do you mean?" Holly asked.

"The wedding." Mildred's eyes remained on the fork. "I think it might be a good idea to wait."

"I disagree." The odd thing was, Holly meant it. All these weeks, she'd been resistant to the idea of Mildred, of a wedding, especially so soon. But after Bridget's bad behavior, Holly had suddenly become Mildred's avid supporter. "Mildred, this is a little bump in the road. Truly." She placed a hand on the crook of Mildred's arm. "Bridget is having other problems right now, issues that have nothing to do with you. She's an emotional teenager. You really can't take this personally. And, to be honest, postponing would only let her have her way. You can't start out your marriage giving her the upper hand."

"You do have a point," Mildred said thoughtfully and moved to the next piece of silverware. "I didn't think this would be quite so challenging."

"I'm sorry about that. It's not an excuse, but I think the girls are still processing everything. They'll come around. I know they will."

Mildred made purposeful eye contact with Holly. "Thank you, dear. For always being so kind to me."

Standing there, it struck Holly, how she wished all these years she had leaned more on Mildred, looked to her for guidance and support, rather than try to do everything alone. It might've made her own burden easier to bear.

Chapter Twenty-Five

I cannot think well of a man who sports with any
woman's feelings; and there may often be a great deal
more suffered than a stander-by can judge of.
*–*Jane Austen

HOLLY SHOULD'VE SEEN IT COMING. Every red flag was there, waving in her face all this time. *Why* hadn't she paid attention? She sat rigid, phone in hand, on the sitting room couch, her leg bouncing to the frantic pace inside her head. When would Fletcher call? He should've arrived in London by now.

She glanced back on the last few hours. They'd been an absolute blur. It had started out a perfectly average Thursday. Girls off to school, Holly off to the gallery, then running errands, then home to wait for them. But when Rosalee and Abbey arrived home, they arrived without Bridget.

After waiting the cursory half hour, giving Bridget every benefit of every possible doubt, Holly reasoned that Bridget was simply taking advantage of the one night their father was in Dublin on a business trip to push her luck. She had likely gone to a friend's house—consciously breaking her curfew. After phoning a couple of Bridget's friends with no success, Holly called Fletcher, suspecting that Bridget's "detour" involved the film set, and Colin.

"I just got on set, myself," he told her. "Don't see her right now, but I can do some checking."

A few minutes later, Fletcher texted: *She and Colin were here. Both gone now. I'll keep checking.*

That was enough to send Holly jumping into her car, leaving Abbey and Rosalee at the house with a vague explanation. The anger rose to her cheeks as she drove to the Manor.

During her steep drive up the hill, she let the worry seep in. *What if it was more than a broken curfew? What if Bridget was running away?*

When she parked at the Manor, she saw Fletcher in the distance, confronting an actor dressed in costume on the front lawn. This couldn't be good. Holly hurried out of the car and approached them, hearing only the last part of their tense exchange.

"That girl is only sixteen," Fletcher told the actor.

The young man on the receiving end of Fletcher's frustration shook his head, put out his hands, "I told you, mate. All I know is they drove to London. He didn't tell me nothin' else."

Fletcher took a step forward, his glare fiery. Holly had never seen him so livid. "That's not what I overheard you tell your friend just now. I heard the word 'hotel.'"

That was when Fletcher noticed Holly.

The actor's eyes dropped to the ground. "The Charleston. That's where he's headed."

Fletcher pivoted to Holly. "I'm going."

"I'm going with you," she insisted.

Fletcher blew out a long breath. "Will you trust me on this? It's better if you don't. I'm... a neutral party. You're her sister. I don't know what I'll find when I reach them, or how Bridget will feel, seeing me there. She might hate me for this. I don't want her to hate you, too. Stay. Please. I'll keep you informed."

Knowing he was right, Holly forced down her natural instinct to handle the situation herself. Fletcher was the best person for this. She handed him the keys. "You'll need a car. Take mine."

On the walk home, Holly tapped out her dad's number, having no idea what to say. Her call went straight to voicemail. Irritated, she clicked off and remembered that tonight's business trip wasn't "just" a business trip but a huge conference he'd been invited to attend at a Dublin castle retreat. He was the guest speaker at this evening's banquet, in fact. She could try him again later tonight, when she knew something.

Almost home, she whispered prayers and tried not to picture every worst-case scenario with Bridget. The weight of responsibility Holly had shouldered for the last six years suddenly began to choke her. Whatever the outcome, she had failed. This was her fault, somehow.

When she arrived back at Foxglove, Abbey and Rosalee peppered her with questions, to which she gave careful, truthful answers without alarming them. "Bridget has broken her curfew. Fletcher's going to make sure she's safe, bring her back home."

"Did she run away?" Abbey wanted to know.

"I think she tried to. But we don't know the full story yet. Let's just wait and see what happened. Everything will be okay."

Then she handed the girls enough money for an Indian takeaway and sent them out to get dinner.

Holly threw herself into some mundane chores—scrubbing the floor in Rascal's laundry room, dusting figurines in the sitting room that had already been dusted that morning, washing an unnecessary load of towels.

Now, sitting on the couch nearly two hours after Fletcher had left—plenty of time for him to arrive in London and start his journey back—Holly shifted positions and waited for the call that would tell her everything was okay.

Hearing her plea, the phone buzzed in Holly's hand.

"Fletcher?"

"We're coming home."

"Is she all right?"

"She's shaken, but she's safe. I got there in time. We'll be home in an hour."

"Thank you, Fletcher."

Holly tapped the phone and sank into the couch with a small groan. The call had brought more anxiety than relief. What did "shaken" mean? If Fletcher had been alone, he could've offered more details. But with Bridget sitting there, maybe it was best he hadn't. In any case, Holly clung to the second half of Fletcher's sentence. *She's safe.*

Holly knew it was best to keep this low-key, so she sent her sisters upstairs to do homework after finishing their curries. With no idea what state Bridget would be in—furious that Fletcher had gone after her, pulled her away? Or grateful to see him, realizing Colin's intentions?—Holly had no way to prepare for what would be coming through that front door.

When she heard the car door slam outside, Holly stood still. She would have to play this by ear, follow Bridget's lead. Unable to wait for a knock, she opened the door and flicked on the outside light.

She saw two figures coming up the stone walkway—Bridget, hunched inside Fletcher's jacket that swallowed her whole, and Fletcher, slightly behind her, his expression serious but otherwise unreadable.

Bridget paused in the doorway, and Holly put a comforting hand up to her shoulder, searching her tear-stained face. "I'm glad you're home."

Bridget reciprocated the brief eye contact then moved past Holly to go upstairs.

Fletcher closed the door behind him then motioned toward the hallway, leading Holly into the kitchen where they could finally talk.

She already had the coffee brewing and poured him a cup. He sat down, and when he took the mug from her, she saw a fresh cut on his reddened knuckles.

"What happened?" she said, wide-eyed, and reached inside the freezer for a bag of peas. "Here, use this."

She sat across and watched him grimace as he held the peas to his knuckles. He brought the mug to his lips and blew on the surface before taking a sip. The suspense was killing her.

"I punched him," he finally said.

"Colin?"

"Yeah. When I got to the hotel—it was shady, in a bad part of town—I saw Bridget in the parking lot, getting out of Colin's car. She looked upset. She slammed the door and was holding onto her wrist, like she'd hurt it."

Holly wondered how but didn't want to interrupt Fletcher's story.

"When she saw me, she looked relieved and walked toward me. But Colin got out of his side and ran over to her. I couldn't hear what he said, but he grabbed her shoulders. He looked angry. Bridget tried to wriggle away, but he wouldn't let her go."

"And then?"

"I moved between them and punched him. I didn't care about his explanations. Her body language was enough for me. It was obvious she didn't want to be near him and she was glad to see me. When I turned around, Bridget had already gotten into your car, and Colin was on the ground. So, I got in the car and sped away." Fletcher shifted the bag on his hand.

"Did Bridget say anything in the car?"

"Only 'thanks.' She stayed quiet the rest of the time."

"I don't want to think what would've happened if you weren't there."

"That guy is scum. I should've seen it coming."

"Exactly what I've been telling myself for the last few hours. I should've seen this coming. I've been beating myself up, going over all the different ways I could've stopped this from happening. Weeks ago." Her throat tightened with regret.

"Bridget chose to go with him. Trust me, there's nothing you could've done to stop her. In fact, prohibiting her to go would've made her want to even more. But, if this helps, I don't think she knew she was going to a hotel. I have a gut feeling Colin lied to her, told her they were going to London for a different reason. Maybe just dinner or something. Because what I saw tonight—Bridget's reaction—was not a girl who willingly wanted to go to a hotel room with someone. She seemed caught off guard."

Holly cupped her mug, its warmth soothing her palms. "I don't know how to do this."

"Do what?"

"Be what Bridget needs right now. A mother."

Fletcher reached across with his non-wounded hand and threaded his fingers through hers. "You don't have to be anything but yourself. You'll know what to say. Just be there for her."

"She hasn't needed me for a really long time."

"But she's gonna need you now."

Holly knew he was right. But she didn't know where to begin.

Reading *Emma* the next morning through new eyes, Holly noticed how much in common "that actor," Colin, had with his character, Churchill. Deceitful, smooth, manipulative. A liar and a bit of a con artist. Someone able to influence Emma in negative ways, bring out her selfish side. No wonder Colin had gotten the role. He was a perfect fit.

She yawned and turned the page, unable to focus on the chapter. Holly had spent a restless night after Fletcher left last night. He'd had a second cup of coffee then walked back to the pub.

She'd checked on the girls, all sound asleep—or, at least, *acting* asleep—then changed clothes, brushed her teeth, and slipped underneath her cold sheets. No matter what tricks she tried—counting sheep, going over business theories, making mental to-do lists—she could only see Bridget arguing, maybe even struggling with Colin in the car, hurting her wrist in the process. Holly would've punched him too.

Early this morning, well before the girls were up for school, she'd kicked off her covers and headed downstairs, full of nervous energy. She tried to phone her father for the millionth time, but the call didn't go through. He'd warned her the reception at the castle might be terrible.

As much as she craved a long and solitary jog, she had to be there for Bridget if she woke up early. So, before the girls came down, Holly channeled her energy into other things: folding the towels from last night, making a full breakfast, studying for a faraway test. When it was time to wake them, Holly peeked inside to see Bridget still fast asleep then decided to ring the school and call in "sick" for Bridget, who would hardly want to face school today. Even with her grades in jeopardy, recuperation today was a priority.

Thirty minutes ago, Abbey and Rosalee had left for the day and Holly sat on the sitting room couch with *Emma* perched on her knees. Rascal had wedged himself between her waist and the cushion, and every now and then, she would reach down to pat his velvet tummy as he snored.

She heard the front door slam and knew it was her father. Jumping up, disturbing Rascal in the process, she hurried to meet him and pointed to his study. He set down his overnight bag, followed her lead, and shut the door—and Rascal—behind them.

"What's going on?" he asked.

"Sorry, I don't mean to be so mysterious. I didn't want Bridget to hear."

"She's not at school?"

"It's not what you think. Well, okay, it's sort of what you think." She tried to figure out how to tell him that last night, his sixteen-year-old daughter broke her strict curfew and went off to London with a boy at least five years her senior. "Have a seat, and I'll tell you."

He went behind the desk and pulled out his pipe. Holly let him light it and puff it before she started. She recounted every detail, from her trip to the film set in search of Bridget, to Fletcher driving to London and punching Colin, to their somber arrival home last night.

With each word, her father's face turned a deeper shade of crimson. By the time she had finished, he'd gotten to his feet, slapping the pipe against the desk so hard that it snapped in two. "That son-of-a-bitch actor! I'll kill him."

"Shh. Dad, she'll hear you." Holly stood to meet him around the desk and placed her hands on his arms. "Calm down. Please. Fletcher got to her in time, and she's safe. I don't want you to do anything rash. You've got to think clearly about this."

"No worries." His voice still crackled with anger. "I'll take care of this myself."

He pushed past her, flung the door open, and exited the house. She could hear his car starting up.

"Oh, great," Holly mumbled, knowing she had a whole new set of troubles on her hands.

She imagined him paying off some thug to beat Colin up, or maybe doing it himself—cornering the actor in a secluded spot on set and beating him senseless. She only hoped her father didn't wind up in jail. Or worse.

Part of her knew he was smarter than that—that he would find a way to punish Colin without getting his hands dirty. This was where his steely business sense kicked in, his street smarts. Rather than worry, she decided to be glad to have a father who was finally taking action without her prompting him.

An hour later, as Holly prepared for a special Friday shift at the gallery, her father walked into the kitchen. His face was back to a normal flesh color, his breathing deep and purposeful. No bruises on his face or hands, no evidence of physical revenge. He took off his coat and hung it calmly on the back of a chair.

"What did you do?" Holly asked, not actually wanting to know.

"I took care of things."

"What does that mean?"

"It means I took care of them."

"That's not very forthcoming."

"The less you know, the better."

He was almost smiling, and she knew that whatever "it" was had been successful. He leaned his thick hands on the chair and pushed back his leg, stretching out his muscles like a runner preparing for a race.

"How's Bridget?" he asked, his focus on the floor.

"I checked on her a few minutes ago. Took her some toast and tea. She's awake, but she doesn't feel like talking yet."

"Should I go up?" he asked, still looking down.

"That would be good. Maybe tap on the door, tell her you're here. No lectures, though. Not now. She really wants to be alone. I need to head to work. Will you be here the rest of the day?"

"Yeah. I was planning to work from home, anyway."

"Good. You can keep an eye on her, then. If she feels like talking, she will."

He straightened up and looked at Holly. "How is she? I mean, how did she seem last night?"

"I think she's embarrassed. And probably heartbroken. She genuinely cared about Colin. It's over now, though, trust me. She was grateful that Fletcher went to get her."

"Do you think...? Am I the one to blame for this? That maybe if I'd made my work less a priority, been less an absent father? Or even maybe the engagement? What if that was the trigger?"

This was a tough one. In some ways, perhaps her father *was* to blame—a lack of fatherly attention over the years, a lack of interest in his daughters' personal lives, an insensitivity to their feelings recently. These all had ripple effects, consequences. But Holly couldn't bear knocking him while he was down. What was the point, anyway?

So, she spoke another version of the truth. "I think we're all a little bit to blame. Me, you, even Bridget. We've all made choices, and some have been the wrong choices. There's nothing we can do about them now. They're done. But we can try harder, listen to each other better. There's still time."

"Maybe you're right. I hope you're right." He reached for his coat again. "My biggest fear is that we've lost Bridget. That all these mistakes—mostly mine—have led to irreversible consequences. Her school, her future—"

"I don't think it's that dire. I saw a softness in Bridget last night and this morning, a vulnerability. It's going to take some time for her to heal, to get past this. But she'll find her way. She's a smart girl, and I think she has a bright future. Plus, she reminds me a lot of someone I know."

"Who?"

"You." Holly grinned. "Stubborn, fierce, strong, confident. How can you not see yourself in her?"

"Never thought of it that way." He squinted, looking at Holly in a side glance. "Those aren't horrible qualities to have, you know."

It was good to see his smirk, a lightness in a heavy day.

The serious face returned. "My only priority," he said, wagging a finger in the air, "is to keep this family safe. Nothing else matters."

"I believe you, Dad. And so does Bridget. Really." Holly noticed the time and reached for her keys. "Sorry, I'm late."

"Okay." He caught her at the doorway and put a hand on her shoulder. "Thank you for taking care of things last night. You made your mother proud. And me. And thank Fletcher when you see him next. That boy is a hero."

"I will. Love you, Dad."

"Love you, too."

Chapter Twenty-Six

But that expression of 'violently in love' is so hackneyed,
so doubtful, so indefinite, that it gives me very little idea.
It is as often applied to feelings which arise from a half-
hour's acquaintance, as to a real, strong attachment.
~Jane Austen

HOPE IN THE STORM. HOLLY stared deep into the painting, her favorite one in the gallery, and studied the realistic detail.

Noelle had painted it two years ago, a perfect English countryside—patchwork lawns divided by quirky, uneven stone walls, sheep dotting the fields in between. But beyond the pastoral landscape, a storm grew. Dark, hateful clouds brewed, threatening the peaceful scene below. The "hope" part of the painting came in the sharp, white rays of sunshine cutting through the other end of the sky—reminding Holly that no matter how dark things became, hope was always visible. The only thing missing was a rainbow.

Distracted by the gallery door, Holly shifted gears, ready to greet the probable tourists, answer their questions, do her job. But instead, she saw Lily—Frank's official girlfriend—enter and wave.

"I didn't know you were coming today," Holly said as Lily reached out for a one-armed hug.

"I brought Frank some lunch. A little surprise picnic." She held up a small wicker basket.

"That sounds fun. He's in the back room," Holly said, stepping aside. "Thanks."

She watched Lily go and knew Frank would be absolutely no use to her the rest of the shift. These days, thanks to Lily, his head was more in the clouds than on the gallery. He'd lost important receipts, miscalculated the budget by two hundred pounds, even forgotten to pay last month's electric bill.

Holly remembered seeing a show on telly once, that proved how being in love could make a person lose control of the rational, practical side of thinking. In an experiment, scientists gave a newly engaged man an MRI and monitored his brain waves as he stared at a picture of his beloved. Instantly, the endorphins kicked in, and the pink blob that represented brain activity used for rational thinking physically shrank. Amazing. And, in a way, something Holly was jealous of. She wanted to feel that way again. In love again. Giddy, intoxicated, irrational. But perhaps not too irrational. That was how Bridget's situation had occurred.

Still, part of Holly wanted to let go, experience the rush, let those endorphins take over.

Someday.

"Do you have any more of those grape tomatoes?" Holly lugged the gallon of milk and bunch of bananas onto the counter.

"No, dear," said Mrs. Pickering. "But I'll get a delivery tomorrow."

"Mind if I set these down? They're getting heavy. I'm not finished shopping yet."

"Certainly." Mrs. Pickering returned to her copy of *HELLO!* and took a bite from a crisp apple.

The market was a compact structure—only two narrow aisles—but adequate enough. The shop carried fresh produce and canned goods and toiletries. The only grocer's in the village, Mrs. Pickering held an almost arrogant monopoly.

"Clean-up on Aisle Two," an odd voice squawked. Holly saw Fletcher, carrying a basket filled to the brim with crisps and biscuits.

"You're eating healthy," she said then winced as she saw his bruised knuckles, evidence of last night's scuffle. She reached out instinctively. "How's your hand?"

"A little sore."

Mrs. Pickering had shut her magazine and was pretending to count pounds at the register. But the obvious strain of her neck gave her eavesdropping intentions away.

"We'd better lower our voices. Or, figure out a code," Holly whispered. "You know she's the biggest mouth in the village."

"I vote for code. It'll confuse her."

Holly nodded and reached for a box of spaghetti.

"So." Fletcher used an unnaturally loud tone. "The rat got the boot at 0900."

Holly scrunched her eyebrows at him. "What does that mean?"

"It's code," he muttered.

"But I don't get it."

Fletcher chuckled and shook his head. "Never mind. Let's talk outside. It's easier."

Holly found the last two items on her list, paid for them, and met Fletcher out in the bright afternoon sunshine. Halfway through July, today would reach an unusually warm eighty-one degrees. Wearing a sleeveless shirt, Holly loved the heat on her arms.

Fletcher suggested the stone gazebo as a rendezvous point, so that was where they headed. Though the structure stood blatantly in the middle of the street, visible to everyone passing by, it still provided a degree of privacy with the thick stone producing heavy shadows inside.

They sat on the cool stone ledge together and set their bags down.

"Spill it." Holly darted her eyes to make sure nobody else was in earshot.

"The rat—that's Colin—was fired this morning."

Holly recalled her father's smug, satisfied expression when he had come home earlier.

"You don't look surprised."

"My father apparently 'took care of things,'" she whispered. Her father's actions still felt covert, even after the fact. "I guess having Colin sacked is what he meant. But I don't have any details. How did you find out?"

"There's not much to tell." He shrugged. "I got to the set a little later this morning, and that's all anybody was talking about. Apparently, the director fired Colin the second he got there. That sparked an argument, and Colin trashed his trailer, then took his stuff and left in a rant, spewing profanities. Wish I had seen it."

"You're wicked." She grinned.

"He deserves to be gone, whatever the reason. Bridget can relax now. How is she?"

"She was still sleeping when I left for work. I'll try to talk to her when I get back home. By the way, Dad said to thank you. That's *two* Newbury sisters you've rescued. He called you a 'hero' this morning."

Fletcher gave one of his aww-shucks head tilts. A flock of tourists, fresh off a tour bus at the end of the street, began to descend on their private gazebo, chatting and snapping pictures.

"I think we're being invaded." Fletcher stood to dust off his shorts.

"Yeah, those obnoxious American tourists. Always interrupting, always making noise." She stood to join him.

"Hey. Those are my peeps you're talking about."

"Did you just say 'peeps'?"

"I believe I did."

They gave a mutual wave and separated, leaving the tourists to ogle the village.

Another restless night. It had been two days since Bridget's escape from London, and in that time, she'd remained inaccessible. Holly had tried to engage her—tap on the door, call her name softly, ask if she wanted to talk. The answer was always a firm but polite "not yet," or a quick shake of the head.

Occasionally, Bridget would sneak downstairs, bundled in her quilt, to sit on the couch and watch telly with her sisters. But her expression was robotic. She wouldn't laugh or react, and when the program was finished, she'd float back upstairs to her bedroom like a melancholy ghost. Still, Holly noticed emptier plates whenever Rosalee would bring the food trays down. Bridget was starting to eat again. Either that, or she'd learned how to push her food around to give the right impression.

Tonight, rather than struggle with sleep, Holly gave in and snuck down to Hideaway Cottage after midnight.

She'd just settled in to her rocking chair with *Emma* when she heard a light tap at the door. Curious, she went to the door and drew it open.

"Hey." Bridget stood in the doorway wrapped in the quilt, her security blanket. Her hair was tousled, her face free of its usual layers of makeup. Her skin was naturally beautiful, youthful. "Can I come in?"

"Of course." Holly stepped aside, closed *Emma.*

"I saw your light on from my window. You come down here a lot, don't you?"

"Yeah. My little getaway."

The seating arrangement was lacking—this room was only meant to hold one person. But that didn't bother Bridget. With some effort, she squatted down on the petite coffee table, the quilt spreading out around her.

"How are you doing?" Holly asked.

Bridget hid her chin inside the flowery fabric.

Deciding to let her sister ease into it, Holly glanced down, moved her thumbnail along a small groove in the rocking chair's arm and waited.

"I feel like a fool," Bridget finally said, her words muffled inside the quilt. She lifted her chin. "I really believed him. That I meant something to him." She closed her eyes so tight that her eyelashes disappeared. Then she opened them again and looked up, unblinking. Her eyes pleaded something, for Holly to understand. "Colin told me he loved me, that we belonged together. He was taking me to see *Wicked* that night, in London. I knew it was breaking curfew, that I'd get in trouble. But I thought it was worth the punishment. Just to be with Colin, go to London, a night I'd never forget. He was so sweet on the ride there. We were talking and flirting and listening to music the whole way. I felt like I was living in a film. But then, when he pulled into the car park of a sleazy hotel..."

Bridget's gaze moved past Holly. "He stopped the car, and I asked him what we were doing there, what about *Wicked*? He said he wanted to surprise me. We could get some dinner there—at the hotel—and then get a room." Her eyes narrowed, remembering. "And that's when I knew. It was his plan all along, a hotel. He'd lied to me, just to get me there. So I told him 'no,' that I wasn't going to a hotel with him. He tried to sweet-talk me, but I was fuming by then. Told him to take me *home.* He leaned in for a kiss, and I slapped him. Hard. I don't know where it came from—but he was suddenly so ugly, so *not* the person I thought he was. He was shocked at the slap and grabbed my wrist—and it hurt. That's when I struggled to get away and left the car. And then I saw Fletcher." She blinked out of the memory. "How did he know we were there?"

"When you didn't come home after school, I called him. He found one of Colin's friends and pressed him for details then went after you."

"Did he know it was to a hotel? Fletcher?"

Holly nodded, and Bridget lowered her eyes again.

"I'm so embarrassed," she whispered. "Such a fool. How could I not have seen through Colin? He always said the right things. I knew a lot of people didn't like him. That should've been the biggest red flag. There were even rumors he had a girlfriend somewhere, but I refused to believe them. I should never have gone with him and put everybody through hell. I can't believe I was so stupid."

Holly stood up to lean over, wrap her arms around her cocooned sister. "You are *not* stupid. You are a bright young woman who thought she was in love. Colin is the fool." She squeezed tightly to emphasize her point. "You're not alone, being deceived by someone you love. It happens to the best people." She thought of Fletcher, his cheating ex-fiancée.

"I'm sorry," Bridget said through sniffs as Holly backed away. "For sneaking off that way. It won't *ever* happen again."

Holly brushed a stray, damp hair out of Bridget's eyes and sat down again.

"I'm ready to go back to school Monday. I'm so behind, I don't know if I'll be able to make up for it, but I'll try." Bridget's voice fell to a whisper. "What if I run into Colin somewhere? In the village, on the street. I can't avoid him forever."

"You won't have to. He's gone," Holly reassured.

Bridget's eyes widened. "What?"

"I wanted to tell you this before, but I was waiting for the right time. I'm not sure of the details, but Dad had something to do with it. Fletcher told me Colin was sacked. The director is scrambling to replace him. They have to reshoot all of his scenes."

"I can't believe it."

"You don't ever have to see him again."

The relief on Bridget's face was palpable. The tense lines around her eyes had softened.

"Have you talked to Dad yet?" Holly asked, wondering if Bridget's new willingness to talk would extend to their father as well.

"I didn't know what to say, how to explain. And I didn't want another row. Isn't he furious with me?"

"He wasn't happy about you breaking curfew. But then when he heard the details, he was relieved you were okay. That trumps everything. Of course, get ready—your new grounding will probably be for life or something. But only because he wants to protect you."

"Fine by me. I've been bloody awful toward him. And Mildred. When you told me about her—about them—all I could feel was this terrible anger, nothing else. I don't know where it even came from."

Holly leaned back to rock a little. "I struggled with everything too, in the beginning. It's still weird, thinking of Dad without Mum. Thinking of him with anybody else."

"Exactly. I mean, Mildred is, you know, fine and everything. As people go. I don't have anything against her. But it's just... replacing Mum that way... I don't know."

"That's what I thought, too," Holly agreed. "That Dad was trying to fill the gap with somebody else. But then, I looked at it a different way. Actually, I have Fletcher to thank for it. He helped me take the focus off me and put it onto Dad."

"What do you mean?"

"Well, instead of thinking about how the engagement affects *me*, I started thinking about how it affects him. Dad. In some ways, he's been lighter these past weeks, hasn't he? Home a bit more, a little less work-oriented. Happier."

"Yeah. He whistles a lot."

"And when I saw that he was happier because of Mildred, then the engagement wasn't something awful anymore. It's not about Mildred trying to take Mum's place. It's about Dad needing someone in his life again. He's waited six years, and now, maybe it's time. He deserves some happiness, doesn't he?"

Bridget pondered this. "Yeah. He does. But…" She looked up at Holly. "All this still makes me miss Mum. So much. I can't help it. It just hurts."

"I know. But Mum would be proud of us for supporting them. She would want Dad to be happy. Especially after all these years."

"That's true, she would." Bridget's eyes brimmed with tears. "But I'm just not there yet. Is that okay? I mean, the idea of someone stepping into Mum's shoes… and then having to call Mildred 'step-mum.' I can't deal with it yet."

"It's understandable. But at least keep your mind open. For Dad's sake."

"I can do that," Bridget promised.

Chapter Twenty-Seven

*The more I see of the world, the more am I dissatisfied with
it; and every day confirms my belief of the inconsistency
of all human characters, and of the little dependence that
can be placed on the appearance of merit or sense.*
~Jane Austen

HOLLY PUSHED THE DOOR OPEN to a picturesque summer day—birds whistling a back-and-forth mirthful tune, sun beaming down on shiny emerald-green grass, a pair of sheep bleating in the next field over. *Pastoral imagery*, she thought, drawing from one of the poetic elements she'd learned last semester in an online literature course.

Sundays should always be like this, she decided. *Nothing but blue skies and halcyon breezes.*

Miraculously, the girls had dressed, eaten, and found their Bibles by 9:55—precisely enough time to walk down the hill and enter the church on the organ's first few notes. Most Sundays, Holly, the girls, and their father found themselves slipping into the back row a few minutes late, clamoring for hymn books, joining the worshippers mid-tune, avoiding Mrs. Pickering's disapproving eyes.

This morning though, only Holly, Rosalee, and Abbey would make the trek down the hillside. Their father spent last evening in London for a brunch business meeting this morning and wouldn't return until mid-afternoon. And Holly assumed Bridget would need one more day at home before venturing out again to face the world.

"Wait up!" Holly heard as she lifted the latch to close Foxglove's gate.

And there Bridget was, looking fresh and clean in a buttercup-colored sundress, walking briskly toward the girls, her hair still damp from a shower.

When she reached them, Holly locked eyes with her and smiled, continuing on.

Bridget paused in the road. "I forgot my Bible," she whispered.

"It's okay," Holly replied, linking arms with her. "You can share with me."

As Mrs. O'Grady poised her fingers to play the first notes of the opening song, Holly and the girls walked down the middle aisle of the old stone church and slipped into the third row, their usual spot. Along the way, Holly waved at all the usual suspects: Mary and George Cartwright, Noelle and Adam, Joe and Lizzie—even Frank was there, seated alongside Lily. Mac, a sporadic church-goer, had made it today, sitting far at the back, away from the others on his row. Everyone accounted for, except Mildred.

When the girls settled in—bags and Bibles adjusted, hymn books plucked from the rack—Holly sensed a presence at her side and glanced up.

"You came," she said with a warm smile.

Fletcher nudged her with his elbow then waved to the girls.

A minute later, the choirmaster asked them to stand and sing, and Fletcher, seeing no hymn books left in the rack, grasped the corner of Holly's to share. Because of his height, she could hear him singing down toward her. And he was good. Surprisingly so. She stopped singing, only mouthing the words, so she could listen.

After another hymn and some announcements, the vicar issued a sermon on the nature of love. He cited verses in Corinthians, "Love is patient, love is kind..." and Holly felt a pinch of sympathy for Bridget, who probably didn't want to hear anything about love right now. Not even from a vicar on a Sunday at church.

When the service ended, Holly assumed Bridget would want to scurry out, back to the safety of Foxglove. But before they could even exit the pew, Riley approached.

"Hey," he told Bridget, his eyes blinking fast. "It's good to see you."

"Thanks," Bridget replied.

"You look… pretty. That's, like, a new dress or something."

"Yeah. Fairly new, thanks," she said again then waited patiently through a long pause and watched Riley shrug.

"So," he said. "Guess I'll see you tomorrow in school? You'll be there, won't you?" For the first time since he approached her, he made actual eye contact, his expression shamelessly hopeful.

"Yes," she replied. "Yes, I'll be there."

"Why do you do this to me?" Holly asked Rascal as he cowered in the corner, watching her scrub the rug.

Her arms ached from trying to remove the latest floor stain. He seemed to save all his bad-dog moments for her.

That's what comes with raising a puppy, she reminded herself. *It's not all fun and games.*

Finishing the task, she held the cleaner and rag with gloved hands and looked over at him. Rascal gave his best pathetic look then wagged his tail like a pendulum. Realizing she wasn't cross anymore, he bent over in his play-with-me position, wiggly butt in the air, and yipped so loudly that he scared himself.

"You *won't* make me laugh," she said, fighting the smile.

At that, Rascal pounced forward and clamped the rag with his teeth, shaking it as he snarled.

"You little maniac." She loved his playful growls. The last ounces of frustration drained away, but she soon remembered her to-do list and wrestled the rag from his tight grasp. "Back to work," she told Rascal, and he followed her, nipping at her heel, trying to chew her trouser leg. She remembered that Border Collies were herding dogs and assumed Rascal was herding her now, begging her to stay and play.

The doorbell rang as Holly peeled off a glove. Before answering it, she pried Rascal carefully off her leg and rushed him into the laundry room to prevent an inevitable distraction.

Finally reaching for the doorknob, Holly realized what an awful state her hair was in, secured in a messy ponytail. Too late to care about it now.

She brushed stray hairs away with her fingers and opened the door.

"Mildred! I didn't see you at the book club this morning." Holly smiled, but her warmth wasn't reciprocated. Mildred remained on the porch, hands crossed in front, her expression stoic.

Holly stepped forward, suddenly concerned that something awful had happened. "Please, why don't you come inside? It's starting to rain."

"No, thank you. I only came to give you something."

She offered a red velvet box, and Holly took it with a question mark.

"Your father's ring."

"I don't understand."

Mildred's words came out in a succession of quick bursts as she struggled to push back tears. "I can't marry your father. It wouldn't be right. I've stayed up all night thinking about it. And I can't. It's impossible."

Holly stepped forward again to comfort her, but Mildred took a firm step backward.

"I won't change my mind. It has to be done."

Holly had never seen Mildred this way before. "Mildred, please. At least *talk* to my father about this first. He deserves to hear it from you. Does he even know how you feel?"

"I can't speak with him. He'll talk me out of it." Her voice became muffled by the steady rain splashing on her wool hat and sliding down her beige raincoat.

"And with good reason. Mildred, you belong together," Holly said, before she had time to censor the words. "My father loves you. You're good for him. I think you're good for each other."

"But I'm not good for this family."

"What do you mean?"

"I know about Bridget."

Holly had wondered if her father told Mildred about the runaway incident with Colin. Apparently, he had. Or else she'd heard it somewhere in the village.

"Don't you see?" Mildred said. "Our engagement has caused too much trouble. It's put such a strain on this family. Unnecessary strain on all you girls. We made a mistake, rushing into things."

"Bridget's going to be fine," Holly said firmly, trying to give back the box, rain pelting her hand.

But Mildred shoved her fists into her pockets, her lips forming a taut, straight line. "I've made up my mind. I'm sorry about putting you in the middle of it. But I simply can't face your father."

She pivoted, and Holly watched the pouring rain swallow her up as Mildred hunched into it. Holly touched the damp velvety box with her fingertips and wished the people around her would stop making irrational, hasty decisions that had such powerful ripple effects on everyone else. It was starting to make her dizzy.

That evening, when her father came back from London, Holly didn't have to say a word, didn't have to tell him that Mildred stopped by, or even relay what she'd said. He knew the minute he laid eyes on the ring box.

He grabbed it from Holly and shot out the door, presumably in search of Mildred. No matter that it was nearly midnight by then. He returned an hour later, shoulders slouched, hair glistening from the rain, box still in hand. Holly watched him go into his study and knew it was best to leave him alone. The engagement was off.

Chapter Twenty-Eight

*There is nothing like employment, active indispensable
employment, for relieving sorrow.*
~Jane Austen

"TWO RULES."

Fletcher popped another crisp into his mouth and crunched it thoughtfully. "Rules? No, no." He wagged his finger. "You can't make rules on a road trip. The whole *point* of a road trip is spontaneity."

"Hear me out. You'll like these rules," Holly assured.

He rolled his eyes and clicked his seat belt. "Okay, what?"

"Rule one, I can't talk about my family drama. Rule two, you can't talk about work. Anything else is fair game."

He paused then agreed. "Fine by me."

This morning, Holly had called Frank early, begging him to let her go to Bath a week earlier than planned, to scope out potential new artists. She couldn't stand the tension in the house and had to get away. Escape. The girls were still in school for one more week before summer break, and today was her father's work-from-home day. He could easily see to dinner, since Holly had prepared and refrigerated it last night.

Immediately after calling Frank, she'd texted Fletcher. She needed some company. *Play hooky w/ me today. Road trip!*

He'd texted back: *When & Where?*

Meet outside Joe's, 30 min. and find out!

When Holly pulled up outside the pub, she saw Fletcher coming from the opposite direction—Mrs. Pickering's shop—with a brown bag in his hand. Inside the car, he set the bag on his lap and said, "Where we goin'?"

"Bath," she told him.

"Bath. Seriously? Umm, isn't that like, ten minutes away?"

"No. It's at least twenty."

"Yeah. So, how does a twenty-minute drive constitute a road trip, exactly?"

"Look, do you want to go, or don't you? It's not too late to back out."

"Actually, Bath is pretty close to Bristol. I could check on my apartment, make sure my cousin hasn't burned the place down." She could see him mulling it over. "Okay, Bath."

As she'd pulled away, she'd given him the "rules" then explained that it was a business/gallery trip, with plenty of room for excursions.

"You look especially nice, by the way," he said now, offering her the final crisp.

The sundress she'd chosen had wisps of yellow and green. In fact, she'd bought it in Bath the last time she was on business for Frank. "Thanks. I was going for artsy-businesswoman meets casual-road-tripper."

"It works."

As she moved onto the motorway toward Bath, she knew it was time for some music. She chose the Bluetooth option with a song shuffle, so they could listen to everything from '80s to classical to coffeehouse rock. The first song was Debussy. A familiar, heavenly, lilting melody.

"That's too sleepy for a road trip," Fletcher insisted. "We need something faster."

Holly clicked the button on her steering wheel for the next Mystery Selection, and a new Katy Perry hit came on.

"Not exactly what I was hoping, but at least it's upbeat." Fletcher wadded up the crisp bag and chucked it into the brown paper bag.

"You're making me hungry," said Holly. "What else is in there?"

He peered inside. "Chocolate or peanuts?"

"No contest. Chocolate, please."

He half-unwrapped a bar and handed it to her. As he did, she knew this was exactly what she needed today. A little music, a little chocolate, a little Fletcher. The perfect elixir for what ailed her.

The few minutes it took to reach the edge of Bath breezed right by. As they approached the city, Holly clicked off the music to concentrate. Because the gallery was located on a narrow cobblestone street—no cars allowed—she had to park blocks away. The crowds were out in full, making the parking situation even more challenging. Even on a weekday, the city teemed with tourists. Bath was always a favorite spot.

When they'd parked the car and walked three blocks to find the right street, Fletcher pointed to a bookshop. "I'll be in here. Come and get me whenever you're done."

The Bath Gallery stood across the narrow street from the bookshop. Holly had been here three times over the past year, so the curator greeted her warmly when she stepped inside. He had three pieces to show her. She snapped pictures of them with her phone, sent them immediately to Frank, then called him to find out the verdict. He okayed two of them, and Holly pulled out the business credit card for the purchase. Twenty minutes after stepping inside the gallery, she'd finished her business for the day. Easy-peasy.

Both paintings were petite, and the curator had wrapped them well and placed them in a roomy bag for her, so lugging them to the bookshop wasn't the trouble it could've been.

Since Fletcher hadn't been outside waiting, Holly assumed he was still wandering the aisles of the bookshop. Oddly, in all her visits to Bath, Holly hadn't ever stepped inside this particular shop before. She'd always meant to, but never took the time. Opening the door now, she smelled the musty-sweet odor of old books and peered at the dark wood bookshelves that rose tall, up to the ceiling. Entering the shop made her crave a bookshop in Chilton Crosse. Sure, Mrs. Pickering sold fairly current books in a wire turnstile at the front of her shop. And sure, Holly could buy any book she desired online, and they'd deliver it right to Foxglove's doorstep in a day or two. Even digital books nowadays were a mouse click away. But nothing could replace the physicality of actual books to skim, browse, and rummage through. Rows and rows of them to explore.

"Hey," Fletcher said, interrupting her daydream. "Are those heavy? You want me to take them?"

"The weight isn't bad, but these plastic handles are starting to pinch my fingers."

"Here," he said, unburdening her.

"Thanks."

"Isn't this place great?"

She could see he was salivating, too. "I love it," she agreed. "I think I could browse all day." She drifted off toward an aisle.

Fletcher followed her. "So, how about some lunch after browsing, then we can head to Bristol? You haven't changed your mind, about stopping by my apartment?"

"No, of course not. I want to see where you live."

Holly wandered around, lost in this glorious world of books, scanning titles, picking one, flipping through pages, then replacing it to find another. She ended up purchasing five books, including a large-print copy of *Pride and Prejudice* for Gertrude.

They agreed on the Pump Room restaurant nearby, located above the Roman baths. After browsing the menu, they decided to share the sea bass.

"Penny... er... pence for your thoughts?" Fletcher mused, buttering a slice of bread.

Holly realized they hadn't spoken since they sat down. "Oh. Sorry. My mind is still back in that book shop, I guess. I had a little epiphany while I was in there."

"What kind of epiphany?" His dark brown eyes had turned amber in the sun's reflection from a nearby window.

"Epiphany's not really the word, I guess. More like a brainstorm."

"What about?"

"I don't want to jinx it yet."

"Oh, sure. Reel me in and then throw me back out."

She smiled, realizing it was unfair. "How about this? You'll be the first to know if anything pans out. Deal?"

"Do I have a choice?"

"No." She reached for her soda. "You don't."

Fletcher drove Holly to Bristol, a thirty-minute ride. She'd been to Bristol before, but it was ages ago. He took the long route, to pass the cathedral, Council House, and university along the way. Finally, they reached a row of tidy flats with stucco fronts.

"Nice area," she said as he parked in the last spot.

"Yeah, it's all right. Next place I live, though, I'll be looking for a house instead of an apartment."

"You might be in the States by then, huh?" she said softly. "And who knows where I'll be this time next year, with everything changing so fast these days." She stopped short. "Sorry. Almost broke rule number one."

"Well, don't let it happen again." Fletcher winked then exited the car.

Inside the flat, nothing surprised her. The living area looked like a bachelor's should, filled with neutral-colored couches and sparse décor. Functional, practical. And messy.

"At least my cousin hasn't trashed the place entirely," Fletcher mumbled, looking over things, seeing crushed, empty cans of ale on the table and a wrinkled T-shirt lying casually over the back of a chair.

"Will I get to meet him?"

"Todd? He's out of town, visiting friends this week." Fletcher sorted through the post on the kitchen bar, stuffing a couple of important-looking envelopes into his jacket pocket. "I'll get a few things from the bedroom while I'm here. Clothes and stuff. Make yourself at home," he said then disappeared down the short hallway.

Holly walked along the edges of the compact space, gazing at the titles in Fletcher's bookcase. On one shelf, L'Amour, King, Ludlum. On another, books about writing screenplays and how to find a literary agent, along with a framed picture. The only one on display.

She reached for it to get a better glimpse. A family picture. Parents, brother, sister, Fletcher. He looked about seventeen and had his arm around his brother's shoulders. They had the same almond-shaped eyes, same height. She would've sworn they were twins, in fact. His mother had reddish-brown hair and leaned into his father lovingly. Holly wished she could meet them, fill in more of the gaps of Fletcher's past. Fletcher knew Holly's entire family well, even Gertrude. She knew so little about his in comparison. It felt lopsided, somehow.

"Ready?" Fletcher stood in the doorway with a bulging duffel bag. "I think I got everything. Thanks for stopping here. Even though it's out of the way."

"No bother." She put the frame back in its spot. "I've enjoyed seeing where you live. It's enlightening."

"Is it?"

"Yeah. Like this picture of your family. They're lovely. It's nice to see where you came from."

Fletcher stepped toward her and looked at the frame wistfully. "That was my brother's graduation party."

"You miss them."

"I do." Fletcher took his eyes off the frame to look down at her. His gaze was longer, deeper than she expected. She wanted to know what he was thinking. Then he cleared his throat. "Yeah. It'll be good to see them again. I will miss England, though."

"Just England? What about *me*?" she said, pinching at his ribs, making him flinch.

"Of course, you. And your sisters, and Chilton Crosse. It's been the best three months I've had in England."

"Even above your Oxford days?"

"Even above those." He looked at the clock on the mantel. "C'mon. We gotta go."

"Are we in a rush?"

"Actually, yes." He switched the duffel bag to his other hand and took the few steps toward the front door, opening it for her. Confused, she stepped through it and walked down the stairs.

"What are we doing?" she asked as he threw his bag into the backseat and held out his hand.

"Mind if I drive again?"

She dropped the keys into his palm. "Okay. But you're being very mysterious."

"Yep. And you're going to love it." He opened the door for her again. "This is a road trip, remember? We're supposed to be adventurous."

"Open your eyes."

Minutes earlier, as they reached the edge of Bath, Fletcher had ordered Holly to cover her eyes. He wasn't taking any chances. Sensing the slight jerk-and-pull of the car here and there as Fletcher made up his mind where to go was starting to make Holly nauseated.

Relieved to be harbored somewhere, she opened her eyes and saw before her a vast, empty field. But far over to her right stood an enormous hot air balloon, newly inflated. Two men were tucking and checking and pulling at the base of it, as a flame danced upward at its core.

"So. What do you say?" Fletcher asked. "Up for a little adventure?"

Holly felt the weight of his stare and tried—in the course of a few seconds—to determine her reaction. She hadn't swallowed, hadn't breathed since she'd seen the balloon. She gathered her thoughts and tried to sound natural. Non-petrified. "When did you arrange this?"

"Inside the bookshop. When you were at the gallery. I remembered a friend of mine recommending it, so I thought I'd call, check into it. Turns out they had an opening. So, back to my original question…"

Despite his incredibly sweet gesture, she had to admit the truth. "I'm sort of… afraid of heights."

"Seriously?"

"Well, not the major-phobia, need-medication level. But yes, heights make me nervous. Very nervous."

"It's safe. I went online, checked it all out. The ride is about an hour, all around Bath."

Listening to his gentle sales pitch and remembering that not only had he taken the time to call and book this ride but that it also probably cost him a small fortune, she knew what she had to do. Fear or no fear, she was going up.

"Okay. Let's do it. I'm up for a challenge," she lied, forcing down the terror.

"Excellent. They're waiting on us. We'd better go."

He grabbed a couple of jackets from inside his duffel bag then held her hand as they walked toward the field. She wondered if he could feel her nerves coursing through her fingertips.

At the balloon, he shook hands with the man in charge, Charlie, and introduced Holly.

Before she had time to prepare, Holly found herself tucked inside the roomy wicker-basket cage underneath the balloon and being handed a flute of champagne—included in the package, Charlie explained. She tried not to drop it as she filtered through all the distractions around her—men busying themselves to prepare the balloon for lift-off, the flame quivering above her, Charlie giving instructions: all limbs inside the cage and no jumping about. The latter struck her funny, in light of her desire to do the opposite—curl up in a fetal position at the bottom of the basket until the ride was over.

Fletcher stood behind Holly with his hand on the small of her back, but even that didn't settle her. She struggled to fight the rising panic as the countdown to lift-off began. A minute earlier, Fletcher had helped her into one of his jackets, and she was grateful now for its size. It covered most of her sundress. It wouldn't offer any protection, should something go terribly wrong, but its fleecy warmth offered an imaginary security.

"You okay? Your face is all white," Fletcher said into her ear, competing with the new roar of the flame as Charlie gave it more gas. "We don't have to do this. It's not too late to back out."

Holly closed her eyes, wishing he hadn't said that, given her an out. Because she was about to take it.

But she remembered Fletcher's excitement when they first stopped the car at the field. Instead of backing out, she found comfort in clichés. *All will be well. It's perfectly safe. People do this every day.*

Charlie was a perfect example. He'd probably given hundreds of these rides. Maybe thousands. He knew what he was doing. She opened her eyes.

"I'm fine," she reassured Fletcher. "Really. Let's do this."

She drank her champagne in two long gulps then handed the glass over to Charlie. When he took Fletcher's empty glass too and instructed the other men, she knew it was time. Holly clutched the top of the wicker cage. She could still feel Fletcher's hand on her back.

The flame made an even-louder shushing noise, and the balloon began to rise, smoother than she'd imagined, slow and gentle. But a breeze brushed by, and she felt a wobble. She caught her breath and watched the men below. *Is it too late to back out?* She could hop out, even at this height, and just sustain a twisted ankle, maybe a few bruises. Better than plummeting to her death later on. But the men were casting off the ropes, already waving goodbye.

Too late.

She gripped the cage tighter—*appropriate name*, she thought, *"cage"—trapped, caught, stuck*—hating this out-of-control sensation. Fletcher shifted his hand toward her waist and squeezed it twice, reminding her he was there.

"Still okay?" he asked.

All she could do was nod.

The trees and people below started to shrink, and Holly closed her eyes, nauseated—*thank you, champagne*—feeling frightened and vulnerable. Powerless, helpless. Why had she let him talk her into this?

"Look at that!" Fletcher said into her ear, competing with the wind and the flame. By now, he had wrapped his hand around most of her waist, the comforting pressure of his body solid against her back.

Curiosity nagged at her, so she forced one eye open. Fletcher was pointing over her shoulder at something below. She opened both eyes to see the Roman baths, now the size of a small swimming pool. She could see the green water and the tourists, now ant-sized. To the left was Bath Abbey, the church in the shape of a cross.

"Oh. Wow." Her voice disappeared inside the wind.

Charlie gave information and history about what they were seeing below. His steady voice soothed Holly's nerves, kept her focused on something besides the fact that they were a hundred meters above ground.

At some point during the ride—she didn't know when or why—she finally let go. Released her fear, the way those men had released the ropes. Her body relaxed. She *was* safe. Charlie knew what he was doing, and Fletcher was here with her, holding on. Somewhere along the way, she'd even un-gripped one of her hands from the cage and placed it on top of Fletcher's, interlocking their fingers.

Now, she dared to look out beyond the city, to see the never-ending countryside, the view she wouldn't *have* otherwise, except for this balloon. She never imagined seeing the world at this angle, rising above it. Things were so small, so manageable. And it made her feel oddly in control.

"This is stunning," she said, hoping Fletcher could hear.

She wondered if her mother had ever seen England this way.

Before long, objects returned to their normal size—trees grew bigger, fields grew wider, and she could see the men preparing for the landing below. Charlie shoved ropes out of the basket so that the men could hold onto them, helping slow the landing.

The nerves came back, and Holly rotated in Fletcher's arms, her face near his chest, pulling him close and gripping at his sleeves with both hands. She squealed as they met the ground with a bobbling thud.

"I've gotcha," he whispered, holding her tight.

She knew it was true in more places than the balloon ride. He had her back, always. She could trust Fletcher with her thoughts and fears, even here, with a safe landing.

She sucked in a quick breath as the cage came to a full stop. Solid ground at last. Fletcher rubbed at her back, kissed the top of her head. "See? That wasn't so bad."

"The opposite of bad." She inched back but kept her grasp firmly on his jacket. She couldn't bring herself to let go. During the last hour, she'd become used to his body, his hands on her waist, the comfort of his voice in her ear. It had ended too soon.

"Well, folks, hope you enjoyed the ride," Charlie said.

"It was incredible," Holly replied, beaming. Exhilaration still pulsated through her system.

Charlie swung the wicker door open for her. She passed through then reached back for Fletcher's hand, still needing something to cling to.

Half an hour later, after an awaiting car took them back to the original field, Holly gave Fletcher the keys again. Even though she'd released her fears, she didn't trust herself to drive in a straight line—not even the twenty miles back to Chilton Crosse. Besides, it was nice, having someone else in the driver's seat. "Would you mind? I'm still amped up from the balloon."

By the time they'd reached the main road back to the village, the sky had turned a dusky blue. The fading of the day, combined with the soothing glow of dashboard lights, left Holly drowsy. She drew her knees up to her chest and hugged them, still wearing Fletcher's coat. She must've dozed off, because when she heard Fletcher's voice—"I had fun with you today"—she looked up to see Storey Road. They were home.

Holly yawned and put her feet back down on the floor, stretching them out. "I did, too. I'm glad you said 'yes' to my road trip."

"I still want to know what your epiphany was. Sounds mysterious."

"Someday," she promised.

Fletcher passed the pub and drove up the hill toward Foxglove.

"What are you doing?" she asked. "I was gonna drop you off at the pub."

"No need. I'll walk. Besides, I think you're too sleepy to drive." He smirked.

"True," she said, yawning again at the mere suggestion.

"I might have to carry you inside." He pulled up beside Foxglove's gate and parked.

She opened the door, and he called back to remind her, "Don't forget the paintings." He reached into the backseat and took them out then met her around the front of the car, where the headlights still shone.

Taking the bag, she rocked forward on tiptoes to give him a quick peck on the cheek. She tilted her head, noticed something in his expression, even though his face was half-covered in shadow.

"You okay?" she asked. "You seem a bit... I don't know... distant, all of a sudden. Pensive."

"Yeah. A little. Had an epiphany of my own on the way home."

"You did? About what?"

Fletcher looked past her, up toward the house. "Naw, I don't wanna jinx it."

"When will you tell me about it?"

"Someday. I promise. Maybe when you tell me about yours."

He opened the gate for her, and she lugged the now-too-heavy paintings up the stone path. When she turned to wave good night, he was already gone.

Chapter Twenty-Nine

We have all a better guide in ourselves, if we would
attend to it, than any other person can be.
-Jane Austen

"THEY'RE BURNING!" ABBEY YELLED, POINTING at the cooker.

"Oh, bollocks," Holly muttered, hoping it wasn't loud enough for the girls to hear.

She shut her laptop and stood to take care of the sausages. Bridget appeared at her side and whispered into Holly's ear, competing with the sizzle, "I need to talk to you."

"Okay. Let me just finish these," Holly agreed, tapping the grease off the last sausage and placing it onto the plate. Not *too* burned. Still edible. She wanted to give the girls an especially good breakfast on their last day of school. Plus, Bridget still had one more exam to take for her A-levels. Holly had never seen Bridget so dedicated, so intense in her studies as these last several days. She had every chance to do well today.

"Now," said Bridget. "Please?"

In spite of being pulled in a million directions—school, breakfast, work—Holly could tell this was important. "Okay. Where?"

"Your cottage. For privacy." Bridget glanced at the girls, absorbed in their meals.

"I'll meet you there in a sec." Holly turned off the range and carried the sausages to the table.

"Need anything else?" she asked Rosalee and Abbey. Seeing them content, with mouths full, she added, "I'll be back in a minute," and left to follow Bridget.

The early morning was misty and cool, more like fall than late July. She trekked the hundred meters to Hideaway Cottage and wondered what all the fuss was about. Especially on such an important school morning.

Bridget sat on the edge of the table, her knee bouncing up and down.

Holly walked to the rocking chair and sat. "Okay, I'm here. What do you need to talk about?"

"Dad. And Mildred."

Holly was so unused to seeing Bridget this way—fidgety, anxious. She was normally so self-assured. Too self-assured, in fact.

"What about them?"

"I know that Mildred gave back Dad's ring."

"Yes," Holly confirmed, remembering the defiant, sad look in Mildred's eyes as she handed over the velvet box a few days earlier.

"It's been weighing on me all night. I couldn't sleep. Mildred would never have broken things off if I hadn't... gone off like that. With Colin."

"Well, that might've been a factor, but you can't blame yourself entirely. Mildred's a grown woman—"

"I've been nothing but horrible to her, ever since we found out about their relationship. I see that now. I want to help make things right."

"What do you suggest? I tried to talk her out of it when she came by with the ring. But her mind was set."

Bridget crossed her leg over her knee. "We have to convince Mildred that Dad wants her. And that *we* want her, as part of the family. And we have to do it together."

"We?"

"You, me, Rosalee, Abbey. We have to be united. And let her know we support the marriage. We have to try..."

Holly heard a crack in her sister's voice and the sincerity inside it. This wasn't only about making things right. This was about redemption. She was doing this as much for her own sake as for their father's.

"Okay. I'm in," Holly said. "And I'm sure the girls will be willing. It's worth a shot. But don't get your hopes up. I mean, we can't make her take the ring back."

"No. But we can try."

It had been Abbey's idea to take a peace offering along. She knew how much Mildred loved banana bread, so she begged Holly to make one this afternoon.

So, after the girls returned from school, they all walked to Mildred's cottage, warm bread in hand.

"Should we knock?" Abbey whispered to Bridget, who stood the closest to the door.

"Right." She lifted up a fist and tapped lightly with her knuckle.

"Having second thoughts?" Holly asked.

"Absolutely not," Bridget said then sucked in a breath as the door opened faster than expected.

"Oh. Girls," said Mildred, clearly startled. "What are you doing here?"

She'd apparently had a lie-in, unusual for her, and she gathered her robe around her waist as she spoke. Her greying hair, normally swirled up into a neat bun, now spilled around her shoulders, making her look years younger.

"We need to speak with you," Bridget said. "Please."

Mildred paused, still unsure.

"We have banana bread!" Abbey shouted, holding up the loaf above her sisters' heads.

Her outburst broke the tension, and Mildred's face brightened a little. "Well, how can I say 'no' to that?" She stepped aside to let them in.

Mildred's cottage, inherited from her parents years ago, was modest and sparse but still cozy. She had none of the fancy antiques of Gertrude's home, or the formal atmosphere of so many cottages in the village. The décor was simple, Mildred-like. Her brother's framed photo sat on the table, a poignant reminder of her still-recent loss.

"Please, have a seat," Mildred said. "I'll put the bread in the kitchen. Shall I cut anyone a slice?"

The girls shook their heads, and Mildred disappeared around the corner. When she returned, she seemed more relaxed, less threatened by their appearance.

She sat in the upright chair close to the couch, where the girls sat. Clasping her hands, she glanced, one face to another, trying to hold an awkward smile.

Rosalee elbowed Bridget.

"Oww!" Bridget yelped then looked at Mildred. "Sorry. Umm, I don't know where to start."

Holly tried to help. "We're here because—"

"Because," Bridget picked up. "Because..." She cleared her throat. "Because we're sorry. Actually, I'm the sorriest." She paused. "Sorriest. Is that even a word? I just finished my A-levels today, so my brain is a little exhausted."

"Take your time, dear. It's all right," Mildred reassured.

Bridget tucked a wayward strand of hair behind her ear. "I know that you gave back my father's ring. He's devastated. And it's mostly my fault, your breaking up."

Mildred shook her head. "No, that's not it."

"I guess I should've said it differently. What I meant to say is that I feel responsible for things, with the way I've been acting. I've caused a lot of people a lot of trouble. The bottom line is that I... that we..." She looked around at her sisters. "Haven't been exactly welcoming to you. We felt threatened, or maybe we were in shock or something. Anyway, it was wrong. We were wrong. We've had a lot of time to think about it, and we're here to ask you back. To invite you into our family. To marry our father."

Mildred stayed silent, so Bridget continued.

"Dad has been really relaxed the past several weeks. I couldn't put my finger on why, but when I found out about your relationship, I knew you were the difference." She paused then made unblinking eye contact, her voice steady. "You make him happy. And that's what matters the most."

Mildred's eyes filled with glossy tears as she shook her head. "Oh, Bridget. I'm pleased to hear you say that. Truly. But I don't think you understood why I gave back the ring."

Holly looked puzzled. "What do you mean?"

"I broke things off, not because you girls were in any way cold or unwelcoming, but because *I* felt guilty, taking him away from you. We kept our relationship a secret from you, and that was so wrong. You deserved to be involved early on, to have some kind of say. Then, when Bridget... had her troubles... it was evident to me that everything was happening too fast. That it wasn't fair to ask you girls to accept something so drastic that quickly. Something we shouldn't have kept from you in the first place."

Mildred peered down at her lap. "I'm the one who should ask you for an apology. I knew it wouldn't be easy, coming into an established family, especially when your mother was so beloved. But I guess I was naive. Your father told me it would be okay, and I believed him."

"It *is* okay," Bridget insisted. "It just took us time." She rose up and fidgeted with something in her pocket. "We want you in our life, in our father's life."

Pulling out the velvet box, Bridget handed it over. "This belongs to you."

Mildred stared at it, then up at Bridget. "Are you sure?" When Bridget nodded, Mildred looked around the room at all the girls. "Are you all absolutely sure?"

A chorus of "yeses" went around the room and Mildred's eyes formed new tears.

"Put it on!" Abbey insisted, and Mildred happily obeyed, reaching for the box.

"That was the easy part," Holly said. "Now we have to figure out how to put on a wedding in three weeks!"

God's living canvas. That's what her mother had called pristine days like this one. Nature, moving in a lazy rhythm, a world unto itself. Breathing and alive and glorious.

Holly had missed her jog this morning. Again. They'd become more sporadic these last few weeks, her solitary outings. Whatever the reason, she was determined to make up for it today, to settle back into some sort of routine. To grasp at her twenty minutes and own them again. So, leaving the girls to sleep late on their first Saturday out of school, Holly found her running shoes and took off.

This time, she took a different route. She recalled a country hillside she used to visit as a teenager, when the frustrations of school or life in general became overwhelming. A fourth-mile from Foxglove House, a haven sat at the edge of the property, looking down onto the valley at the backside of the village. From this particular spot, she couldn't see a single cottage, or a road, or another human being anywhere. She was the only person on earth.

Five minutes ago, she'd jogged to the peak and sat on the stone wall, watching clouds drift and hover, creating splotchy shadows on patchwork fields below.

Something specific had drawn her here today—something that urged her to carve out a place of solitude so she could think, sort things out. That "something" seemed harmless enough at first. When she awoke this morning, Holly had gone to her calendar, uncapped a Sharpie, and flipped ahead to circle the wedding date in August. To count the days, to make it real. But when she did, she saw something else. Days that lay afterward—all blank, all unpredictable. There it was, in little square grids, proof that life as she knew it was about to change.

And like the clouds above her now, the future seemed vast and endless, free-floating.

Should she even *stay* in the village? What was here for her now? Perhaps she should venture back to Kingston, get a Master's degree in something.

But then what? Taking courses was the easy part—open a catalogue, point your finger to what sounds interesting, enroll. But how to utilize those courses was an entirely different matter. How would they translate into a career for the rest of her life? She still didn't know what to be when she grew up.

She had reached at least one definitive conclusion in all this. There was no way she could remain at Foxglove House after Mildred moved in. Yes, her father had offered an open-ended invitation, to stay as long as she wanted, but Holly knew better. After the wedding, she'd no longer be necessary to the ebb and flow of the household. If she stayed, she knew the awkward dance she and Mildred would do, trying to navigate their different roles. Holly would always end up feeling intrusive. In the way, underfoot. No, she owed it to Mildred to step aside. And to herself. It was time.

Even last night, Holly had attempted to tell her father that, but he was too giddy over Mildred's reacceptance of the ring to hear anything about it. This morning at breakfast, he'd walked into the kitchen, moving around the table to pause at each daughter and give a kiss on the head.

"Thank you." Four kisses, four thank-yous. In his mind, all was right again with the world.

And, he was naive enough to believe things could stay the same in that world—that making room for Mildred, while keeping Holly there, wouldn't rock the boat a single iota.

Holly took one last look at the ever-changing purples and greens and greys of the stunning valley and pushed off the stone wall to resume her jog. And to feel the pinch of regret that she couldn't stay in this beautiful limbo forever.

Chapter Thirty

All the privilege I claim for my own sex (it is not a very enviable one; you need not covet it), is that of loving longest, when existence or when hope is gone.
~Jane Austen

"**I** CAN'T BELIEVE WE ONLY HAVE three meetings left after this one." Mildred clucked as she opened the box of blueberry scones Julia had brought.

"It went so fast," Holly agreed. "I'm thinking we could tack on one more meeting—stretch it out—sort of a 'closing ceremony' where we talk about the whole book. Like a wrap party."

"I love that idea! Oh, and Gertrude already asked me this morning—what book are we doing next?"

Holly didn't have the heart to tell her that in these next few weeks, she wasn't entirely sure if she would even still *be* in the village, much less in charge of the book club.

"Maybe *Pride and Prejudice*?" Holly offered. "I think Aunt Gertrude should be introduced to Mr. Darcy."

Mildred snickered. "Excellent choice."

"We could even show her the DVD, with Colin Firth, that wet shirt clinging to his chest…"

"Eww," Fletcher offered, walking up from behind, reaching for a scone. "Glad I won't be around for that."

Mildred chuckled and went to answer the door for the next arrival—Noelle, looking adorable and radiant in her pregnancy dress. The whole village knew her secret by now. They couldn't help but know it, as she'd started to show last month. The other book club members had already discussed tacking on a surprise baby shower during one of the meetings.

Four other members followed Noelle inside, chattering away, filling Gertrude's stuffy cottage with conversation and laughter.

Over the weeks, Holly had fully expected the book club's attendance to wax and wane. People would surely get too busy or forget, or even fall regrettably ill, or have emergencies arise. But there had consistently been no fewer than eleven people at each meeting, sometimes reaching up to fifteen.

Today, Frank opened the discussion with his question, "Why did it take Harriet so long to destroy her mementos of Mr. Elton? He'd been married for weeks when she finally decided it was time for closure. Why would she hang onto something that was so clearly over and done with?"

Gertrude, who now enjoyed responding to his questions as though they were personal affronts, spoke up. "My dear Frank, you are a man, and could therefore never understand the deep underpinnings of the female heart. Simply put, Miss Smith held onto the idea of Mr. Elton for so long because it was too painful to let him go."

Holly watched Gertrude's face change. The arrogance faded, replaced by a wistfulness Holly had never seen.

Gertrude stroked Leopold's white fur and shifted her gaze off of Frank and onto the floor, her voice lowering to a gravely whisper. "Women can hold an affection for years, even decades. Even after the hope of a love is long dead and gone. A woman could be jilted at the altar—for example—left humiliated in front of her family and friends and still believe he might return someday, begging her forgiveness…"

The cottage had never been so silent. Holly waited along with everyone else, for clarification, for explanation.

But none came. Gertrude blinked and looked again at Frank. The arrogance returned. "Therefore, it is perfectly acceptable for Miss Smith to take as long as she likes to get over a man. Even one as despicable as Mr. Elton."

Frank's mouth was still slightly agape, and Holly knew he wouldn't be any help transitioning the group from awkwardness back to normality.

So she shuffled the notes she'd scribbled last night on her makeshift bookmark and said, "All right. Okay. Why don't we talk about the next chapter? We can discuss more about Churchill's behavior with the letters of the puzzle and what Mr. Knightley concludes from it."

Fortunately, Lizzie took the baton Holly had offered, pointing to specific quotes she found confusing then addressing a particular question to Fletcher, the resident *Emma* expert.

Gertrude remained silent the rest of the hour, and Holly hoped she hadn't regretted being so open with the group. For the first time in her life, Holly felt a pinch of regret, for ever judging Gertrude too harshly.

"You're still awake," Holly said, seeing her father walk in. She had just finished editing a paper for her business course. She hit "submit" and shut the laptop.

"Couldn't sleep." He yawned and joined her at the kitchen table.

"Oh, I wanted to ask you something. About Gertrude." She told him about the book club discussion, the jilting example, the faraway stare. "Is it true? I didn't know she'd ever had a boyfriend."

He rubbed the back of his neck, as though deciding how much he should tell her. "It's not something she's ever spoken about. It was a very painful time for her."

Holly could see him measuring his words carefully.

He folded his hands on top of the table and said, "His name was Andrew. He was in the military—navy, I think. She was nineteen, and it was this whirlwind romance. They were engaged after six months. The story goes that Gertrude's parents had an expensive wedding planned, here at the church in Chilton Crosse. The entire village was in attendance. When it was time for the ceremony, Andrew was a no-show. The next day, she got a note saying he'd run off with another girl. Rumor was that he'd gotten the girl pregnant."

"Unbelievable."

"Gertrude was devastated. I think she even swallowed some pills, but they found her in time. She's been holed up in that cottage ever since, crotchety and hating men."

"She tried to kill herself?" Holly stared at the table, processing it, picturing Gertrude as a pretty young girl, brokenhearted to the point of suicide. "It explains so much."

"I hate how she's wasted her life away, staying isolated. I don't think she's allowed herself to trust anyone since that day at the church. But you and Mildred have helped her the most, hosting that book club of yours. It's forced her to deal with people."

"I can tell it's been good for her. Not that she'd ever admit it, of course. Mildred wants to keep it going, assign another book after *Emma*."

"Speaking of Mildred and the wedding..." He shifted in his chair. "I've made a decision. Well. *We've* made a decision."

Holly braced herself for yet another surprise. Or the ripple effects it would undoubtedly bring.

"We've moved the wedding back."

"Dad...." Holly protested, but he put his hand up.

"It's not what you think. We don't have cold feet. We simply can't put a wedding on this quickly. Mildred wants a bit more time."

"Well, that's understandable. I was wondering how she'd be able to pull it off. Even with mine and the girls' help."

"Exactly. So, how does the first of September sound?"

"Fine by me. Good decision."

"And there's something else," he continued. "I can't stop thinking about what you said. About moving out of Foxglove right after the wedding."

"Dad, it's for the best. Really."

"Where will you go?"

Holly shrugged. "I'll find a place."

"That's not good enough." His eyes squinted to make his point. "I will not have my daughter pushed out of this house because of my remarriage. It's unacceptable."

"It's my choice, Dad. You're not pushing me out. I'm going of my own accord. I'm a grown woman, anyway. It's time."

"What about your sisters? Sure, the twins are nearly grown, but there's Abbey. I'm worried about how she'll transition. There's got to be a compromise."

242

Holly rested her chin on her hand and smiled. "It'll all work out. Abbey's stronger than we think. And Bridget is doing so much better. And the last thing you should be worried about right now is me. You've got a wedding coming up!"

"Hard to believe, your old man getting hitched." He raised himself with another yawn. "G'night, love. I think I'll try to get some sleep."

She watched him go and opened her laptop again, to the Cotswold real estate search engine she'd bookmarked last night. Part of her ached inside at the thought of leaving her home, her sisters and dad, of making it real. But the other part of her knew she had no choice. As she'd told her father, it was time.

Chapter Thirty-One

One does not love a place the less for having suffered in it.
~Jane Austen

O F ANY MAKEUP, HOLLY HATED applying mascara the most. Ever since she first attempted it at age fifteen, she'd never been able to master it. She didn't quite understand the whole "wand" aspect. And this lack of understanding often created globs that stuck to her lashes, or produced black splotches under her eyes when she blinked at the wrong time.

This morning, she paused at the mirror, having applied what could possibly be the most perfect coat of mascara of her life, when a thunderous "crash!" made her blink, leaving black dots, as if a miniature caterpillar had walked underneath her eyes after inking its little feet...

"Blast," she grumbled and forced the wand back into the tube. As she found her eye makeup remover, unscrewed the lid, and pulled out a moist disc, she suddenly got curious about the crash. It was only 7:30 in the morning. There shouldn't *be* any crashes at this hour. There should only be birds tweeting or leaves shushing.

From outside her bedroom window, she could see the corner of Hideaway Cottage—and three, no, four men standing around it with tools. One of them took something in his hand and bashed it up against the side. Her beloved cottage!

Alarmed, Holly threw on a robe and wiped her eyelids with the disc as she flew down the stairs, her heart pumping fast.

Rounding the corner, she nearly smacked right into her father, who steadied her with his hands. He should've been on the road to London by now, she remembered.

"Dad!" she said, out of breath. "What are those men doing to my cottage?" She pointed toward the back door.

"Honey, calm down." He squeezed her shoulders reassuringly. "I asked them to come."

"You asked them to come? They're destroying it!"

"No, no…" He chuckled. "It's the 'compromise' I told you I'd find. I'm not destroying the cottage. I'm renovating it."

"I don't understand."

"I'm adding on a bedroom and bath. And a mini-kitchen. You can choose all the colors and tile—whatever you want. I've got the men working 'round the clock. It should be ready in time for the wedding."

"Oh, Dad…"

"You can stay as long as you like, now. No awkwardness. Problem solved."

When the shock wore off, she warmed to the idea instantly, even knowing it wasn't a permanent solution. Her cottage. She could stay there, at least for the near future. No enormous rush, no drastic life change until she was fully ready. Until she knew what that next step even was. This was possibly the sweetest, grandest gesture anyone had made for her. Usually when her father took a bull by the horns without anyone's consent, she felt nothing but aggravation. But this time, she flung her arms around his neck in a tight squeeze.

"You're the best, you know that?"

Her father shrugged in mock modesty.

She backed away and gripped his shoulders. "As much as I appreciate this, you must admit—it *is* a bit underhanded."

"What do you mean?"

"Well, you do this incredible thing, spend all this money, all without telling me. Of course I'm going to *want* to stay now."

"That's all that matters, isn't it?" He pecked her cheek and took a step toward the front door. "I'm late. See you tonight."

She gathered the belt around her robe and tied it then walked back toward the garden, where the banging and crashing and thudding ensued. She saw Mac pointing fingers to the men, describing something to them. She should've known he would be involved. He tipped his cap when he saw her.

For a moment, she went forward in her mind, visualized their finished work. Hideaway Cottage, a real cottage. Even if it were temporary, even if she only used it for a few months, this gave her a place to be. All her own. Finally.

The last layer of freshly whipped cream resembled a white layer of new-fallen snow. Holly spread it gingerly on top, creating even ridges across. A bottom layer of graham cracker crust, then cream cheese, then chocolate pudding, then whipped cream. Her mother's special recipe for the ultimate comfort food—Chocolate Layered Delight.

Holly hadn't made this dessert in ages but had gotten a craving for it today. She deserved something special—she'd finished her summer course last night, submitted the final paper.

An odd sensation, ending a semester. Even a brief one. The exhilaration of finishing was clouded by the disbelief that it was really over. No more textbooks or study groups, no more papers or online quizzes. At least not until the fall, when she hoped to finish up her online coursework and graduate in December.

As Holly set down the spatula and reached for the glass pan, she thought about texting Fletcher—seeing if he was free to celebrate later tonight. They'd hardly spoken in the couple of weeks since the hot air balloon ride but not for lack of trying. He'd been put to work on the set, rewriting three scenes at a moment's notice, and she'd worked extra shifts at Joe's and at the gallery, in between writing her paper.

She paused with the glass pan, hearing steps in the hallway, then a muffled thud. Rascal bounded into the room, tail wagging, tongue hanging out. Holly expected Abbey right behind him, but no one was there. Abbey and Rascal had been playing in the garden on this peerless Saturday afternoon, while their father had taken the twins out to the cinema in Bath—a film Abbey was still too young to see.

"Abbey?" Holly called, an odd concern nagging at her.

She set down the pan, scooped Rascal up and placed him gently into the laundry room, then walked around the corner. There stood Abbey, empty hands dangling at her side. Tears rolled down both cheeks, splashing onto the wood floor, where two peaches lay.

"What happened? Are you hurt?" Holly raced to kneel at Abbey's side, examining her arms, her legs, looking for any sign of bleeding or injury. She saw a couple of minor scratches on Abbey's knees, but that was all. Nothing to explain the tears. Except the peaches.

At Holly's touch, Abbey heaved with sobs, her eyes now shut tight.

"Abbey, please. Talk to me," Holly begged, her hands on Abbey's waist, wishing her father was here. She wasn't quite certain what to do, as many times as she'd pictured this moment in her mind.

Eyes still closed, Abbey pointed down at the peaches on the floor, confirming what Holly already knew. Abbey had remembered.

Holly racked her brain for all that information she'd looked up online when she realized Abbey had blocked out the memory of her mother dying in front of her. What to do in case the memory flooded back.

"Mummy," Abbey said through a trembling lower lip, sounding six years old again.

"It's okay, Abbey," Holly whispered. "I'm right here."

"Mummy fell down."

Holly watched Abbey's closed eyes flicker, move erratically behind her lids. She seemed to be watching that day like a motion picture in her mind, minute by minute, frame by horrifying frame.

"I'm here. You're safe."

"Don't leave. Mummy, please! Don't leave me."

Holly's own eyes brimmed with tears, wishing she could enter that world too, that horrible memory, and scoop Abbey up, whisk her away.

Eventually, Abbey's sobs calmed, and the tears weakened. She leaned into Holly's embrace and went limp, like a rag doll, grasping the fabric of Holly's shirt with tight fingers.

"I'm right here." Holly rubbed her sister's back. "Right here."

Holly stayed firm, letting Abbey quietly sob, even through the burn that began in her thigh muscles as her sister clung to her. Abbey's grasp loosened, and she started to back away. Holly's knees ached from the hard floor, but she didn't stand. She wanted to remain face-to-face. When she saw Abbey's gaze, she knew Abbey had come back to her. Though red and watery, Abbey's eyes were clear, coherent.

"Are you okay?" whispered Holly.

Abbey nodded and rubbed at her eyes with her fist.

"You wanna talk about it? What happened outside? We don't have to."

"I saw a perfect peach," Abbey said, "up on a high branch. I jumped and tried to touch it, but I couldn't reach. So, I climbed the tree and leaned closer and grabbed it. And then, all of the sudden, I saw Mum in my head—like a memory. She was reaching for a peach, too, standing on tiptoes. Then she fell down on the ground. I guess I fell, too." She looked down at her scraped knees.

"I'm so sorry, love…" Holly moved a strand of hair that had clumped into an S on Abbey's moist cheek.

"That's why you kept peaches away from me, isn't it?" she asked. "Because of the tree."

"That's why. We wanted to protect you."

Abbey suddenly seemed very grown-up as she said, "She died right in front of me."

"I know." Holly's voice cracked as she willed more tears away. She had to be the strong one.

"I watched her fall, but then she was still. She looked asleep. Then… I think Mac rushed over."

"Yes. He tried to save her."

"But it didn't work. And then he took me into the house, to get me away. But later, I snuck my head out the door and watched some men cover her face with a sheet. They took her away."

"Yes." Holly stroked her sister's hair as she spoke, hoping this was the right thing to do, letting her talk about it. But Abbey seemed so calm, so detached now.

"Why did she have to die?" Abbey asked, looking directly at Holly for the answer. "Why was she taken away?"

"I don't know." And it was the truth. Of the thousands of times she'd asked that question, the answer had never come. "All I can say is that she's not totally gone. I feel her all the time—remember things she said, the way her perfume smelled, or how she hummed 'Fiddler on the Roof' when she washed the dishes."

"I remember that!" Abbey smiled.

"See? She's still here with us. She's in this house, inside all our memories."

"I miss her," Abbey said, barely audible, her eyes downcast again.

"I miss her, too."

Abbey fell asleep on the couch minutes later, and Holly took the opportunity to sneak away upstairs and track down Mrs. Harrison, the school counselor, for some advice. On the phone, Holly explained the situation, the peach tree, the flood of memories.

Mrs. Harrison listened patiently then said, "You've done the right thing. Each person is different with repression and how they handle coming out of it. You were patient, to let her work through it on her own. Talking about it was good."

"What do I do now? I mean, do I bring it up again, or leave it alone? I'm so afraid she's going to be traumatized. That I'll do something wrong."

"Actually," Mrs. Harrison said, "she's been more traumatized the last few years, during the repression. It was her mind's response to the horror she experienced. Her mind must think she's old enough to handle the memory, for it to come on so suddenly. I think it's the beginning of healing and closure for her."

"Do you think she needs some counseling?"

"It certainly wouldn't hurt. I have an opening Monday."

Holly agreed then thanked her and hung up, taking a moment to breathe.

In a sense, Holly's own mind had been protecting her, too, all these years. Anytime Holly thought of her mother for more than a minute or two, the moment she experienced that ache of missing her too much, Holly would nudge the memory away, if it ever threatened to come too close. She had always managed to distract herself from the details in the nick of time. But recalling details through Abbey's eyes, Holly felt the anguish all over again of losing her mother. And now, in private, Holly let it come—watched the casket being lowered into the warm earth that unbelievable day. Groaned as they all walked away from the gravesite, abandoning her mother, leaving her there, alone in the ground. Holly remembered the helplessness then. Nothing could bring her mother back. The ultimate loss of control.

She heard a door slam downstairs and knew her father and the twins were home. Somehow, Holly snapped back to the moment, remembered the situation, and made this about Abbey again. She wiped the tears she hadn't felt falling and reached for a tissue.

The pub was the last place Holly wanted to be right now. Too boisterous and merry for her frame of mind, but her father had insisted. When he'd seen her puffy face and tired eyes, when she'd told him everything that had happened with Abbey, he ordered her to get out of the house. He would take over now—feed the girls, get them to bed.

She had nothing left to give, anyway. Drained, she'd shut the front door of Foxglove to walk down the stone path. It was suppertime, and though she didn't have much of an appetite, she knew she needed something. The pub seemed the most logical choice. The easiest choice.

She also didn't want to relay the entire story to Fletcher all over again, but she craved his company. Almost as much as Abbey had needed her, she needed Fletcher now. He would know what to say. His kind eyes, warm smile, strong embrace—all good medicine.

Minutes later, making her way around Joe's mahogany bar, she weaved through the dense crowd around the dartboard, and made her way up the stairs to Fletcher's room. She hadn't even bothered to powder her nose, hide the red patches on her cheeks from crying too hard. Fletcher wouldn't care.

She knocked twice before he finally opened the door.

"Oh," he said when he saw her.

Not exactly the reaction she was hoping for.

"Wow. You look fancy." She walked past him and sat on the edge of the bed. He was buttoning his Oxford shirt. He wore shiny loafers and creased tan slacks. His hair had even been jazzed up with some sort of mousse.

"I didn't know you were coming," he said, flustered. "Did you text me?"

"Oh. No. Sorry. I just wanted to see you. Hope you don't mind."

He patted at his hair self-consciously. "No, I don't mind…"

"You have other plans, don't you?" Here she was, assuming he was completely free on a Saturday night, at her beck and call. Clearly, he was going out. With someone else. Cindy, she suspected. Still, for some reason, it came as a jolt, a shock.

"Well, sort of. Yeah. I do."

Holly rose and moved toward the door. Before she reached for the knob, she said, "It's a date, isn't it?"

Fletcher paused. "Sort of, yeah."

"Okay, well, have fun. I'll text you later."

Fletcher stepped in front of her before she could open the door. "Are things okay?"

The awkwardness subsided, and Holly recognized the warmth in his voice.

"I mean, you look a little frazzled," he explained.

"It's nothing that can't wait. I wanted a chat. That's all."

"Holly, I'm sorry. I should've told you."

"What? That you're going on a date? Good on you! We can talk later. Wasn't important, anyway."

She nudged her way around him before he had a chance to stop her, not turning around to see if he would even try, the faint scent of his musky aftershave staying with her as she walked away.

Chapter Thirty-Two

She could not endure that such a friendship
as theirs should be severed unfairly.
~Jane Austen

FOR YEARS, HOLLY HAD BEEN excited about the prospect of planning a wedding someday. But she had always assumed the wedding would be her own. This morning, after the book club meeting, she'd spent two hours with Mildred, solidifying plans—at the bakery to pick out cakes then the florist's to choose arrangements. Even though her father had pushed the wedding back, Holly and Mildred had no time to waste.

Holly had hoped this would be a bonding time with Mildred, but the pressure of decision-making and the vast array of choices superseded any real conversation. Holly suggested a lunch at the pub afterward, but Mildred had a higher calling—Gertrude needed her to run some "urgent" errands.

So, Holly picked up an order from Joe's to go, and enjoyed the noon-day sun on her bare arms as she headed home. The rest of her afternoon was oddly free. No papers to write, no gallery to work for, no pressing household chores to finish. The girls were sleeping late today and having leftover pizza for lunch, all arranged.

Her knee-jerk reaction, of course, had been to ask Fletcher to join her at the pub. But before she even pulled out her phone to text, she hesitated, changed her mind. Something was "off" with him these days, and she knew it was fruitless to ask. He hadn't answered her last three texts, hadn't shown up at today's book club. As childish as it seemed, she wanted Fletcher to seek her out, make the first move.

Earlier, Holly had tried to pinpoint when things had changed—when he'd suddenly had less time for her.

The shift seemed to occur sometime after the balloon ride in Bath. Holly spent the better part of this morning's jog retracing their conversations that day, wondering if she'd said something, anything, to make him uncomfortable, to make him back away. But, she'd come up empty. Perhaps his "epiphany" that night was that he'd be leaving Britain soon, and thus it would be smarter or safer to back away from their friendship? To start the inevitable detachment process early? Some people couldn't handle goodbyes. Perhaps Fletcher was one of them.

And then, of course, there was Cindy. Odd, that he would keep her from Holly, when before, they'd been so free to discuss their love lives. And odder still, that he would go out with Cindy in the first place, when he'd proclaimed himself "taking a break" from all women. Plus, he was leaving, anyway, in a couple of weeks. Had Cindy's fake eyelashes been *that* persuasive?

Whatever the case, Holly didn't have the foggiest idea why Fletcher had backed away, so she should give him the benefit of the doubt. To make another effort, to be the bigger person. Yes. She would grab Fletcher's attention later in the week, catch him up about Abbey's situation, get things back to normal. Epiphany or no epiphany, she made up half of this friendship and still had certain rights to claim. There was still time...

Reaching the end of Storey Road, thoughts still on Fletcher, Holly stopped cold. She noticed a handwritten sign on Mrs. Mulberry's antique shop, and read it, openmouthed:

Going Out of Business Sale! Everything Must Go!

Mrs. Mulberry had said she was planning to retire but never this—never selling the shop. Holly always assumed it would remain, that the shop would be handed down to someone in her family, probably to Lizzie, a smooth transition. Holly felt a wave of unexpected sadness as she peeked inside to see Mrs. Mulberry tagging a piece of antique furniture. The end of an era.

Holly touched the door handle and stepped in. "Hello?"

Mrs. Mulberry turned around, black marker in hand. "Well, Holly. How nice to see you."

"So, you're doing it, then. Selling the shop."

Mrs. Mulberry capped the marker with a sigh. "Yes, it's time."

She knew it was delicate, private, but for some reason, it was important for Holly to know more. "I always assumed the shop might be passed down. To Lizzie?"

"Yes, well, since she's married Joe and has become involved in the pub, I assumed she wouldn't want the shop. Or, rather, have time for it. And, I was correct."

Though Mrs. Mulberry attempted to disguise her disappointment, Holly could see what an emotional decision it had been. "I'm sorry," she said. "That you have to sell. I really hate to see this place go."

"Thank you, dear." Mrs. Mulberry fidgeted with the collection of tags in her hand. "Please feel free to look around. Some wonderful sales going on. I've already put on half the tags, but if you have a question about a piece, ask me."

"I will, thanks."

They parted, and Holly was free to roam about. Currently the only customer in the shop, she wondered if anyone else even knew about the sale yet. She felt privileged, as though she'd been let in on a secret meeting before everyone else found out.

She wandered, knowing that a piece of her childhood was about to be snatched away. The large placards on shelves, on furniture, that shouted, "DISCOUNT!" or "HALF OFF!" or "ALL SALES FINAL!" only made it worse.

But as she roamed in the middle section of the shop, through shelves of delicate lace tablecloths, toy wooden soldiers, costume jewelry, bins of old-fashioned sweets, something came to her again. Holly recalled her brainstorm a couple of weeks ago, the epiphany. The one she had in Bath. How she so desperately wished their little village had a decent bookshop of its own.

It returned. That seed of an idea that seemed so impossible. She paused in the aisle and looked around at the shop. Really looked.

Then, she reached forward in her imagination and pictured a different kind of shop. Bookshelves—lots and lots of them, high up to the ceilings. Over in that corner, where an antique Aga stood, she saw a coffee bar, maybe baked goods, too. At the register, she visualized specialty gift items for book lovers and writers. And over in that special niche, she saw a children's story corner, with posters of beloved classics. *Anne of Green Gables, Little Women, Charlotte's Web.*

Her heart beat fast, and her face beamed. Could it really be this simple? Was she standing right in the middle of her future? Handed to her on a silver platter by a "Going Out of Business" sign?

All those business courses could measure up to something important, something tangible. No longer just words in a textbook. She wouldn't even have to hire a manager. She could be her own manager.

The start-up capital would be no problem at all. On her twenty-fifth birthday, her father had surprised her with a generous trust fund, to be used at her discretion. At the time, she was absorbed in helping with her sisters, making sure their needs were met. Money was the last thing she cared about then—she already had all she ever needed. She'd decided to save the fund for a day when it would be important to her.

And today might be that day...

"Holly? Are you all right?" Mrs. Mulberry's bird-like voice broke into her thoughts.

Holly realized how zoned-out she probably looked, standing in the middle of the shop, daydreaming.

"Yes, I'm actually terrific," she said, still beaming. "Do you have a buyer yet? For your shop?"

"Oh, no, dear. It's only been on the market since yesterday. Why? Do you know someone who might be interested?"

"Yes," she said, feeling a rush. "Yes, I think I do."

"Let this meeting come to order."

Holly snickered, staring at her father across his desk.

"What?" he asked. "You told me this was about business. I'm trying to set the tone."

After leaving the antique shop, Holly had become obsessed with the idea of turning it into a bookshop. She hopped online for research, dug up some papers high in her wardrobe that told her, to the penny, how much her trust contained, and then she'd phoned her father. She knew she didn't need his permission, but she needed his expertise. Of anyone she knew, he would be the one to tell her bluntly whether she was making a sound business decision or an insane, impulsive one.

When he arrived home, she set a plate of chicken and dumplings before him, anxious to discuss her business proposal.

"So, I know the basics of what you want to do," he said now, between bites. "Let's talk specifics."

Holly rattled off some figures, showed him a preliminary budget, told him Mrs. Mulberry's price, then sat back and awaited the verdict.

He ate as he listened to her presentation then took a long gulp of lager, sat back in his chair, and threaded his fingers together on top of his very-full stomach.

"I think you might have something here," he said.

"Something good or something barmy?"

"Definitely not barmy. You've thought everything through, have the capital to back it up, and laid out a solid plan for the future. Very sensible."

"Isn't it too impetuous, though? Isn't it wild and crazy and impossible?"

"Are you trying to talk yourself out of it?"

Holly considered this. "No. No, I'm not. Just because it's impulsive doesn't mean it's not viable."

"Precisely. Some of the best business decisions I've ever made were after a moment of impulsive creativity." He leaned forward. "So. What are you going to call this little venture of yours? You need a name. Something catchy."

"I haven't thought that far ahead." She looked down at her lap, at the stacks of papers and internet research, then looked up at him again. "This could really be something, couldn't it?" she asked, hesitant.

"It can be anything you want it to be."

Holly pushed down the anxiety that came along with making such a spontaneous, expensive decision. Even knowing she had her father's approval, this had happened so fast. Almost too fast. "Thanks, Dad. For your help. I needed a sounding board."

"You're welcome. But, you know I have an angle of my own here, too," her father confessed. "This venture of yours will ensure that you stay close by. I was afraid you'd run off and leave the village for good. Even with your renovated cottage."

"Oh, Dad. Even if I left Foxglove, I could never be too far away. It's home. It always will be."

She started to gather her documents together and leave him to finish his meal in peace but then remembered something. "I meant to tell you," she started. "Abbey's counselor, Mrs. Harrison, spoke with me this afternoon."

"She saw Abbey this morning, didn't she?"

"Yes. And she said that Abbey is handling things pretty well. She suggested another session this week. Just to make sure."

"Sounds good to me. I still can't believe her memory came back the way it did." He shook his head.

"It was frightening to witness it. Like the memory forced its way in, all at once. I didn't know what to do."

"You did everything right. I'm glad you were with her."

"Me, too. But..."

"What?"

"Well—I'm still worried. In some ways, she's experienced Mum's death as though it happened a few days ago. For all of us, it's been years. But for Abbey, it's fresh. I think time is what she needs the most. We have to give it to her."

"And so we shall."

Holly pushed back from the desk to stand and held her papers at her side. "I can't believe I'm going to be an entrepreneur."

"And a proper one, at that. You've always been the best at everything you do. I have no doubt this will be the same."

Holly exited her father's study with a breathless rush she hadn't experienced in years. Or maybe ever. Something was finally happening. A purpose, a direction, something to reach for. A dream to fulfill.

The next morning, brushing her hair, getting ready for work, she knew she couldn't let today go by without seeing Fletcher. As busy as she was lately, something important had been missing from her days, and it was him. She had so much to tell him, so much he didn't know—Abbey's memory recollection, the new business venture, even the renovation of the cottage.

After spending a slow, tedious morning at the gallery, with Frank mostly online, chatting with Lily, Holly left work early and headed for the Manor. She hadn't been there since that awful day she'd gone storming in to retrieve Bridget from Colin's trailer.

The walk wasn't as pleasant as she'd hoped. The first week of August, any rain that fell usually became a sticky, humid mess. It was probably her least favorite time of year, as far as weather was concerned. She much preferred the chilly days of autumn.

Seeing the Manor ahead, Holly noticed the film production was closer to wrapping than she'd realized. One day, all the heavy lorries and equipment, the glamorous actors and actresses, the constant barrage of crewmembers would disperse. Where had summer gone?

The brightness she'd felt at the beginning of her walk began to fade as she saw Fletcher in the distance, standing near the front door. Soon, he wouldn't be this accessible, only a half-mile down the road. No, he would be back home, in West Texas, selling condos and getting his teaching certificate.

Holly heard a squeaky giggle and knew that Fletcher was talking to Cindy. She wore a beautiful beige dress and matching bonnet, and she laid a gloved hand at the crook of Fletcher's arm, leaning in to laugh at something he'd said. When Holly saw Fletcher flash his dimples in response, she knew he was smitten. And knew she didn't wish to interrupt this intimate scene. But before she could walk away, Fletcher glanced up.

"Hey," he said from a distance. Cindy glanced to see who was competing for Fletcher's attention. When she noticed Holly, she flashed her actress-smile, whispered something to Fletcher, then squeezed his elbow and floated away.

"Hi," Holly said, suddenly self-conscious. "Didn't meant to interrupt."

"You didn't. Wanna come inside?" Fletcher asked. "They're setting up the dinner party scene."

"Umm, I guess. Okay…" She couldn't think of a reason fast enough to say no.

She followed him though the generous doorway and into the reception area, recently transformed into an elegant banquet room. An elongated table had been constructed, and two women were placing cutlery and cloth napkins at each setting, while another woman lit candles all over the room. Two miniature triangular trees made of cranberries and ivy stood on each end of the table.

"It's beautiful," Holly said. "This must be for the Christmas dinner party?"

"That's the one."

He led her over to a rose-embroidered chaise against the wall and they sat, watching the lighting techs set up around the room.

"How's that working out, by the way?" she asked him. "Having a new actor play Churchill? I assume Colin left quite a hole in the production."

"They had to reshoot about five scenes, not too bad. Colin's hole was thankfully fillable."

As the silence persisted, Holly grew hesitant, even though she was brimming with things to tell him. The conversation seemed forced, small talk to fill the gaps in pauses.

To spice things up, or maybe just to crash right through whatever stupid wall had been erected between them, Holly asked, "Did you have a good time? On your date?"

Fletcher nodded. "Yeah, it was good. She's a sweet girl."

"Mmm-hmm," Holly said, as though she knew. But she didn't know. She'd hardly ever said two words to Cindy, and truth be told, she didn't much like the look of her. The tossing back of hair extensions, the vapid-actress capped-teeth smile. Not exactly what Holly pictured as Fletcher's "type."

From the silence, it was obvious Fletcher didn't want to reveal more about the date, which forced Holly to change the subject. This wasn't the place to discuss something as serious and dark as Abbey's breakdown, so she chose something lighter.

"I'm about to have a new home," she said. "Dad is renovating the cottage behind Foxglove for me. It'll be ready in a few weeks, I think."

Fletcher looked at her sideways. "Really? So I guess that means you're staying here, in the village."

"Where did you think I would go?" Was he implying she *shouldn't* stay? That she was choosing the comfort of home over being adventurous enough to leave? And why did she care so much what Fletcher thought? It shouldn't bother her so much, especially since he didn't seem to care much about her life these days.

He shrugged. "I don't know. I thought that with the Mildred thing, your options were wide open. You'd mentioned going back to Kingston."

"Yeah, well, lots of things have changed since we last talked. In fact, it looks like I'm going to be here pretty permanently."

She wanted to tell him about the bookshop, but a brisk voice interrupted, "Okay, everyone. If you're not in the scene, it's time to leave. We've got rehearsals in five minutes."

"I guess I'd better let you go." Holly stood up, swallowing her frustration.

"I'll catch you later." He stood with her, hands in his pockets.

"Okay. Later." She watched him move his attention to the actors gathering around the table. He would be leaving in a couple of weeks, but right now, she felt as though he was already gone.

"I can't believe it sold this quickly," Mrs. Mulberry said.

"Me either, actually," Holly agreed. "I think it was meant to be."

Last week, one day after Holly spoke with her father about her new business venture, Holly made an offer on Mrs. Mulberry's shop, which was eagerly accepted. After signing all the paperwork and having the proper inspections performed, the shop was officially Holly's.

Today's meeting at the shop was simply an informal passing of the torch—Mrs. Mulberry's idea—to share a cup of tea. They sat in two antique chairs beside an antique bed in the back of the shop.

Mrs. Mulberry was prepared to move out within five days. She'd sold most of her inventory by now, after slashing prices from fifty percent to eighty percent off. Holly had already made inquiries about adding bookshelves and stocking books. She'd also bought some pieces from Mrs. Mulberry to stay in place—the chairs they sat in, an old coat rack near the front door, a hand-painted *Alice in Wonderland* bench that sat in the children's nook. Echoes of a place that still meant something to

Holly, and probably most of the villagers, as well. A nice transition. Things were well on their way.

"I'm so pleased the shop has gone into local hands." Mrs. Mulberry dabbed the corner of her mouth with a napkin. "I was petrified it would fall into an outsider's lap. Be turned into some tourist trap."

Holly smiled. "No, no. This will be in keeping with the spirit of the village. My bookshop will have class. Mixed with a bit of whimsy."

"I like it already."

After their chat, Holly gave Mrs. Mulberry a tight squeeze and knew that the next time she walked through those doors, the space would be fully hers.

On the way home, giddy, Holly received a text from Fletcher: *4got to tell U. Wrap party this Sat. Whole fam invited.*

She stood still at the entrance of Foxglove to text him back: *Thanks. 4got to tell U. Dad's wedding Sept 1. You're invited.*

Waiting, she heard the buzz and looked at the screen.

Will b gone by then.

Not what she wanted to hear. Couldn't he stay another week, for the wedding? Didn't her family mean enough to him for that, at least? She wanted to call him, but knew he could be in a place he couldn't talk, on set, during an important scene. Hence, the texting.

Slipping the phone into her pocket, Holly mulled over the great paradoxes, how something so good, so perfect and wonderful—the bookshop, the wedding—could occupy space with something so depressing and upsetting—Abbey's traumatic memory recall, Fletcher leaving, probably forever. Why couldn't life just make up its mind? Why couldn't one day be entirely filled with goodness? Nothing but goodness.

Chapter Thirty-Three

*The memory is sometimes so retentive, so serviceable, so
obedient; at others again, so tyranic, so beyond control! We are,
to be sure, a miracle every way; but our powers of recollecting
and of forgetting do seem particularly past finding out.*
~Jane Austen

Tourists were out of luck this evening. If they attempted
to have a pint at the pub, or buy a scone from the bakery,
or even purchase cigarettes from Mrs. Pickering's, they would
find nothing but dark interiors and locked doors. The whole of the
village had shown up for the *Emma* wrap party at the Manor. Children,
adults, even elderly villagers had all been invited by the producers to
show the crew's gratitude for the warm welcome they'd received over the
past three and a half months.

Even Holly's father had decided to attend tonight's festivities,
bringing Mildred and all four daughters. He drove slowly, up close to
the Manor, and parked in a prime spot. Holly wondered if he'd bribed
someone for it.

Holly was relieved to peel herself out of the backseat, where all four
sisters had been crammed together for the past few minutes. They'd
picked up Mildred at her cottage then headed for the Manor. Duncan
had also asked Gertrude to join them, already knowing her answer. An
emphatic "no." Too cold, too hot, too crowded, too loud—who knew
what the real excuse was.

Walking up to the Manor's entrance, Holly grasped Bridget's hand to squeeze it, trying to offer a little surge of confidence. Earlier, Bridget had sat in Holly's bedroom, watching Holly select the perfect earrings for tonight. Bridget confided that she wasn't sure how she would react, entering the Manor again, the place she and Colin had been together, the place they had met. In fact, she hadn't made the decision to attend the wrap party until the very last minute.

Holly had no idea what one would wear to a wrap party, but in the end, she assumed a little black dress would be a classic choice. Her sisters, walking ahead toward the Manor as she followed behind, also chose dresses, though theirs were more summery and youthful.

At the entrance, Riley saw Bridget and met her with a nervous, lanky hug. For the first time, Holly noticed, Bridget didn't squirm or cringe at seeing him. In fact, her smile seemed genuine, and they even walked inside together, chatting. Two months ago, Bridget would've shunned Riley, left him to fend for himself while she went in search of more handsome, "interesting" company. But the Colin incident seemed to have made Bridget examine the world—and people—in a new light. Her priorities had shifted in the right direction.

Entering the main hall, they branched out to the enormous ballroom, where the majority of partygoers bobbed and danced to the beat of Kylie Minogue. A stark difference from the Austen-era string quartet during the ballroom dance scenes weeks ago. In fact, the Manor had been stripped bare of all its Austen-esque trappings. Everything was nearly back to normal, as it had been before the film crew had first arrived.

People talked above the throbbing bass, laughed at each other's jokes, held plastic cups of ale, and talked in louder-than-usual voices. Holly spotted Joe and Lizzie in the far corner, working the keg. A cracking good time.

She wasn't looking for him, but her eyes found Fletcher at once. He stood at the fringes of the party, leaning against the wall, talking to Cindy. His eyes wandered out then latched onto Holly's. Before she could wave, he'd shifted his attention back onto Cindy. Well. At least she knew ahead of time how this evening would play out. She would evidently be Fletcher-less. Again. And it stung, more than she'd expected it to.

Holly separated from her sisters and headed over to Joe and Lizzie, at the far end of the room.

The music changed to something even livelier than before, and as Holly took a sip of the ale Lizzie handed her, she ached for someone to dance with, even chat with. She spotted Frank and started to walk toward him but saw Lily at his side. They were hunched together, oblivious to anyone else.

Noelle and Adam danced in the center of the room. He reached up to twirl her, catching her off guard. She giggled and fell into his arms, holding her baby bump while Holly tried to contain her envy. It wasn't working.

Finishing off her drink, she set down the half-empty cup and gravitated back through the ballroom's double doors where she'd first entered. As she passed through, she caught a sliver of someone's conversation rising above the other mumbles of the crowd. A couple of actresses talking. Holly kept moving but slowed her pace, curious, as she heard Cindy's name mentioned.

"Bought her ticket today," one of the girls said.

"For America?" the other asked. "I'm so jealous! Lucky, lucky girl."

If they'd been people she actually knew, Holly might've been comfortable enough pausing to get the details. But she didn't know them, so she moved on as though she'd never heard.

Cindy. Going to America? Surely not. Fletcher wouldn't... surely he hadn't...

Holly stopped before she could draw the inevitable conclusions and made her way to the back gardens. Fresh air awaited. Stepping onto the stone porch, she recalled that this was the exact spot she and Fletcher had danced in their Jane Austen attire a few weeks before.

Continuing on, not knowing where she wanted to go but knowing she wanted to keep moving, Holly walked down the marble steps and wandered out into the lush garden. She slipped off her shoes and felt the cool, manicured grass between her toes as she walked toward the center fountain, the rushing sound of water filling her ears. The sky was nearly pitch black by now, but the generous floodlights that shined down from the Manor lit up most of the garden, creating long, uneven shadows on the lawn.

She'd worn a light shawl and now wrapped it tighter around her bare shoulders, obliterating the chill.

She reached the fountain and saw something shimmer beneath the water. She couldn't remember her specific wishes as a little girl, visiting the gardens here with her mother, dropping in coins. But they surely had something to do with fairy tales: a prince or a castle, or even a pony.

What would her wishes be now? They would probably be wishes for other people. That her father would find supreme happiness with Mildred. That Abbey would grow into her own self, comfortable with how smart and special she was, that she would make peace with the memory of their mother. That the twins would find their individual ways and grow to be selfless, goal-oriented women who made good, rational choices.

And for herself? Maybe to enjoy her life, rather than overanalyze it. To look at her life for what was, what it had been, and accept it, then and now, flaws and all.

"Holly?"

She gasped and twirled around to see Fletcher, standing a few feet away.

"Sorry, didn't mean to startle you." He slipped his hands into his pockets and rocked on his heels. He wore a tan blazer—the same one he'd worn to her garden party ages ago. His hair was longer now, touching the back of his collar.

"No, it's fine," she said, willing her pulse to slow to a normal rate. "I didn't hear you. I guess turnabout's fair play."

"What do you mean?

"Remember?" she prompted. "That first day when you were rehearsing your lines here, at the back of the garden"—she pointed behind them—"and I snuck up on you?"

"Oh, yeah. Only you got to catch me looking like a raving lunatic, while I get to catch you looking, well... beautiful."

She blushed at the unexpected compliment. He seemed back to himself, his old self, relaxed and charming and easy to be with.

But then Holly remembered Cindy and America, and her insides churned.

Fletcher stepped toward her and turned to sit on the fountain's edge, hands on his knees. She could finally see his face in the floodlights.

"Sit with me," he coaxed, patting the fountain's edge.

"Promise you won't tip me in?"

"Well, the thought hadn't crossed my mind until just now." He grinned.

She sat beside him, gathering her shawl a little tighter. "Where's Cindy?"

"Not sure. Probably saying goodbye to the director." He rubbed his hands along his jeans a couple of times then crossed his arms, banishing the chill. He seemed fidgety. "I saw your sisters inside. They look well. Happy."

"Yes, they're good. In spite of everything." She remembered that he still didn't know about Abbey's memory recollection, or all the drama surrounding her father's engagement, or even her purchase of the bookshop. In the past few weeks, it seemed he'd disappeared from their lives as suddenly as he'd entered it.

The petty side of her wanted Fletcher to fish, to have to work for it. To ask individual questions about Holly's life, pull the information out of her. He owed her that, didn't he? For all the times since the balloon ride that he'd avoided her texts, or brushed her aside in favor of something—or someone—else more important. Even now, the pause lingered, and he still didn't seem interested enough to ask her. To catch up. To resume their carefully built friendship. She'd invested time into it, and now, looking at him, distant and disengaged, she wasn't entirely certain it had been worth it in the first place. To have opened up her life to someone who seemed now not to care at all. Someone who was leaving, going across the ocean in a couple of days, anyway. With someone else.

Fletcher uncrossed his arms and stood. She couldn't tell whether he was about to leave or was about to say something profound—his expression was uneasy, his eyes frustrated. He parted his lips as he took in a breath. "Holly, I—"

Holly's phone buzzed, and out of habit, she glanced down. A text from Abbey, using Rosalee's phone. *I'm tired. Walk home?*

Holly turned the phone over, wanting to give Fletcher a chance to finish. But all he said was, "Go ahead and answer. I need to get going, anyway." He ran a hand through his hair with a shrug.

"It's just Abbey," she said, quickly texting back: *Meet you at front door.*

Fletcher had already taken a couple of steps toward the Manor when she looked up again. Before he disappeared, she wanted to stand up and grab his sleeve, spout the truth in one long breath. *I miss your friendship. I miss your hugs, our talks. I don't want you to leave yet. I'm not ready for you to go. Please stay a little while longer. I have so much to tell you...* But something kept her from rising. "You'll be at the book club on Monday, the final meeting?" she asked. A mundane question. A safe question.

"Yep. I'll be there."

In the split second before he walked away, Holly saw in his eyes something that looked like disappointment. But maybe it was something else entirely. Once upon a time, she knew him so well she could read the details in his eyes. But not anymore. Those days were gone.

The next morning, Holly heard a knock at the door, well before her alarm would go off for church.

"Come in," she called, groggy. Then, "Hey you," as she saw Abbey peek in.

Holly rose up on her elbows as Abbey approached, holding a wriggly Rascal—he was getting *so* big. Abbey let him loose on the bed, and he immediately pounced on Holly's stomach, knocking the wind out of her as he leapt to plant a wet kiss on her cheek.

"Ugh! Ridiculous dog." She pushed him playfully away. "What a wake-up call." She turned back to Abbey. "What are you doing up so early? Church isn't for hours."

"I couldn't stay asleep. Guess what Bridget wants to make tonight?"

"I have no idea."

"Casserole."

"Really?"

"Yeah. One of Mum's recipes that she found in a drawer last night."

Holly hadn't ever seen Bridget wield a cooking utensil in the kitchen—except to clean it during mandatory dishwashing duty. "I'm impressed. And a little bit scared..."

"She invited Riley over for dinner. Is that okay?"

"Riley? More than okay. He's a nice boy."

Rascal burrowed underneath the covers with his nose and became a hump of fabric gliding along the length of the bed.

"I wanted to ask you something." Abbey traced her fingertip along the thread of the quilt.

"Sure, anything."

"Mrs. Harrison said it might be good to do something... an activity... to help me with Mum, with facing the memories."

"That sounds like a good thing."

"And I've decided on something. I want to have a service for her. At the peach tree."

Holly raised her eyebrows and studied Abbey's face, still focused on the thread. "You mean, a memorial?"

"Uh-huh. I didn't get to go to the funeral. I want to say goodbye like the rest of you did."

Holly clutched her sister's hand and fought the tears.

"So," Abbey continued, unfazed, "this would be just the family. Underneath the tree. We can have cards and flowers and say something about Mum."

When she was able to find her voice again, Holly whispered, "I think that sounds amazing. Come here." She leaned in to wrap her arms around her sister, snuggling her face into Abbey's hair. "I love you. You know that, don't you?"

"I love you, too."

"You're an inspiration to me."

"I am?" Abbey backed away and looked at her sister sideways.

"You are."

Rascal, still under the sheets, bumped against their legs. He whimpered then growled, desperate to find the opening.

"Silly dog." Holly lifted the sheet to see his black, wet nose poking out.

"Can we have it tonight? The memorial?" Abbey asked.

"We can have it whenever you're ready."

The order of things had been entirely Abbey's idea. After church, she had called a family meeting and told exactly how the ceremony would go. She wanted each person to name a quality they remembered best about their mother then place at the base of the tree an item that symbolized that quality.

So, several hours later, Holly joined her father, Abbey, and the twins at dusk as they gathered near the peach tree.

Holly squeezed Abbey's hand. Abbey squeezed back, keeping her eyes stoically ahead. Holly caught her father's gaze and nodded reassuringly.

The absolute silence of the cool evening seemed profound, almost sacred. Nobody moved for several minutes, until Abbey cleared her throat and spoke toward the tree.

"I loved Mummy for her kindness. Once, we were sitting in the garden, and she saw a baby blue bird on the ground with a broken wing. She picked it up and put it inside a box, and we fed it and got it healthy until its wing healed. She taught me to treat everything with kindness and love." Abbey walked over to the tree and propped up a picture of a blue bird, soaring in the sky, against the trunk. She had drawn it this afternoon, and Holly had helped her frame it.

Abbey stepped back beside Holly. Her turn.

"I remember Mum best as hopeful. She never looked at any situation with negativity. She would find the bright side in everything. Which was occasionally annoying." She heard her father chuckle softly. "I feel like I get that hopefulness from her. Whenever things become unbearable, there's always a strength inside I can draw from. And she had a big faith in God that I admired. So, whenever I feel down or lonely, I remember that there's nothing too big or too impossible for God to do."

Holly stepped forward and placed beside the frame a carved wooden cross her mother had given her when she was sixteen. She'd taken it with her to Kingston then hung it in Hideaway Cottage when she came home so unexpectedly. It was the first thing she'd unpacked.

Next was Rosalee's turn, who honored her mother's generous nature by placing a ceramic Father Christmas beside Holly's cross, reminding them of when their mother would help them deliver clothes and toys to the less fortunate every Christmas. Then, Bridget remembered her mother's sense of humor and placed down a toy clown she'd received as a child. "I remember her smile more than anything else," Bridget whispered as she moved back to the circle. "I can still see it in my mind sometimes…"

Finally, it was their father's turn. He took his time, scratched at his beard, fought back the quiver in his jaw. Holly understood how difficult this must be for him, going back to that dark place, if only for a few moments.

"Your mother was eighteen when I met her. Bonniest lass I'd ever seen. The free spirit who married a cynic. I don't know how she put up with me all those years." He smiled up at the tree, watching the gentle rustle of leaves in a new breeze. "But she did. So, here today, I honor her great capacity for love—with every cell of her being. There wasn't a day I spent with her that I didn't know, with absolute certainty, that she loved me. And I was a better man because of it. Asking her to marry me was the single best decision I ever made."

He stepped toward the trunk and set down a petite jewelry box that Holly could only assume contained their mother's wedding ring. The girls had all been strong during each part of the memorial, but watching him with the box created a surge of emotion. Holly let the tears fall, unashamed, and noticed her sisters were all crying as well.

Seeing this, Duncan said, "Come here…" and stepped toward them, reached out his long arms, and encompassed all his daughters in a warm group hug. Holly shut her eyes, still crying, and felt him kiss the top of her head then heard him kiss the twins then Abbey. He lifted his face to the sky and said, "Thank you, Hannah, for leaving me four pieces of you."

Chapter Thirty-Four

I cannot fix on the hour, or the look, or the words, which laid the foundation... I was in the middle before I knew that I had begun.
~Jane Austen

FOR THE FIRST MONDAY IN months, Holly awakened but remained in bed, staring at the ceiling. She let her mind wander, go wherever it may. No throwing off covers, rushing about, no going over the day's events in her head before her feet even hit the floor. And, for the first Monday in months, she didn't sense that compulsive, anxious need for a jog. Not even a quick one.

Maybe it was yesterday's memorial, the odd sense of closure it had brought. Or maybe it was the image of her family, standing in front of that tree, finally united. Whatever it was, it left Holly with an oddly foreign calm. So foreign that she wanted to fight it. But instead, she attempted to embrace it. And when she finally did roll out of bed, she put on her robe, made a cup of coffee, opened the French doors, and let Rascal out to play in the garden. All without checking the clock once.

The girls, still on holiday from school, had planned to sleep late, anyway. Holly could hear the snores drifting through their bedroom doors when she wandered downstairs.

The only thing nagging at her, still, was Fletcher. As the hours counted down to his leaving, she'd become resigned to the fact that their friendship had run its course. That Fletcher had served a unique purpose in her life these past months, and now it was time for him to move on. Like some sort of fairy godmother, whose job here was complete. She told herself that the unexpected gifts he'd given her—an outlet to vent her troubles, a supportive shoulder to lean on, another person her age to talk to—were more than enough for him to leave behind. She should be grateful for what they'd had and leave it at that.

Rinsing out her coffee cup, she tried to be mature. To look at the facts. Fletcher was leaving. He couldn't stay here the rest of his life, meeting her needs, rescuing her sisters from danger, being her friend. He had a life of his own to live. But standing at the sink, trying her best to be brave, she could only feel sad. She looked at the clock and realized their goodbye at the final book club was only two hours away.

"You can't *do* this to me!" Frank wailed, prompting Holly to shush him in the roomful of people.

She had tendered her resignation a minute before.

"I'm sorry," she said. "It's something I have to do. I need to devote all my time to the bookshop now. You knew this was coming. And I'll only be a few shops down from you."

He gave her a pout then a half-smile. "I know. But I'm only upset because you're… irreplaceable."

Holly reached out for a hug. "Thank you, Frank."

They stood in Gertrude's reception room along with the other book club members, chatting and eating the delicious tarts Julia had brought along. Though Julia had never uttered a word during book discussions, her dog-eared copy of *Emma* and her faithful attendance since Week Three spoke louder than anything.

Gertrude waved Holly over to her chair. "Are they up yet?"

"Are what up?" Holly asked.

"The posters, of course!" Gertrude growled. Two days ago, she'd phoned and insisted that Holly place posters all around the village, to advertise their next book, *Pride and Prejudice*. Gertrude didn't even want to skip a single week and told Holly to announce the date as a week from today.

"Yes, they're up. Frank helped me yesterday."

"Excellent." Satisfied, Gertrude popped another biscuit into Leopold's impatient mouth.

Holly surveyed the room, wondering where Fletcher was. A couple of minutes before the start of the meeting and still no sign of him. No text, no nothing. Feeling her aggravation rise, she turned to Frank again.

"Where's Fletcher? He was supposed to be here."

"I thought you knew," he whispered. "He's gone."

"What?!" Holly said, louder than she intended. "When did he leave?"

"Yesterday, I think. At least, that's what I thought I heard Joe say."

"I can't believe it. He didn't even say goodbye," she muttered.

"It's time!" Gertrude insisted, from across the room. She tapped her cane twice. "Let this meeting come to order!"

Holly still hadn't absorbed this latest Fletcher information when she was forced to sit down and lead the meeting. She did her best to clear her head, focus on *Emma,* on this group of people staring at her.

She cleared her throat and said, "Since this is the last meeting, I thought we could share our thoughts on favorite characters. Anyone want to start us off?"

Immediately, eagerly, Frank and the ladies thumbed through their well-worn pages to find their favorite parts in support. Holly tried to pay attention as Mrs. Pickering chose Emma's father—she enjoyed his quirky traits. Or as Mrs. Farraday chose Miss Smith, who maintained character and dignity through all sorts of maltreatment. Or even when Frank chose Miss Bates, a character who withstood criticism and gossip with head held high. Gertrude chose Mrs. Elton, for her ability to be outspoken and candid.

Finally, it was Holly's turn, and she felt unprepared, unnerved. Still, it was an easy question to answer, her favorite character.

"Well," she started, the book perched on her lap, "I guess my answer is a bit of a cheat. I could say my favorite character is Emma, for her wit and her growth throughout the novel. Or that it's Mr. Knightley, for his chivalry and integrity. But instead, I'm going to say that my favorite character in *Emma* isn't a character at all. It's a relationship."

She explained. "I think the dynamic between Emma and Mr. Knightley is more powerful and complex than any other relationship or single character in the book. Maybe in *all* of Jane Austen's books, in fact. Their love story is intriguing because they were friends first. Genuine friends, with no romantic nonsense getting in the way. They were able to be themselves with each other—as evidenced by Emma's childish behavior in many situations. She wasn't afraid to be who she was, didn't try to give Knightley only her best parts. She showed him her flaws, as well. But all that time—even within the friendship—their love was buried just beneath the surface, neither one realizing it until the very end."

She saw some heads bobbling in agreement and continued, more relaxed, more focused. "I adore Knightley's chivalrous nature. He was such a gentleman—rescuing Miss Smith at the dance then walking away with Miss Bates at the lawn party, another rescue, of sorts..."

Holly trailed off, hearing her own words. Rescued. A similar image came to her mind, a real-life one—Fletcher, swooping up Abbey with an injured foot. Then another—bringing Bridget home from London after punching out Colin. *That boy is a hero*, her father had said...

She looked around and saw the ladies waiting. She cleared her throat again and took her thoughts back to the novel. "And, as for Emma, I like her cluelessness the best. Her complete denial over Knightley, the entire length of the book. She was fighting her feelings for him all along. I mean, it took him going away to London before she finally realized how much he meant to her."

Holly thumbed through to the page she had marked in Chapter Forty-Eight and read aloud slowly, "'Till now that she was threatened with its loss, Emma had never known how much of her happiness depended on being first with Mr. Knightley... and only in the dread of being supplanted, found how inexpressibly important it had been...'"

She shrugged off a nagging sensation, the image of chocolate-brown eyes, the Southern accent she'd grown accustomed to, the dimples, the warm hugs. Things that had too suddenly vanished from her life, possibly forever.

Holly ignored her quickening heartbeat as she picked another section to read, eager for a distraction. "'Mr. Knightley to be no longer coming there for his evening comfort!—No longer walking in at all hours... How was it to be endured?'"

Holly stared at the words, feeling the uneasy panic rise again, feeling Emma's panic as if it was her own. She didn't know it until now, but the longer Fletcher had been absent these past few weeks, the more he had become present in her thoughts. Mostly on the fringes of them, but always there. Always. He was the first one she wanted to go to when something happened, good or bad. She noticed the girls had started missing him too, asking when they could see him again.

All this time, she had assumed she was frustrated because she missed his friendship. But now, staring at these pages, she knew it was something else she missed. Something deeper. The realization shocked her like cold water in the face. Fletcher was gone, and she didn't get to say goodbye. He'd boarded a plane that would carry him an ocean away. And the thought of never seeing him again left an ache she knew she couldn't tolerate. An ache that touched deeper than friendship.

He had become irreplaceable.

"Holly?" Frank muttered beside her. "What's wrong? You look flushed."

She looked at him with wide eyes, hit fully with the connection. "It's Fletcher." She pointed to the book.

"Whatever do you mean?"

"Fletcher... he's Knightley," she told Frank, as though he would completely understand her babbling.

She shifted back to the group, her breathing hurried, clutching the book. She said it slowly, punched each word with meaning. "Fletcher... is... Knightley," she repeated and stood. "How could I have been so blind?" She turned again to Frank. "I need to find him. Are you sure he's already gone?"

"Not a hundred percent sure. It was secondhand information. I could be mistaken."

"Then maybe it isn't too late."

"What about Cindy?" Frank asked. "You told me they went together. To America?"

"It doesn't matter. I have to talk to him. I have to try."

Some of the ladies had stood too, chattering to each other, confused about what was happening.

Frank braced Holly, hands on her shoulders. "Go and see Joe. He'll know where Fletcher is." Then added with a firm nod, "Go get him."

She rushed out the door, not caring that the ladies were probably planning how to snatch her later and take her to an institution.

Jogging down the hill, around the corner to Storey Road, she stopped short before she reached the pub. Must try the obvious, first. She dialed Fletcher's number and got his voicemail. Clicking off, knowing she didn't want to leave some incoherent, scattered message, she decided on another idea, to ring Fletcher's flat in Bristol. It wouldn't hurt to try. She scrolled through the numbers on her mobile—he'd used her phone once, to call his cousin—then hit "call," and held her breath.

"Hello?" an American voice answered. *Not* Fletcher.

"Hi, is this Todd?"

"Yep. Who's this?"

"You don't know me, but I'm a friend of Fletcher's—my name is Holly Newbury."

"Oh, sure. Holly. I know who you are."

"Where is he? Fletcher? I think he flew back to America yesterday?" She didn't care that her voice was laced with desperation. This was too important.

A pause produced hope. But then—"No idea, sorry. I just got back from the States, myself, this afternoon. Haven't spoken to him in a couple of weeks."

Deflated, she said, "Okay, thanks. Would you please have him call me if you do talk to him? It's really important."

"Will do."

She clicked the phone off, undeterred.

A minute later, she found Joe. The pub was empty, and she remembered there had been a note on the door as she'd opened it that she hadn't bothered to read.

"This is inventory day, isn't it?" She winced, seeing the stack of boxes he was counting. "Sorry, I'll go."

"No. Stay. You look a little… rough around the edges." He poured her a pint and set it on the bar. She wedged herself between the high stools and took a couple of sips, still out of breath from the trek down to the pub.

"What can I help you with?" he asked.

Suddenly at her wit's end, she felt unexpected tears and dove right in, knowing her chances were miniscule. "Is Fletcher gone? Did he really leave?"

"He checked out yesterday morning. Thanked me for my hospitality and gave me a generous tip." Joe handed her a cocktail napkin, and she used it to dab her eyes. "Why did you need him? Did he leave something behind?"

She didn't want to say something as cheesy as, *Yes, me.* So instead, she said, "We had some unfinished business."

Maybe it was seeing Joe standing behind the bar, poised patiently to listen, rag slung over his left shoulder, or maybe it was the gesture of the cocktail napkin. But the cliché rang true. She wanted to pour out all her troubles to the barman. And so, she did.

It came out in fast, rambling sentences. She told Joe all about Fletcher's confusing distance, about Cindy, then this morning's book club epiphany.

"That's when I realized it—I didn't only miss his friendship. It was more than that," she added. "I have a terrible confession to make, Joe. I think I'm in love with him. I think I've loved him for a while, actually. I just didn't know it."

"Why terrible?" Joe prompted.

"Because he's gone. Because I've lost him, an ocean away." Tears threatened again, but the phone buzzing in her hand distracted her. She'd been clutching it tightly this whole time. Maybe it was Todd, remembering something.

Tilting the screen to see it, blinking to clear her vision, Holly froze as she saw the text message.

Turn around.

Holly did as the text commanded and swiveled her head to see. And there he was. Fletcher, standing at the pub door. Not thousands of miles away.

Without even thinking, she pushed away from the bar, untangled herself from the stools, and rushed into Fletcher's arms. He reciprocated her hug, one hand tight around her waist, the other cradling her neck.

"Hey there," he whispered then kissed the top of her head.

"I thought you were gone." She pushed away to look up at him. "Back to Texas."

She could still feel his hand on her waist as he explained, "I went to London last night, to confront Finn. I had to see him in person, hash things out. Get some closure before I left England."

"Without saying goodbye?" It was so un-Fletcher-like, skulking away without as much as a note or a phone call. To her, or to her sisters. Had they meant anything to him?

He brushed a stray hair from Holly's face. "I tried to say goodbye—after the wrap party. It was late, and I went to your house and noticed your lights were on at that little cottage. I walked all the way up to your door, raised my hand to knock, and then... realized I had no clue what to say. I couldn't imagine forming the words to say goodbye to you."

Holly smiled. *This* was the Fletcher she knew so well—self-effacing and sincere.

He continued. "I'd planned to fly to Texas this afternoon, maybe send you a text from the plane. But I couldn't go through with it. The flight. I needed to come back here. See you again."

Even as she felt comfortable in his arms right now, their familiar connection returning, something horrifying occurred to her. She remembered what she'd spilled to Joe—all the vivid details and heightened emotions that poured out—only seconds before Fletcher's text. She quickly became *un*comfortable.

"How much of that did you hear, my talk with Joe?" she whispered, pointing behind at the bar, suddenly self-aware, seeing it all again through Fletcher's eyes. She realized that Joe had discreetly taken his leave. They were alone.

"Most of it," Fletcher admitted.

She took a step back, exposed and embarrassed. He'd wriggled out of their friendship weeks ago. Made himself scarce, backed away. It was incredibly likely he never felt anything *but* friendship for her. Which was why he'd almost left the country without so much as a goodbye. She was a fool for letting her guard down.

But before she could make excuses or wrench herself out of his grasp, Fletcher stepped forward and closed the gap. "I have a confession of my own to make."

"What?"

"Remember my epiphany? On our trip to Bath?"

"Yeah. You never told me what it was."

"That's because the epiphany was *you.*"

"What do you mean?"

"During the balloon ride, I dunno, something... shifted for me. I started realizing I had feelings for you. Deep feelings. And I guess I didn't know what to do with them. Or how you felt about me."

"But... you stopped returning my texts. You avoided me after that."

He grimaced. "I couldn't handle it—the pressure of rejection if you didn't feel the same. I was going to tell you how I felt... at the fountain. But I chickened out."

She remembered his awkwardness, and now it made sense. The silence, the fidgeting. She had interpreted them as indifference. "But what about Cindy? You two were looking pretty serious. I heard you were taking her to America."

"What?" Fletcher shook his head. "No, never. Maybe she has a new acting gig over there or something, but it has nothing to do with me. Holly, she was a distraction. We went out one time. She made everybody think it was something it wasn't. Well, if I'm honest... okay, this is horrible."

"What?

"On some completely sophomoric level, I think I was using her. Trying to make you jealous. Testing your feelings."

More of the pieces suddenly snapped together.

But there was one final piece to fit into place. One that would tell her everything she needed to know. "What would you tell me now, if we were back at the fountain? If you hadn't chickened out?"

"I would've told you this..." Before she had time to process it, Fletcher leaned in close and pressed his lips to hers. It took a moment to find her equilibrium, but when she did, she returned his kiss and felt a shot of adrenaline. Inside the warmth of his lips, she experienced every paradox at once, all mingled together: strong and weak, hot and cold, delirious and rational. Scared and happy.

"Did that answer your question?" he said, backing away too soon.

"Mmm. Not quite," she said, dizzy, smiling. "I think I need a *bit* more clarification."

Fletcher took his time and leaned in again, kissing her with certainty, making sure she understood. Even though his kisses were brand-new to her, they felt entirely familiar. Because *he* was familiar. Her friend, her companion. And now, something much more.

His hand moved up to touch her cheek, his urgency changing into something gentle and slow. And when he ended the kiss, his face still close, he whispered, "I'm in love with you too, Holly."

She let the words sink in, let herself believe them. Let herself realize that every moment they'd had together led up to this moment, this confession.

"Well, it's about damn time!" she heard someone exclaim from behind. She stretched her neck to see Joe, standing with Lizzie at the back, both of them beaming.

Holly turned back to Fletcher, leaning in for another kiss, and said, "I couldn't agree more."

Chapter Thirty-Five

*It is such a happiness when good people get
together—and they always do.*
~Jane Austen

S HE WOULD NEVER TIRE OF it—getting shipments of books, all brand-new. Unwrapping them, cracking them open, smelling that beautiful, polished new-book smell.

Holly smiled as she opened the last box, at least for the foreseeable future, and picked up the first copy on top: *Emily of New Moon.* Just as she was about to open the cover and inhale, she heard the click of Rascal's paws on the hardwood floor, coming to take a whiff, too.

"Hey, boy," she said, rubbing at his ears. He sat beside her and panted. Those obedience lessons Mr. Elton had given were working wonders. No longer the frisky, out-of-control, un-potty-trained puppy. He was maturing every day.

"Where do you want these?" Abbey yelled from across the shop, holding up two dolls in the children's nook. She and Rosalee had been shelving children's books and gifts for the past hour.

"Inside the shelves. Any position you want," Holly called back.

The second half of August and first half of September, every day, Holly had been inside this bookshop, preparing for tomorrow's Grand Opening. She couldn't believe it was already here. The buzz in the village had been at a fever pitch. She couldn't get better publicity than an enthusiastic Frank and a gossipy Mrs. Pickering. She really should pay them a commission.

The uncomfortable pull in her lower back told Holly it was time to take a break from this final box and get some food.

"Abbey, call Rascal over to you, please!"

"Rascal! Here, boy!" Abbey said, and immediately, his ears perked up, and he took off in her direction.

On her way back to the cashier's desk, Holly paused, took it all in. The bookshop—with many people's help—had been transformed. New floors, new paint on the walls, softer lighting. She'd filled the space with bookshelves upon bookshelves. All different heights, to add some variety. She'd created reading areas, cozy corners where people could sprawl out. She'd put Rosalee in charge of the music—her choice, but Holly suggested something light, like jazz or classical.

Bridget wanted to be in charge of the décor, so Holly let her be. For the most part. Bridget always had a good eye for fashion, so Holly trusted her eye for design, as well. They'd spent many hours together, pouring over furniture and accessories in catalogues, until they'd agreed on color schemes. Bridget had also been the one to come up with the bookshop's name. The entire family had brainstormed for weeks, thinking of every possible name: *Books 'n Such; Books, Books, Books; Ye Olde House of Books*. Finally, Bridget—who hadn't, to Holly's knowledge, contributed a single name up until that moment—piped up nonchalantly with "Why not just 'The Book Shoppe?' That's what it is, isn't it?" And that had been that. Simple, straightforward, and to the point. Much like Bridget.

Now, Holly reached the cashier's desk to see Bridget giggling as she draped a string of miniature white lights over Riley's neck.

"Umm, I think those are for plants, not people." Holly grinned.

Riley looked embarrassed, but Bridget smiled. "I think they look better right here." She kissed Riley on the cheek, turning him bright red. They had been officially dating for two weeks, because Bridget finally asked *him* out. She knew he'd never gather the courage, so she'd asked him to see a film. They had been inseparable ever since.

"Would you two volunteer to get us some food?" Holly found her bag on the bottom shelf and fished out several fivers. "Maybe some sandwiches?"

"Sure." Riley removed the lights and took the money. He and Bridget disappeared around the counter and held hands as they walked out the door.

Holly looked behind her at the new painting, ever-so-slightly off-center. She reached up to touch the corner and straighten it. She remembered visiting the gallery three weeks ago, on a mission. *Hope in the Storm.* That painting belonged here, with her.

The bell at the front door tinkled. "Excuse me, ma'am? Where do you want this?"

Holly saw Fletcher and Mac, each holding the end of a heavy, aubergine chair. A "cushy" chair, an exact copy of the one in the gallery.

"Over here," she pointed, guiding them to the corner.

They angled the chair and set it down carefully, then Holly adjusted the small coffee table in front of it.

"Perfect. Thank you. Bridget's bringing sandwiches. Mac, please stay and have some," she said.

"Aye, I will. Thank ye."

"There's also tea over there, if you want some."

Mac tipped his cap and headed in the direction of the beverage bar, dead center of the shop.

"Hey there, beautiful." Fletcher put his hands on Holly's waist and pulled her close. "This is really happening. *Your* shop." He gave her a soft kiss on the lips.

"I'm still in shock."

"It'll be an instant hit. Tomorrow will be insane."

She thought ahead to the Grand Opening, the joy and chaos and anticipation. Like Christmas morning. "I don't think I'll be able to sleep a wink tonight. Oh! How did your interview go?"

Last month, Fletcher had become a permanent Chilton Crosse resident. While Holly lived in Hideaway Cottage for the time being, Fletcher would stay on at Joe's Pub, renting his room, while taking the rest of his history courses online, working toward teacher certification. This time next year, he would be a qualified history teacher. And in the meantime, he'd interviewed for a full-time tutoring position at the school. He and Holly had discussed their future together—both the near-future goals, such as flying to Texas to meet Fletcher's family at Thanksgiving, and even the more faraway goals, such as marriage.

"I think the interview went well," Fletcher replied. "I should hear something by tomorrow." He leaned in for another kiss.

"Is this where the party is?" a voice boomed.

Holly loosened her grasp on Fletcher to see her father walking toward them, a bottle of something in his hand, raised high. Mildred followed slightly behind, hand threaded through her husband's other arm.

"The newlyweds are back!" Holly met them halfway.

"Daddy!" Abbey said from the nook and raced over, Rosalee following.

"I heard your good news," Duncan told Rosalee as he received a squeeze from Abbey. "Congratulations on the film. When does production begin?"

"Next month. I've already talked to Mrs. Clementine about missing school. I'll have a tutor on set."

"I'm proud of you," he whispered, giving her a kiss on the cheek.

"So, tell us, you two! How was Paris?" Holly grasped Mildred's other hand, squeezing it, then took the champagne her father offered. Fletcher extended his hand to Duncan.

"Hello, son." Duncan shook Fletcher's hand. "Paris was incredible. I'd been there before, on business, but seeing it this way, with my new bride, was—"

"Indescribable," Mildred finished for him.

"I'm so happy for you both." Holly still couldn't get over seeing her father in love. And looking back, she couldn't believe there was ever conflict surrounding this union. It was nothing short of meant to be.

"A toast!" said her father.

Within a couple of minutes, Fletcher had popped the cork and found a stack of Styrofoam cups, while Holly opened a two-liter of soda for the girls.

"Wait for us!" Bridget said, returning with Riley and bags full of sandwiches. She hugged her father and then Mildred.

"Mac, where are you?" Holly called. "Join us!"

Typical Mac, he'd faded into the woodwork, pretending to scope out the shop, giving the family some private time. Now, he walked meekly toward the gathering, removed his cap, took a cup from Holly, then stepped back again.

Fletcher and Holly poured champagne and soda until everyone had a cup of something.

Duncan held his hand high. "A toast. To this family—including my beautiful bride—and all those in this room who have worked so hard to make my daughter's dream a reality. May 'The Book Shoppe' be nothing less than a stunning success."

"Hear, hear," said Fletcher, and squeezed Holly's shoulders.

Holly had to hold her champagne and wait for the lump in her throat to dissolve before even thinking of taking a sip. She watched the smiles around her, stepped back in her mind, an observer of them, these people in her life. All the new additions to her family over the span of a few months. How far they'd all come, just to be in this moment.

Seeing her family happy, at peace, and watching Fletcher—her partner, her friend, the love she'd been looking for—Holly knew her life's cup was filled to the brim. And bubbling over.

Other Books by Traci Borum

Painting the Moon

Acknowledgements

To my family—my heart and soul. To my late father, supportive and brilliant and loving. The best role model a girl could ever have. I miss you every day. To my beloved grandparents, Della and Perry Sandifer, Lillian and Val Borum. Your love and support all through the years have been invaluable. To my sister, Karen Ratekin. I'm so honored that you've read my books and offered such encouragement. It means more than you know.

To my dearest friends, who continue to be supportive of my writer's journey: Augusta Malvagno, Sandy Graham, Mary Lou Robinson, Becky Bray, Karen Peterson, and my Commandos and Pitizens.

To the entire Red Adept team, but particularly Lynn McNamee, Suzanne Warr, Michelle Rever, Jessica Dall, Streetlight Graphics (especially Glendon Haddix), and all the acquisitions editors and proofreaders. This novel is what it is because of your diligence and dedication and talents. I'm so grateful to you.

To Renina Baker at MotoPhoto for my author photo.

Finally, all thanks to God, whose guidance and inspiration made this book entirely possible. He's the Source.

About the Author

TRACI BORUM IS A WRITING teacher and native Texan. She's also an avid reader of women's fiction, most especially Elin Hilderbrand and Rosamunde Pilcher novels. Since the age of 12, she's written poetry, short stories, magazine articles, and novels. Traci also adores all things British. She even owns a British dog (Corgi) and is completely addicted to Masterpiece Theater—must be all those dreamy accents! Aside from having big dreams of getting a book published, it's the little things that make her the happiest: deep talks with friends, a strong cup of hot chocolate, a hearty game of fetch with her Corgi, and puffy white Texas clouds always reminding her to "look up, slow down, enjoy your life."

Made in the USA
Monee, IL
02 November 2019